Full Moon City

Full Moon City

Edited by

Darrell Schweitzer
and Martin H. Greenberg

GALLERY BOOKS

New York   London   Toronto   Sydney

G

Gallery Books
A Division of Simon & Schuster, Inc.
1230 Avenue of the Americas
New York, NY 10020

First Gallery Books trade paperback edition March 2010

GALLERY BOOKS and colophon are registered trademarks of Simon & Schuster, Inc.

For information about special discounts for bulk purchases, please contact Simon & Schuster Special Sales at 1-866-506-1949 or business@simonandschuster.com.

The Simon & Schuster Speakers Bureau can bring authors to your live event. For more information or to book an event, contact the Simon & Schuster Speakers Bureau at 1-866-248-3049 or visit our website at www.simonspeakers.com.

Designed by Renata Di Biase

Manufactured in the United States of America

10 9 8 7 6 5 4 3 2 1

ISBN 978-1-4165-8413-1
ISBN 978-1-4165-8500-8 (ebook)

Contents

Children of the Night

Mostly, we fear them.

When Bela Lugosi's vampire Count praised wolves in the 1931 film, this was used to emphasize Dracula's inhuman, otherworldly nature. It produced some of the most memorable lines ever uttered on the silver screen:

The children of the night. What music they make.

I doubt it was ordinary wolves he had in mind, either. The uncanny must surely be sensitive to the uncanny, even though, one imagines, vampires might well envy werewolves. After all, vampires are *dead*, forced to steal vitality to maintain a shadow existence, whereas werewolves are very much alive, maybe even *too* vital.

Dracula had lycanthropic powers. He could transform himself into an enormous wolf when need be.

The wolf remains a symbol of power and fear. Very likely this is programmed into our genes from the days of our barely-human ancestors, who once had to take on the fanged and clawed world with no more than a club, a pointed stick, or, at best, a piece of sharpened flint. One wolf, when the odds are more or less even like that, can be formidable. An organized pack can bring down a moose, or a man, with ease. It is hard to believe that in times of famine, in the depths of winter, they didn't occasionally do so. Wolves remain, in folklore, stories, and fairy tales, one of the

terrors that come in the night, despite the efforts of naturalists such as Farley Mowat (*Never Cry Wolf*) to convince us that
wolves have gotten entirely too much bad press.

The more traditional image of the wolf emerges clearly in
Daniel P. Mannix's *The Wolves of Paris* (1978), a nonfiction account of how, in the midst of the Hundred Years' War (four-
teenth century), great hordes of wolves roamed the devastated
French countryside, devouring man and beast alike, until they
actually besieged the walled city of Paris. Understandably, the
enormous creature at the head of this wolf pack was assumed to
be a werewolf.

Belief in shape-shifters is as old as mankind. (Not just
werewolves, either; in some parts of the world you can find
wereleopards, werehyenas, and so on.) You can well imagine the
caveman, huddled around his fire with the rest of his tiny band,
listening to the cries of animals in the night—their music—and
knowing that, to him, the night landscape was forbidden territory. To wander far from the fire meant death. He'd had that
hammered into his head since childhood. For the survival of the
tribe, it was crucial that he teach his children the same thing.
What could be more impressive and terrifying than a human
being who transformed into the very creature everyone else
feared and ventured out into that forbidden night-realm?

Of course, not all cultures see werewolves as the enemy. Some
Native Americans viewed them as benevolent. This may have
been because Native Americans were better outdoorsmen than
medieval French peasants and had less to fear, although certainly
American werewolves still must have been seen as creatures of
awe and mystery.

The werewolf has been in literature for a long time. The best-
known example from Antiquity is very likely the werewolf story
told over the dinner table in the *Satyricon* of Petronius, written
in the time of Nero. Here we see a very familiar motif: A man

turns into a wolf and commits his depredations. His guilt is proven afterward when, back in human form, he bears marks of an injury inflicted on the wolf.

Gene Wolfe, in his meticulously researched novel *Soldier of the Mist* (1986), tells us that in Greece in the fifth century B.C., it was common knowledge that Scythians were werewolves.

I don't doubt it.

There are werewolf stories from the Middle Ages, too. "The Lay of the Werewolf" by Marie de France (twelfth century) presents a sympathetic werewolf who confides his secret to his wife one night, whereupon she hides his clothes so that he cannot return to human form and she can run off with her lover. The werewolf acts the role of a tame "beast," wins the favor of the king, and eventually regains his humanity. The wife is punished, but the werewolf is not, even after everybody learns what he is.

Nevertheless, werewolves are feared more often than not, if only for their propensity for eating people. (Whether *wolves* have ever eaten anyone is a subject disputed among naturalists. That werewolves do so is not.) If anything, the werewolf is an embodiment of uncontrolled rage and lust. We define our "humanity" precisely by our ability to control our "bestial" tendencies. The werewolf, therefore, may be seen as ourselves, with every trace of civilization and social inhibition stripped away.

While there is no single werewolf story or novel that defines the whole genre in the way that Bram Stoker's *Dracula* defines the vampire, two books do stand out and represent different strands in the development of the literary werewolf.

The Werewolf of Paris by Guy Endore (1933) is the classic novel of the supernatural werewolf, set in nineteenth-century France. The protagonist, Bertrand Caillet, is the offspring of a woman raped by a priest, who is himself of an accursed line. Bertrand has all the classic werewolf characteristics, including eyebrows that meet and hairy palms. He experiences blackouts, excessive urination (possibly to mark territory; this detail is also mentioned in Petronius), and hunts animals first, then people. The climax of the book finds him in Paris during the turmoil of the Commune (1870) and its bloody suppression, against which background—as is very much the author's point—one small werewolf seems quite insignificant amid an orgy of human cruelty.

Jack Williamson's *Darker Than You Think* (magazine version, 1940; expanded as a book, 1948) presents the "scientific" werewolf, based on the notion that a rival, shape-shifting race, *Homo lycanthropus*, lives alongside mankind and is poised to regain the world mastery it once enjoyed in prehistoric times. Other more recent books, notably Whitley Strieber's *The Wolfen* (1979), expand on Williamson's thesis.

The werewolf has also been equated with that very contemporary horror icon, the serial killer, with whom, indeed, he has much in common. (What was Ted Bundy but a werewolf without the excess hair?) Yet Stefan Dziemianowicz makes an excellent case in his entry on werewolves in S. T. Joshi's *Icons of Horror and the Supernatural* (2007) that the predominant image of the werewolf in Western culture stems, not from literature or folklore or true crime, but from Lon Chaney Jr.'s portrayal of the unfortunate Larry Talbot in the 1941 film *The Wolf Man*, which defines the "rules" against which subsequent werewolf stories are measured, even when those rules are broken. We all know the "standard" Hollywood werewolf: the unwilling victim who was very likely bitten by another werewolf, who cannot control his urges whenever the full moon rises, who kills and cannot be stopped by anything other than a silver bullet. Wolfbane may repel him, but it's the silver bullet that's needed in the end, very often delivered in a moment of tragedy, as in the 1961 film *The Curse of the Werewolf*, by someone near and dear to the raging man-beast. Perhaps the most significant change the movies have made on our image of the werewolf is that, due to technical limitations not fully overcome until *An American Werewolf in London* (1981), most movie werewolves move about on two legs. They are hulking, hairy, clawed, wolf-faced *men*. Werewolves in folklore and literature have generally been *wolves*, with four legs and a tail, even if sometimes very large. Since the printed page does not have the same limitation, most literary werewolves, even post–Lon Chaney, are of the four-legged kind.

There's another great line from the film *Young Frankenstein*, that springs to mind. The heir to the Frankenstein legacy (Gene Wilder) is being driven from the train station by hunchbacked, pop-eyed Igor (Marty Feldman). A wolf howls.

"*Werewolf*..." says Frankenstein with obvious dread.

Igor nods to one side. "*There*, wolf..."

It's a great throwaway, but, Dear Reader—*here wolves*.

Inherently, a werewolf anthology must have werewolves in it. The present volume has plenty, and at least one, by some stretch of the definition, in every story. The one narrative strategy that will definitely not work in this context is the Ultimate Shocking Revelation: "My God! He really was a werewolf!"

We know that. Having gotten such superficialities out of the way, then, the authors, who include some of the most prominent fantasists of our time, can still render any number of changes on the werewolf theme. Each story addresses the question of the werewolf in a city environment. It is one thing for the wolf-man to undergo his transformation, then race howling across the relative privacy of the rural countryside, killing sheep, deer, and the occasional hapless peasant. But, we wonder, as the world changes and as populations move off the land and into vast, artificial jungles of stone and concrete, what is a werewolf to do? How can he (or she) blend in?

The resultant stories repeatedly break the Hollywoo There is a notable shortage of silver bullets. Most werewolves live in the contemporary big city, in a world of cell phones and subways. There are terrifying werewolves, funny ones, sympathetic ones, unsympathetic ones, and more. You can meet a werewolf on the Internet. Greg Frost shows what happens when a werewolf just happens to be among the bystanders at a bank robbery. Carrie Vaughn's continuing character Kitty (already the star of a series of novels) is a werewolf who has been outed in the national media and who hosts a late-night talk show for uncanny creatures. The werewolf packs of Kitty's world have a great deal in common with biker gangs. Esther Friesner's werewolf is a child who lives among the very rich in the best part of Manhattan. Lisa Tuttle's Austin, Texas, werewolves attend a support group. Holly Black provides a striking portrait of the modern warewolf as performance artist. Ian Watson returns to Eastern Europe, the home of so many of our scariest legends, but it is the modern Romania of the post-Ceauşescu era. Tanith Lee suggests that a modern British werewolf might want to live comfortably in the city while commuting to the countryside to carry out his bloody business.

The possibilities multiply. Lycanthropy can be a curse, a lifestyle, or even, in some cases, a solution.

The wolves are there, lurking in the dark of our own minds.

Happy hunting!

—*Darrell Schweitzer*

Full Moon City

The Truth About Werewolves

LISA TUTTLE

The first meeting of the Lycanthropy Support Group came nowhere near Mel's best fantasies; in fact, it barely missed disaster.

Besides herself, only seven people turned up, a number that made the classroom she'd reserved at the Town & Country campus of Houston Community College look ridiculously, over-optimistically large.

She watched them straggle in: two couples, two single men, one single woman. Mel took an immediate dislike to that one. She was pretty, in a blonde and doll-like manner, very petite, and way overdressed in a beige cashmere sweater, stiletto heels, and gold jewelry. None looked anything like Mel's idea of a were-wolf, but the woman was the worst of all, a designer-accessorized Chihuahua.

She was shopping, Mel decided; drawn by the lure of the supernatural to seek out something ahead of trend, not available in any store, soon to be a must-have bit of arm-candy: a werewolf boyfriend.

Just like me, said the bitchy voice inside her head. You're nothing special, just desperate to hook up with somebody who is.

Mel ignored that self-hating part of herself. It always cropped up when she got nervous—or when she might just be about to win. Her feelings about werewolves ran much deeper than idle

curiosity. What she felt was more than interest; it was a compul-
sion. People talked about choice—about choosing what you did
and how you lived and who you loved and what you wanted, as
if life were a restaurant, and anyone who wasn't happy with the
menu must be sick. Well, after years of unhappy, failed relationships, and several months of therapy, she'd decided she needed to
visit a different restaurant.

Some things just could not be changed, and it was a waste of
time to try. Take homosexuality. Some would rather deny its existence, or treat it as an illness, but that never worked. Whether allowed to flourish or forced underground, by now it was obvious
that homosexual desires were every bit as real as heterosexual,
and no more amenable to a "cure."

Her fascination with lycanthropy was like that; so deeply-
rooted, so much a part of herself that she couldn't have changed
it if she'd wanted. Some things couldn't be denied, and you ignored them at your peril. It wasn't like she hadn't tried; she was
twenty-seven years old and had been dating since she was fifteen.
But not one of the men she'd met had been right for her. There
was always something missing, making true love impossible.
Something that was not to do with personality or sexual technique; something that could not be fixed with good intentions.

She'd finally realized it was not her fault that her relationships
never lasted—and it wasn't the guy's fault, either. It didn't matter how physically attractive he appeared, no matter how kind
or understanding he was at heart, no matter how clever, rich, or
creative; she could never be satisfied with a man who was just a
man. She wanted something else.

Mel remembered the magazine advice columns she'd read
when she was younger, when she hadn't yet figured out why
none of the men she'd met made her happy. The first step to
finding "the right man" was to put yourself in a position where
you'd meet men—lots of men. Forget quality; think quantity.

Sooner or later, amid all the disappointing strangers, there'd be one who suited you. That could never happen if you stayed home dreaming about Prince Charming. You had to get out there and hunt. In another evocative phrase: You have to kiss a lot of frogs to find your prince.

Mel stood beside the coffee urn, which had seemed so necessary to create a hospitable ambiance that she'd paid extra for it, and regarded her potential prey through narrowed eyes. They were a disappointing bunch, and not simply because they appeared so indifferent to the presence of a hot, caffeinated beverage.

Not one had the faintest trace of anything lupine or feral in his or her demeanor. The two wives (judging by body language) were mere ordinary mortals like herself who'd come along to support (or keep hold of) their partners. Seeing as they were attached, Mel politely crossed the husbands off her mental list. The whiff of danger she hoped for in a sexual relationship had nothing to do with the boring clichés of adultery.

That left two guys in their late twenties, each one unattractive in his own way. One was fat and pale as a grub, with wet, too-red lips. He wore a dingy white button-down shirt, with a pocket protector beneath the pens that bristled from his swelling breast. The other was reasonably fit but filthy, and not in a sexy way: unshaven, hair long and greasy, he had black half-moons of dirt under his fingernails and crusty yellow stains on a baggy T-shirt advertising Galveston's Rain Forest Café.

Everyone kept a clear distance from everyone else, the couples making still islands near the center, while the singletons prowled nervously, avoiding eye contact. Mel thought this might reflect wolf-like behavior, but maybe she was getting desperate, searching for scraps of faith.

She still believed werewolves were real—she just wasn't sure there were any in this room.

Meeting werewolves didn't seem like it would be that hard, at first. You could find anything on the Internet. There were chat groups and mailing lists dedicated to every precise and peculiar subdivision of the supernatural: transgendered vampires; gentle ghouls; bloodthirsty, cross-dressing fairies; elves with a fetish for whipping cream; werepanthers wanting to be bottle-fed by little people . . . It was in this otherworldly bazaar that she'd made contact with real, live werewolves—or, at least, with some men who said they were. They also claimed to live about as far away from her home in Houston as possible—Alaska, Calcutta, Newfoundland—even though when one gave her his phone number during their slow progression toward intimacy, it had a Kansas City area code.

Only one of these cyber relationships had progressed to an actual, face-to-face meeting. The vibes between them were good, and the sex wasn't bad, and he had suggested that his next visit to Houston would fall around the time of the full moon . . . but she never heard from him again. She guessed he was married. She had no way of knowing if he'd also lied about being a werewolf.

You could be anyone, anything, on the Internet, and if you were careful, no one could catch you. She'd been honest herself, but when, after nearly two years, she was still no closer to attaining her desire, she took a cold, hard look at how she was presenting herself, and wondered if it could be her own fault.

So she tried something else: "Lonely werewolf, based in Houston, longs to run with a pack. It can't be right to be all alone. Anyone else feel the same? Get in touch."

She got a lot of responses. Most were not werewolves at all, as they readily admitted; just curious. Many were from elsewhere in the state, or even lived abroad. But she persisted, stressing the importance of area as much as lycanthropy, until, eventually, she had a core group of twenty she believed were genuine, Houston-resident werewolves, and she proposed a get-together.

LYCANTHROPY SUPPORT GROUP
FIRST MEETING: THURSDAY, MAY 15, 7:30
ROOM 203
HCC, TOWN & COUNTRY CAMPUS,
1010 WEST SAM HOUSTON PARKWAY, NORTH

In retrospect, looking with dismay at the small turnout, she wondered if she should have selected a more central location. The price of gas had gone through the roof recently; people were being more cautious about long journeys. But where in this enormous, sprawling city was central? She had started with the idea of staying inside the Loop, close to Memorial Park (which had always seemed to her the ideal place for a midnight wolf-pack gathering), but the prices of the few venues she'd investigated had put her off. Houston Community College was more accommodating, and although they had campuses dotted around the city, this was the one where she'd been a student, it was easy to find, and, maybe most important, it was in the northwest, her own territory, just ten minutes from her apartment in one direction, ten minutes to Memorial Park in another.

No, she decided, the location was not at fault. Some of those who'd responded lived out by the airport, some were closer to downtown, while others lived in the south, and there was at least one who'd mentioned Deer Park. This was a city of drivers, used to judging distances not in miles but in minutes by freeway. Those who had stayed away must have had other reasons. Maybe they'd never intended to come. Maybe they shared an occult, insider knowledge that let them know she was a fake. Maybe real werewolves didn't use the Internet. Or maybe, unlike their wild brethren, they were naturally loners.

Mel continued to lurk and prowl, hoping the crowd would grow, hoping that one of the others would take charge, so she wouldn't have to put herself on display. But no one made a move. Clearly, there were no alpha males in this sorry excuse for a pack, so at seven minutes to eight, Mel went to the front of the room, cleared her throat, and invited everyone to please take a seat.

Suddenly the little scattering of people, all so disparate they might have wandered in here by mistake rather than design, coalesced into her audience.

Under their collective gaze, Mel wondered why she'd ever thought this a good idea. She only wanted to meet one werewolf—not be stared at by a whole pack of them. And to have to go on pretending to be one! What had she been thinking? If she revealed her ignorance now, asked the wrong questions, let the mask slip, she'd be at their mercy. She clutched the edge of a table, feeling like Little Red Riding Hood as she stared at the gleam of their eyes.

"Take a picture, it'll last longer," muttered the Chihuahua.

"What?" Dislike stiffened her spine; Mel glared. "Would you mind speaking up? I'm not sure everyone heard you."

The tiny nose wrinkled disdainfully. "I wondered if you were going to tell us why you called this meeting. What you hope to accomplish."

"I hoped you would tell me. I mean," she amended hastily, "all of us. Maybe we could each say what we hope to get out of this meeting. That's really all . . . I thought . . . it seemed like a good idea just to get together and talk," she finished rather lamely.

The Chihuahua shrugged. "You start."

"It doesn't have to be me first." But as no one else volunteered, she took the plunge. "I guess, like I said online, I felt lonely. I wanted to meet others in the same situation."

"Why?"

"Why? Well . . . we are pack animals. Aren't we? I think so, anyway. It's not natural to be alone."

"It's not natural to be like this!" cried one of the wives. Her husband ducked his head as she spoke. "I don't see how getting together with others is going to make anything better. I don't want him to be part of a pack; why should he? He's not a wild animal; he's my husband!"

"Is he allowed to cross the street by himself?" It was the dirty man who replied. "Chrissake, he's your husband the rest of the time. What's wrong with you? You can't let loose, can't let him be something else, for just one night a month? What about you, man, how do you feel? You totally whipped? You let your woman talk for you?"

The husband's head jerked up, and, even though she wasn't the target, Mel took an instinctive step back.

"She knows how I feel," he said softly. "I feel like she does. I don't like it. I didn't ask for it to happen. I want to be a man all the time, not lose control, lose myself, when the moon is full." He sneered suddenly. "You like it?"

The other man shrugged. "Like, dislike, it just is. It's part of who I am. I don't have a problem with that."

"No problem. Well, aren't you the lucky one." He moved suddenly in his seat as if about to rise. "It's a disease, pea-brain! And I don't accept that some disease is part of me—like my— my nose. I mean, if my nose was deformed, like a pig's snout, I wouldn't feel like, oh, I got no problem, that's just me—hell, I'd go to a doctor and get it fixed! Who wouldn't?"

"So go to a doctor."

"You think I haven't? Seriously, you think a doctor can fix what we've got?"

"I already told you. I don't think it needs fixing."

"The doctors think it's in our heads. In my head. They think I'm crazy. I go to the doctor, and all he can do is give me pills, make me sleepy and dumb—they don't change anything. They just make me feel stupid. I tried to show him—"

"You tried?"

The other man made a low groaning sound. "I showed him, all right? I got him to check me into a hospital and keep me overnight."

There was a collective catching of the breath. The dirty man tensed, and for a moment Mel, her skin tingling, thought he would attack his adversary. Then he relaxed a little and slowly, slowly shook his head. "Man, you are . . . something else."

"But the doctor didn't think so. Still thinks I'm crazy. He offered to run some tests—which by the way my insurance wouldn't cover—but all he could advise was I should keep taking the happy pills and also talk to a psychiatrist."

"None so blind as he who will not see," said his wife.

She must have seen, thought Mel, breathless. She must watch her husband transform from man into wolf every single month. And still she thought it not a wonder but a disability. But how could she appreciate what she had in him if he didn't want it? And how could a doctor not realize what he was seeing? She supposed there must be people, even very smart people, who denied the evidence of their senses if it conflicted with what was supposed to be possible. How else could werewolves have survived into modern times without being recognized by science?

The dirty man shrugged. "My advice to you—"

"I don't want your stupid advice," the married man snapped back. "All I want—the only reason we came here tonight—is to hear somebody say there is a way out, there is a cure." He swiveled around in his chair to fix his gaze on Mel. She tried not to flinch. "I thought you were talking in code," he said. "Your ads. First you say you wanted to join a pack, then you advertise this support group."

"Lyncanthropy," said the Chihuahua, her mouth twisting into a smile that might have been pained, or mocking.

"That, too. A medical term, right? So, see, I thought there

might be a drug, a new drug, to repress the symptoms—maybe even gene therapy . . . ?"

Mel stood frozen, with no idea of what to say. It turned out her lack of response said it all.

"No," he said flatly, as his expression changed, blood shining dully in his cheeks. "So obvious—what you are—stupid of me—I see now."

His wife was already standing. He got up, too, and they left without another word. The single woman went after them, and then the other couple. Only the two single men remained.

Mel looked at them, wanting to pass off the defection of the others with some light comment, but afraid. She'd given herself away. Judging from the woman's reaction, *lycanthropy* was not a term they used among themselves. And somehow *pack* was wrong, too, and maybe even *werewolf*. What did they call themselves? She tried to get some clue from the argument she'd witnessed, running it back through her head, but she'd been silent too long; she must have seemed utterly defeated, with nothing more to say, because the dirty man got up to go.

"Wait!" she called out. "Please don't leave."

He stopped and looked at her. She saw, beneath the grease and dirt and stubble that he might be quite attractive, and was spurred to make an effort. "I'm not . . . what he thought. And . . . maybe I did it wrong, the way I proposed this meeting and all, but I still . . . there's a good reason for it," she went on, desperately improvising. "I'd really like to talk to you. Can we just talk?"

His eyes bored into hers until she felt dizzy. "Okay," he said, and stood there, relaxed, light on his feet, arms loose at his sides, waiting.

"Well . . . want to go for a drink somewhere?"

He shook his head, and her heart plummeted. But he plucked at his filthy T-shirt and smiled wryly. "I'm not fit for human company now. I came here straight from fixing my truck. I should have cleaned up first, but I was running late. We could make it another night."

Her heart gave a hopeful leap. "Fine, yes, let's. When?"

"Uh . . . how about Tuesday?"

She knew—they both knew—that would be the night of the full moon. Her mouth dried. She could only stare back at him with widening eyes and nod her head.

"All right. You like barbecue?"

"Sure."

"Goode Company, on Kirby . . ."

"I know it."

It was her favorite place for a sliced beef sandwich, even if it was always crowded at lunch. It was well inside the Loop, not far from where she worked. She wondered if that was home territory for him, or—deliberately? —not.

"Five-thirty all right with you?"

That would give him plenty of time to get far away from her after they'd eaten, long before the moon would rise, if he decided he couldn't trust her. Fair enough. She nodded again.

"See you then," he said. She stood watching the space where he'd been until a small sound reminded her she wasn't alone.

The overweight young man in the short-sleeved white shirt stood up, his red lips stretched into a predatory smile. "I'll take you up on that drink, right now," he said. "I'd like to talk."

She didn't want to, but she made herself smile back in a friendly way.

"There's coffee here," she pointed out.

He wrinkled his nose. "Bet it's nasty. Anyway, I'd rather have something cold. There's a TGIF just off the feeder, how about that?"

"All right . . ."

"Devon. I'm Devon."

"I'm Mel." They walked out together.

"What's that short for, Melanie? Melissa? Melinda? No? Um, Okay, let me think. Melody? Melanctha?"

As they exited the building into the parking lot, he abandoned his guesses to suggest it would be a sensible, gas-saving measure to go in one car. "I have to swing back this way anyway on my way home."

"Well, I don't," she said. "And I'm not leaving my ride." She put on her helmet as she spoke, and indicated her Honda Nighthawk. "Meet you at Friday's."

TGIFs could be crowded and noisy at certain times, but a quarter to nine on a Thursday night was not one of them. Devon ordered a beer and a plate of nachos, and pressed her to have a specialty cocktail when she said she didn't like beer, but she stuck to iced tea.

"Worried you might get drunk? Scared I might take advantage of you?" He gave her a loose-lipped leer. "You got a long way to go? I'd be happy to drive you home."

"No thanks." What a creep. She couldn't see herself putting up with this human personality even if he did turn into a wolf once a month, but he let fall various comments that made her feel sure he was another supernatural groupie, like herself. She had no idea if he believed her claim to be a werewolf, or if it was enough for him that she was female and hadn't actually run away screaming.

Half an hour of his undiluted company was more than enough. Even though she brushed off his attempts to get her phone number and made it clear that she had no interest in seeing him again, she left by the back alley—an easy route for the Nighthawk, but it might be tricky for his Suburban. Instead of following the tollway feeder as usual, she took off into the nearest neighborhood, accepting the thirty-mile-per-hour speed limit and a meandering journey home for the certainty that she had well and truly lost her unwanted companion.

Ari—that was the formerly dirty man's name—cleaned up beautifully. She wouldn't even have recognized him on Tuesday if he hadn't been waiting for her in the Goode Company parking lot and said hello as she was about to walk past.

His voice was the same, but—shaved, hair washed and fluffy, exuding a faint aroma of green tea and figs, attired in faded jeans and a snug black T-shirt—he was a different person, really quite dangerously attractive. Luckily, he noticed the Nighthawk, and that gave her a moment to recover outside the full beam of his attention.

"Wow, you have a bike."

"Uh-huh. You?"

His lips pursed and he shook his head. "I wish. Maybe, if I make a little more money this year, I could afford . . ."

"You have a car, don't you?"

He frowned. "So?"

"I mean, you could trade it in. You don't need more than one set of wheels, do you?"

He shrugged uncertainly. "I'd rather just use it for fun, especially if I had somebody to ride with." He gave her a look that was a reminder of her public claim to be lonely, wanting a pack to run with, and she became aware she was on a precipice, with no idea of how to talk herself down from her lie.

"Let's go in," she said quickly. "I'm starved, and the smell of meat is driving me crazy!"

Despite her words—and the fact that she'd had nothing to eat all day but a banana-pecan muffin and a skinny latte—Mel managed to consume barely half her sandwich, and that was a struggle. The sheer physical excitement of being close to this handsome werewolf, along with the fear that at any moment she'd say something to reveal her true nature and drive him away, made it tough to swallow.

They sat out on the patio to eat—the open air was humid and hot, but far from the unbearable sauna it would be in a few weeks—and while James McMurtry's latest songs played in the background, they talked about themselves. Neither so much as hinted at the W-word, but concentrated on ordinary, ground-laying stuff about jobs and schools, musical preferences, and the best things on YouTube this week. It could have been any ordinary first date. Except that she'd never felt so nervous and excited, never had so much pent-up emotion invested in the out-come of any other date in her life. Maybe this was how women had felt in the olden days, when to sleep with a man was to seal your fate.

She heard very little of what Ari said; her attention was too involved with monitoring his responses to her. She knew he was attracted to her, and it was clearly no simpler for him than it was for her—she could feel the wary tingling of his nerves as he tried to make his mind up, which instinct to follow, to trust her, or not? It was all very nerve-wracking, but, in the end, as she'd hoped, he went with the physical attraction.

It was barely six-thirty, still daylight, when he suggested going back to his place.

"It's not far," he said. "We can have coffee, and I've got some Ben and Jerry's in the ice box."

"You give good directions?"

"No, I'm going to drive."

She shook her head. "I'm not leaving my ride."

He smiled slyly. "You don't have to leave your ride. Wait'll you see mine."

It was an old Ford pickup truck, really old, like something her grandfather had owned. The back panel lay down to form a ramp; she could have ridden the Nighthawk up and in if she'd cared to. "There's even a blanket to keep it warm, and a tarp to keep it dry if it rains. Not that it will rain."

"Very cozy."

"My neighbors think it drives down property values when I park it out front, but I've never had a more useful vehicle."

"I bet."

"So, are we on? Will you trust me to take you there?"

It seemed like a test, like, what would a real werewolf do? Maybe she should insist on keeping her own independence, but the connection between them was still so tenuous, she was afraid of losing him in the diabolical traffic that clogged the freeways at this time of day. What if she missed the exit and never saw him again?

"We'll trust you," she said.

"All right!"

They didn't have to go on the freeway at all; it turned out that Goode Company really was Ari's local barbecue place. His house was in an old neighborhood a few blocks off Bissonnet. Although several houses on his street were huge, recent constructions likely valued at half a million or more, his was the original bungalow built on the lot back in the 1950s. She remembered he'd told her he was an orphan, his mother having passed just a year ago, and wondered if it had been his childhood home.

But, inside, it had the feeling of a place not long occupied. The walls were a freshly painted white, with no pictures or ornaments, and the furniture was sparse and new-looking.

He made coffee, and they made meaningless small talk, standing in the kitchen while they waited for it to brew. She could tell that he was nervous and excited, too, and she wondered how much time they'd have to make love before he began to change. How sudden would it be? And how much conscious control would he have? Would he attack her? And if he did, would it be with the aim of changing her, or to kill? Was she crazy to put herself at his mercy like this?

"Are you cold? I left the air-conditioning on, but—"

"No, I'm not cold. Not at all. The opposite, really." Her gaze locked on his until he came forward and put his arms around her. They kissed for a while as her legs grew weak, and finally he suggested they move to the bedroom.

The bed faced an uncurtained window onto a backyard screened by a privacy fence.

"I can close it if you want, but nobody can see in, and with it open like this, when the moon comes up . . ."

"Mmm, nice," she said quickly, sensing she was meant to finish the sentence and not knowing how. To distract him, she stripped off her top.

They made love, and the room grew thick with shadows as, outside, evening darkened into night.

When would it happen? Mel wondered as they lay tangled together, resting. She was alert, too tightly wound up with anticipation to truly relax, but she guessed from the laxness of Ari's muscles, and the slow rhythm of his breath, that he'd fallen asleep. Presumably he'd wake up before he changed—wouldn't he? Surely he couldn't be so casual about it that he'd risk sleeping through the big event! But maybe it made no difference.

She tried not to fidget, tried not to be impatient, but her leg, trapped beneath one of his, began to cramp. She had to push him to free herself. "Sorry," she whispered, and kissed his shoulder. No response. When she let him go he flopped back, a dead weight, and as she listened, she became aware of how silent the room had become; she could no longer hear his breathing.

"Ari?" She bit her lip, then laid her ear to his chest. Inside, his heart went on beating, and when she held her own and strained to hear, she could just make out the slow exhalation of his breath.

She looked out the window and saw the silver gleam of the full moon hanging low above the treetops.

She pressed his bare upper arm, squeezed it, tried to shake him awake as she said his name, but there was no response. She gently nibbled his ear, then blew in it, before giving it a sharper nip, but he didn't so much as flinch or groan. If she hadn't been able to feel his warmth and the continued slow thump of his heart, she could have thought him dead. Turning on the light, she leaned over him, lightly slapped his cheeks, then clapped her hands.

"Ari! Get up now!"

Not a twitch in reply. Lifting his eyelids, she saw his eyes were rolled up in his head.

She sat back on her heels. Her vision blurred, and then hot, fat tears rolled down her cheeks. Now she understood how a werewolf could spend the night under observation, and the hospital staff would never see anything they could not explain. Nothing happened, except inside his head, or inside the head of anyone who thought he was a werewolf.

For a while she wept, mourning the loss of her long-cherished dream. Then she went to the bathroom, had a shower, and dressed herself. When she came out, Ari was still lying as flat and motionless as a corpse on the bed. She supposed he'd be like that until dawn, when he'd wake up believing his wolf dreams were true.

Her hands clenched as she looked at him, and she felt a terrible urge to take revenge on his body; not to kill him, but to slash and cut and mutilate, to leave the mark of her anger and disappointment in a way he'd never be able to forget.

But that would not be fair. Of the two of them, she was the only liar.

So she forced down her fury, and turned away and went out into the night.

She was too angry, unhappy, and restless to go home; a long ride was the only thing that might make her feel better. She got on Highway 59, then took 45 going south. The flow of this main artery took her through the heart of the city and out, through south Houston, past old Hobby Airport, and down through the sprawling coastal suburbs, until she finally, truly felt she'd left the city behind. Past League City and La Marque, and then over the bridge to Galveston Island.

Tooling along Seawall, she spotted the giant shrimp on top of Casey's and realized she was hungry, so she stopped for a big plate of cold shrimp with Cajun hot sauce and plenty of Saltine crackers, washed down with a light beer. Afterward, she rode the whole length of the island, all the way through the state park at the far end, where the darkness of night and the warm salty air and the empty space all around combined to soothe her troubled soul.

It was very late—or very early—when she left the island. She'd just come off the bridge on the mainland and was powering across the flat, empty marshland bordering Jones Bay when she saw the pack. Seven or eight large, doglike creatures loped along, parallel to the road—empty except for her—their fur gleaming softly in the moonlight.

Wolves, she thought, and then immediately sneered at herself. She had wolves on the brain. Obviously it would take a while before the truth about werewolves seeped through to her unconscious mind. That these might be real wolves was just as unlikely, since that species had been hunted to extinction in Texas many decades before she was born. These animals must be something else—coyotes, most likely, or maybe a new coyote-dog hybrid, which would explain why they looked so big.

She remembered an item on a local news program about the urban coyote. As its traditional habitats were built over, instead of being pushed farther out into increasingly smaller, less hospitable territories, the coyote had adapted to the urban environment. This was not such good news for the small pets that got preyed upon, and because of the plentiful and rich diet offered by people's trash, not to mention cross-breeding with stray dogs, the new breed of urban coyote was not only bigger and stronger but more dangerous, being less shy of people than their wild ancestors had been.

Even as she recalled the serious face of the newscaster, warning Houstonians that these animals were a threat, Mel felt no fear. She could easily outrun them on her bike, and in any case, the pack showed no interest in her. Soon enough they vanished into the distance behind her and she was alone again in the moonlit night, with nothing to prove she'd ever seen them at all.

The road did not stay hers for long. After she passed League City, traffic began to trickle onto the highway, until, by the time she'd entered Houston city limits, there was a light but steady flow of vehicles. Because traffic was so light, most of the people on the road were driving faster than usual. Ordinary cars and trucks zoomed past Mel at speeds much higher than her bike could manage. She couldn't help but find this annoying—she was used to being the one doing the zooming and zipping through heavy traffic—but since there was nothing she could do about it, she slowed down. There was no hurry for her to get home.

She'd just left 45 and filtered onto 610 going north when she saw the wolf.

This time, there was no chance of convincing herself it was a big coyote, rare breed of dog, or anything except a fully grown northern gray wolf. The hairs rose on her arms and the back of her neck as her awed gaze locked onto the creature. She eased off on the gas.

The wolf was far enough ahead that her bike was no threat to it, especially not at this speed. At the moment that it began to cross the freeway, all four lanes were empty of traffic. It should have been perfectly safe. But then, with shocking suddenness, a car appeared, coming out of nowhere, it seemed, and hurtling past Mel at nearly a hundred miles an hour.

It was a stupidly big car—one of those overpowered tanks designed for people who thought of themselves as road warriors, in need of protection—going stupidly fast, and the bare, unarmored creature trotting along so smoothly never had a chance.

The SUV just clipped the wolf as it was crossing the road; a quick, brutal touch that barely impacted on the machine (it kept on going without pause or wobble) but knocked the animal off its feet, lifted it, and flung it across two lanes, smack into the concrete barrier.

Did the driver even see what he had done? If so, he gave no sign as he roared away. The wolf subsided into a shrunken heap of fur and bones.

Mel felt as if she'd been struck herself. Not giving a thought to the dangers of stopping on the inside lane of a major freeway, she pulled in and dismounted.

Even though it seemed clear death must have been immediate, she couldn't help hoping there was still something she could do to help.

Close up, she saw no blood, but the magnificent head was twisted around in a way that told her the neck was broken, the spine snapped. One open eye—the only one visible—was already glazed in death. She peeled off one of her gloves and touched the still-damp nose, from which no breath issued. She laid her hand on the thick fur, feeling the body heat that hadn't yet had time to dissipate. Tears pricked behind her eyes, and she blinked rapidly and swallowed hard.

But along with the sorrow she felt at this senseless, brutal, accidental death came a rising excitement, a sense of awe at what it meant.

A wolf had died. A wolf, on the Houston freeway.

That pack she'd seen down by the coast—not coyotes at all.

How many others were there, loping across shadowed suburban lawns or through the wild, wooded acres of Memorial Park at this very moment? Twenty, thirty, maybe even more? Most of them would be smart enough to avoid spending much time out in the open, where they might be seen, and especially to avoid the freeways with their killer cars.

And as they roamed, wherever they went, their human bodies would be lying unconscious in their beds, waiting for their souls to return after a night existing in the forms of wolves. This very physical form. She touched the rapidly cooling body again, assuring herself of its reality. This was no dream. She understood now how, through so many centuries, werewolves could be real yet remain hidden from scientific enquiry. It was easy to see why doctors and hospital staff had been blind to the truth, just as she had been herself.

But how did it work? Suddenly, she had more questions than ever. And what happened to the wolf bodies after the sun came up? She wondered if anyone knew.

Gazing down at the dead wolf, she thought that at this moment, in some house or apartment, a human being must be lying dead. One of those mysterious, sudden deaths you sometimes heard about: no suspicious circumstances, a man in the prime of life . . .

All at once she thought of Ari.

She looked down at the crumpled heap of flesh and bone, and went cold. What if . . . what if she'd somehow been responsible? What if, instead of staying safe in his usual haunts, he'd ventured out across the city in search of her?

She was shaking as she got back on her bike. She had to force herself to take it slow and easy—it would just be too stupid, too Romeo and Juliet, if she managed to get herself killed, and all along he was still safe where she'd left him, slumbering away.

It was one of the most difficult rides of her life. She arrived back at his house, soaked in sweat, her muscles achingly tight. As she dismounted on his driveway, she noticed that her bell was missing. This struck an ominous note. The little brass bell had been a token given to her by the man who'd taught her to ride. It was meant to protect her from the evil spirits of the road, and even though she didn't really believe it—not literally—still, that it should be absent now was sinister.

When she left, Mel hadn't been intending to return, so she was relieved to find that the door hadn't locked automatically behind her.

Ari lay in bed just as she had left him, motionless, on his back, naked beneath the dark brown sheet. She sank to her knees at the bedside and laid her head on his chest. At first, through the rushing of blood in her ears and her own, too rapid breathing, she couldn't hear or feel anything else, but gradually, forcing herself to calm, she became aware of the steady beat of his heart inside his warm chest, and then of his faint, shallow breathing. He was safe.

Tears filled her eyes. She wept a little, for release. She'd imagined keeping a wakeful vigil over him for what remained of the night, but a wave of tiredness washed over her, and not bothering to undress, she lay down beside him and slept.

When she awoke, the room was light with morning, and she was alone. She sat up quickly and followed the scent of fresh coffee to the kitchen.

"Good morning," she said cheerily, but froze at his baleful stare. "What's wrong?"

He made a show of considering. "Nothing, I guess, if you don't think it's wrong to lie." His brows came together. "Did you think I wouldn't know? That you could get away with it? But, wait, why should you care? You got what you wanted: a night with the freak. Tell me, Miss Melly: did it live up to your expectations? Was it as exciting as you'd hoped?"

"It was good for me," she said, feeling her cheeks get hot. "I thought you seemed to be enjoying yourself, too."

"Don't change the subject. If this was just about sex you could have told me the truth."

"Oh, really? If I'd told you over barbecue that I wasn't a were-wolf, would you still have invited me back here?" She saw him wince. "What? Oh, the W-word. You don't use it. I didn't know."

"Obviously."

"An easy way to weed out the groupies and other liars?"

He shrugged.

"Okay, so you don't like people like me. But you came to my meeting."

"Um. Well—I just wasn't quite sure. I didn't want to pre-judge, just in case. You know what that guy said—Mr. It's-a-disease—about a code? That's what I wondered. I thought it was just possible somebody else, one of my own kind, was trying to find me."

She thought of the pack she'd seen when she was out riding. "But can't you find each other when you're, you know . . . I mean, you must meet each other all the time."

He grimaced. "Hardly 'all the time.' Once a month, in our other forms. It's rarely planned, although when you find a good place to roam, you tend to go back again and again. Is that terri-toriality? Or just common sense? I don't know. I mean, you want to be able to roam around freely, maybe hunt, definitely play, and you don't want to be seen by the—by anyone. Memorial Park is great. I can't remember how many square miles of land that cov-ers, lots of places to run, easy to get lost in, and after dark, there really is just nobody else around. And right smack dab in the middle of town. But even so, this is a big city, and a short hop in the car translates into a damn long run on four legs. And leaving your car overnight, somewhere it shouldn't be, even just once a month, is risky."

There were so many questions she wanted to ask: why hadn't his wolf materialized inside the house? Where did it appear, and could he control that location at all? How did it work? How much did he remember? But even if he'd lightened up a little, she didn't think he'd put up with her questions for long. She watched as he poured himself a cup of coffee without offering her any or indicating that she should help herself.

She spoke as neutrally as she could. "If two people are in the same place, together, when the moon rises, their wolves will be in the same place."

"Seems you know all about it."

"No, I don't, but I want to."

"Oh, and I'm supposed to be grateful for your curiosity?" With a jerky movement suggesting he was repressing a more violent response, he set his mug down hard on the counter. "I'm not here to be your personal freak-show!"

Seeing the strong fingers of his empty hands, she felt a thrill of fear. "I don't think you're a freak. I think . . . I think you're wonderful. I've never met anyone more . . . more . . . oh, please, Ari, I love you!"

She hadn't meant to say it so soon or so bluntly, but there it was, her final throw of the dice; she had nothing else to offer.

His shoulders sagged, and he was unable to meet her gaze. "That's a little dramatic, isn't it?"

"It's true."

"You hardly know me."

"What about last night? Doesn't that count?"

She felt more confident now, knowing she'd disarmed him. Of course he didn't love her yet, but he might come around to it in time. She already knew his secret, and, far from a barrier between them, it had brought them closer. It was true she'd lied to him at first, but since it had brought them together, surely that was forgivable?

She had been hovering in the doorway, but now she took a step forward. "You don't have to share anything you don't want to. I'm not asking for a big commitment, just a chance. I mean, why not? You can't pretend you don't like me—I mean, you asked me out."

His eyes flashed. "Only because I thought you were someone else."

That hurt a little. "Well, okay, but who's being prejudiced now? Is that fair? You thought I was . . . like you. I'm not, but I'm still a nice person—"

He shook his head savagely. "I don't mean I thought you were different—I thought you might be someone else. Someone I'd already met—just once—and really, really wanted to find again."

She flashed on the "missed connect" classifieds in the weekly press: You were the blue-eyed princess in tight blue jeans at Hooters' Happy Hour who made me spill my beer . . .

Her chest felt hollow as she understood. He was in love with someone else. "You thought maybe she was looking for you, too, and might use the same language I did: 'Lonely werewolf, longs to run with pack.' Not a code, because you don't have a code, but almost."

He nodded slowly. "I knew how unlikely it was, and I was pretty sure, really, as soon as I saw you that you weren't . . . her . . . but . . . well, I'd been looking for her for so long, and you're an attractive woman, and, let's be frank, I was horny." He shrugged. "Well, we're both grown-ups. No need to apologize."

"Love means never having to say you're sorry," she said, a bit hopelessly.

"I don't love you, Mel."

"And I don't love you, either," she snapped. "As you helpfully pointed out, I hardly know you. I could say the same about your lost love. You don't even know her name or what she looks like. We're both in love with fantasy figures."

"Mine is real."

"So is mine; I just haven't met him yet." She tried a gentler approach, softening her tone. "But look—we could still have fun together."

"Like last night? I'm sorry, Mel, but even if it doesn't creep you out, the idea—"

"So change me," she said quickly. "I mean it! Make me like you. It's what I want. Next month, you could bite me . . ."

He recoiled. "No!"

"Why not? If I ask you to—and then we could be together—"

"It doesn't work like that! We're not vampires, you know."

"How does it work?"

But it was clear, from the hard look on his face, that he was not going to share any more secrets with her. "Forget it," he said. "I'm not trying to make you feel worse, but there's no future for us. It's not your fault. Even if I could do it—even if you managed to change some other way—it wouldn't change the way I feel. I'm sorry."

There was no point in arguing about it; it was never possible to argue someone into love with you—she knew that all too well from being on the other side of these miserable, final conversations.

So she took her leave of him. He probably thought her heart was broken, and maybe it should have been after such a disappointing end. But in fact she felt quite ridiculously cheerful as she rode away from his house. She knew this was not the end, but only the beginning. She'd finally learned the truth about werewolves, and now the hunt was on.

Innocent

GENE WOLFE

You promise not to throw that stuff on me again, Father? Really promise?

Okay. It burns, but if you promise, you can come on in. What I wanted to tell you last time was that I didn't do anything they say. None of it is true. One of the cops said I was the kind who hangs around school yards, so that part's true. I did. Sit down on the other bunk and I'll explain.

It isn't that I want to make love with little girls like they say. I never, ever wanted that. I will tell you the truth, and if you want me to swear on that prayer book I'll do it. I have never wanted sex with anybody I've ever seen. Not little girls, or boys either. And not women, or not very much. Not with men. Just thinking about it makes me sick.

I was sick a lot when I was a kid. I had a delicate stomach is what the doctor and everybody said. Everything I ate made me sick. It tasted awful, too. There was this nice girl next door. Her name was Nancy. She felt sorry for me, so she gave me a little piece of her chocolate bar one time. She said how good it was and how much I'd like it.

Well, I wanted to make her happy, so I made myself eat it. It smelled horrible and tasted the same way, and you know what chocolate looks like. But I got it down just the same and told her how good it was. I was still puking that night a long time after Bradley went to bed.

Him? Oh, he was my foster father back then. I grew up in foster homes. There were three or four, maybe five, because nobody really wanted me ever, and I guess I ought to have told you.

No, I never knew my real mom, or my dad either. Some garbage man found me in a trash can—

Sorry my laugh bothers you, Father, but I can't help laughing every time I think about it. It is just so funny. I've seen the old TV news. The library helped me look them up. They are nice like that.

No, not even that old. I was premature, and my mother just threw me away, whoever she was. They never did find her, only a policeman—this was another policeman, an old guy—told me one time that they thought it was this one girl who'd hung herself a couple days before they found me. That's what they thought because her body looked like she'd just had a kid, only the doctors said I couldn't have lived that long without being fed and kept warm.

Only I'm never cold. Are you, Father? How does it feel?

I've picked up pieces of ice and even put them in my shirt in the winter. It doesn't bother me. You know what does, Father? Wearing a shirt. Wearing anything. Can I take mine off?

Thanks. Yes, I'm hairy, and I suppose that helps.

Oh, yes. I hate hot weather. You know what I really like? I like winter nights, those cold, clear nights when the stars shine and shine, and there's frost everywhere.

Or snow. Snow is good. That's when I pray.

Sure I believe in God, Father. For me, God is the moon.

Wait!

I know all that. He's not really the moon, and it's just a sort of island up in the sky. People have been up there. You know that crucifix you're holding up is just wood and metal, but it *means* God to you. That's how the moon is to me. God hung the moon, and since I can't see Him I pray to Him there.

Sure. Ask me anything you want. What do you want to ask me about?

Here? In jail? Well, to tell you the truth, I don't eat anything much, which I guess is why they told you I was on a hunger strike.

No way! I am not. Give me something that won't make me sick and just watch me eat! Only the food in here is like what they had in the cafeteria at school. It's just garbage. Some of it might have been good meat when they got it, but they ruin it on purpose.

So what I would do back then was go to a little café I knew about where they'd bring me what I asked for. It was pretty bad, sure, but I could eat it and not puke it up. That way I did not starve. When I was older and had more money, I would just buy meat at the butcher's and eat it. Sometimes I was so hungry I would open the package there in the store. He didn't like it, but I was a good customer. Later I used to snack on the job. You get a nibble here and a nibble there, and if you keep it up all day it's enough.

Do you want to hear about this, Father? About what I really like?

Okay, let me tell you how I found out. I was down at this one dump with this guy Paul. We were climbing over the junk looking for something we might like and looking for rats, too. We looked for the rats because they would bite you if you didn't see them first. We had sticks, and we would whack rats with them any time we could. Mostly we missed. You probably know how that is. They run fast, and they're always getting under something.

Paul got a rat, a big one. He knocked it over toward me,

knocked it off its feet, you know, and I whacked it with my stick, too. After that, Paul killed it, or thought he had. He whacked it two or three times and it lay there like it was dead. Then he picked it up, and it bit him . . .

I should not be telling you all this, Father. Bending your ear like this is what I mean. I know you don't care about all this. The thing is, I'm just so lonesome. Hungry and lonesome, like a lost dog. I know it seems pretty funny for me to be lonesome in a place as noisy as this, with doors slamming and people yelling all the time, but I've got nobody to talk to. No visitors, either.

No, I'm not in solitary, Father. Or I'm not supposed to be. Who told you that?

Well, I'm not. It's all a big lie. They would have told me, wouldn't they? Besides, I haven't done anything, really. I mean since I have been in here. If you get put in solitary, it is just about always because you hit one of the screws. I have never done that, or bit one either.

You want to know the worst thing I've ever done in here? They won't let me go out to where the others eat, they just pass my tray in with their stinking garbage on it. So a couple of times I have thrown all their garbage on the floor and walked on it.

Why? I just wanted to show them what I thought of it. That's all. Besides, I wanted them to have to talk to me. Which they did, and brought me a bucket and a mop and made me clean it up. It gave me something to do. Two of them tried to twist my arms the first time, and it scared them. That was the most fun I've had since I got stuck in here.

Oh, I'm strong, real strong. Take my hand, Father, and I'll show you.

All right, but I would not have hurt you bad. I had this cell-mate. His name was Paul, only I do not remember his last name. Really I have had eight or maybe ten. Can I tell you what they do here? How they use me?

Well, suppose they want to put somebody in solitary, but they know he has this good lawyer. He's got money, right? So if they do, that lawyer will go to a judge and try to get him out. Well, what they do is put him in here with me. In a couple of days he will be begging them for solitary.

Oh. Yeah. I guess I think of all these guys as Paul because Paul was the first, the kid the rat bit. He was bleeding pretty good and naturally it made me hungry, so I said don't you know rats are poison? I got to suck out the poison or you'll die.

He let me. I got it in my mouth, and it was the best thing I had ever tasted. Man, it was so good! So I kept drinking and drinking until Paul said you never spit the poison out. I said yes I did. That was a mistake, because he knew I hadn't. He got mad and jerked his hand away, and I bit his neck.

That was where I started learning about meat, right there in the dump. Meat doesn't really go bad as fast as people think. It depends on a lot of things, like can the sun hit it. I didn't know about that then, but I knew that if I left my meat there in the dump, the rats would get at it and it would be no use coming back for some the next time I got hungry.

Well, Father, there was this old factory near there where nobody worked anymore. It was supposed to be locked up, only Paul and me had found a way to get inside. We thought there would be a lot of rats in there, but there wasn't because there was nothing in there for them to eat.

So I went in there and the basement seemed like the best place. It was dark down there, and nobody would see my meat unless he went poking around down in that basement with a flashlight. So I left it down there and went home.

The next day I came back and there were rats, so I got some rope and hung it up where they couldn't get to it. It was dark and cool down there, so I felt like that would be a friendly place for me. It was, too. My meat lasted down there until I had eaten just about everything. I'd come back every day or maybe every two days. Or twice a day, sometimes.

No, they thought he'd run away. The police do that a lot, say he has run away, because then they don't have to look.

What you really need is a good freezer, but if you don't have one, there is still a lot you can do. You can rent a locker, too. That is what I did for a while. I knew how a butcher would wrap meat. The paper they use and the tape. I got a guy at work to tell me.

So I got some. And when I had meat I would cut it up and wrap it neat and everything. Then I would take it to my locker and people would think that I had paid for a side or killed a deer or something.

But like I said, I still had a lot to learn about meat. Old people are not good, did you know that? They are not. Younger is better until you get down to about ten, Father. After that, younger is just smaller.

You take this old guy Paul, or Bradley or whatever his name was. He was my foster father for a while, and I never did like him because he was generally mad about something, and I swear, Father, I could taste his pipe tobacco. I got some ketchup from the supermarket—just taking it you know because I didn't have much money then. I put that on the meat because it was a pretty color and I thought it would cover up the taste. It didn't, and he was the only one I ever put anything like that on.

Sure. All of it because I didn't want to waste him.

Well, they put me in a different foster home after that, because with him gone the lady had to go to work. Only I remembered the old place and came back for this one girl. She was really, really sweet. It started me wising up. Younger was better, and girls were better than boys. They are not so tough, they don't have that boy taste, and the fat runs all through everything. That's the good way.

No, I have never felt sorry about it the way you mean, but I kind of missed a few of the people afterward. Then, too, when it was somebody that I knew the police would come around sometimes and say when did you see her? Was there any reason for her to run away? All that stuff. It always made me kind of nervous, because I knew they would never understand. So it was better if it was somebody I did not know at all.

Of course, that was the trouble with Paul, the guy who used to sleep in that bunk. He was locked in with me, so they'd know right off. Besides, I'd only get one meal off him before they took the meat away.

Yeah. Sometimes I would get up when the moon was coming in through the window. I would stand beside his bunk and just look at him. How would this part taste and how would that part taste? Would it be better to boil the hands and feet? I knew I couldn't do it, but it was fun to think about just the same. Some nights I would think yes, and some nights no. Just eat the fingers, chewing up the bones.

Only some nights he'd wake up and get mad about me being there, and then I'd have to shut his mouth for him.

No, it's not so bad being alone. I walk up and down the cell, three steps this way and three steps that way. It drives them crazy. Then at night I yell out the window and listen. Nobody has ever yelled back, but if somebody ever does, I'll get out. I don't know how, but I will. You watch.

Oh, sure. I know all about those psychologists. They bring one in because they want to get rid of me, only I do not want to get sent where I will be with crazy people all the time. So I smile and answer all their questions right; what day is it and why am I in here and all that. It's all the same, and by now I know it better than they do. No, I don't ever hear voices, doc—only sometimes I wish I did. Well, doc, I'm me. I give them my name and tell them about foster homes and going to vocational school and all that. Only not about Paul, or Nancy, neither. After that I explain how I am innocent and it is all a big mistake anyway. By the time I've finished with them I know they will say, "Dull normal" when they get out.

Well, I am not a child molester no matter what the screws say. All right I guess I am a murderer, maybe. That part is probably right. Only not a child molester. No way!

Sure, I went to school. My middle school grades were not so good, so I went to Braciola Vocational. They had meat-cutting. It was really big there, and it was what I took. The teacher said I was a natural, and I'll tell you, Father, if my old teachers at the middle school had seen my grades, they would not have believed them. I got out pretty close to the top of my class. Only I used to see this one little girl.

You know where Braciola is, Father?

Well, it's right next to Glazier Elementary School. So when we went out to play softball or anything I would see the little kids playing there on the other side of the fence. If my team was at bat, I'd have plenty of time to look at them. There was this one girl, pretty and filled out nice without being too fat. You know what I mean? She looked tender, but she looked solid, too. I kept thinking how nice it would be to follow her home. Not close, you know, but just keeping an eye on her. See where she lived and all that. She'd be heavy, but not so heavy that I'd have trouble moving her around. I could even pack her in this one duffel bag I had. That's how I thought while I was still at Braciola.

Only I never did get to follow her because she got out of school before I did. So I thought probably she rides the school bus anyhow, and what good is that?

She was so pretty! You should've seen her, Father. Those wide eyes and that beautiful, innocent little face. You would have wanted her just like I did.

How old? Oh, I don't know for sure. Eight, maybe. Or she could have been seven. But so beautiful. And not big, but solid.

Father, I thought she could never be mine unless I could figure out some way to find out where she lived. Only I didn't want to ask any of the other kids about her. You understand what I mean? They would have remembered later. So I just watched her and thought someday I'll get one just like that.

You never know, Father. God arranges this stuff. It's not us, and it sure wasn't me. I got out of school like I said, and I got a job at the packing plant. I joined the International Brotherhood of Meatworkers and everything. This teacher I had recommended me, and anytime he recommended a guy, the Human Resources guy at the plant jumped at him. Everybody told me that, and when I applied and gave him my letter, I found out it was true. It said I was good-natured, hardworking, and reliable. On the next page it said I had a natural aptitude few students possess. That was the big finish, you know? I still remember it, and I'll bless Mr. Johnson to the end of my days.

I was walking back home from work one day and there she was. I guess she'd been kept after school for being naughty, or maybe there had been some kind of special thing at her school after classes. Practice for a school show, maybe. Something like that.

Anyway, there she was, and I followed her. It was broad daylight, so I wasn't planning to do anything at all. That day I just wanted to find out where she lived. I had this little apartment by then, and a nice new freezer.

So I followed her, and this car came along. The guy stopped and said her momma had sent him to get her and take her home.

Sure I could hear him, Father. You would be surprised how good my ears are. It's funny because I have a lot of color blindness. I know because they tested me at Braciola Vocational. So you would think my ears might be bad, too. Only they are a lot better than most people's.

Well, I heard him, like I said, and I knew right off that he was lying. He was going to steal her and he was real scared somebody would know it. I could hear it in his voice, but she could not. She got into the car with him, but I had the smell of him by then and I had seen the car and the license number. I wrote it down as soon as they had gone so I would not forget it.

No, Father. I have never owned a car. I never got that much money together before they put me in here. If I had owned a car I would have driven it to work, probably, and I would never have seen him stealing her.

So I borrowed somebody else's—just pulled him out when he was getting in and took his keys. Only I never meant to keep his car, which would be stealing. I was going to leave it someplace where he would find it.

I looked for an hour, maybe, before I found them. They were in a trailer park where one of the guys I worked with lived. So I got out and knocked on the door of the trailer. He opened it, and when he saw how mad I was, he just ran away out the back door and I let him go.

Well, Father, maybe most of them don't have back doors, but this one did.

She was in there on the floor crying. He had tied her hands and there was a rope around her neck that was tied to the bed so she couldn't get away. Besides, he had torn off all her clothes and she was bleeding from down here.

Sure I did. You would have, too, Father. It tasted great.

So I said, don't cry, please don't cry, he's gone now and you don't have to worry about him anymore. Now you listen to me. I am going to leave you here until dark. It won't be long. When it is dark, nobody will see that you are naked, so then I can get you into my car and it will be all right.

No, Father. I wasn't going to hurt her at all.

So then I drove out to that factory where I had kept Paul. I had my paper and tape there, and a cleaver and some knives. You know. After that I went back home and put some in my freezer.

By then it was dark so I came back for her just like I had said. She was so sweet! She had finished crying by then, and the way she looked up at me . . . If you had seen her little face then, Father, you would know I would never hurt her. I untied her and got her into my car, only the police stopped us and here I am.

So I am not a child molester like they said. Not at all. He was the one that did her like they were married, only nobody could marry a girl as little as she was then.

Maybe ten. Not much older.

She'll be older now. I know that. But if you'll find her and talk to her, she'll tell you I never did. It was him. I just licked her where she was bleeding. You know. That was all I did.

Well, tell her to tell the truth, please. She won't lie to you, I know. And tell her I will get out someday and when I do I am going to look her up and make sure she's all right.

I didn't mean to scare you, Father. Really I didn't. I just laid my hand on your shoulder—you shouldn't be so touchy. Just tell the screw you want out.

Kitty Learns the Ropes

CARRIE VAUGHN

I hit play on the laptop DVD software and sat back to watch.

This was a recording of a boxing match in Las Vegas last year. The Heavyweight World Championships, the caption read. I was glad it did, because I knew nothing about boxing, nothing about who these guys were. Two beefy, sweaty men—one white, with a dark buzz cut and heavy brow, the other black, bald, snarling—were pounding on each other in rage. I winced as the blows against each other sent sweat and spit flying. As sports went, this was more unappealing than most, in my opinion.

Then the white boxer, Ian Jacobson, the defending champion, laid one into his opponent, Jerome Macy. The punch came in like a pile driver, snapped Macy's head around, and sent the big man spinning. He crashed head-first into the mat. The crack of bone carried over the roars and cheers of the crowd. I resisted an urge to look away, sure I was witnessing the boxer's death.

The arena fell silent, watching Macy lie still. Jacobson had retreated to an empty corner of the ring, looking agitated, while the referee counted down over Macy. Ringside officials leaned in, uncertain whether to rush in to help or wait for the count to end. Macy lay with his head twisted, his body crumpled, clearly badly injured. Blood leaked out his nose.

Then he moved. First a hand, then an arm. He levered himself up, shaking his head, shaking it again, stretching his neck back into alignment. Slowly, he regained his feet.

He turned, looking for his opponent with fire blazing in his eyes. Jacobson stared back, eyes wide, fearful. Obviously, he hadn't wanted Macy to be seriously hurt. But this—rising from the dead almost—must have seemed worse.

The roar of the crowd at the apparent resurrection was visceral thunder.

They returned to the fight, and Macy knocked out Jacobson a minute later, winning the title.

A hand reached over me and hit the pause button on the laptop.

"That wasn't normal," said Jenna Larson, the woman who had brought me the recording of the match. She was a rarity, a female sports reporter with national standing, known for hunting down the big stories, breaking the big news, from drug scandals to criminal records. "Tell me that wasn't human. Jerome Macy isn't human."

Which was why Larson was here, showing me this video. She wanted to know if I could tell Macy was a werewolf or some other supernatural/superhuman creature with rapid healing, or the kind of invulnerability that would let him not only stand back up after a blow like that, but go on to beat up his opponent. I couldn't tell, not by just watching the clip. But it wouldn't be hard for me to find out if I could get close enough to smell him. I'd know if he was a werewolf by his scent, because I was one.

She'd brought her laptop to my office. I sat at my desk, staring at the frozen image of Macy, shoulders slouched, looming over his fallen opponent. Larson stood over me—a position of dominance, my Wolf side noted testily—waiting for my reaction.

I pushed my chair away from the desk so I was out from under her, looking at her eye to eye without craning my neck. "I can't say one way or the other without meeting him."

"I can arrange that," she said. "His next bout is here in Denver this weekend. You come meet him, and if there is something going on, we share the scoop on the story."

This was making me nervous. "Jenna. Here's the thing: even if he is a werewolf, he probably doesn't want to advertise the fact. He's kept it hidden for a reason."

"If he is a werewolf, do you think it's fair that he's competing against normal human beings in feats of strength and endurance?"

I shrugged, because she was right on some level. However talented a boxer he was, did Macy have an unfair advantage?

It also begged the question: in this modern age when werewolves, vampires, witches, and other things that go bump in the night were emerging from shadows and announcing themselves—like hosting talk radio shows that delved into this secret world—how many other people had hidden identities? How many actors, politicians, and athletes weren't entirely human?

Larson was in her thirties, her shoulder-length brown hair shining and perfectly arranged around her face, her makeup calculated to look stunning and natural, like she wasn't wearing any. She wore a pantsuit with high heels and never missed a step. She was a woman in a man's profession, driven to make a name for herself. I had to respect that. The territorial side of me couldn't help but see an alpha female on the prowl.

She was brusque, busy, and clearly didn't have time to hang around because she shut down the laptop and started packing it into her sleek black shoulder bag.

"I know you're interested in this," she said. "If you don't help me, I'll get someone else. One way or another, with or without your help, I'm going to break this story. How about it?"

There wasn't even a question. She called me pretty well: I wouldn't let a story like this get away from me.

"I'm in," I said.

· · ·

I came within a hair of changing my mind outside the Pepsi Center the night of the bout. The crowd swarmed, jostling around me as they elbowed their way through the doors. This many people, all of them with an underlying aggression—they had paid a lot of money to watch two guys beat the crap out of each other—was making me want to growl. The Wolf side of my being didn't like crowds, didn't like aggression. I wanted to fight back, snarl, claw my way free to a place where I could run, where no one could touch me.

Concentrating, I worked to keep that part of me buried. I had to keep myself together to do my job.

I still wasn't sure I wanted to do this job. If Larson turned out to be right and Macy was a werewolf, what if he didn't want to be exposed? Should I step in and somehow talk her into keeping his secret? He had a right to the life he was carving out for himself. I'd been in his position once. On the other hand, maybe Macy would be okay with exposing his werewolf identity. Then I could claim his first exclusive interview for my radio show. Larson could break the story in print, I'd get the first live interview—part of me really hoped Macy was okay with telling the world about this.

The other part hoped he wasn't a werewolf at all. Luck had saved him during that bout in Vegas.

Larson met me inside the doors with a press pass that got us close to ringside. I wasn't sure I wanted to be ringside. Flying sweat and spit would hit us at this range. The arena smelled of crowds, of old sweat and layers of energy. Basketball, hockey, arena football, concerts, and circuses had all played here. A little of each remained, along with the thousands of people who watched. Popcorn, soda, beer, hot dogs, semi-fresh, semi-stale, ground into the concrete floor, never to be erased. And the echoes of shouting.

The arena filled. Larson talked with her colleagues, talked on her cell phone, punched notes into her laptop. We waited for the gladiators to appear.

"You look nervous," she said to me, fifteen minutes into the waiting. I'd been hugging myself. "You ever been to a fight?"

I shook my head and unclenched my arms, trying to relax. "I'm not much into the whole sports thing. Crowds make me nervous." Made me want to howl and run, actually.

The announcer came on the booming PA system, his rich, modulated voice echoing through the whole place and rattling my bones. Lights on scoreboards flashed. The sensory input was overwhelming. I guessed we were starting.

The boxers—opponents, combatants, gladiators—appeared. A great cheer traveled through the crowd. Ironically, the people in the upper bleachers saw them before those of us with front row seats. We didn't see them until they climbed into the ring. The challenger, Ian Jacobson, looked even more fierce in person, glaring, muscles flexing. Already, sweat gleamed on his pale skin.

Then came Jerome Macy.

I smelled him before I saw him, a feral hint of musk and wild in this otherwise artificial environment. It was the smell of fur just under the skin, waiting to break free. Two werewolves could smell each other across the room, catching that distinctive mark.

No one who wasn't a werewolf would recognize it. Black hair cropped close to his head, he looked normal as he ducked between the ropes and entered the ring. Normal as any heavyweight boxer could look, that is. He seemed hard as stone, his body brown, huge, solid. In his wolf form, he'd be a giant. He went through the same routine, his manager caring for him like he was a racehorse.

Just as I spotted him, he could sense me. He glanced over the ropes, scanning for the source of that lycanthropic odor. Then he saw me sitting next to Jenna Larson, and his eyes narrowed. He must have known why I was here. He must have guessed.

My first instinct, wolf's instinct, was to cringe. He was bigger than I, meaner; he could destroy me, so I must show deference. But we weren't wolves here. The human side, the side that needed to get to the bottom of this story and negotiate with Larson, met Macy's gaze. I had my own strengths that made me his equal, and I wanted him to know that.

As soon as Macy entered the ring, Larson leaned over to me. "Well?" She didn't take her gaze off the boxer.

Macy kept glancing at us and his mouth turned in a scowl. He must have known who—and what—I was, and surely he knew about Larson. He noted the conspiracy between us and must have known what it meant. Must have realized the implications.

"Yeah, he is," I said.

Larson pressed her lips together in an expression of subdued triumph.

"What are you going to do?" I said. "Jump in and announce it to the world?"

"No," she said. "I'll wait until the fight's over for that." She was already typing on her laptop, making notes for her big exposé. Almost, I wanted no part of this. It was like she held this man's life in her hands.

But more, I wanted to talk to Macy, to learn how he did this. I knew from experience—vivid, hard-fought experience—that aggression and danger brought the wolf side to the fore. If a lycanthrope felt threatened, the animal, monstrous side of him would rise to the surface to defend him, to use more powerful teeth and claws in the battle.

So how did Macy train, fight, and win as a boxer without losing control of his wolf? I never could have done it.

The bout had started. In the ring, the two fighters circled each other—like wolves, almost—separated only by the referee, who seemed small and weak next to them. Then they fell together.

Gloves smacked against skin. I winced at the pounding each delivered, jackhammer blows slamming over and over again.

Around me, the journalists in the press box regarded the scene with cool detachment, unemotional, watching the fight clinically, an attitude so at odds with the chaos of the crowd around us.

I flinched at the vehemence of the crowd, the shouts, fierce screams, the wall of emotion like a physical force pressing from all corners of the arena to the central ring. Wolf, the creature inside me, recognized the bloodlust. She—I—wanted to growl, feeling cornered. I hunched my back against the emotion and focused on being human.

The line between civilized and wild was so very thin, after all. No one watching this display could argue otherwise.

They pounded the crap out of each other and kept coming back for more. That was the only way to describe it. An enthusiast could probably talk about the skill of various punches and blocks, maybe even the graceful way they danced back and forth across the ring, giving and pressing in turn in some kind of strategy I couldn't discern. The strategy may have involved simply tiring each other out. I just waited for it to be over. I couldn't decide who I was rooting for.

Catching bits of conversation between rounds, I gathered that the previous fight between Macy and Jacobson had been considered inconclusive. The blow that had struck Macy down had been a fluke. That he had stood up without being knocked out—or killed—had been a fluke. No one could agree on which of the two had gotten lucky. The rematch had seemed inevitable.

This time, Macy clearly had the upper hand. His punches continued to be calculated and carefully placed, even in the later rounds. To my eyes, Macy looked like he was holding back. A werewolf should have been able to knock an enemy across the room. As a werewolf, *I* could have faced down Jacobson. But Macy couldn't do that. He had to make it look like a fair fight.

Jacobson started to sway. He shook his head, as if trying to wake himself up. Macy landed yet another solid punch that made Jacobson's entire body quiver for a moment. Then the big boxer went down, boneless, collapsing flat on his back and lying there, arms and legs splayed.

Chaos reigned after that. The crowd was screaming with one multilayered voice; the referee knelt by Jacobson's head, counting; Jacobson's trainers hovered in the wings, waiting to spring forward. Around me, journalists and announcers were speaking a mile a minute into phones or mikes, describing the scene.

Macy retreated to a neutral corner, bouncing in place a little, arms hanging at his sides. He hunched his back and glared out with dark eyes that seemed fierce and animal. Maybe they only did to me.

The referee declared the fight over. Jacobson was knocked out, and only started climbing to his feet when his trainers helped him. Macy raised his arms, taking in the crowd's adulation.

That was it. The whole thing started to seem anticlimactic. There was some chaotic concluding business, strobe lights of a million cameras flashing. Then the journalists started packing up, the crowd dispersed, and the cleaning crew started coming through with garbage bags. A swarm of fans and reporters lurched toward Macy, but an equally enthusiastic swarm of guards and assistants kept them at bay while trainers guided Macy from the ring and down the aisle to the locker area, which was off limits.

Larson slung her laptop bag over her shoulder and tugged my sleeve. "Come on," she said.

Walking briskly, snaking through the mass of people, she led me to a different doorway and from there to a tiled corridor. This was the behind-the-scenes area, leading to maintenance, storage, and locker rooms, from the other side. Larson knew where she was going. I followed, willing to let her lead the way, quietly hanging back, observing. Other reporters marched along with us, all jostling to get in front, but Larson led the way.

She stopped in front of a door, where a hulking man in a security uniform stood guard. Other reporters pressed up behind us.

"Mr. Macy isn't giving interviews now." The bear of a man scowled at the crowd.

"I'm Jenna Larson," she said, flashing an ID badge at him. "Tell him I'm here with Kitty Norville. I think he'll talk to us."

"I *said*, Mr. Macy isn't giving interviews." The other reporters complained at that.

Larson pursed her lips, as if considering answers, then said, "I'll wait."

"You'll wait?" I said.

"He's got to come out sometime. Though, if he gives an interview to one of the guys, I swear I'll—"

The door opened, and one of the trainers leaned out to speak a few words with the guard.

"Is who here? Her? Really?" the guard said, glancing at Larson. Grudgingly, he stood back from the open door. "He's asking for you. Come on in."

I stuck close to Larson as she slipped through the door, while the guard held back the rest of the reporters, most of whom were protesting loudly.

Male locker room. There's no other smell like it. Lots and lots of sweat, new and old, stale, baked into the flat carpet, into the paint on the walls. And adrenaline, like someone had aerosolized it. Like someone had lit a scented candle of it. Pure, concentrated, competitive maleness. Wolf didn't know whether to howl or whine.

"This way," the trainer said, and guided us through the front, a brightly lit area filled with lockers, to a smaller, darker side room with only one light in the corner turned on.

The smell of alcohol almost overpowered the smell of

maleness here. It looked like an infirmary. Cabinets with clear doors held gauze, cotton balls, bandages, and dozens of bottles. On a padded massage table in the middle of the room sat Jerome Macy.

A shadow in the dim light, he smelled of sweat, adrenaline, maleness—and wolf. His eyes were a deep, rich brown. I could almost see the wolf in them, sizing me up. Challenging me. I didn't meet his gaze, didn't give him any aggressive signals. This was his territory. I was the visitor here, and I didn't have anything to prove.

"It's okay, Frank," Macy said to the trainer, who lingered by the door. The man gave a curt nod, then left, closing the door behind him.

So not even Macy's trainers knew. The three of us were alone in the room, with the secret.

His hands were raw, chapped, swollen. Tape bound his wrists. He leaned on his knees and let the limbs dangle. Werewolves had rapid healing, but he'd still taken a beating. Macy kept his challenging stare focused on me. I started to bristle under the attention. I crossed my arms and lurked.

Larson drew a small digital recorder out of her pocket and made a show of turning it on. "Mr. Macy. Is it true that you're infected with the recently identified disease known as lycanthropy?"

His gaze shifted from me to her. After a moment, he chuckled. "It's not going to do me any good to say no, is it? You planned this out pretty good."

He was almost soft-spoken. His voice was hushed, belying the power of his body. It gave him a calculating air. Not all brute force, this guy. I wanted to warn Larson, *Don't underestimate him.*

"I think the public has a right to know," Larson said. "Don't you?"

He considered. Sizing her up, like a hunter deciding whether this prey would be worth the effort, gazing at her through half-lidded eyes. He was making a challenge: the stare, the shoulders, the slight snarl to his open lips, showing teeth—all pointed to the aggressive stance. I recognized it. There was no way fully-human Larson could. For all her journalist's instincts, she wouldn't recognize the body language.

He said, "What would I have to pay you to keep you quiet?"

I was betting he couldn't have said anything that would make her more angry. She said, "Bribery. Real nice. Be smart about this, Macy: you can't suppress this. You can't keep this quiet forever. You might as well let me break the story. I'll give you a chance to have your say, tell your side."

She approached this the way she would any other stubborn interview; she turned on her own aggressiveness, glaring back, stepping forward into his space. Exactly the wrong response if she wanted him to open up.

The boxer didn't flinch. His expression never changed. He was still on the hunt. He said, "Then what would I have to *do* to keep you quiet?"

That threw Larson off her script. She blinked with some amount of astonishment. "Are you threatening me?"

I stepped between them, trying to forestall what the press would call an "unfortunate incident." Glancing between them, I tried to be chipper, happy, and tail-waggy.

"Jerome! May I call you Jerome?" I said, running my mouth like always. "I'm really glad Jenna asked me to come along for this. Normally I wouldn't give boxing a second thought. But this. I'd never have believed it if I hadn't seen it. How do you do it? Why don't you shape-shift when you're in the ring?"

I had seen animals in cages at the zoo look like this. Quiet, glaring. Simmering. Like a predator who was prepared to wait forever for that one day, that one minute you forgot to lock the cage. On that day, God help you.

"You're Kitty Norville, right? I've heard about you."

"Great!" I said, my bravado false. "Nothing bad, I hope. So are you going to answer my question?"

He straightened a little, rolled his shoulders, and the mood was broken, the predator image slipped away. His lip turned in a half smile.

"I think about my hands," he said. Which seemed strange. I must have looked bemused, because he explained, "I have to punch. I can only do that with human hands. Fists and arms. Not claws, not teeth. So I think about my hands. But Kitty—just because I don't shift doesn't mean I don't change." Some of that animal side bled into his gaze. He must have carried all his animal fighting instinct into the ring.

That was creepy. I had an urge to slouch, grovel, stick an imaginary tail between my legs. *Please don't hurt me . . .*

"So you do have an unfair advantage?" Larson said.

"I use what I have," he said. "I use my talents, like anyone else out there."

"But it's not a level playing field," she said, pressing. "Tell me about the fight in Vegas. About taking the punch that would have killed a normal human being."

"That fight doesn't prove anything."

"But a lot of people are asking questions, aren't they?" Larson said.

"What exactly do you want from me?"

"Your participation."

"You want to ruin me, and you want me to *help*?" This sounded like a growl.

The trouble was, I sympathized with them both. Jenna Larson and I were both women working in the media, journalists of a sort, ambitious in a tough profession. She constantly needed to hustle, needed that leg-up. That was why she was here. I could understand that. But I'd also been in Macy's shoes, struggling to do my job while hiding my wolf nature. I'd been exposed in a situation like this one: forced to, against my will.

I didn't know who to side with.

"Here's a question," I said, gathering my thoughts even as I talked. "Clearly you have a talent for boxing. But did you before the lycanthropy? Did you box before, and this gave you an edge? Or did you become a werewolf and decide a werewolf would make a good boxer? Are you here because you're a boxer, or because you're a werewolf?"

"Does it matter?"

Did it? The distinction, the value judgment I was applying here was subtle. Was Macy a boxer in spite of his lycanthropy—or because of it? Was I sure that the former was any better, more noble, than the latter?

"This isn't any different than steroids," Larson said before I could respond. "You're using something to create an unfair advantage."

"It's different," Macy said, frowning. "What I have isn't voluntary."

She continued, "But can't you see it? Kids going out and trying to get themselves bitten by werewolves so they can get ahead in boxing, or football, or anything."

"Nobody's that stupid," he said. The curl in his lips was almost a snarl.

Larson frowned. "If it's not me who breaks the story, it'll be someone else, and the next person may not let you know about it first. In exchange for an exclusive, I can guarantee you'll get to tell your side of the story—"

I saw it coming, but I didn't have time to warn her or stop him.

He sprang, a growl rumbling deep in his throat, arms outstretched and reaching for Larson. She dropped her recorder and screamed.

He was fast, planting his hands on her shoulders and shoving her to the wall. In response I shouldered him, pushing him off balance and away from the reporter. Normally, a five-six, skinny blond like me wouldn't have been able to budge a heavyweight like Macy off his stride. But as a werewolf I had a little supernatural strength of my own, and he wasn't expecting it. No one ever expected much out of me at first glance.

He didn't stumble far, unfortunately. He shuffled sideways, while I kind of bounced off him. But at least he took his hands off Larson, and I ended up standing in between them. I glared, trying to look tough, but I was quivering inside. Macy could take me apart.

"You bastard, you're trying to kill me!" Larson yelled. She was wide-eyed, breathing hard, panicked like a hunted rabbit.

Macy stepped back. His smile showed teeth. "If I wanted to kill you, you'd be dead."

"I'll charge you with assault," she said, almost snarling herself.

"Both of you shut up," I said, glaring, pulling out a bit of my own monster to quell them.

"You're not as tough as you think you are," he said, looking down at me, a growl in his voice, his fingers curling at his sides, like claws.

"Well, I don't have to be, because we're going to sit down and discuss this like human beings, got it?" I said.

Never taking his eyes off Larson, he stepped back to the table and returned to sitting. He was breathing calmly, though his scent was musky, animal. He was a werewolf, but he was in complete control of himself. I'd never seen anything like it.

He was in enough control that Larson would never talk him into an exclusive interview.

She'd retrieved her recorder and was pushing buttons and holding it to her ear. By the annoyed look on her face, I was guessing it was damaged. "I don't need your permission," she muttered. "I've got Kitty to back me up. The truth will come out."

I frowned. "Jenna, I'm not sure this is the right way to go about this. This doesn't feel right."

"This isn't about right, it's about the truth."

Macy looked at me, and I almost flinched. His gaze was intent—he was thinking fast. "Kitty. Why did you go public?"

"I was forced into it," I said. "Kind of like this."

"So—has going public helped you? Hurt you? If you could change it, would you?"

I'd worked hard to keep my lycanthropy secret, until I'd been forced into announcing what I was on the air. It hadn't been my choice. I could have let it ruin me, but I made a decision to own that identity. To embrace it. It had made me notorious, and I had profited by it.

I had to admit it: "I don't think I'd be nearly as successful as I am if I hadn't gone public. I'd still be just another cult radio-show host and not the world's first celebrity werewolf."

He nodded, like I'd helped him make a decision.

"We're not here to talk about Kitty," Larson said. "Last chance, Macy. Are you in or out?" She was still treating this with aggression, like she was attacking. She was only offending him.

"Write your story," he said. "Say what you need to. But do it without me. I won't answer any questions. Now, get out." He hopped off his table, went to the door, and opened it.

"You can't do this. You'll have to talk to someone. Sooner or later."

I hooked my arm around hers and pulled her to the door, glancing at Macy over my shoulder one last time. I met his gaze. He seemed calm, determined, without an ounce of trepidation. Before I turned away, he smiled at me, gave a little nod. He was a wolf confident in his territory. I'd do best to slink away and avoid his wrath.

Larson and I left, and the door closed behind us.

Silent, we made our way back to the lobby of the arena. I said, "That went well."

She'd gone a bit glassy-eyed and had lost the purposeful energy in her stride.

"Are you okay?" I said.

"I think I'm going to be sick," she murmured.

"You need to get to a bathroom? Go outside?" I started hurrying.

She shook her head, but leaned against the wall and covered her face. "This must be what the rabbit feels like after it gets away from a fox."

Post-traumatic stress from a simple interview? Maybe. Most people considered themselves the top of the food chain. Few of them ever encountered something that trumped them.

"I don't know," I said. "I'm usually not on the rabbit side of things."

She stared at me and didn't have to say it: I wasn't helping.

"Is he going to come after me? Was he really threatening me? If I run this story, am I in danger?"

I urged her off the wall and toward the doors, so we could get outside and into the air. The closed space and pervasive odor of sweat was starting to get to me.

"No. It's intimidation." It was what people like him—boxer or werewolf—were good at. "He can't touch you without getting in trouble, even if he is a werewolf."

A few more steps brought us outside, into the night. I turned my face to the sky and took in a deep breath of fresh air, or as fresh as city air ever got.

"What are we going to do?" she said. "The story's going to look pretty half-assed without a statement from him."

The lack of an exclusive interview wasn't the end of the world. I'd dealt with worse. We could still break the story.

"You'll have a statement from me," I said. "And I'll have one from you. We'll do the best with what we have." What Larson had told Macy was true: the truth would come out eventually. Maybe by being part of the revelation, I could mitigate the impact of it—mitigate Larson's ire over it.

"It's not fair," she grumbled. "It's just not fair."

I wondered if Macy was thinking the same thing.

As it turned out, Jerome Macy scooped us both. He held a press conference the next morning, revealed his werewolf identity to the world, and promptly announced his retirement from boxing, before anyone could kick him out. Jenna Larson's exposé and call to action, and my interview of her on my show, were lost in the uproar. Almost immediately there was talk of stripping him of his heavyweight title. The debate was ongoing.

About a month later, I got a press kit from the WWE. For the new season of one of their pro wrestling spectacle TV series, they were "unleashing"—they actually used the word *unleashing*—a new force: The Wolf. Aka Jerome Macy.

So. He was starting a new career. A whole new persona. He had chosen to embrace his werewolf identity and looked like he was going gangbusters with it. I had to admire that. And I could stop feeling guilty about him and his story.

This changed everything, of course. He was going to have to do a lot of publicity, wasn't he? A ton of promotion. Sometimes, patience was a virtue, and sometimes, what goes around comes around.

I picked up my phone and called the number listed in the press pack. I was betting I could get that interview with him now.

No Children, No Pets

ESTHER M. FRIESNER

I am Emmeline. I am six.

I am a city werewolf. I live in Central Park. It is very near the Plaza Hotel.

I don't like the Plaza because it is full of all these people who are always asking, "Where are your mommy and daddy, little girl?" when they see me in the lobby. It is absolutely annoying. Then I have to scootle right out of there as fast as I can go on two legs, which is not as fast as I can go on four, but if I were scootling around the lobby on four legs, I would not even get in the front door of the Plaza Hotel, or the side door or even the delivery entrance, for Lord's sake.

Lily Packmother says that when I am older and have got some self-control, I will be able to walk right in through the front door of the Plaza Hotel and march right through that lobby and straight up to that check-in desk and tell them "One room with a view of Central Park, a dozen raw prime sirloin steaks, a fat bell-boy, and charge it, please." Then I will be able to get right onto that big elevator and ride up to the very top floor—even if my room is not on that floor—and get off and find the best place to lurk until the moon turns full. Then I can eat people.

Oooooh, I absolutely *love* eating people! I am much too small to eat a whole big one now, but when I get older, I will be able to eat sixty-eleven dozen of them without so much as batting an eye. Lily Packmother says, "Emmeline, you can't be serious about eating so many people. You will give yourself a tummy ache." But I am mostly entirely serious, even if it takes us werewolves longer to get old than people. Lily Packmother says it is something to do with dog years or backwards dog years or something. All I know is I will have to wait. I am good at waiting. It is all a matter of seeing it through until the Revolution. That is what my daddy says.

Central Park is my most favorite place in the whole city. It is full of all of these trees that are very good to hide behind in the dark and also to pee on if you are a boy werewolf, which I am not, thank heavens. Boy werewolves do not have any good manners like me, Emmeline, even if they are my fellow proletary fighters in the workers' struggle and Daddy would say that I owe them solidarity. Solidarity is awfully important but boy werewolves smell bad and sometimes they try to rip your throat out to establish pack dominance. I completely dislike them.

There are lots of good smells in Central Park. Sometimes I am able to find the hot-dog man and take some mustard right off his cart to put on my food because everything in New York City tastes much better with mustard. I never eat the hot-dog man. There would be no more hot dogs. I am enormously fond of hot dogs. Central Park also has all of these pigeons, which are not very good to eat even if you completely slorsh them all over with every drop of mustard in the entire universe. Lily Packmother says that they are all right when you are incredibly desperate and about to starve to death right this very minute, which happens more than you might imagine when you are a werewolf. She says beggars cannot be choosers and that there are werewolves starving to death in China, so we should count our blessings because we are living in America and not Communists.

Then I hit her on the ankle with the leash I took off the last doggie I ate and remind her that my daddy is a Communist.

Lily Packmother doesn't want me to grow up to be a Communist. She says that it is bad enough I am a poor motherless cub without my daddy having been a Communist and doing something as stupid as what he did when he heard about the Rosenbergs getting lectricuted. I don't know what she is talking about. I don't know what he did. I don't know who the Rosenbergs are. No one in our pack is named Rosenberg. I think maybe they live in the Plaza Hotel and that is where my daddy is, too.

I wish he would come out. Nine months is an awful long time to be visiting people and leaving your daughter all by herself in the middle of Central Park one night when it was absolutely dark and there were all of these big monster sea lions from the zoo rampaging through the trees everywhere. My daddy told me to sit down on that park bench and not to move even *one inch* from there, because someone would come to find me eventually. He said that he was sick at heart about the Rosenbergs and witch hunts and all of those clowns and lapdogs in Washington, D.C., and that there was only so much one man could take, for Lord's sake.

Here is what I like to do: pretend I know what grown-ups are talking about.

Then he said it would be better if I were raised by the System because he couldn't get a job anywhere on account of the witch hunt and there was no way he could provide for me, so the System won, which was not fair at all and Marks was right. After that he went into these bushes and I sat on that park bench until I heard a very loud bang somewhere in the dark and I decided I had sat on that bench, not moving even *one inch*, long enough and I had to go somewhere else, in case those sea lions found me and stamped on me and absolutely devoured me. With mustard.

I ran and ran and ran until I came out onto a place by a fountain where I met this doggie who looked like a frog and he bit me. Then I ran away and I stopped bleeding almost right away instantly, which was completely strange, and I ran back into the park, which was where Lily Packmother found me.

She said, "Hello, little girl, I see you have been bitten and turned into a werewolf. That means you are one of us now and we will look after you."

I said, "Hello, my name is Emmeline and are you the System?"

When you are bitten by a werewolf or even a wolf and you go on and the moon gets full, you have to turn into a wolf, too. That is the law. I was not bitten by a wolf. I was bitten by a dog that had this curly little tail and these big googly frog eyes, but Lily Packmother said that she could smell wolf on me, which means that dog must have had a lot of wolf in him somewhere. I do not know where; he was much too small to have a lot of anything in him anywhere, let alone a whole wolf.

Here is what Lily Packmother likes to say: "The acorn does not fall far from the tree."

Here is what I say: "I was not bitten by an acorn."

And here's the thing of it: when the next full moon came, I turned right into a werewolf and went out and caught and ate three squirrels and a collie and part of a sleeping man on a park bench who smelled funny and tasted like old shoes, so Lily Packmother was right about that dog.

Lily Packmother says she is always right. She says this is because she has the most spearience of anyone in the whole pack because she was bitten by another werewolf hundreds and thousands and billions of years ago, in the 1920s right before the stock market went to Hades. I don't know where Hades is. I think that it is somewhere in California or Detroit. I am very specially good at geography. I know how to take the crosstown bus all by myself.

There was this time that one of our pack said that Lily Packmother was wrong and they had this duel and Lily Packmother tore his throat right open with her teeth even though she was not a wolf at the time, which was highly inconvenient, and there was this blood slorshing all over everywhere, for Lord's sake, and my dress was entirely ruined.

Lily Packmother said, "Emmeline, you can't be seen in public like that even if you are a werewolf because blood will tell." I asked, "What will it tell?" and she said, "The police," and I remembered what Daddy says about the police being capitalist tools to repress the proleterrycats, so I said, "I need a new dress."

Lily Packmother went away and came back with this very fawncy frilly dress for me. I asked her where she found it and she said some people should learn to watch their children better. I put it on and said, "Thank you very much, it fits perfectly, and I hope this is not the product of the sploitation of the working classes." Then I spun around and around to make the skirt go whoosh all swirly and I fell down into the bushes and skinned my knee.

Here's what I can do:

> Climb trees
> Spell
> Curtsy the way Mama taught me before Daddy told
>> her it was an affectation of the boorshwazee and
>> she died
> Slurp the insides out of squirrels
> Make fur hats
> Howl
> Quote Marks
> Fight for the Revolution and the workers and topple
>> the capitalist pigs and destroy the oppressive System
>> when I get older
> Draw a horse

There are lots of horses near Central Park. They pull these handsome cabs filled with people through the park at all hours of the day or night. I like horses, specially the brown ones. My fur is brown. It sprouts all over my body and grows soft and plushery when the full moon rises over the trees and the buildings and the fountain in front of the Plaza Hotel. At first it itches on my face. That is where the fur entirely bursts out before it grows anywhere else on me at all. Then I have to scratch it with this broken rattle that this baby who had it before me wasn't going to use anymore.

A broken rattle makes a very good back scratcher.

Lily Packmother says, "Emmeline, you must stop scratching your fur! If you break the skin, you will get the mange, and then where will you be?"

I say, "I will be in Central Park." I don't know what the mange is, but I am pretty sure it is something I can blame on the capitalists.

Lily Packmother says that it's a good thing that all of us in the pack itch when the full moon rises, because the itching gives us fair warning that the Change is upon us and we should wriggle out of our human clothes just as fast as we can or else they will rip themselves to pieces right off our bodies in utter shreds when we turn into wolves. This is specially true of the pack males, who all wear trousers, which do not grow on trees.

I want to wear trousers, but Lily Packmother says they are not the proper attire for a young lady and she ought to know. She was a deb-you-tont before she got bit by that man from Rumania or Bohemia or Astoria or someplace else they talk with that accent. That man met her at a big dance at the Plaza Hotel when Lily Packmother was still just Plain Lily and her younger sister Marie Isolde was getting married in the White and Gold Room. Everyone was saying what a dreadful shame it was that Plain Lily's sister was getting married before she was, and she couldn't even tell them it was on account of how Marie Isolde stole her boyfriend by being no better than she should be and having round heels.

I still want to wear trousers.

Here's what Lily Packmother likes: Doris Day movies.

Here's what I like: *The Adventures of Robin Hood* with Richard Greene on television even though we don't have a television in the park so I can't see him anymore.

One day I was walking through Central Park and I came to that zoo and went to look at those ravaging sea lions for a while. It was very hot and sunny and I was absolutely dying of thirst and shriveling up into ashes like a bug when all of a sudden I saw that dog with those frog eyes who bit me that time. He was with this little girl and this rather large and musty woman so I went right up to them and said, "I am Emmeline, your dog bit me, and now I am a werewolf, do you want to play?"

The woman looked down her nose at me and said, "Our Louise cawn't cawn't cawn't be playing with just any child who comes along, her mother *knows* people."

I said, "That is all right because my daddy knows the Rosenbergs."

That was when the woman just scooped up that little girl and vrooshed away with her over one shoulder and that dog running after them on little tiny scootly legs because everybody dropped that leash, and it was dragging on the ground for anyone to grab so I did. I held on to it with two hands and absolutely yanked it. That frog dog stopped—*goink!*—just like that, and his legs all kept going but his neck didn't and he landed on his back looking up at me so I said, "Hello, I am Emmeline and you bit me. That is boorjwa oppression and what do you intend to do about making restitution to the prolethingiat?"

And that frog dog looked up at me and said, *"You're* the One!" He sounded just like David Niven.

Ooooooh, I absolutely adore David Niven! I sneak into all his movies.

Just then that musty lady came back with that little girl walking behind her howling and blubbering and having the worst temper fit I have ever seen in my entire whole life. The little girl ran right up to that frog dog and scooped him up in her arms and made this most hideous ugly face at me and said, "Don't you dare steal my dog! Do you want to play?" So we did.

Her name is Louise. She is six. She lives in the Plaza Hotel. She wanted me to go to the Plaza with her to play but the musty lady said, "You cawn't cawn't cawn't possibly just go waltzing off with us like this, child. Your Mummy and Daddy will become concerned."

I said, "I don't know how to waltz, but I can curtsy, my daddy is still in the Plaza Hotel and my mommy is dead." That made the musty lady creak right down on one knee in front of me and hug me to her chest, which is all fluffy. She said some people should never have children and called me a poor little lost lamb. I tried to tell her I am not a lamb, but it was extremely difficult with all that fluffiness. Then the little girl thwapped the musty lady on top of her head with her fist so hard that she crunched her felt hat and said, "Stop blubbering, you old prune, you're wasting our time. If her daddy's in the Plaza, she can come play in my room *now!*"

So I did. We went right up to those big front doors and across that lobby and straight up to the very top floor in that elevator. Then we just raced right down that hall and Louise kicked on the door to her apartment until that musty lady caught up to us and let us in with a big metal key. It took her too long, so Louise kicked her in her ankles and said, "Amanda, you are ugly and you stink and as soon as my mother calls I am going to tell her to have you fired and sent back to Hell or England."

Amanda is Louise's governess. She looks like pillows. She

takes care of Louise because Louise's mother is always someplace more important.

Louise and Amanda live in these big rooms at the very top of the Plaza Hotel. Louise has millions of toys and is bored a lot. She asked me what I wanted to play and I said dolls because I can't remember the last time I had a doll to play with, for Lord's sake, but the absolute instant I touched one of her dolls she snatched it right out of my hands and smashed its head against the wall and said dolls were stupid and we were going to play something good.

We played Davy Crockett and she shot me. Then we played cowboys and Indians and she stuck an arrow in me. Then we played that she was the queen of everything in the whole world and I had to fetch her a cup of tea on a silver tray or else she was going to cut off my head and hang me up by my tongue and push me off a cliff and utterly *squonk* me. I had to act like I didn't mind about any of those stupid games she made me play because I wanted another chance to talk to the frog dog that bit me. I told Louise we should play with the frog dog but she said she was the queen of everything and I was a mere slave and how dare I speak up like that to her majesty and that is when she hit me right over the head with that silver tray.

I am a werewolf. I hate silver. Silver hates me.

I started to cry and Amanda came in and took the silver tray away from Louise and said, "Louise, what what what have you done to your little playmate, and with the silver tray that my dear grandmamma gave me? It is of great sentimental value to me and completely irreplaceable. Look, you have bent it. It will cost a lot of money to have fixed."

That was when Louise grabbed the silver tray back and ran to the window and just flung it open and threw that tray right out into the air like it was a paper airplane. Then she said, "Look! I just saved you a lot of money. I want some chocolate ice cream now. Call Room Service and charge it, buzzard-face."

Here is what Amanda said: "They don't pay me enough to put up with this sort of crap."

Here is what Louise said: *"What* did you just say?"

Here is what else Amanda said: nothing.

Louise smiled. "That's what I thought." And we had chocolate ice cream.

While we were eating, the frog dog came over and bit me on the arm. He didn't do it hard enough to make me bleed, like when he turned me into a werewolf. He did it just enough so I would look at him. Then he rolled his googly eyes at me and at the door to the bathroom.

I got up and said, "I have to go to the bathroom."

Louise said, "Who cares?" She grabbed my chocolate ice cream before I could take even one half of a step away from it and gobbled it down as I was walking away, but I didn't care because the frog dog was walking right beside me all the way into that bathroom.

I shut the door behind us and sat down on the toilet lid. The frog dog sat down on a big pink fluffy bath mat and looked at me tilty. "It's a good thing you found me," he said. "You never should've run away after I bit you. Something could've happened to you, and you're the One!"

"I am not one," I said. "I am six."

He said, "Spare me the cute stuff. I have been around this town since before Peter Stuyvesant learned how to pee without getting any on his wooden leg and I know my stuff. I am the Vessel of Lycanthropy, which makes me like the Holy Grail for werewolves everywhere in the greater New York metropolitan area, except for Staten Island. I am the immortal blood descendant of the great she-wolf who suckled Romulus and Remus, and the Fenris wolf who will bring the doom of Ragnarok upon the gods themselves, *savvy?*"

I said I savvied. I didn't know what that meant but Louise wasn't going to be eating my chocolate ice cream forever and I wanted to find out more before she came and banged on that bathroom door at us.

The frog dog said I was the Chosen One because he did not just go around biting every Tom, Dick, and Harry unless the Spirit of Lycanthropy told him to. So far he had been around for twenty million hundred and two years and bitten an awful lot of people but nothing much came of it because someone always shot them with a silver bullet and he was losing hope. He said that when I got older I would be able to turn into a wolf without having to wait for the full moon because rank has its frilly edge. He made me promise not to get shot with a silver bullet and I did because right then I would have promised anything just to get him to stop yapping at me.

That made him happy. He said I was going to bring about the Kingdom of the Werewolves through the spawn of my loins, and that we were all going to lay waste to New York City, including Staten Island, and roam the streets in wolf form by day as well as by night and every single day, too, for Lord's sakes, and devour the human beings and crunch them and absolutely skrink their bones.

Here's what he said: "Your coming is Foretold and Inevitable."

Here's what I said: "Like the Revolution."

Then he asked me if I had even been paying any attention whatsoever to everything he'd been telling me and I said maybe and he snorted so hard that big glops of wet spray came out his nose and spackled all over me and the shower curtains. That was when Louise started banging on the door.

The frog dog said, "You will be the Chosen One and you will like it." Then he peed on the bath mat.

Louise's governess got all mad about that, but Louise just got on that telephone and called Housekeeping and told them, "Get one of your lazy maids from Refugeeland right up here pronto, cleaning up dog pee is all they are good for, I bet they are all Communists. My mother knows Senator Joseph McCarthy and he will get their fat bottoms shipped right back to Commieville before you can blink, same to you, and move it, Stupid." Then she told me to come back next day to play more.

That night in the park I told Lily Packmother about what the frog dog told me, including about how rank has its frilly edge. She said, "Emmeline, I think you must mean rank has its *privilege*," and I said that was all right by me as long as I got to be a wolf whenever I wanted to. Then she said, "I am so proud of you for being the Chosen One. I always knew you were special. You will be the salvation of all werewolfkind someday through your progeny."

I said, "Is that the same thing as the spawn of my loins?" and she said that, yes, it was and that I would understand when I was older and went into heat. So I guess that means next summer unless we get to live somewhere that has air-conditioning. Then she gave me a nice haunch of mounted policeman for my dinner and scolded me when I left the bone marrow because that chocolate ice cream at the Plaza Hotel had spoiled my appetite and werewolves were *still* starving all over the place in China. That is all they seem to do over there, for Lord's sake.

The next day I wanted to go back to the Plaza Hotel and play with Louise some more. She has all kinds of toys, even if she is a pill. Lily Packmother said it would be all right if I went but that I would have to come right straight home to Central Park before it got dark or she would like to know the reason why. She said that now it was known that I was the Vessel of Lycanthropy, it was very important for me to come to the big pack meeting that night and receive homage.

I think homage is all very well and good but I like chocolate ice cream better, mostly because I know what that is.

So that morning I went right in through those big doors and straight across that lobby and right into that elevator and all the way up to the top and down that hall and knocked on that door until Louise's governess opened it and said, "Oh, it's you. I thought you knew better than to come back for more of the same with that little bastard."

I said, "Why are your eyes all red?" and she said she had really tied one on last night, and I wanted to know one what, but then there was Louise with scrambled eggs on her face so I never did find out.

Louise ate up all her breakfast and didn't offer me any except the toast crusts. I told her I was hungry and there were werewolves starving in China. She said that was tough toenails and threw her juice glass at me. Then we went to her room and she said we were going to play Davy Crockett again.

I said, "I want to play Robin Hood instead and you can be Richard Greene."

She told me fat chance, and Robin Hood was a big pansy. She laughed at me when I said he was not a flower just because he wore green all the time, on account of living in Sherwood Forest where it was important for camelflog. Then she told me what she meant about Robin Hood being a big pansy and laughed at me some more when I said that sounded absolutely ugh.

"That's nothing, you baby," she said. "You should hear what your mommy and daddy did together to get you born." And she told me that, too, and it was even more ugh.

"My mommy and daddy never did that," I said. "My daddy told my mommy that the Revolution needed more soldiers to fight the boorjwah oppressors so they got me from the Workers' Collective because from each according to his ability to each according to his needs and they needed me for the Revolution, so there."

Here is what Louise did then: stare at me like her frog dog.

Here is what she did next: turn to me and say, "I bet you are the daughter of that stupid Commie who shot himself in the park last year. The police were looking for you. You're going to be put in an orphanage."

I said, "No, I am in the System and my daddy is in this hotel visiting the Rosenbergs. He told me to sit on that park bench and he went away and he is in here somewhere. I am going to find him before I am one single minute older. That will show you. Good-bye." But when I tried to walk past Louise, she shoved me back so hard I fell on some of her broken toys, which are everywhere, and it hurt.

She said, "You're nuts. He's dead. It was in all the papers last summer. I read all about it. So did Amanda. I'll prove it to you." Then she hollered for her governess to get into the room fast or else and when she came rushing in Louise told her, "This is that dead Commie's kid. She's stupid and crazy and she thinks her daddy's coming back. *Tell* her!"

First Amanda stared at Louise. Then she stared at me. Her eyes were all soft and watery. She said, "Miss Louise, you cawn't cawn't cawn't expect me to tell a child such a thing until I am sure this is the child in question. I would like to speak with her alone, if you please."

Louise said, "No. I wanna watch."

Amanda said, "There is a large box of petty force in my room, which I was saving for myself," and Louise scootled away to utterly lay waste to the whole thing. Then Amanda turned back to me and asked me all of these questions about my name and my daddy and what happened in the park that night. I told her everything she wanted to know except about how the frog dog bit me and the rest of it. She gasped a lot.

Then she said, "Oh, you poor child, I am afraid that everything that wretched little beast told you is true. My heart breaks for you, but your daddy is indeed No More By His Own Hand and you match the newspaper descriptions of that unfortunate man's lost little girl." She put her arms around me and hugged me tight again like when she thought I was a lamb. That was nice. She smelled like lilac bath powder and lemon candies. She cried in my hair. I cried, too, because now I knew my daddy was not coming back ever again at all and I was utterly heartbroken.

Louise came back in with a whole bunch of petty force grundled up in her fists. Her fingers were leaking pink and green icing and yellow cake. When she saw Amanda and me crying on each other she threw those lumps of squooshed petty force at us and laughed. She said I was a crybaby and I should stick my head in gravy and wash it off with ice cream and send it to the Navy.

Amanda said, "Miss Louise, you ought not not not mock this poor orphaned child. You are Privileged and you should use what you have to help those who do not have as much and be thankful your lot in life is not theirs."

I wiped my tears on Amanda's blouse and said, "Yes, like Marks said, from each according to his ability to each according to his needs or else."

Louise showed us this absolutely *rank* grin all smoolied over with melted petty force icing and said, "She is a Commie just like her stupid dead daddy and you are a Commie sympathizer and I am going to turn you both in to the police and my mother *now.*"

I said, "Thank you for a lovely time, Amanda. You have been very nice to me and I will do my best to see that you are not devoured by the spawn of my loins, but I really must be going now." I shook Amanda's hand and headed right for that door but Louise grabbed me and twisted my arm hard and said,

"You're not going anywhere, except an orphanage and *jail*." Then she knocked me down and sat on me.

Amanda said, "Miss Louise, you cawn't cawn't cawn't be serious about any of this. Get off the poor child this instant!" But Louise said that if Amanda did not move her fat rump the Hell out of there, she was going to call the police herself and tell them Amanda was a big lady pansy and then she could keep me company in jail and see how she liked it.

Amanda said that was a dreadful lie, but Louise asked her if she felt like seeing who the police believed, some old English bag or someone whose mother had more money and influenza than God Himself. That was when Amanda burst into tears all over again and ran out of the apartment and Louise and I were left alone.

Here is what I said: "You better get off me now."

Here is what she said: "Make me."

Then I said, "Maybe I can't make you get off me now, but just you wait until the moon is full and I start to itch all over and I completely burst right out of my clothes if I do not get them off in time and I become a wolf and rip your throat out."

That was when she laughed at me some more and called me a looney and said I would wind up in an orphanage *and* jail *and* the nut house, but that it came as no surprise to her because everyone knows all Commies are crazy. She asked me, "Do you know what would fix you right up, you big screwball? A lobotomy. Would you like a lobotomy?"

I said, "What I would like is to be old enough to be Foretold and Inevitable so I could start itching right now this very minute and—ow! Stop bouncing on me!—and not have to—ow! I told you, *stop* that, you're making me mad!—and not have to wait until full moon to grush y'r froab in my powfur zhaws ob def an'—Ow! *Ow*! Ow-owOOOOOO!"

Oh my Lord, Lily Packmother simply would *not* approve of

what happened. She says that just because we live like savages in Central Park and become ravening, murderous, bloodthirsty beasts every time the moon is full is no reason not to respect Tradition or we would be no better than Trade Unionists. But I could not help any of it. It was all enormously Foretold and Inevitable and fun. I did not have a warning itch even one little bit and it was still daylight outside let alone time for the full moon when my clothes simply burst *right off* before I knew it, and I think I was lots and lots bigger than I usually get when the Change is upon me, and Louise screamed but not for long because I am very 'fishent.

That was pretty much that. Louise tastes like old hardboiled eggs and does not have any trousers I could borrow to cover my shame afterward, which is what Lily Packmother calls it, only more of those stupid dresses.

Here's what I can do: Burp up patent-leather shoe buckles.

It took me utterly forever to find one drop of mustard in that whole apartment, for Lord's sake.

I am Emmeline. I am six. I live at the Plaza Hotel.

I have to. Louise's mother does not visit often, but when she does, it would be a good idea if there were a little girl of approximully the right age to say hello and what did you bring me? I will have to get used to having a different name now. Lily Packmother says so. She says it is the least I can do so Amanda can keep her job and not have to face a lot of uncomfortable questions from the police. Besides, Amanda says it isn't as if that rich sow will ever catch wise, not for how little she has ever cared about having a child in the first place, and some people are not fit to raise a begonia let alone a little girl.

I am not a begonia and I am really not Louise. I am still me, Emmeline.

I am going to have *lots* of toys.

I visit Lily Packmother in Central Park all the time. She and Amanda have become very good friends. They both say how proud they are of me for being a big girl and solving a big problem all by myself even if I did solve it with a very messy solution. But Lily Packmother says that is all water and other liquids under the bridge and Amanda says she is only sorry in theory about what I did to that little bitch, no offense meant to Lily Packmother and none taken.

The Vessel of Lyncanthropy has a new name, too. I gave it to him. He is Frankie because that is a lot easier to spell on my drawings of him and also because I still love hot dogs. He says the fact that my power to turn into a wolf in broad daylight manifestoed so soon means that I was the Chosen One and how! He says once I grow up and get the ball rolling, ordinary humans won't have a snowball's chance in Hell. Amanda says he should not not not use such language in front of a mere child.

That makes Frankie sad because I am going to take whole entire *ages* to get that ball rolling, on account of the backwards dog years and me being as young as I am to start with. Then he cheers up because he is immortal and good things are worth waiting for and the twenty-first century is not *that* far away. He says the humans may be harder to catch then, on account of all the flying cars and jet packs strapped to their backs, but we werewolves will manage.

I say, "Hello, Housekeeping, send someone up to clean our room there are lots and lots of stains all over from the roast beef dinner I had that exploded please give yourselves a gigantic huge tip thank you and charge it please."

Now all I have to do all day is play in the Plaza Hotel and not give Amanda too many headaches and see to it that the rest of the pack gets a fair share of any leftovers we have from dinner. Then I watch television. I get to watch *Robin Hood* all I want.

Oh my Lord, there is absolutely too much for one small child to do while waiting around for my loins to spawn and bring about the Kingdom of the Werewolves or to infiltrate the power base of the moneyed classes and overthrow Capitalism, whichever comes first. It will be fun.

Tomorrow I think I'll write *Comes the Revolution!* on all the tabletops in the Palm Court with Amanda's Hazel Bishop red lipstick.

Ooooooh, I absolutely *love* waiting for the Revolution!

I am Emmmm . . . *Louise*. I am six.

For now.

Sea Warg

TANITH LEE

One dull red star was sinking through the air into the sea. It was the sun. But eastward the October night had already commenced. There the water was dark green and the air purple, and the old ruinous pier stood between like a burnt spider.

Under the pier was a ghostly blackness, holed by mysterious luminous apertures. Ancient weeds and shreds of nets dripped. The insectile, leprous, wooden legs of the pier seemed to ripple, just as their drowning reflections did. The tide would be high.

The sea pushed softly against the land. It was destroying the land. The cliffs, eaten alive by the sea (smelling of antique metal, fish odour of Leviathan, depth, death), were crumbling in little pieces and large slabs, and the promenade, where sea-siders had strolled not more than thirty years ago, rotted and grew rank. Even the *danger* notices had faded and in the dark were only pale splashes, daubed with words that might have been printed in Russian.

But the sea-influencing moon would rise in a while.

Almost full tonight.

Under the pier the water twitched. Something moved through it. Perhaps a late swimmer who was indifferent to the cold evening or the warning *danger—keep out*. Or nothing at all maybe, just some rogue current, for the currents were temperamental all along this stretch of coast.

A small rock fell from above and clove the water, copying the sound of a rising fish.

The sun had been squashed from view. Half a mile westward the lights of hotels and restaurants shone upward, like the rays of another world, another planet.

When the man had stabbed him in the groin, Johnson had not really believed it. Hadn't *understood* the fountain of blood. When the next moment two security guards burst in and threw the weeping man onto the fitted carpet, Johnson simply sat there. "Are you okay? *Fuck*. You're not," said the first security guard. "Oh. I'm—" said Johnson. The next thing he recalled, subsequently, was the hospital.

The compensation had been generous. And a partial pension, too, until in eighteen years' time he came of age to draw it in full. The matter was hushed up otherwise, obliterated. Office bullying by the venomous Mr. Haine had driven a single employee—not to the usual nervous breakdown or mere resignation—but to stab reliable Mr. Johnson, leaving him with a permanent limp and some slight but ineradicable impairments both of a digestive and a sexual nature. "I hope you won't think of us too badly," said old Mr. Birch, gentle as an Alzheimer's lamb. "Not at all, sir," replied Johnson in his normal, quiet, pragmatic way.

Sandbourne was his choice for the bungalow with the view of the sea—what his own dead father had always wanted, and never achieved.

Johnson wasn't quite certain why he fitted himself, so seamlessly, into that redundant role.

Probably the run-down nature of the seaside town provided inducement. House prices were much lower than elsewhere in the south-east. And he had always liked the sea. Besides, there were endless opportunities in Sandbourne for the long, tough walks he must now take, every day of his life if possible, to keep the spoilt muscles in his left leg in working order.

But he didn't mind walking. It gave extra scope for the other thing he liked, which had originally furnished his job in staff liaison at Haine and Birch. Johnson was fascinated by people. He never tired of the study he gave them. A literate and practiced reader, he found they provided him with *animated* books. His perceptions had, he was aware, cost him his five-year marriage: he had seen too well what Susan, clever though she had been, was up to. But then, Susan wouldn't have wanted him now anyway, with his limp and the bungalow, forty-two years of age, and two months into the town-city and walking everywhere, staring at the wet wilderness of waters.

"I see that dog again, up by the old pier."

"Yeah?" asked the man behind the counter. "What dog's that, then?"

"I tol' yer. Didn' I? I was up there shrimping. An' I looks an' it's swimming aroun' out there, great big fucker, too. Don' like the looks of it, mate. I can tell yer."

"Right."

"Think I oughta call the RSPCee like?"

"What, the Animal Rights people?" chipped in the other man.

"Nah. He means the RSPCA, don't ya, Benny?"

"'S right. RSPCee. Only it shouldn' be out there like that on its own. No one about. Just druggies and pushers."

The man behind the counter filled Benny's mug with a brown foam of coffee and slapped a bacon sandwich down before the other man at the counter. Johnson, sitting back by the café wall, his breakfast finished, watched them closely in the way he had perfected, seeming not to, seeming miles off.

"An' it's allus this time of the month."

"Didn't know you still had them, Benny, times of the month."

Benny shook his head, dismissing—or just missing—the joke. "I don' mean that."

"What *do* ya mean then, pal?"

"I don' like it. Great big bloody dog like that, out there in the water when it starts ter get dark and just that big moon ter show it."

"Sure it weren't a shark?"

"Dog. It was a dog."

"Live and let live," said the counter man.

Benny slouched to a table. "You ain't seen it."

After breakfast Johnson had meant to walk up steep Hill Road and take the rocky path along the clifftop and inland, through the forest of newish high-rises, well-decked shops, and SF-movie-dominated cinemas, to the less fashionable supermarket at Crakes Bay.

Now he decided to go eastwards along the beach, following the cliff line, to the place where the warning notices were. There had been a few major rockfalls in the 1990s, so he had heard; less now, they said. People were always getting over the council barricade. A haunt of drug-addicts, too, that area, 'down-and-outs holing up like rats' among the boarded-up shops and drown-foundationed houses farther up. Johnson wasn't afraid of any of that. He didn't look either well-off or so impoverished as to be desperate. Besides, he'd been mugged in London once or twice. As a general rule, if you kept calm and gave them what they wanted without fuss, no harm befell you. No, it was in a smart office with a weakened man in tears that harm had happened.

The beach was an easy walk. Have to do something more arduous later.

The sand was still damp, the low October sun reflecting in smooth, mirrored strafes where the sea had decided to remain until the next incoming tide fetched it. A faintly hazy morning, salt-smelling and chilly and fresh.

Johnson thought about the dog. Poor animal, no doubt belonging to one of the drugged outcasts. He wondered if, neglected and famished, it had learned to swim out to sea, catching the fish that a full moon lured to the water's surface.

There were quite a few other people walking on the beach, but after the half mile it took to come around to the pier-end, none at all. There was a dismal beauty to the scene. The steely sea and soft grey-blue sky featuring its sun. The derelict promenade, much of which had collapsed. Behind these the defunct shops with their look of broken toy models, and then the long, helpless arm of the pier, with the hulks of its arcades and tea-rooms, and the ballroom, now mostly a skeleton, where had hung, so books on Sandbourne's history told one, sixteen crystal chandeliers.

Johnson climbed the rocks and rubbish—soggy pizza boxes, orange peels, beer cans—and stood up against the creviced pavement of the esplanade. It looked as if bombs had exploded there.

Out at sea nothing moved, but for the eternal sideways running of the waves.

At the beginning of the previous century, a steamboat had sailed across regularly from France, putting in by the pier, then a white confection like a bridal cake. The strange currents that beset this coast had made that the only safe spot. The fishing fleet had gone out from here too, this old part of the city-town, the roots of which had been there, it seemed, since Saxon times. Now the boats put off from the west end of Sandbourne, or at least they did so when the rest of Europe allowed it.

Johnson wondered whether it was worth the climb, awkward now with his leg, over the boarding and notices. By day there were no movements, no people. They were night dwellers very likely, eyes sore from skunk, skins scabrous from crack.

And by night, of course, this place would indeed be dangerous.

As he turned and started back along the shore, Johnson's eye was attracted by something not the cloud-and-sea shades of the morning, lying at the very edge of the land. He took it at first for some unusual shell or sea-life washed ashore. Then decided it must be something manufactured, some gruesome modern fancy for Halloween, perhaps.

In fact, when he went down the beach and saw it clearly, lying there as if it had tried to clutch at the coast, kept its grip but let go of all else, he found it wasn't plastic or rubber but quite real. A man's hand, torn off raggedly just behind the wrist bone, a little of which stuck out from the bloated and discolouring skin.

Naturally he thought about it, the severed hand.

He had never, even in London, come across such an item. But then, probably, he'd never been in the right (wrong) place to do so.

Johnson imagined that one of the down-and-outs had killed another, for drugs or cash. Maybe even for a burger from the Alnite Caff.

He did wonder, briefly, if the near-starving dog might have liked to eat the hand. But there wasn't much meat on a hand, was there?

That evening, after he had gone to the supermarket and walked all the way back along Bourne Road, he poured himself a Guinness and sat at his table in the little 'study' of the bungalow and wrote up his find in his journal. He had kept a journal ever since he started work in Staff Liaison. Case-notes, histories . . . *people*—cameos, whole bios sometimes.

Later he fried a couple of chops and ate them with a green salad.

Nothing on TV. He read Trollope until 11:36, then went to bed.

He dreamed of being in the sea, swimming with great strength and ability, although in reality he had always been an inadequate swimmer. In the dream he was aware of a dog nearby, but was not made afraid by this. Instead he felt a vague exhilaration, which on waking he labeled as a sort of puerile pleasure in unsafety. Physically he had long outgrown it. But there, deep in his own mind, perhaps not so?

The young man was leaning over his motorbike, adjusting something apparently. The action was reminiscent of a rider with his favourite steed, checking the animal for discomfort.

Johnson thought he had seen him before. He was what? Twenty-five, thirty? He had a thick shock of darkish fair hair, cut short the way they did now, and a lean face from which the summer tan was fading. In the sickly glare under the streetlight his clothes were good but ordinary. He had, Johnson thought, very long fingers, and his body was tall and almost athletic in build.

This was outside the pub they called in Sandbourne the "Biker Inn."

Johnson didn't know the make of the bike, but it was a powerful model, elegant.

Turning off Ship Street, Johnson went into the *Cat In Clover*. He wasn't yet curious as to why he had noted the man with the bike. Johnson noted virtually everyone. An hour into the evening he did, however, recall where he had twice seen him before, which was in the same launderette Johnson himself frequented. Nice and clean then. Also perhaps, like Johnson, more interested in coming out to do the wash than in buying a machine.

During the rest of the week Johnson found he kept seeing the man he then named, for the convenience of the journal, Biker. The rather mundane region where Johnson lived was one of those village-in-city conurbations featured by London journalists writing on London—like Hampstead, for example, if without the dosh. You did get to be aware, indirectly, sometimes, of the locals, as they of you, perhaps. Johnson believed that in fact he wasn't coincidentally and now constantly "bumping into" Biker, but that he had become *aware* of Biker. Therefore he noticed him now each time he saw him, whereas formerly he had frequently seen him *without* noticing, therefore without consciously *seeing*.

This kind of thing had happened before.

In the beginning, when in his teens, Johnson had thought it meant something profoundly important, particularly when it was a girl he abruptly kept on seeing—that was, *noticing*. Even in his thirties he had been misled by that idea, with Susan. He had realized, after their separation, that what had drawn him to her at first wasn't love or sex but her own quirkiness and his observation of it. She had worked it out herself, eventually. In the final year of their life together she came to call those he especially studied (including those at Haine and Birch) his "prey." "Which of your prey are you seeing tomorrow?" she would ask playfully.

Now grasping that it was some type of acuity in him that latched on to certain others in this fashion, Johnson had not an instant's doubt that he had reacted differently to Biker.

So what was it then, with Biker? *What* had alerted Johnson there under the streetlamp on that moonless night?

During the next week, Johnson took his washing to the launderette about 6 p.m., and there Biker sat.

Biker was unloading his wash, but raised his eyes. They were very long eyes, extraordinarily clear, a pale, gleaming grey.

"Cold out," said Johnson, dumping the washing.

"Yeah," said Biker.

"Damn it, this machine isn't working."

"Yeah," said Biker. He looked up again. "Try kicking it."

"You're joking," said Johnson placidly.

"No," said Biker, and he came over quite calmly, and did something astonishing. Which was he jumped straight upward with enormous agility and power, and fetched the washer the lightest but most expressive slap with his left foot. Landing, he was like a lion—totally co-ordinated, unfazed. While the machine, which had let out a rattling roar, now gulped straight into its cycle. Biker nodded and returned to his wash.

"Wow," said Johnson. "Thanks."

"Don't mention it."

"I owe you a drink. The girlfriend's refused to come round till I get these bloody sheets done."

Biker glanced at him.

Johnson saw there was neither reluctance nor interest in the smooth, lean face, hardly any expression at all. The eyes were only mercury and white china.

"I'll be in the *Victory*," he said.

Once Biker left, Johnson, not to seem too eager, stayed ten minutes with his washing. He had chosen the crank machine on purpose. And what a response he had got! Biker must be an acrobat. At the very least a trained dancer.

Perhaps, Johnson thought, he shouldn't indulge this. Perhaps it was unwise. But then, he usually did indulge his observation. It had never led to anything bad. Except once.

Had being stabbed and disabled made him reckless? He thought not. Johnson *wasn't* reckless. And he could afford the price of a couple of drinks.

When he got into the pub, the place was already full. The music machine filled the air with huge thuddings, while on every side other machines for gambling flashed like a firework display.

He looked round, then went to the bar and ordered a drink, whisky for the cold. He could already see Biker wasn't there.

Which might mean *he* had distrusted Johnson, or that something else had called him away. Or anything, really.

Johnson was not unduly disappointed. Sometimes *not* knowing was the more intriguing state. Besides, going out of the door he heard a man say, as if signaling to him, "Yeah, there's something out by the old pier sometimes. I seen it too. Big animal. Dolphin p'rhaps. But it was dark."

Yet another week after the exchange with Biker, Johnson was leaving the smaller Sainsbury, near the Odeon, when he glimpsed his quarry, bikeless, driving by in a dark blue BMW.

Johnson knew he would thereafter keep his eyes open also for the car, whose number-plate he had at once memorized. He was sure, inevitably, that he had often seen the car as well. He was struck by an idea, too, that Biker, in some strange, low-key way, wished to be visible—the bike itself, the car, the habit of the launderette. And that in turn implied (perhaps) a wish to be less visible, or non-visible, on other occasions.

With his groceries Johnson picked up one of the local papers. He liked to glance at it; the doings of the city of Sandbourne amused and puzzled him. Accordingly he presently read in it that another late-season holiday maker had gone missing. There had apparently been two the previous summer, who vanished without a trace. Keen swimmers, they were thought to have fallen foul of the wild currents east of the town. The new case, however, one Alice Minerva McClunes, had been a talented lady from New York. On the south-east coast to visit a niece, she had gone out with her camera and sketch-pad and failed to return. "She wanted to stay on the beach," the presumably woebegone niece reported, "till moonrise. It was the full moon." Alice was, it seemed, known for her photography of moonlight on various things.

This small article stayed intransigently with Johnson for the rest of the evening. He reread it twice, not knowing quite why.

Johnson the observer had made no friendships in Sandbourne, but he had by now gained a few acquaintances to say "hello" to.

He went to the local library the next day, then to the fishmarket above the beach. There, in between the little shops, he met the man he knew as Reg. And then Biker appeared walking along from the east end of the town, from the direction actually of the eldritch pier. And Reg called out to him, "Hi, mate. Okay?" and Biker smiled and was gone.

As one might, Johnson said, "You know him? I've seen him around—nice bike. Drives a car, too, doesn't he?"

"Yes, that's Jason. Don't know his other name. Lives in one of the rock-houses. Got a posh IT job in London—only goes up a couple of times a week. Oh, and once a month, three days and nights in Nores." Reg pronounced this neighbouring, still parochial, town in the proper local way as *Nor-ez*. "Bit of money, yes."

"A rock-house? They're the ones built into the cliff, aren't they?"

"Yep. Caves in back with pools of seawater. Pretty trendy now. Not so good when we get a freak high tide. Flooded out last year, all of 'em. Only, he was off at Nores—three days every time. Thought he might come back to see the damage but he never did. When I saw him he just says, I'll just buy a new carpet. Okay for some."

"Yes," said Johnson regretfully.

But his mind was busy springing off along the last stretch of habitable Sandbourne, mentally inspecting the houses set back into the cliffs. Smugglers had put them to good use in the 1800s. Now renovated and "smart," they engaged the wealthy and artistic. He was curious (of *course* he was) as to which house was Jason's—Jason, who, after all, must be rich. He thought of the pools of sea that lay behind the facades, and the great stoops of bending cliff that overhung them. Johnson had seen photographs of these structures in *History of Sandbourne*.

He visualized acrobatic Jason leaping straight down into a glimmering, glittery, nocturnal pool, descending like a spear, wriggling effortless and subtle as an eel out through some pipe or fissure, and so into the black-emerald bowel of the sea. He pictured those cold silver eyes under the glazes of blind green water, and the whip of the two legs, working as one, like a merman's tail. But somehow, too, Johnson pictured Jason as a sort of dog—hairy, unrecognizable, though swimming—as if there had been a dream of this, and now he, Johnson, recalled. As gradually he had remembered, was remembering all the rest, the sightings in launderette, car—all, everything.

Turquoise, blood-orange, daylight snagged the drips of nets under the skeletal arm of the pier. Bottle-green light gloomed through rotted struts, shining up the mud, debris, the crinkle of water like pleated glass . . .

And the day lifted to its zenith, and folded away. It was November now. Behind the west end, the sky bled through paintwork themes of amber and golden sienna. The sea blued. Sidelit, long tidal runners, like snakes with triangular pale indigo heads, swarmed inward on the land. Darkness began to stir in the east.

They forgot, people, how the dark began there, eastward, just as light did. The sun, the moon, rose always from the east. But so did night.

Never mind that. Soon the moon would be full again.

Under the pier, the mind was lying in its shell of skull. As dark filled in on dark, dark was in the brain, smooth and spontaneously ambient as the ink of a squid.

Under the pier.

Overhead the ruin, and the ancient ballroom, which a full moon might light better than sixteen chandeliers.

Something not a wave moved through the water.

Perhaps a late swimmer, indifferent to the cold.

• • •

Jason lived in the house behind the courtyard. It had high gates that were, most of the time, kept shut and presumably locked. A craning tree of a type unknown to Johnson grew up the wall, partly hiding with its bare, twisted slender branches an upper-storey window. Johnson discovered the correct house by knocking at another in the group, asking innocently for Jason, the man with the bike. An uninterested young woman said the man with the bike lived at the one with the courtyard. She didn't want to know Johnson's business. Johnson guessed the BMW would be parked in one of the garages above that corresponded with the rock terrace. The bike, according to the woman, was kept in the yard.

Having walked past the relevant house, he walked back and up Pelling Road to the clifftop. He sat on a bench there, looking down at the winter shore and the greyling sea. From here, away along the saucer curve of the earth, he could make out the pier like a thing of matchsticks. They said any storm destroyed always another piece of it. And yet there it still was, incredibly enduring.

He had visited the library again, looking at back numbers of the local papers. There had been a few disappearances mentioned in those past years he had viewed. But he supposed only tax-paying citizens or visitors would be counted. The coast's flotsam might well vanish without a trace.

That night the moon came up like a white plate in the tree at the end of the bungalow's small fenced garden.

The disk wasn't yet full, but filling out; in another couple of nights it would be perfect.

Johnson put down the Graham Greene novel he was reading and went out into the dusk.

Sea-influencing, blood-influencing, mind-influencing moon.

He thought of Jason, perhaps in his rich-man's house just

above the beach, behind the high gates and the yard, inside stone walls with the sea in the back of them.

By midnight Johnson was in bed asleep. He dreamed clearly and concisely of standing inside the cliffs, in a huge cave that was pearl white, lit by a great flush of brilliance at either end. And the far end opened to the sea, long thick rollers combering in, and where they struck the inner floor of the cave, white chalk sprayed up in the surf. But then out of the sea a figure came, riding fast on a motorbike. He was clad in denim and had short and lustrous hair, but as he burst through the cave, brushing Johnson with the rush of his passage, anyone would have noticed that the biker had the face of a dog, and in his parted jaws, rather delicately, he held a man's severed hand.

Waking from this, Johnson found he had sat bolt upright.

There was a dull, groaning ache in his lower gut and back, which he experienced off and on since the stabbing. He was barely aware of it.

Johnson was thinking of the changes the moon brought. And how something so affected might well share an affinity with the lunar-tidal sea. But also Johnson thought of an old acquaintance of his, fussy Geoffry Prentiss, who had been fascinated by the sightings, detailed in papers, of strange fauna, such as the Beast of Bodmin. He'd coined a term for such a phenomenon: *warg*. An acronym, WARG stood for Weird Animal Reported Generally.

With a slow, inevitable movement, not really disturbing, Johnson got up, went into the bathroom, and presently returned to put on his clothes and boots.

By the time he reached St. Luke's, the clock showed ten minutes to 3 a.m. There had been almost no one on the upper streets, just a young couple kissing. Soon though, a surreal distant pounding revealed the area of the nearest nightclubs, and outside the *Jester* a trio of youths were holding up another, who was being impressively sick. Compared to London, Sandbourne was a mild place. Or so it had seemed.

He wondered, when he turned east along the promenade, under the high lamps already strung with their Christmas neons of holly and stars, if he were sleepwalking. He considered this with complete calm, analytically. Never before had he taken his study of others to such an extremity. Had he in fact had a breakdown, or in more honest words, gone mad?

But the night was keen. He felt and smelled and saw and *experienced* the night. This was not a dream. He walked in the world.

The moon had vanished westward in cloud, as if in pretense of modesty. Beyond the line of land, the sea was jet-black under jet-black sky, yet the pale fringes of wavelets came in and in. Constant renewal. Repetition of the most elaborate and harmonious kind. Or the most *relentless* kind.

In the end, the seas would devour all the landmasses of the earth. The waters would cover them.

Several elderly men, drunk or drugged, sprawled on a bench and swore at him as he passed, less maliciously than in a sort of greeting for which, by now, they lacked other words.

Gulls, which never slept, circled high above the town, lit underneath translucently by the lamps.

Johnson went down the steps and into the area where the fishing fleet left its boats and sheds. The sand, the sheds, the boats, were sleeping. Only a tiny glow of fire about fifty feet away showed someone there keeping watch, or dossing.

The shadows clung as he passed the fish shops and turned into the terraced street above the shore. The lamps by the rockhouses were greenish and less powerful. They threw a stark quarter-glow on the stone walls, then on the many-armed tree, the two high gates. One of which stood ajar.

Jason, the acrobat with metallic eyes. And the gate was open.

Inside, the yard had been paved, but the bike wasn't to be seen. Instead a single window burned yellow in the lower storey, casting a reflected oblong, vivid and unreal as if painted there, on the ground.

Johnson accepted that it was impossible not to equate this with a trap, or an invitation, and that it was probably neither.

He hesitated with only the utter silence, the silence of the sea, which was a sound, to guide him. Such an ancient noise, the clockwork rhythm of an immortal god that could never cease. No wonder it was cruel, implacable.

He went through the gate and stepped softly over the yard until he reached the window's edge.

The bright room was lit by a powerful overhead source. It showed banks of computers, mechanical accessories, a twenty-first-century nerd's paradise. And there in the middle of it Jason kneeled on the uncarpeted floor. He was dressed in jeans, shirt, and jumper. He was eating a late supper.

A shock passed through Johnson, quite a violent one.

Afterwards, he was slightly amazed at his own reaction.

For Jason was not dining on a severed hand, not on anything human at all, and yet— Yet the *way* he ate and *what* he ate—a fish, evidently raw and very fresh, head and scales and fins and tail and eyes and bones all there, tearing at them with his opened jaws, eating, gnawing, swallowing all, those metal eyes glazed like those of a lion, a *dragon*— This alone. It was enough.

Not since London had Johnson driven, but his license was current and immaculate. Even his ironic leg, driving, gave him no problems.

He hired the red Skoda in town. It wasn't bad, easy to handle.

On the afternoon of the almost full moon, having waited on the Nores Road for six and three-quarter hours, he spotted Jason's blue BMW instantly. Johnson followed it on through forty minutes of country lanes, between winter fields and tall, bare trees, all the way to a small village known as Stacklebridge. Here, at a roundabout, the BMW turned around and drove straight back the way it had come.

Johnson, however, drove on to Newsham and spent an hour admiring the Saxon church, sheep, and rush-hour traffic going north and south. He had not risked the obvious move of also turning and tracking the other car homeward. Near Sandbourne, he was sure, Jason would park his vehicle in concealment off the road, perhaps in a derelict barn. Then walk, maybe even *sprint* the last distance, to reach his house or the pier before moonrise.

The nature of his studies had often meant Johnson must be patient. He had realized, even before following the blue car, that he could do nothing now, that was, nothing *this* month; it was already too late. But waiting was always part of watching, wasn't it? And he had been stupidly inattentive and over-confident only once, and so received the corrective punishment of a knife. He would be careful this time.

He didn't need to dream about it now. He was forewarned, fore-armed.

But the dream still occurred.

He was in the pier ballroom, and it was years ago because the ballroom was almost intact, just some broken windows and holes in the floor and walls, where brickwork and struts and darkness and black water showed. But the chandeliers burned with a cold, sparkling lemon glory overhead. All about were heaps of dancers, lying in their dancing clothes, black and white and rainbow. They were all dead and mutilated, torn, bitten, and rotted almost to unrecognizability.

Jason came up from under the pier, directly through the floor, already eating, with a savage hunger that was more like rage, a long white arm with ringed fingers.

But his eyes weren't glazed now. They were fixed on Johnson. They *knew* Johnson. And in ten seconds more Jason would spring, and as he sprang, would become what he truly was, even if only for three nights of every month. The nights he had made sure everyone who knew of him here also thought he spent in Nores.

Johnson reacted prudently. He woke himself up.

He had had dreams about other people, too, which had indicated to him some psychological key to what was troubling them, far beyond anything they had been able to say. Johnson had normally trusted the dreams, reckoning they were his own mechanism of analysis, explaining to him. And he had been very accurate. Then Johnson had dreamed that gentle, tearful Mark Cruikshank from Publicity had come up to him on the carpark roof at Haine and Birch and stuck a long, pointed fingernail through his heart. The dream was so absurd, so out of character, so *overdramatic* that Johnson dismissed it as indigestion. But a couple of days later Mark stabbed him in the groin, with the kind of knife you could now buy anywhere in the backways of London. For this reason Johnson did not think to discount the dreams of Jason. And for this reason, too, Johnson had known, almost at once, exactly what he was dealing with.

Christmas, personally irrelevant to Johnson for years, was much more important this year. Just as December was, with its crowds of frantic shoppers—not only in the festive, noisy shops, but in their cars racing up to London and back, or to Nores and back.

Moonrise on the first of the three nights (waxing full, declining to gibbous) was earlier in the day, according to the calendar Johnson had bought. It was due at 5:33 p.m.

Not knowing, therefore, if Jason would set out earlier than he had the previous month in order to beat the rush-hour traffic after four, Johnson parked the hired Skoda in a lay-by just clear of the suburbs, where the Nores Road began.

In fact the BMW didn't appear until three-thirty. Perhaps Jason had been delayed. Or perhaps, as Johnson suspected, a frisson of excitement always ruled the man's life at this time, adding pleasure to the danger of cutting things fine. For, once the moon was up, visible to Jason and to others; the change must happen. (There were plenty of books, fiction and non, to apprise any researcher of this point.)

On this occasion, Johnson only followed the blue car far enough to get out into the hump-backed country lanes. Then he pulled off the road and parked on a narrow, pebbly shoulder.

He had himself to judge everything to within a hair's breadth.

To begin the manoeuvre too soon would be to call attention, and therefore assistance and so *dispersal*. Indeed, the local radio station would doubtless report it, and so might warn Jason off. There were other places after all that Jason, or what Jason became, could seek refuge in.

Probably Jason always turned round at the Stacklebridge roundabout, however. It was the easiest spot to do so.

Johnson kept his eye on his watch. He had made the trip twice more in the interim, and it took consistently roughly eighty minutes to the village and back. But already there was a steady increase in cars buzzing, and frequently too quickly, along the sea-bound lane.

At ten to four the sun went. The sky stayed a fiery lavender for another thirteen minutes.

At four twenty-five Johnson, using a brief gap in traffic, started the Skoda and drove it back fast onto and across the narrow road, simultaneously slamming into reverse. A horrible crunching. The car juddered to a permanent halt.

He had judged it on his last trip: stalled and slanted sidelong across the lane, the Skoda blocked the thoroughfare entirely for anything—save a supermodel on a bicycle.

Johnson got out of the car and locked the doors. He made

no attempt to warn the next car whose headlamps he could see blooming. It came bounding over the crest of the lane, registered it had about twenty yards to brake, almost managed it, and tapped into the Skoda with a bump and screech. Belted in, the driver didn't come to much harm. But he had buckled a headlight, and the Skoda's bodywork would need some repairs, aside from its gearbox. The driver scrambled out and began to swear at Johnson, who was most apologetic, describing how his vehicle had gone out of control. They exchanged details. Johnson's were the real ones; he saw no need to disguise them.

As they communicated, three more cars flowed over the crest and, not going quite so fast, pulled to a halt without mishap. Meanwhile two other cars coming from the direction of Sandbourne were also forced to stop.

Soon there was quite a crowd.

The police must be called, and the AA, plus partners and others waiting. Lights from headlamps and digital gadgets flickered and blazed. Mobiles were out all along the verges, chattering and chiming and playing silly tunes under the darkling winter trees.

All the while, the back-up of trapped cars on either side was growing.

Covered by this group event, Johnson absented himself carefully, slipping off along the tree-walled hem of the fields, making his way back up the static vehicular line towards Stacklebridge.

People asked him if he knew what had happened, how long help would be in coming. He said some idiot had crashed his gears. He said the police were on their way.

It was full dark, five-fifteen, eighteen minutes to moonrise, when he noted Jason's BMW. It was boxed in on all sides, and people were out of their cars here, too, shouting, making calls, angry, frustrated, and only Jason still there, poised over the wheel, staring out blankly like something caught in a cage. *He* didn't look angry. He wasn't making a call. Standing back in darkness under the leafless boughs, Johnson observed Jason and timed the moon on his luminous watch.

In fact, the disk didn't come up over the slope to the left until the dial showed 5:41. By then the changes were well advanced.

Afterward, Johnson guessed no one else had noticed much what happened *inside* the BMW. It was the Age of Solipsism. You cared only for yourself and what was yours. The agony of another, unless presented on celluloid, was missed.

But Johnson saw.

He saw the flurry and then the frenzy, planes of half light and deep darkness fighting with each other like two vultures over a corpse. And he heard the screams.

And when the creature—and by then this was all one could call it—burst out, straight out the side of the BMW, none of them could ignore that they might have to deal with it.

Jason had become his true self. He—it—was about seven feet tall and solidly built, but as fluid in movement as an eel. The head and face, chest and back and arms were heavily hairy, covered in a sort of pelt through which two pale, fishlike eyes and a row of icy teeth glared and *flamed*. The genital area was also sheathed in fur, but under that the legs were scaled like those of a giant snake or fish. When the huge clawed hands rose up, they, too, had scales, very pallid in the blaze of headlights. It snarled, and it stank, rank, stale, *fishy*. This anomalous thing, with the face of a dog and the eyes of a cod, sprang directly against the crowd.

Johnson, cool, calculating, lonely Johnson (to whom every human was a type of study animal), had deemed casualties inevitable, and certainly there were a few. But then, as he, student of humanity, had predicted, they *turned*.

Subsequent news broadcasts spared no one who heard, saw, or read them the account of how a mob of already outraged people had ripped the monstrous beast apart. Questioned later they had been nauseous, shivering, crying, but at the hour, Johnson himself had seen what they did, and how they stood there after, looking down at the mess smeared and trampled on the roadway. Jason of course, given half a chance, would have and had done the same to them. And contrary to the myth, he did not alter back in death to human form, to lie there, defenseless and accusing. No, he, it, had retained the metamorphosis, to puzzle everyone for months, perhaps years, to come. Naturally, too, it hadn't needed a silver bullet, either. Silver bullets were the product of legends where the only strong metal, church candlesticks, was melted down to make suitable ammunition. If Johnson had had any doubt, Jason's own silvery eyes would have removed it.

That night, when the howling tumult and the flying sprays of blood had ceased, Johnson had stood there under the trees. He had felt quite collected. Self-aware, he was thinking of Mark Cruikshank, who had stabbed him, and that finally he, Johnson, for once in his bleak and manacled life, had got his own back on this bloody and insane world of aliens—werewolves, *human beings*.

Country Mothers' Sons

HOLLY PHILLIPS

Now we live on the edge of the bombed quarter of the Parish of St. Quatain in the City of Mondevalcón. The buildings are crooked here, tall tenements shoved awry by the bomb blasts and scorched by the fires. At home in our valleys we whitewashed the houses every spring, even the poorest of us, brightening away the winter's soot. Here, for all the rent we pay, the landlords say they are too poor to paint, and we live in a dark gray, soot-streaked world, leaning away from the wind and the dirty rain. Spring comes as weeds sprouting in the empty lots where no one has yet begun to build. Build what? We are outside the rumors, we who only moved here after the war. My village was only a hundred miles away, but I am a foreigner here. Stubbornly, like most of us, I am still in my heart a native of my village; I only happen to live in this alien place.

Elena Markassa lives high at the top of a creaking staircase, in her "tower," she says, where she can look far out and down. They are bright rooms, though cold and restless with the wind that sneaks in through the broken and never-mended panes. But the rest of us live lower down, out of the reach of the sun, so we often gather there, wrapped in our sweaters and shawls. Lydia Santovar huffs and puffs after the climb, but Agnola Shovetz and I are mountain women and too proud, even carrying a sack of potatoes between us. Elena Markassa never leaves her flat;

she's an antiquated princess in her gloomy tower, waiting for her perennially absent son to come home.

We all have absent sons.

"These boys!" Agnola Shovetz says with a toss of her hands and a note of humor in her voice, but Elena Markassa's broad face is heavy as she brings the flour tin from the pantry. We are making peroshki today, a long and fussy chore demanding company.

"They need work," Lydia Santovar says.

"My boy works," Agnola Shovetz says, ready for a mild quarrel.

"I don't mean that kind of work. Waiting tables! I can't blame my boy, even grown men take what they can find these days, but what kind of work is that for a man? And all for a pocketful of small bills. I hardly saw a coin from one end of the month to the other, back home. Who needed it? We worked the land, and it gave us what we needed. The apple trees and the barley fields and the cows: there was always something that needed doing at home. That was work, all of us together, building up the farm. That was where the wealth was, and you always knew where the boys were . . ."

At home. Is this all we talk about? Home. The war took it away from us, or took us away from it. The land we all thought eternal was ruined or lost, simply lost, as if the mountains had closed in, folding the valleys away out of reach. It's true, the word conjures our small house with the walls of plaster over stone, and the icon of St. Terlouz growing dark as an eclipsed sun over the hearth. But it's also true that when I hear that word I think of Georgi out on the mountain slopes, running through the streams of moonlight that splash through the spruce boughs and shine off the patchy remnants of snow. How he could run! Not a handsome man, my Georgi, and with a shy, hostile look with strangers, as if he were poised between a snarl and a fast retreat, but oh, to see him moving across the steep meadows, dancing from rock to rock above the backs of the scurrying sheep. Our son moves a little like that, so that it hurts sometimes to see him hemmed in by all these stony walls. *Mountains, buildings,* my boy says to me, *it's all rock, Mama. Either way, it's only rock.*

It isn't the buildings, his father would have said. It's the walls.

Lydia makes a well in the mound of flour on the table and I start cracking eggs while Elena fills the big kettle at the tap.

"This morning," Elena says, pitching her voice over the rush of the water, "I had to hear from my neighbor across the hall on the other side, she looks over the roofs going down to the harbor. She says all last night she heard the boys out on the roof, drinking, fighting, God knows what they get up to—"

"My boy's not a fighter," Agnola says.

"Whatever they do," Elena says, "this morning the roofs were covered with dead birds. Feathers like a ruined bed, that's what my neighbor said, and the birds all lying there like a fox went through the henhouse, dead."

"They keep hens on the roof over there?" Lydia says. Her strong arm is pumping as she beats the eggs into a yellow froth.

"Not hens," Elena says. "Pigeons, seagulls. Should I know? City birds. Nobody keeps hens here."

"People keep doves," Agnola says. She has a worried look, always on the verge of hunger.

"Not for eating," Elena says authoritatively. Perhaps living in her tower has made her an expert on the city's heights. "They're racing pigeons, for sport."

"We used to snare wood doves and cook them into pies," Agnola says.

"You can't eat city birds," Lydia says. She's a little short of breath. "No better than rats, with what they eat."

"It's the *dead* birds I'm talking about." Elena bangs the kettle down on the stove and turns to us. "Of course I had to hear it from my neighbor. *He* comes home almost at dawn, when all night I hardly slept for wondering where he is, and 'Where were you?' I say, but it's 'Mama, I have to go to work, do I have any clean socks?'"

"Oh, but my boy's just the same," says Lydia. "They're all the same, aren't they, Nadia?"

They look at me, because they think my boy is the ringleader, the troublemaker, the one whose role in life is to lead the innocent astray. But what can I say? That, no, unlike their boys he tells me everything, sitting on the edge of my bed in the dark?

The clouds blew away before midnight last night, and the moon shone so bright the birds mistook it for day. Down below, far below the height of rooftops on the hill, the harbor looked like a circle of sky, black water and moon sequins embraced by a lunar crescent of headlands. The water trembled under the wind that cleansed the air of its night smokes, and the birds, confused by the brilliance of the moon, lifted their wings, half aloft as the sea air flowed over and around them. Multitudes of pigeons on the roof leads leaned silently into the wind, bright eyes colorless, ruffled feathers like pewter. They stood in ranks like a congregation waiting for the hand of God to part the curtain of sky and sweep them away to another world; city doves, gray as the pavements, waiting for the right hand of God. And all around, like lumps of creosote on chimneys, finials on church spires, heat-slumped lightning rods and weather vanes frozen by the cold light, perched the owls.

If you move slow enough, not stalking-slow, but easy, you have to have some humor about it, be a little careless—but if you're easy, you can walk right among them. They're used to people; it's like feeding them in the square, except they're so still, in a trance, soft around your feet. In the cold you can feel the warmth of them against your ankles, the soft feathers of their breasts.

I can feel it. I can see the sleepy shutter-blink of their eyes as they stare out to sea, bemused, be-mooned.

The boys climbed the roofs as if tenements were mountain peaks and they were wolves climbing into the thin air to serenade the moon. And what happens to the hundreds of souls under the roofs when the roofs are no longer roofs, the buildings no longer buildings but hills, and the streets are only ravines, black with moon-shadow? What happens to all the dreamers when our boys are alone with the birds on the high hills? Do we dream beneath their feet like the dead dream, locked in the solid earth?

The boys stood on the steep roof slope, feet warmed by pigeons and faces icy in the wind. The pigeons with their wings half-spread, and maybe the boys, too, with their arms thrown wide, so many saints on so many crosses of moonlight, waiting for the right hand of God. And the owls, their yellow eyes the only color in the world, lifting free from chimney and spire, more silent than the blustering wind.

> *And you'll never know, Mama, you'll never know how*
> *it is to see the plunge, the hard short fight, the feathers*
> *flying like confetti at a wedding, and feel the hot*
> *bloody claws clench your arm. They're so strong.*
> *They're so strong.*

But I do know. You can't tell your son that, not when he's sitting on the edge of your widow's bed with his young blood running so hot and fast in his veins. But I know. I can see it still and breathe the cold air that pours like slow water off the edge of the snowfields. Spring in the valleys, but winter on the heights, so cold there is ice in the air to catch the light of the moon. The waning snow is so white it turns the rest of the mountain to shadow; and the broke-neck grouse, wings wide and head lolling below a halo of scattered feathers; and my Georgi, a shadow, with only his eyes bright with moon. Is that why I left the mountains? Not because there was nothing left but scarred fields and a gutted house, nothing for my son but the choice between brigandage and hunger. But because as long as I am here, or anywhere else, I can see my husband there—as if I had to leave before he could come home from the war.

But the women, my country friends, are looking at me, waiting for an answer. "Yes," I say with just the right sort of sigh, "these boys, they're all the same." And I reach for a potato and a paring knife, taking my share of the chore.

When you're trudging through the gray streets, with maybe a shopping basket in one hand, an umbrella in the other, bumping along with all the other umbrellas on the way to market to buy vegetables off a truck without even a crumb of good dirt in sight—when you're walking the daytime streets, you'd think there's only two kinds of animal in the world: the pigeons and the cats. Maybe if you look hard, you see the little house sparrows, brave as orphans snatching up what the pigeons are too slow to grab, and the seagulls lording it up on the gutters and the gable ends; and there are cormorants down in the harbor, drying their wings like so many broken umbrellas on the pilings; and of course there are the poor city dogs, tugged about on leashes when they're not trapped inside; and rats you only ever hear scrabbling in the walls. But the city belongs to the pigeons and the cats, like rival armies in a battle as old as the city, and this city is very old. Very old. And somehow, it's the pigeons that believe themselves in the ascendant, though you'd think it would be the cats, arrogant with their superior armament of teeth and claws. But it's the pigeons who bustle around like women on market day, keeping a sharp eye out for a good bit of gossip and a bargain, while the cats slink about on the edges of things, holding themselves equally ready for a fast retreat or a lightning raid. Only at night, when the pigeons hide from the dark and the streets are quiet, do the cats quietly take command.

Mondevalcón is a snarl of streets, a tip-tilted tangle running across the hills that rise between the harbor and the high black mountains inland. Even with the new electric streetlights going up, there is a lot of darkness here at night, and of course the streetlights are going up first among the palaces on the hill and the docks down by the water. In between, where most of us live, there is still darkness, deep as the sea. Only, sometimes the moon slips in, canny and elusive as the little gray tabby that comes to my balcony for her saucer of milk or her bit of egg every morning. Yes, moonlight comes like a cat, easing silently down one street angled just so, skipping across the battered roofs, running rampant in the bomb sites, then darting, sudden and bright, down an alley so narrow you would have sworn it hadn't been touched by natural light for a thousand years. And one night the foxes from the wild mountains followed the moon into town.

You should have seen them, Mama! my son says in the dark of my curtained room. I can hardly see him for the darkness, just the shape of a gesture or the glint of an eye, but I can smell the sharp sweat of him, still more boy than man, and the fruit tang of the liquor he shares with his friends. I hear, too, the wild energy that still has him in its grasp. He won't sleep until it lets him go, so I prop a second pillow under my head and listen. *You should have seen them,* he says.

Cats are solitary creatures and seldom gather, so it's a curious thing when they do. They came so quietly, as if they gathered substance out of the night air, appearing like the dew on the cobblestones of the street, on wide marble steps and the lofty pediments of the grand old buildings, the banks and palaces and guild halls, that survived the war. There is one wide avenue on the seaward face of the Mondevalcón hill, Penitents Climb, that rises, steep and nearly straight, from the harbor front to

Cathedral Square. It runs on from the square, the same wide street though its name has changed, down the back side of the hill, past the townhouses of the rich, and up again, past the train yards and coal depots and feedlots, and up still more into the harsh black rock country of the high mountains, shaded here and there by the juniper and pine. This was the road the foxes took as they came dancing on their long black-stockinged legs, their grinning teeth and laughing eyes bright in the light of the moon. They were not silent. Like soldiers marching into town with a weekend leave before them, they stepped with a quick, hard tapping of claws and let out the occasional yelp or a vixen scream to tease the lapdogs barking and howling from the safety of their masters' houses, and so their coming was heralded.

The cats waited where Penitents Climb runs into the square. The bombed cathedral stood in its cage of scaffolding, as if it were half a thousand years ago and it was being raised for the first, not the second, time. The cobblestones, where light once fell from jewel-toned windows, were dark, and the square, domain of pigeons in the daylight, was a black field waiting for battle to be joined. How did the boys find themselves there, so far from their usual harborside haunts?

We followed the moon, my son says, though perhaps they only followed the cats.

The silent cats. In the moonlight you could see the wrinkled demon-masks of their small faces when they hissed, the needle-teeth white, the ears pressed flat, and the eyes. Eyes black in the darkness, black and empty as the space between the stars. Even in the colorless light of midnight you could see all the mongrel variety of them, small and dainty, long and rangy, big and pillow-soft in the case of the neutered toms; and the coats, all gray, it's true, but showing their patches, their brindles, their stripes. All the cats of the city, alley cats and shop cats and pampered house cats, thousands of cats, as many and as silent as the ghosts of the city's dead, so many killed by the bombs, and all gathered there to repel the invasion of the mountain wilds.

The foxes came skipping into the square, long tongues hanging as they drooled at the daytime scent of the pigeons. Is that what drew them down from the mountains? Or did they, like our mountain sons, only follow the moon?

Battle joined. One fox makes a meal of one cat, if the cat is surprised before it can climb. Foxes are long-legged and long-jawed, clever and quick, and born with a passion for mayhem. But for every fox there was a dozen cats or more, and a cat defending its nest of kittens is a savage thing, with no thought for its own hurt.

The foxes took joy in it, you could see that, the way they pounced four-footed or danced up on two. It almost seemed the cats were the wild ones. No fun in them, no quarter, no fear of death but no thought for anything else, either. Your heart could break for them when they died. You could love them for it, thrown broken-backed and bleeding from some grinning dog-creature's mouth, but they were fearsome, too, so many of them in such a bloodthirsty crowd. I could imagine them turning on us like that. One black she-cat turned such a face to me, with her white, white teeth and the eyes black as holes, that I was almost afraid, forgetting how small she was. Like a lioness.

And so they prevailed, the cats, though terribly many of them died. As the moon slipped away behind the black mountains, the foxes seemed to lose the fun of the thing, or maybe it was only that the moon's setting called the signal for retreat. And so the sun rose and the pigeons, never knowing the battle that was fought for their safety, gathered to hunt for crumbs on the bloodstained cobbles of the square.

• • •

"And now there are police about asking questions!" Lydia Santovar says.

It is just the two of us today. Elena Markassa, up in her leaning tower, has pleaded a headache, and Agnola Shovetz is cleaning offices, to her chagrin, so Lydia has come to my small flat to
make our pies. We have wrinkled apples from the winter store,
rhubarb—crisp and fresh with sour juice—and hard little raisins
that look like nothing so much as squashed flies. This has a sat-
isfying appearance of bounty spread out on my counters along
with the sacks of flour and sugar and the tin of lard, something
to take pleasure in, in the face of all our worries about money.
Beyond homesickness, I am thinking more and more about
our weed-choked fields and ruined barns back home. I have
rented our pastures to the shepherds and that gives us our tiny
income—that and my son's small wage from cleaning trolley
cars—but oh, to have enough to hire a man to rebuild the house
and plow the fields! Oh, to have a man, my man, back again! So I
am not listening very closely to Lydia's tale.

"You have had a theft in your building, Lydia? I hope you lost
nothing yourself."

"You aren't listening, Nadia Prevetz."

Well, this is true.

"It's the cats I'm speaking of. Surely you must have heard!"

What I have heard is what my son tells me, but nothing more,
so to play safe I say, "Someone has been stealing cats?"

Lydia looks at me strangely. Does she doubt my innocence,
or my sense? "Killing them, Nadia. Someone has been killing
the cats all over the city. The police say nothing, you know how
they are, but everyone has been talking. But you must have heard
this?"

I have a slice of apple in my mouth and can only shake my
head no.

"Everyone says it is the work of a madman, or perhaps even a wicked gang, and now with the police everywhere asking about men seen out late at night, and in the newspaper today a letter about bringing the curfew back into force . . . Well, you can see what they think, that soon it won't be just cats but people that are getting killed."

"But surely . . ." I keep my eyes on my hands, the neat curl of apple peel sliding away from the knife. "Isn't it just as likely to have been animals?"

"That's what I say! It's just animals. Even if it is some gang of fiends."

It's clear what kind of newspapers Lydia reads. I bite my lip to keep from smiling. "What I mean to say is, isn't it likely that it was dogs or some such that killed the cats? I think a pack of dogs roaming the streets makes more sense than a gang of cat-murderers."

Lydia refrains from giving me another look. I can feel it, though her hands are as busy as mine.

"Maybe that's all it is," she says. "But the police are about, with their questions and their eyes, and I'm keeping my boy in at night until it all settles down."

"Well, you can try," I say, with the smile fighting free. Try to keep the young men indoors with spring on its way!

"Maybe you should try, too," Lydia says, her voice sharp as my paring knife. "To be on the safe side."

Still she forcibly refrains from looking at me, and my smile dies.

For here is another memory of home, and one I wish I could forget. Why is it that I need to build my memories of our house piece by piece, like our bedroom: so small that our marriage bed, too big to fit through the door, had to be built inside the room—that room, warm as a hen's nest in winter, with its white plaster walls and black beams and tiny two-paned window set to catch sunrise and moonrise in the east—I have to build it one eye-blink at a time, yet the bad memories leap sharp and wounding to the front of my mind. There is Georgi, with his hunted look and restless body, and there are the shepherds complaining of sheep dead in the shearing pen, and there is our son, so small and his eyes so wide, never understanding why these angry men have come to accuse his father . . . of what? Even they did not seem to know, except that we were the only people in the valley who did not raise sheep. My poor Georgi! I had to take them out and show them our goats, that I kept for milk and for the finer wool, and such a clamor did the does raise when they smelled the sheep blood on the men's clothes that the boy started to cry and the men went away ashamed. But by then Georgi was also gone, back up into the high trees. The best hunter in the valley—as if he had to demean himself by slaughtering sheep penned and helpless! It was two sheep dogs that went bad, the way they sometimes do, and leapt the fence to savage the sheep they were meant to be guarding. The dogs were shot, but no one apologized to my Georgi. I don't think he ever noticed, but I did, remembering how our little boy cried.

And now my boy, his father's son, refuses to stay inside on nights when the sky is clear.

> *I spend all day in the maintenance shed with the stink*
> *of oil and paint, Mama, I wouldn't know if it was*
> *raining or snowing or dropping fish from the sky except*
> *that the trolley cars come back all covered with scales.*
> *I have to see the sky sometimes, don't I? I'd go crazy!*
> *Listen, Mama, don't ever let them lock me away. If I*
> *wasn't a lunatic when I went in, I would be before I*
> *could come out again.*

And why would anyone lock him away? But I can see his eyes are dancing with mischief, he's only teasing his sad old mother, and so I laugh with him about the fish. *But think, Mama,* he says solemnly, *those scales had to come from somewhere.*

Like the foxes did.

Oh, these bright nights of spring! For the spring is well advanced now, and for all I thought it would be invisible here in the midst of the gray old city, there seems to be sweet new green everywhere. Workers clearing the bomb sites must cut the wiry vines to free the rubble, and even the heaps of wilting greenery show white trumpet flowers still trying to open with the dawn. Every balcony has sprouted an herb garden, rosemary already dressed in faded blue, bergamot opening in orange and red, mint in vivid green despite the soot that dusts everything indoors and out. And at night, when the onshore wind drives the clouds onto the high mountain peaks and the blazing moon robs the world of color, the tenements are like cliffs seeming too sheer to climb but beckoning with tender leaves in every cranny and on every ledge. And the cloud-heavy peaks are still barren with snow.

> *Do you remember, Mama, how Papa used to take us up through the woods to the high meadows below the cliffs? He was always the one who saw them first. Do you remember? The way they would leap, you would swear, from nothing to nothing where the rock was so steep even stonecrop could barely cling. The way they would leap . . .*

Do I remember? The steep meadows strewn with the earliest flowers, the yellow stars of avalanche lilies and the pale anemones too tender, you would swear, for the harsh high winds; and the black cliffs with their feet buried in the rubble of stone broken by ice in the winters when no one was there to see it fall; and the sharp-horned chamois like patches of dirty snow where no snow could cling, until they moved, leaping, as my son says, from nothing to nothing, or so you would swear. The chamois made my neat-footed goats look clumsy and earthbound, the tame and more than tame cousins condemned to valley life: debased. Or was that how I felt, trailing in the wake of my husband and my son, who seemed to have been born for the heights? But even they were banned from the steepest cliffs.

It was the challenge, Mama. You don't know, you don't know . . .

The longing for the high places, the hot-blooded joy of risk.
The chamois came across the rooftops in the full noon of the moon. Did they ever touch the city ground? Perhaps they stepped from the mountain slope onto some steep outlying roof and leapt from there to the next, roof-edge to ridgepole, gutter to gable, never dropping to the mortal earth. I can see them under the moon, skirting the dome of some palace on the hill, leaping over skylights with a patter of hooves. I wonder what they thought, those people living in the topmost floors. Maybe they heard it as a sudden fall of hail. And then the airy descent to the window-box gardens, the heady herbs, the alarm of the reflection in the moonlit window glass, and the far greater alarm, the shock of prey, when the window slides up and the young man tests his weight on the high iron landing loosened by bomb blasts and eaten by rust.

You have to keep moving. It's the only rule: keep moving, and always go up instead of down.

The chase, the glorious moonlit chase. Buildings are crowded here on the seaward face of the Mondevalcón hill. They press upwards like trees starved for sunlight, confined by the streets that are so narrow, some of them, a strong boy can leap from gutter to gutter like a mountain chamois, that nimble goat with horns so sharp they can stab through a wolf's hide like a twin-bladed spear. So the chamois fled before the silent hunting pack, a light thunder of flinty hooves that drowned the quieter thump and pad of bare feet; running in fear, perhaps, but in challenge, too, the challenge their kind has always offered the would-be predators of the mountain heights. They fled across the hill and upwards, the way instinct led them, and the moon followed to its setting among the clouds trapped by the western peaks, and the late dew fell, the heavy dew of the ocean shore—

> —and when we looked he was gone. Just gone. He must have fallen without a sound. We didn't know until we looked down and saw him on the street there, ten stories down.

Lydia Santovar's son. Lydia Santovar, my friend, who came from a village on the flat plain far inland, and whose son had never even seen mountains before the end of the war.

"It was the war," Elena Markassa says outside the church on the funeral day. "These poor boys, too young to fight—thank God! —but old enough to know what the fighting meant. And always with the threat of a bomb falling or the wrong partisan band coming through any day or night, the end of the world, for all a child knows, coming maybe today, maybe tomorrow or next week, next year. No wonder they grew so reckless. Poor boys!"

"They need their fathers," Agnola says, and we stand in silence a moment before going in, the three of us already in our widow's black, ready for a funeral any day, today or tomorrow or next week. A funeral every day.

My boy has come with me, as all the boys have, and I can feel him beside me as we stand and sit and kneel to the priest's sure

direction. He is a reassuring presence, the solid living weight of
him, and it is hard for a widow with an only child not to clutch
him, not to scold in mingled relief and fear. But I can feel the
restlessness in him. For the first time, I see his father's hunted
look in his clear young face, the dark wariness that prepares
itself for fight or flight at any moment. (*Maybe today, maybe tomorrow* . . . Elena's words haunt me, drowning out the priest.)
What does this mean for him, for his future life? I watch the
priest, I watch my friend Lydia, stony in her grief, but I see our
mountain-shadowed home, the roofless house and weedy fields,
the green pastures hemmed not by fences but by the dark mass of
the trees. At the same time I see a doubled image, a shadow, the
dark tenements hemming in the greening bomb sites, and I remember my son saying, *Mountains, buildings, it's all rock, Mama.
Either way, it's only rock.* But this place cannot be home to my
Georgi's son. Surely this tragedy proves as much? No matter that
the wilderness has followed us—followed him—into the city.
Surely, to such a boy, such a man, the city can never be home.
Yet, even as he ducks away from Lydia's accusing, tear-washed
stare, my son refuses to admit we must go.

Well, it is my mistake. It was my doing that brought us here,
fleeing the burnt house and the ex-partisans and the hunger. It
is my fault. I have no one to blame but myself. Perhaps even this
death should lie heavy in my hands.

The sun is shining above the inland peaks, the last long slant
of sunlight before the mountain shadow comes, the last bright
heat of the first warm day of spring, and we have made a feast of
farewell. There are peroshki, of course, stuffed with potato and
bacon, potato and sauerkraut, potato and onion, and drenched
with melted butter. There are roast beets and sour cream. There
is the stewed pork, red with hot paprika, and the baked cockerel,
and the leek and rabbit pie. There is soft white bread and bread

as dark and thick as molasses, and hard cheese, and pink sausage reeking with garlic, and red sausage studded with black pepper-corns, and butter packed in a little bowl of ice. There are pies, tart rhubarb and sweet apple, with crusts bubbled with golden sugar. And there is wine, the harsh, sour country wine that is as familiar and as vital as the blood in our veins. The boys follow us, half-unwilling, drawn as much by the smell of the food as by any sense of obligation to their fallen friend. He has been buried nine days, Lydia's son, and it is time to make his final good-byes before he moves on.

We have spared no expense, and two black taxicabs carry us up to the cemetery gates and stand there while the drivers, be-mused, help us unload our hampers. The city parishes have long since run out of room for their dead; the Mondevalcón cemetery stands high above the city, above even the palaces, on the first slope of the mountains. The grass is very green here, well fed and watered by the heavy fogs that haunt this coast, and there are flowers among the graves, roses and irises already blooming, and tiny white daisies scattered across the lawn. The black mountains rise above us in their scanty dress of juniper and pine; below us the city swells in a wave of dark roofs to the shining palaces with their towers and domes, and falls, roof piled against roof, to the blue water of the harbor; and beyond the dark headlands lies the sunlit blaze of the sea. There are seagulls crying, even this far from the water, and a clanging from the train yards, but there is still a great silence here, the enduring quiet of death and the open sky.

The three boys are abashed by the amusement of the taxi driv-ers (this farewell feast is a country rite, it seems, and the men make them feel so young), but they help carry the big hampers through the iron gates and down the gravel path we all trod nine days ago. The smell of the food follows us, mingling with the scent of cut grass, mouthwatering in the open air. Seagulls perch on monuments nearby, white as new marble on the grimy little palaces of death.

The boy's grave is humble, still showing dirt beneath the cut sod, with only a wooden stake leaning at its head. Lydia straightens this with a countrywoman's practical strength, as if she were planting a post for a new vine, while Elena Markassa, Agnola Shovetz, and I organize boys and hampers, and spread blankets politely between the neighboring graves. There will be a headstone in the fall, once the turned earth has settled; they don't know it yet, but the boys will be saving the money they have been spending on liquor and cigarettes to help Lydia pay for a good marble stone.

We spread the feast upon the blankets and the grass, open the bottles and toast the dead boy's name. Lydia tells stories of his none-too-distant childhood, and the living boys seem to shrink in their clothes, becoming even younger than they are, until they are children again, enduring their mothers' company. They eat, guilty for their hunger; we all eat, and for us women, at least, there is a deep and abiding comfort in this act. There is no mystery here, and no great tragedy, just another family meal. We are all family now, with this spilled blood we share among us, and Lydia is at once ruthless and kind to the living boys, speaking bluntly about the life and death of their friend. There are four mothers here, and four sons, though one of them lies silent in his bed and leaves his plate untouched.

The sun makes a bright crown on the mountain's head, and then falls away, spilling a great shadow across the city as a vanguard of the night. We feel the chill even as the sunlight still flashes diamonds from the distant sea. The food has cooled, sparrows have the crumbs. The air is sweeter than ever with the smell of turned earth and new grass, and even the haze of coal smoke from the train yard adds no more than a melancholy hint of distance and good-byes. The first stars shine out. The wine has turned sad in our veins. It is nearly time to shake out the blankets, stack the plates and pots and sticky pie tins, find the corks and knives and cheese rinds that have gone astray in the grass, and begin the long walk home.

My son stands and looks above the monuments with their weeping angels to the mountains. They are very black now, clothed in shadow. He moves towards them, weaving among headstones and walking softly across the graves. I am struck again by how like his father he walks, that supple prowl, and in the fading light he looks older, almost a man, walking away from us, the mothers, old already in our widow's shawls. I watch him with a pang in my heart, as if to see him thus is to lose him, as I lost his father, who walked away one day and never came home. I will call him in a moment to come and help me fold the blankets. The other boys have also stood, watching with a bright attention that excludes their mothers, and soon they have followed him, vanishing among the tombs, leaving us in the ruins of our feast while the color drains out of the world, into the deep clear blue of the sky.

The moon is rising, out on the eastern rim of the world. The horizon gleams like a knife's edge, the ocean catching the light even before the moon herself appears. So beautiful, that white planet, that silver coin. They tell us she is barren, nothing more than rock and dust, but there must be something more, something that calls out to the heart. How else could she be so beautiful? How else could she exert such force over the oceans of the world, and the hidden oceans in our veins? She rises, and all my longing comes over me again. Maybe here, whispers my most secret hope. My Georgi has been lost for so long. But maybe here, at last, he will follow the moon's call to the eastern edge of the world and find me once again.

We watch the moon rise, silent at last, while the boys wander out of sight among the graves. And as we sit here, wrapped in our nighttime thoughts, we hear the first voice lifted in a long lament. A voice to make a stone weep. Surely the moon herself would weep to hear such a cry! A rising and a falling note so long it seems it will never end, and then a silence so deep we can hear the grass rustling to the passage of the worms. And then the voice sings again, and is joined by another, and a third, in a chorus of grief, of longing, of love so wild it trembles always on the edge of death. They sing the moon up into the zenith, and fall still so that the silence folds gently about us, as deep and as peaceful as the grave. The rustling comes again, so quiet you would swear it was beetles or mice, but then we hear the paws striking the gravel path, the huff of breath and the faint clicking of claws, as the wolves follow the moon's path into the city. We see them for only an instant, two shadows, three . . . four? . . . we sit a while, waiting to see if there are more to come. One more is all I pray for. Oh, please! Do I pray to God or the moon? One more of those quiet gray shadows come down from the mountains to pass among the graves. Please, let there be one more. But we are alone now, four widows with absent sons, and soon we must rise and pack away the remains of our feast, and make our last good-byes.

A Most Unusual Greyhound

A Harry the Book Story

Mike Resnick

How it begins is that I am sitting there in my office, which is the third booth at Joey Chicago's 3-Star Tavern, sipping an Old Washensox and taking care of business, which this particular evening concerns doping out the odds on the Horrendous Howard–Kid Testosterone rematch. Gently Gently Dawkins, all 350 pounds of him, is sitting across from me working out a crossword puzzle, and for the past fifteen minutes has been stumped trying to come up with a three-letter word for "morbidly overweight." Dead End Dugan, who is still not used to being a zombie, is standing in a corner, wondering why he isn't thirsty anymore. It is at that precise moment that Joey Chicago tells me that I've got a phone call.

"Should I come over to the bar to get it?" I ask.

"The cord is four feet long," says Joey. "What do you think?"

So I walk over to the bar and pick up the receiver, and who should be at the other end than Benny Fifth Street, but it is hard to hear him because there is a lot of barking and even more yelling going on, and I remark that I did not know they brought telephones along on fox hunts and that, unlike Joey Chicago's, it must have a mighty long cord.

"I am at the dog track," says Benny. "Tell me that you do not book bets on dog racing."

"I am Harry the Book," I say with a note of pride. "I book bets on everything."

"All right," says Benny. "Tell me you do not book a bet on tonight's dog races for Tabasco Sanchez."

"As a matter of fact, Tabasco Sanchez bet five large on the feature race of the night," I tell him. "Is there anything else I should not be telling you?"

"Yes," says Benny. "Tell me that Tabasco Sanchez does not lay the five thousand dollars on an animal called Devil Moon."

"I cannot tell you that," I say, "and I do not think I want to hear what you are going to tell me next."

"What odds do you give him?" asks Benny.

"Twenty to one," I say. "After all, the dog is a first-time starter. He has never run before."

"Well, he is now a first-time winner, though he has still not broken out of a trot," says Benny. "It is a most unusual race and this Devil Moon is a most unusual greyhound, which is why I have called you."

"What is unusual about Devil Moon?" I ask.

"I have never seen a shaggy brown greyhound before," says Benny. "Furthermore, he has a pot belly, just like Sanchez himself."

"Maybe I am hearing you wrong," I say, "because otherwise I would be inclined to ask how a shaggy, pot-bellied dog can beat all the fastest greyhounds at the track."

"It is somewhat out of the ordinary," agrees Benny. "He is in an eight-dog field."

"And?" I say.

"He kills five of them on the way to the post."

"This is clearly a new form of strategy," I say. "But that still leaves two healthy greyhounds, does it not?"

"They are two healthy, terrified greyhounds," confirms Benny.

"Devil Moon just stares at them and shows his teeth. One of them climbs into the stands and will not return to the track. He is still whimpering when last I see him."

"And the other?" I ask.

"He jumps the outer fence and is still running. I figure he must be nearing the state line by now."

"The New York state line is not that close," I say.

"I am referring to the state line of Colorado, or maybe Burma," says Benny. "I have never seen a dog run that fast. Devil Moon has turned him into the Secretariat of dogs. Unfortunately, he has also turned him into the Wrong-Way Corrigan of dogs. Anyway, the race begins and Devil Moon starts trotting leisurely around the track. The mechanical rabbit makes a complete circle and is bearing down on him when Devil Moon bites its head off. He crosses the finish line and goes back to the barn, which they call a kennel here, and then he seems to vanish, because nobody can find him, although between you and me I don't know why anyone goes looking for a dog that eats his rivals and damages valuable track property."

"Do you know who owns him?" I ask.

"It says right in the program book," answers Benny. "He is owned by someone called Sylvester Sanchez."

"That is Tabasco Sanchez," I say.

"It says Sylvester," insists Benny.

"Mighty few mothers christen their children Tabasco," I note.

"You know," says Benny thoughtfully, "now that you point it out, I'll lay plenty of nine-to-five that Kid Testosterone is also an alias."

"I would stay on the phone and discuss aliases all night with you," I say, "but who should I see entering Joey Chicago's other than Tabasco Sanchez himself?"

"Perhaps he will solve the mystery of his real name," says Benny hopefully.

"I think he is more interested in collecting one hundred large from me," I say, "which I do not have any intention of paying off until all the circumstances have been explained to my satisfaction, which I put on a probability scale right up there with anacondas tap-dancing and politicians turning away from cameras."

I hang up the phone just as Tabasco Sanchez enters the bar.

"Hello, Harry," he says with a big smile on his face. "I trust you have heard the results of this evening's sporting events."

"Yes," I say. "Benny Fifth Street was out at the dog track and has so informed me."

"Have you got my money?" he asks.

"Before we talk money," I say, "we have to talk about the race, because the condition book says it is for greyhounds and I am told that Devil Moon does not exactly resemble your everyday greyhound."

"He is a most unusual greyhound, I will admit," agrees Tabasco. "But the fact remains that he wins the race."

Suddenly he coughs, and what should come out of his mouth but a bunch of dog hair.

"I thought that only cats choke on hairballs," observes Gently Gently Dawkins.

"And those are gray hairballs, are they not?" I say.

"I must have picked them up when I was back at the kennel, kissing Devil Moon for winning my hundred large," says Tabasco nervously.

"This is most interesting," I say, "because I have it on good authority that Devil Moon differs from most greyhounds in that he is brown."

"So I am nearsighted," says Tabasco. "I kiss the wrong dog."

"I am beginning to think that nearsightedness is the least of your physical problems," I say. "I am told that Devil Moon sports a pot belly just like yours."

"That is why I bet on him," says Tabasco defensively. "He reminds me of me."

"He reminds me of you, too," I say accusingly. "Especially if your name is Sylvester."

"My name is Tabasco."

"Show me your driver's license," I say.

"Nobody in Manhattan drives a car," he says. "But I am booked as Tabasco on my last three arrests."

"What are you on the first seven?" I ask.

"I don't remember," he says stubbornly.

"Gently Gently," I say, "what do you think his name was?"

"Sanchez," says Gently Gently promptly.

"You see?" says Tabasco. "Nobody knows that I was Sylvester Sanchez." He stops. "I mean, nobody remembers it." He frowns. "That doesn't sound much better, does it?" he concludes.

"So perhaps now you will deign to tell me about it," I suggest.

"Tell you about what?" he asks, suddenly scratching his left shoulder.

"About you and Devil Moon."

He leans down and scratches his thigh. "Damned fleas!" he mutters.

"So how long have you been a wolf?" I ask.

"Ever since I start noticing girls," he says, trying to smile, and I see more gray hair stuck between his teeth.

"Why don't you just admit that you are a werewolf?" I say.

"Do I look like a werewolf?" he scoffs.

"Yes," I say.

"Oh," he says unhappily. "I was hoping it wouldn't show."

"I wonder just how many rules, regulations, and laws you have broken tonight, Tabasco," I say. "You have destroyed track property. You have killed five competitors. You have chased a valuable greyhound off of the premises. You have impersonated a greyhound yourself . . ."

"I do *not* impersonate a greyhound!" he says heatedly. "It is not my fault that the track steward took my entry fee. I never claimed to be a greyhound."

"All right," I say. "I will amend impersonating a greyhound to impersonating a wolf."

"I didn't impersonate a wolf," he replies adamantly. "I *am* a wolf."

"Okay, then," I say. "You have impersonated a human . . ."

"I'm a human, too!" he insists.

"The court is going to have a difficult time with this one," I predict. "They will not know whether to put you in jail or the dog pound."

"Have you any suggestions?" he says.

"Yes," I tell him. "I suggest you redeem your marker and pay me the five large before I decide to testify against you."

"But I *won* the race!" he says.

"Do you think the track lets the result stand once I tell them what you are?" I ask.

"Would you do that?" he says.

"Absolutely, if you don't redeem your marker," I say. "I booked a bet on a greyhound. You were at best a brownhound."

"I thought we were friends," says Tabasco.

"I am very fond of you," I assure him. "It is just that I am even fonder of the five large you owe me."

"We have a problem here, Harry," he says. "I am ashamed to admit it, because I always pay my debts, but I am tapped out. I prowl all night, which is not even a minimum-wage job, and it tires me out so much that I fall asleep at my desk during the day so often that I am given my walking papers three weeks ago. This is why I came up with the dog track idea. I am desperate for money. You would be surprised at how little a wolf can earn between midnight and six in the morning."

"If this is the case," I say, "why did you choose to become a werewolf?"

"It is not a matter of choice," says Tabasco. "I fall in love with this beautiful Gypsy woman named Yolanda Schwartz . . ."

"Yolanda *Schwartz?*" I say.

"Well, she is half Gypsy," he replies. "And for some unknown reason her father disapproves of me."

"Unknown," I say.

"Well, it was unknown at the time," answers Tabasco. "Only later do I find out that it is his Cadillac that I steal and sell to Straight Deal Sheldon's chop shop."

"I can see where this might cause him to view the situation with some concern," I agree.

"And a modicum of fury," adds Gently Gently.

"He winds up and hits me with his high hard one—a Gypsy curse," says Tabasco. "And from that day to this, I have had a secret identity, just like Clark Kent and Bruce Wayne, the difference being that Clark Kent is gainfully employed and Bruce Wayne is independently wealthy, and what is more, they climb into their costumes while I grow into mine."

Benny Fifth Street walks in just then.

"Hi, Tabasco," he says. "Nice race, all things considered."

Tabasco buries his head in his hands and starts crying. This causes him to choke, and he spits out still more gray hair.

"You've got to help me, Harry!" he says desperately. "This curse is ruining my life. I only enter the race to raise enough money to have the curse removed so I can get back together with Yolanda." A tear runs down his face. "She still loves me, but it is a very smart curse."

"Smart in what way?" asks Benny.

"She's allergic to dogs!" he wails, crying and coughing up hair again.

"Boy, that's some Gypsy curse," agrees Gently Gently.

"Have you talked to Big-Hearted Milton or Morris the Mage?" I suggest. "They are masterful if mendacious magicians. Possibly they can remove the curse."

"Possibly they can," echoes Tabasco. "But they will not do it for free, and I have already explained my plight to you."

"Well," I say, "it appears we must help you find a way to make a living, if only so you can pay off my five large and have enough left over to speak to Milton or Morris." I think of all the things I see dogs do in the movies. "Can you save a dying man in a blizzard?" I ask.

"I cannot even *find* a dying man in a blizzard," says Tabasco, "and besides, when I am busy being a wolf, I tip the scales at no more than ninety pounds. Can you imagine me pulling Gently Gently to safety?"

"I cannot imagine you pulling him across the room unless you know how to operate a crane," says Benny.

"Is there a market for Seeing Eye dogs?" I ask.

"I am nearsighted and I have astigmatism," says Tabasco unhappily.

"I have never noticed you wearing glasses," I say.

"I do not wish to spoil my manly good looks, especially once I meet Yolanda," he says.

I am about to tell him that he is in no danger of that, that his manly good looks have gone the way of the dodo and the five-cent beer, but instead I concentrate on the problem at hand. "What else can you do besides eat greyhounds?" I ask.

Tabasco frowns. "Give me a for-instance," he says.

I shrug. "Do you herd sheep?" I say.

"That is wrong," says Gently Gently.

"How can a question be wrong?" says Benny. "It is answers that are wrong."

"Do you herd sheep is wrong," insists Gently Gently. "Have you heard sheep is right."

"Get him some calories," I say to Benny. "The crossword puzzle has sapped his mental strength, and he is now operating on two cylinders, three at the most."

Benny leads Gently Gently off to the bar for nuts and pretzels, and I go back to considering Tabasco's problem, except Tabasco isn't there anymore. I look down and there is Devil Moon, panting and drooling and looking mournfully into my eyes. Mournfully, and maybe a little hungrily, too.

"Tabasco, do you still understand me?" I say.

Tabasco stares at me and yawns. He has very white teeth.

"Tabasco, howl once if you understand me and twice if you don't."

Tabasco walks over to a nearby chair and lifts his leg on it.

"I like him better as a guy," says Gently Gently, staring at Tabasco from the bar.

"Hell," adds Benny, "I even like him better as a greyhound."

"You know," says Joey Chicago, "other guys decorate their places with the stuffed heads of lions and tigers and mooses and things like that, but me, I am too gentle and too sensitive to ever show off the remains of an animal in my establishment." He raises his voice. "But if somebody lifts his leg in here again, we're going to display a mounted wolf's head over the bar." He turns to Benny and Gently Gently. "And that goes for you, too!"

All the while this is going on, I am staring at Tabasco and trying to think of how to put his transformation to economic gain. For a while I think of the movies, but even though Rin Tin Tin has gone on to his reward, I can foresee numerous problems, because out there time is money, and once they get all the actors and cameras in position and yell, "Action!" it would not do for the new Rin Tin Tin to appear as the old Tabasco Sanchez.

I know that guard dogs are always in demand, but I also know Tabasco Sanchez, and whether he is busy being a man or a wolf, I would not want to put him near anything that was worth guarding.

I am beginning to think that maybe he has got a handle on the situation, that there is no way for a wolf to make a decent living working the third shift, especially in Manhattan, when a newspaper delivery truck drives by, and plastered all over it are ads for the forthcoming Southminster dog show, and suddenly I see a way for Tabasco to pay off his debt to me.

"Tabasco," I say, "if you can understand me, I think I have the solution to your problem. I do not know quite how you can answer me. Clearly you do not howl on cue, and telling you to lift your leg once or twice will clearly put you in dutch with Joey Chicago. Maybe you could paw the ground once if you understand me and twice if you don't?"

Tabasco stares at me and remains motionless.

"Is that a yes or a no?" asks Benny.

"Maybe you should make it multiple choice," suggests Gently Gently.

"Tabasco," says Joey Chicago, "if you will stop being a wolf for the next ten minutes, you can have an Old Peculiar on the house."

"I call that damned sporting of you," says Tabasco, who is a man again so fast that I do not even see him change.

"How do you do that?" asks Benny.

"And how come your clothes vanish when you are a wolf and come back when you are a man?" asks Gently Gently.

"You will have to ask Big-Hearted Milton or Soothsayer Solly," replies Tabasco. "I do not seem to have any control over it—or over anything else, for that matter."

"Do you remember what I say to you while you are being Kazan of the North?" I ask as he downs his Old Peculiar.

"Yes, and I am very grateful."

"Then why did you not respond?" I say.

"When I am a wolf, I think wolfish thoughts, and I am concerned with wolfish things. I hear you say that you have solved my problem, but as a wolf I am much more interested if you had tell me where all the rabbits or the lady wolves were hiding." He pauses for a moment, then continues: "But I am interested now."

"I see that the Southminster dog show is coming up, and that first prize is six large, which means five for me and one for you. All we have to do is win it."

"Win against the best-bred, best-conditioned dogs in the world?" says Tabasco doubtfully. "I haven't got a chance."

"Where would America be if Alexander Hamilton had had that attitude?" says Gently Gently reproachfully.

"Pretty much where it is today," answered Tabasco. "And so, come to think of it, is Alexander Hamilton."

"I don't know, Harry," says Benny. "I know what he did in an eight-dog field, but Southminster has thousands of dogs. How many can he kill and eat before someone gets wise?"

"Or before he gets full?" says Gently Gently.

"Tabasco," I say, "are you willing to try, or do I pass the word that you will not make good your marker?"

"I will try," he says. "I cannot have you spreading it all over town that I am a deadbeat."

"Or that he is only occasionally a human being," adds Gently Gently.

So the next morning I buy a leash and collar, making a note to add it to what Tabasco owes me, and then I go to the Madison Square Garden, where they are holding this canine beauty contest that night, and ask to see the condition book, figuring I will enter Tabasco in a field for nonwinners of two, and they explain to me that this does not work like Belmont or Aqueduct, and I have to enter him in the proper breed, so I request the entry form for timberwolves, and they laugh and ask me what I really want.

"I do not much care," I reply, "so long as he competes after dark."

"That is a most unusual request," says the steward.

"He burns easily," I say.

"Here is a list of the breeds that will show at night," says the steward, handing me a sheet of paper. "Is he on it?"

I look, and I do not see timberwolf or even werewolf listed, but one of the breeds is greyhound, and I figure, well, he has won a race as a greyhound so he might as well remain consistent and win Southminster as a greyhound.

I go back to Joey Chicago's and kill some time there before we are due in the ring, and then, about an hour before post time—at Southminster they call it ring time—Benny and Gently Gently and Tabasco and I all go over to the Garden.

It is a very unusual sport, this dog-show game, because they do not even have a tote board on the infield, and in fact they do not have an infield at all. There are dogs everywhere, and Benny hunts up the ring we are to appear in, and I turn to Tabasco.

"It is time to turn into a wolf again," I say, "and it would not hurt things a bit if this particular wolf happens to look just like a greyhound."

He closes his eyes and grunts.

"I am trying," he says. "But nothing is happening."

"Try harder," I tell him.

He tenses and grunts again, but when he opens his eyes he is still Tabasco Sanchez.

"This is most embarrassing," he says.

"I do not wish to be the bearer of bad tidings," says Benny, "but you are due in the ring in three minutes."

"I am sorry, Harry," says Tabasco. "It does not seem to be working tonight."

"I pay a twenty-five-dollar entry fee," I tell him, "and I am going to get my money's worth." I put the collar around his neck and attach it to the leash. "Let us go."

"This is humiliating!" he says as I start dragging him toward the ring.

"Give me my five large and I will cease and desist this instant," I say.

He does not reply, and I look back at him, and he has become a wolf again.

We enter the ring with six sleek greyhounds. Tabasco looks at them and growls. It is a loud, ominous, hungry growl. Two of the greyhounds begin dragging their owners to the far side of the ring, three start shaking, and one just lays right where he has fainted.

The judge comes over and stares at Tabasco.

"I believe you are in the wrong ring, sir," he says at last.

"I am in the right ring," I answer.

"This is not a greyhound," he says.

"He is from the Mexican branch of the family," I say.

"He is not a greyhound," repeats the judge. "I am going to have to disqualify him."

"He *is* a greyhound," I insist. "He has just been out in the sun too long, and has acquired a tan."

"Get out of my ring!" says the judge, pointing to the exit.

For a minute I think Tabasco is going to bite the judge's finger off, but I jerk on the leash, and suddenly all the fight goes out of him as he realizes that we have failed and he still is penniless, and he docilely follows me out of the ring.

We are on our way to the exit when we pass a ring where they are judging these little silken-haired dogs, and suddenly Tabasco stops and digs in his heels, which is a lot of heels to dig in all at once, and I can tell he is taken with one feminine little dog.

I ask a ringsider what this kind of dog is called, and he says,

"Shih tzu," and I say, "Gesundheit!" and he says, "No, that is the name of the breed."

I pull on Tabasco's leash again, and he pulls back, and before long most of the ringsiders are no longer watching the Gesundheit dogs but are laying bets on who will win our tug-of-war, and at the moment Tabasco is a seven-to-five favorite, and then suddenly there is a cheer, and Tabasco and I both stop pulling for a minute to see what the cheering is about, and it seems that the little dog he has been watching has won.

On the way out of the ring she makes a beeline for Tabasco, and then they touch noses, and then she is led away and I start to walk to the exit again, and Tabasco bites his leash in half and runs to the big ring in the center of the building, and I have no choice but to follow him since he is five thousand dollars on the hoof, or on the claw as the case may be, and I am not letting him out of my sight until I collect.

I am not sure what is going on, but dogs keep coming and going into the big ring, and finally there is an enormous cheer, and all that is left in the ring is the little Gesundheit dog and thirty-seven photographers. Finally the crowd starts dispersing, and as it thins out I spot Tabasco on the far side of the ring, and I race around it to reach him before he can run off, and when I get there he has forgotten to be a wolf and is just plain old Tabasco Sanchez again, still attached to a leash and collar.

"What are you trying to pull?" I demand.

"Just wait, and all will be revealed," he says.

A minute later Benny catches up with us, and I can see all 350 pounds of Gently Gently rounding the far turn and heading for home, and then suddenly we are joined by as pretty a dark-haired girl as I have ever seen. She walks right up to Tabasco and plants a kiss on his cheek.

"Harry the Book," he says, "I want you to meet the woman I intend to marry, Yolanda Schwartz."

"You must have just arrived," I say, "because surely I would have noticed someone of your good looks before."

"You have been looking at her for the past hour," says Tabasco.

"You are mistaken," I say. "I would not forget someone like her."

"She just went Best in Show," says Tabasco. "I recognize her the second I see her, for even a change in species cannot disguise the love of my life from me."

I stare at her, and there is not a touch of Gesundheit dog to be seen, except maybe for the silken hair.

"It is true," says Yolanda. "I am so mad at my father for what he does to poor Tabasco that I run away from home, so he curses me, too." She holds up a fistful of money. "It turns out to be a blessing, because now Tabasco and I can be together forever, and he can pay off the five thousand dollars he owes you."

"No," says Tabasco. "We need that money to set up house-keeping."

"Think, Tabasco," says Yolanda. "If we take our human forms, Daddy will just find us and break us up again. But if we stay a Shi Tzu and a wolf forever, he will never find us. We will sleep all day and love all night."

This sounds as good to Tabasco as it would to any red-blooded male of any species, and he turns over the money to me.

"You only owe me five large," I say. "I will invest the rest where it will do the most good."

I do as I promise, and the next day I give them their very first wedding present, which is a thousand-dollar line of credit at Morgan the Gorgon's Meat Market.

The Bitch

P. D. CACEK

Oh, God."

Karin had heard Russ say those two words in a number of ways for a number of situations. It would be an explosive murmur while making love, a groan after she told a bad joke, or an epithet when he discovered a new oil spot on the driveway—but the way he said it this time sent a chill racing through her, freezing her hand halfway against her wineglass.

"Russ?"

His eyes moved slowly from some point over her right shoulder to her eyes, then down to his plate, his mouth set in a firm, bloodless line. Suddenly the restaurant's ambient sounds—the quiet conversations from the other tables, the soft click and clatter of flatware against plates, the sweet, seductive music that hung in the air . . . all of it became a distraction as Karin leaned forward. "Russ, what *is* it?"

He looked up and said one word: "Lily." The chill deepened.

"Shit."

"Yeah."

For the six months they'd been dating, Lily—the ex who wouldn't go away—had been a constant, determined, and, up until that night, discreet rival for Russ's affections . . . even though he'd made it clear to Karin that he no longer felt anything for the woman.

Karin believed him.

Lily, apparently, did not.

They'd be at a movie and—surprise—Lily would be sitting two rows back. They'd be at a party and Lily would be standing across the room, glaring at Karin until Russ turned around, at which time tears would magically form in her pale gray eyes and she'd leave in a flurry of weeping and garnered sympathy. For six months Lily would show up, accidentally, wherever they were. Karin should have expected it, but somehow, she thought tonight would be different.

"Ah, Jesus . . ."

Karin didn't have to look, she knew when the air, suddenly scented with lilacs and musk, moved between them and the candle flame shuddered as a shadow fell across the table.

Russ shook his head. "Karin, this is Lily."

Karin's hand finally reached her wineglass as she looked up. *Fragile* was a term she heard most from people, including Russ, used to describe her. *Broken* was another, but from where she sat, looking up at the pale woman with thick black hair and bloodred lips, Karin couldn't see it.

Except for the tears glistening in her eyes, and the flowing, über-feminine dress the color of ash, Lily seemed as hard—and invulnerable—as marble.

Smiling politely, Karin cleared her throat and nodded. "Hi."

The sadness in Lily's eyes crystallized momentarily when she glanced at Karin, before melting back into twin pools of dejection as she looked at the table.

"Oh," she whispered, voice hoarse with emotion, "I see you're having dinner."

It was a flat statement that made Karin feel as if she'd done something horribly wrong . . . or simply *was* something horribly wrong. She lifted the wineglass and took a quick sip to wash the taste out of her mouth.

"Yes. The food's very good here."

Lily brushed at her coal-dark hair, dismissing Karin and her comment, before turning her full and undivided attention back to Russ.

"I always thought so; it was one of our favorite places."

Russ made a sound that was halfway between a cough and groan. "We never ate here, Lily."

"Oh?" Confusion deepened the slight—very slight—wrinkle between the woman's eyes. "That's strange . . . I thought we had. Well, we ate at so many good restaurants I guess I got . . ." She sighed and Karin fought the urge to applaud. "Anyway, I was just driving by and saw your car in the parking lot and thought I'd stop in. To say 'hi.' "

Karin's stomach tightened uncomfortably around the portion of the night's meal that she'd already eaten. "How nice."

Lily gave her a small, weak smile before utterly dismissing her. Again.

"You look good, Russell."

"Thanks."

"And you've put on some weight. *She* must be a good cook."

The color deepened along Russ's cheeks as the *she* in question finished off the wine in her glass and toyed with the idea of *accidentally* spilling the rest of the bottle down the front of Lily's dress.

Russ grinned but pushed his plate away. "Is there something you need—"

"I saw Ben and Dee the other night," Lily interrupted with the precision of a surgeon removing a tumor. "They said you seemed happy. *Are* you happy, Russell?"

Russ smiled at Karin and winked. "I'm working at it."

"Oh, dear. That's rather an evasive answer, isn't it? You're either happy or you're not. You shouldn't have to *work* at it, Russell."

Despite the obvious chill that had descended, Karin felt a slow burn creep up along her throat, but managed—somehow—to keep her voice light. "Oh, I think Russ is doing okay in that department."

"Really?" Lily said, then reached down and helped herself to the piece of roast beef on Russ's fork.

He shook his head when Karin started to say something. Holding herself still, she watched the woman's lips slowly part to reveal a set of strong white teeth that closed over the meat with a kind of predatory finality.

"Well." Lily handed Russ back the empty fork and leaned over, kissing his cheek. "If you're not going to invite me to join you . . . It *was* good seeing you again, Russell."

Turning, she gave Karin one last withering, *dry-eyed* glare before walking away. Karin watched the rest of the performance— Lily wiped at her eyes a number of times between their table and the door—before she could force herself to look away. Russ was busy looking at nothing in particular.

"Join us?"

Russ was toying with his wineglass but never picked it up. "Sorry about that. Sorry."

"Did she *seriously* think we were going to ask her to join us?"

"I don't know, yeah . . . maybe. That's just Lily being Lily."

Karin poured another glass of wine and finished it in one long, continuous swallow.

He reached across the table to take her hand when she started to refill the glass. "Don't. She was just trying to rattle you."

"Well, it worked. How could she see your car? We parked in the back."

"I don't know . . . she has a way of doing things like that."

"She's . . . barged in on your other dates?" Karin did a quick mental rundown on the things Russ *had* told her about Lily and couldn't remember that particular point of interest.

"What? Oh . . . no, no, but for the first couple of months after we broke up I'd go somewhere—to the market or hardware store

134 | P. D. Cacek

or, even a fast-food drive-thru—and I'd see her. We wouldn't talk or anything, but she'd be there. And when I'd get home, there'd be a message on my answering machine or a text message on my cell . . . We never actually spoke but she wanted me to know she was there . . . that she'll always be there."

Russ let go of her hand and finished his wine.

"And, in case you're wondering why this happened to-night . . . I suspect it's because I've been with you longer than any of the other . . ."

Karin took pity on him and nodded. "Six whole months, going on seven."

"And that bothers the hell out of her . . . because this is real."

She couldn't say anything and it was probably just as well when, instead of letting the moment continue, he added:

"We started dating just a few months after her husband died and that was a mistake. She was so devastated by his death, so helpless . . ." He shrugged. "I don't know, but she *needed* me and, I guess, I liked the feeling, so I stayed even after I knew the relationship wasn't what I wanted. A couple years into it and I'd really had enough and tried to break it off . . ."

Karin leaned forward but didn't say anything. This was the first time she'd heard about that.

"She threatened to kill herself if I left. And . . . I believed her."

"So you stayed."

"For another eighteen months, and then . . . Christ, I couldn't take it. She thought she had me so she felt she could do or say anything to belittle me and I'd take it. We were at an office party and my boss's wife—who was a bit drunk and flirty at that point—was complimenting me on my suit when Lily walked up. 'Oh yes, the poor man knew nothing about fashion or . . . much of any of the social skills until *I* showed him. He's so helpless without me.'"

"Yikes."

Russ nodded. "Yeah, and Lily made sure everyone in the room heard it. When I took her home . . . back to *her* home, that is, I told her how I felt and she laughed and said it was only a joke and she felt sorry for me if I didn't know that. I walked her to her door, then turned around and left."

"Wow."

"I didn't answer the phone for three days, and on the fourth, she showed up at my office in hysterics . . . making me the bully, of course. Then—Christ, I don't want to talk about this anymore, okay?"

Karin nodded. She could get the rest of the story from friends. "Sure."

They ate the rest of their meal making careful small talk about safe subjects and were laughing and holding each other as they walked to his car. But later that night, when they made love, Karin had the distinct impression that there was another person in bed with them.

A woman with long dark hair and sad gray eyes and sharp white teeth: a bitch in flowing sheep's clothing.

"So . . . you met Lily?"

Karin could hear the pity in her friend's voice and almost wished she hadn't called. But what's the use of having a girlfriend, especially a girlfriend who knows all the players and doesn't have to be brought up to speed?

"Yes," Karin said. "Yes, I did."

"And?"

"Scary lady."

"You think so?" Karin was a bit surprised by the comment. "I just think she's sad. And, yeah, okay, maybe a little . . . pathetic. I mean, it *has* been three years. I keep telling her it's time to move on."

"You still talk to her?"

"Oh, sure. Ben and Russ worked together, so I knew Lily from the start and . . ." Her friend's sigh echoed softly in Karin's ear. "Well, she still calls sometimes to ask about Russ. Last night she was in tears, sobbing her heart out because she saw the two of you together and how could Russ go to *their* restaurant with another woman and—"

"It wasn't their restaurant. Russ said—"

"—do this to her because she still cared so much. Yadda, yadda, yadda. Same song, different verse. Don't let it get to you."

Karin heard a snap and looked down at the broken mechanical pencil in her hand. "Uh-huh."

"C'mon. It's just her way of trying to get sympathy. I know she probably hoped I'd call Russ and tell him, but I told her to knock it off instead. She got real quiet and then hung up."

"Why does the word 'manipulation' come to mind?"

"Yeah, but she's just running scared. Ben and I haven't seen Russ this happy in . . . a long time, and I'm sure Lily notices that, too."

The mailbox icon flashed in the upper corner of her computer screen and Karin smiled. Russ liked to send her jokes or cartoons or just "Hi, miss you" messages to brighten her workday. Setting the broken pencil down, she clicked open the e-mail . . . and stopped smiling.

"Oh, joy."

"I know." Dee sighed. "But don't let her get to you. It's hard when someone won't let go, but she's really only hurting herself."

"I know . . . and I can understand how Lily doesn't want to give up. Russ is a wonderful man and I don't intend to simply walk away."

"It may get rough."

Karin nodded and reread the message on her screen:

I simply don't understand why you're with him. You're nothing. You're average at best and Russell requires a woman who is much more than that. I'm saying this only as a friend, but if you continue to burden him with your presence, you'll only bring him down to your level, and one day he'll notice that and leave you. Show me I'm wrong. Leave him now and gain my respect—Lily

"Oh," Karin said into the phone as she pressed the *delete* key, "there's no doubt about that."

"Excuse me?"

Russ smiled weakly. "She wants all of us to be *friends*."

"And you know this because . . ."

"She called me at work this afternoon . . . weeping and asking me to forgive her for last night. She said she'd be happy and be able to get on with her life if we could be friends."

Karin took a deep breath and pretended to think about it without adding any comment about aeronautically gifted swine. She also didn't mention Lily's e-mails—five in total, all along the same "you're not good enough for him, leave now, you pitiful excuse for a woman" lines—or the phone message on her answering machine:

> *"I don't think Russell will ever know just how much he meant to me . . . but he was my world and I—I—"* (sound of weeping) *"I hope you both know that I only want him to be happy. If not with me, then . . . I hope you can make him happy but I worry because he should have said that last night. If a man is happy, he wants to tell the world. Has he ever told you? He told me so many times how happy I made him . . . but he must have lied. He must still be lying—to himself. Please, Karin,*

call me and let's talk. There are so many things you
apparently don't know about him . . . that only I can
tell you. We need to talk. Please call. My number is—"

She'd erased the message and, just for the annoyance factor, turned off the machine before heading over to Russ's for the night. The woman was obviously nuts . . . or not.

"The lady does get around . . ."

Russ stopped tearing lettuce apart and looked at her. "Excuse me?"

Karin shook her head and stole a grape tomato out of the bowl. "Nothing. So she wants us to be friends, huh? What did you tell her?"

He looked down so quickly Karin thought she heard his neck pop. "I . . . told her I'd ask you—but that I didn't think it was a good idea."

"Uh-huh."

Russ finished dismembering the lettuce and picked up a homemade cheese crouton and held it out to her . . . an offering she couldn't refuse.

One of the many things Karin loved about Russ was his skill in the kitchen. The man could cook, and while she managed well enough to keep from starving, her meals tended to be of the simple boil-in-the-bag variety. Russ, on the other hand, prepared *real* food, from scratch, using recipes that required more than "place in pot" and "turn on heat."

If ever a man knew the way to a girl's heart . . .

Karin sighed—a bad mistake, considering the mouthwatering aromas that filled the kitchen. She took the crouton and crushed it between her back teeth. "It's not going to happen you know . . . the friends bit, I mean."

"I know."

"Then why didn't you tell her?"

He shrugged. "I don't want to hurt her any more than I already have. Lily may seem strong, but she's not, Karin . . . not like you."

Karin concentrated on chewing and swallowing and not destroying his obvious delusions about his *fragile, broken, weak* ex. "Yeah, well . . . I guess she'll figure it out eventually."

"Here's hoping." He leaned across the island counter and planted a kiss on her nose. "Now, how'd you like to do me a favor?"

Russ generally didn't need any help when it came to cooking, so Karin had already toed off her croc sandals and had made herself comfortable on one of the counter's tall bistro-styled chairs—where she could filch the occasional nibble while he worked. She was already looking for a glass when he picked up a wine bottle and upended it. A lone drop, the color of ripe plums, landed on top of the lettuce.

"I thought I had another bottle of Cabernet when I made the dressing. How do you feel about running out and getting some wine? Do you mind?"

Karin snagged her purse off the back of the chair and slid her feet into the plastic shoes. "I can do that. Need anything else?"

"Not a thing. Thanks. Now scoot."

She left him wreathed in a cloud of steam and paused only a moment to listen to the utterly domestic sounds coming from the kitchen. They were good sounds, echoes of hearth and home and refuge—sounds that she had missed and hadn't even realized until that moment.

"I don't hear the door closing," he shouted, and it made her smile.

"Yes, sir. Right away, sir. At once, sir." Karin stepped out into the bright late-summer evening and made sure the door banged shut behind her. Smiling, she walked past her car and continued down the drive to the sidewalk. It was too pleasant a night to drive the quarter mile to the wine-and-spirit shop.

One of the benefits, if there were any, of living in a "covenant-controlled planned community," aka 'acre-o-condos,' was that there was *always* a strip mall within walking distance.

Not that many of the community-dwellers seemed to take advantage of it, as was evident by the number of cars that filled the parking lot. Their loss, she thought, and waved the right-of-way to a harried-looking woman in an SUV that could have housed a family of six, plus pets. Given the choice, Karin preferred feeling the ground beneath her feet.

He called her cell just as she'd finished signing the credit card receipt.

"You walked, didn't you?"

"Can't put anything over on you." Mouthing her thanks to the salesclerk, Karin picked up the bagged wine and began weaving her way through the crowd to the door. "I won't be five minutes . . . start dishing out the salad."

Russ *humphed* through the phone. "Okay, but the wine's supposed to breathe before it's served, you know."

"I'll jog and we can give it CPR when I get there."

Karin snapped the cell phone shut and dropped it back into her purse. She had no intention of jogging, even though the sky had grown considerably darker while she'd been perusing the wine aisles. Night didn't bother her. And even if the city planners had attempted to keep the original "country feel" of the area by leaving the sidewalks tree lined and avoiding the overuse of streetlights, it was still upper-middle-class suburbia, for God's sake.

Once she left the strip mall, with its ring of sodium security lights, Karin had only the full moon to guide her way, and that was fine. What could happen to her?

She'd only gone two blocks when she heard a soft scuff on the sidewalk behind her. It could have been a dog or a cat or a deer or a—

When a second, then third, then fourth scuff condensed into steps, Karin felt the hairs stand up on the back of her neck. Someone was following her, and that someone was getting closer.

Tightening her grip on the wine, Karin forced herself to look straight ahead and continue with the same easy, unhurried stride, as if she hadn't heard a thing. Every college self-defense lecture she'd ever heard came thundering back to her, along with each possible reaction's chance of actually working:

Run—50 percent, if you were faster than your assailant.

Turn and confront—30–65 percent, depending on who was behind you.

Scream "rape" or "murder"—0 percent.

Scream "fire"—75 percent, but only if you were near a building.

Fall down and play dead—minus 5.3 billion percent.

Fight—100 percent, but a bad idea for a number of reasons.

The breeze shifted and carried with it the scent of lilacs and musk . . . and a low, trembling growl that slowly, very slowly formed into words.

"He's . . . mine."

Before Karin could react, something cold and hard and sharp raked down her back, shredding her shirt and the skin beneath.

Karin spun to the left, only partially aware of the squeal of brakes and blaring car horn as she darted out of the tree shadows and into the street.

Russ was setting the table when she walked in.

"A couple of minutes? I was about to send out the . . . *Jesus*, what happened to you?"

Setting the bottle down on the table, she glanced over her shoulder at the tattered remains of her T-shirt and gave him a sheepish grin. "You won't laugh?"

There was only concern in his eyes. "Of course not."

"I . . . slipped and fell into some bushes. Never said I was overly coordinated."

"God, apparently not." Turning her, Russ gently examined her back. "You're lucky you only got scratched. They don't look very deep, skin's hardly broken, but you'd better let me put some antiseptic on them just in case."

"After dinner?"

"Now."

While Russ went to fetch the disinfectant and cotton swab, Karin opened the wine and poured herself a glass.

She didn't give it so much as a moment to catch its breath.

Lily was in the book, too. She answered after the third ring.

"Hello?"

"Hello, Lily. You're right, we need to talk."

"Who is this?"

"You know very well who this—"

"Oh, *Karin*, of course." The laughter was condescending. "Yes, I suppose we should talk if you want to. Frankly, I thought you'd have already gotten my message. But if you insist . . ."

"I do."

"All right, then." She yawned. "Where and when?"

"Now's good for me. Open your front door."

She wasn't dressed for company—cutoffs and a shapeless purple tank top, no makeup, hair in a tangle—but the look on Lily's pale face, although she was trying hard to suppress the shock when she opened the door, made Karin wish she'd brought a camera. It was one of those precious moments she'd want to remember.

"There's a law against stalking, you know."

Karin closed her cell phone. "Funny you should mention that."

Pushing past the startled woman, Karin walked into the living room and sat on the edge of an overstuffed white sofa. The room was all cream and beige and lace and soft pillows; silk lilies in china vases and scrollwork furniture; knickknacks and framed pastels. There were no hard edges in the room, nothing sharp or prickly or that in any way reflected the true nature of its owner.

Karin found that interesting and wondered if Russ ever noticed.

"Oh," she said when her hostess finally arrived, "and before you say anything, I know there's also a law against breaking and entering . . . and even if I didn't have an uncle on the police force, I could always say you invited me in. But don't worry . . . I haven't said anything to my uncle *or* to Russ. This is between you and me."

Lily stood like a queen—head held high, movements sure, her eyes as hard as slate and just as brittle. Karin couldn't help but admiring that.

"But where are my manners?" Lily asked, hand dramatically placed at her chest . . . undoubtedly to reinforce the fact that she wasn't wearing a bra. Karin fought the urge to look down at her own size 34Bs, knowing the comparison wouldn't be in her favor. "Please forgive me. May I offer you something to drink?"

"No. Thanks."

"Well, since you've already made yourself at home . . ."

Silence—profound and heavy—filled the moments until Lily had settled herself in the chair directly opposite Karin.

"So you wanted to talk." Lily crossed one leg over the other. "Go on, then. What did you want to talk about?"

Karin sat a little straighter. "Let's cut the bullshit, shall we? I want you to stop bothering Russ."

Lily smiled. "I've never bothered Russell. We're friends."

"No." Karin smiled back. "You're ex-lovers—emphasis on *ex*—and that's all you are. Now, I know sometimes people can remain friends after a relationship, but, lady, I am positively certain you're not one of those people."

Lily's pantomime smile faded, and before Lily could control herself, Karin saw the hardness beneath her skin. It was impressive.

"You don't know how right you are. However, you should be very careful about saying things like that. It could be dangerous."

"Oh?"

"I'm not like other women. I can't be intimidated or shoved aside. When I want something, I get it . . . and when I have it, I keep it—until *I'm* tired of it."

"So what you're saying is that Russ hurt your pride and you're going to try and get him back just so you can . . . what, return the favor? Do you think I'd let you do that?"

"You don't have a choice."

Lily's voice deepened until it was a growl more menacing than the one Karin had heard the night before.

"Russell belongs to me. I decided that the first moment I saw him. I never expected to find anyone after my husband died, but Russell . . . managed to fill the void very nicely. We were good together, he's just forgotten that."

"But he still left you."

"No, he ran because he realized what I am."

"And what is that?"

"Dangerous. Poor Russell, but I forgive him for his weakness and will continue to do so until he finally comes to his senses."

Lily smiled and ran a hand languidly through her hair while Karin dug her nails into the palms of both hands.

"Meaning," Karin translated, "when he comes back to you?"

"It's only a matter of time."

"And until then, you continue to harass us?"

Lily laughed, tossing her head like a schoolgirl. "I won't dignify that with an answer."

"Okay, then," Karin said, "how about this—from this moment on, you will leave Russ and me alone."

Lily smoothed down her hair. "No."

"He doesn't want you."

"He doesn't know what he wants."

"I'm warning you, Lily—get out of his life."

She blinked her sad gray eyes. "Oh, I can't wait to tell Russell. I knew I'd find your weak spot. You're just like all the others. I only want to be friends and you . . . and you come into my house and threaten me. He'll be so disappointed when I tell him."

If Lily hadn't started laughing, things might have gone . . . differently.

Karin opened her hands and watched the blood that had filled the small crescent-shaped cuts in her palms reverse direction as the flesh regenerated. "You know, I had a strange feeling you were going to say something like that."

She leaned back against the white sofa cushion and Lily gasped.

"Don't!"

"It's okay, I'm house-trained. Oh . . . wait, you're worried about what you did to my back, all that bloody seepage and stuff like that. Well, you don't have to be."

Karin stood up, lifting her shirt as she turned around . . . and wished she could see the woman's face. There wasn't a scratch, or a scar, or the faintest hint of the four jagged wounds that had cut her to the bone. Nothing but solid, healthy, unmarked flesh.

"We heal quickly. It's part of some inherited survival trait, I guess. *People* were always trying to kill us." Turning, she tucked her shirt back into her jeans but remained standing. "What did you use? My guess is a cultivator, right? And I have to say, I admire the restraint you showed, although it could have done some pretty serious damage if I were human."

"Hu-hu—"

"Yes, me, but we're talking about *you* right now. I hate to say it, even though it's already been established that you're not a wholly rational, understanding woman, but I can't leave a body.

The trouble is, Russ would think he was responsible for your killing yourself."

Karin extended her jaw, sighing with pleasure as the canines elongated to their full and deadly length. They made her lisp a little, but she didn't have any choice.

"He would blame himself until the day he died, and frankly, lady, you've already hurt him enough."

Lily's mouth kept opening and closing, but fortunately for both of them, she didn't say anything.

"So, you see, I really have no choice. Hope you understand."

Karin didn't have to do it—it was an absolute, unadulterated, and selfish indulgence on her part and she knew it. Over the generations, her kind had learned it was easier, and much *safer*, to transform after the prey animal was dead . . . but she'd wanted Lily to see what a *real* Alpha Bitch looked like.

Right before Karin snapped her neck and dragged her body into the bathroom.

Tile was much easier to clean than carpet . . . especially white carpet.

While Russ turned the steaks on the firepit's grill, Karin used the sizzling flames to reread the words that she'd so carefully scripted in Lily's beautiful forward-slanted handwriting. It had taken her a bit more practice, but once she'd found a sample, she had to admit, she'd done a pretty good job.

> *Russell . . . and I hope you noticed I didn't add "dear" or "dearest" or "my beloved" . . . because I'm finally tired of this. It's over. Foolish me, but I thought you were a different sort of man. I need a man who is my equal, and, let's face it, Russell, you are hardly that. Still, I can't bear the thought of seeing you with . . . her, so you'll be pleased to know, I'm sure, that I won't*

be around to witness the charade any longer. There's a
wide world out there, and perhaps, if I'm lucky enough,
I'll find someone truly worthy of me. The best to you and
what's-her-name—

Karin handed him back the note, the scent of Lily's perfume—
lilacs and musk—that she had liberally dabbed onto the paper
competing with the aroma of roasting meat.

"Ouch."

Russ shook his head and, laughing, fed the note to the fire.
"Yep, a real bitch to the end."

Karin smiled. "Well, I know it's selfish of me . . . but I'm glad
it's over."

"Amen, sister." Russ poked at one of the steaks with a long-
handled fork and got quiet for a minute. "Tell me you're not
the . . . possessive type, are you?"

She thought about telling him how werewolves, like their *lupine* cousins, mate only once and for life . . . but it was still too
early in their relationship to get into all that family stuff, so she
just gave him an "are you kidding" look and sniffed the air.

"Mmmm . . . steaks smell done to me."

"Only if you like 'em red and runny."

"My favorite."

"Okay then." He slid the thicker of the two steaks onto her
plate and grimaced. "Christ, I've seen cows hurt worse than that
get better."

"Oh, ha-ha."

"Yeah, well, just remember—you are what you eat."

Karin belched softly and smiled. "Not necessarily."

The Aarne-Thompson Classification Revue

HOLLY BLACK

There is a werewolf girl in the city. She sits by the phone on a Saturday night, waiting for it to ring. She paints her nails purple.

She goes to bed early.

Body curled around a pillow, fingers clawing at the bedspread, she dreams that she's on a dating show, a reality television one. She's supposed to pick one boyfriend out of a dozen strangers by eliminating one candidate each week. After eliminations, she eats the guy she's asked to leave. In her dream, the boys get more and more afraid as they overhear screams, but they can't quite believe the show is letting them be murdered one by one, so they convince each other to stay until the end. In the reunion episode, the werewolf girl eats the boy who she's picked to be her boyfriend.

That's the only way to get to do a second season, after all.

When she wakes up, she's sorry about the dream. It makes her feel guilty and a little bit hungry, which makes her feel worse. Her real-life boyfriend is a good guy, the son of a dentist from an ancestral line of dentists. Sometimes he takes her to his dad's office and they sit in the chairs and suck on nitrous oxide while watching the overhead televisions that are supposed to distract patients. When they do that, the werewolf girl feels calmer than she's felt her whole life.

She's calling herself Nadia in this city. She's called herself Laura and Liana and Dana in other places.

Despite having gone to bed early, she's woken up tired.

Nadia takes her temperature and jots it down in a little notebook by the side of the bed. Temperature is more accurate than phases of the moon in telling her when she's going to change.

She gets dressed, makes coffee and drinks it. Then goes to work. She is a waitress on a street where there are shirt shops and shops that sell used records and bandannas and studded belts. She brings out tuna salads to aged punks and cappuccinos in massive bowls to tourists who ask her why she doesn't have any tattoos.

Nadia still looks young enough that her lack of references doesn't seem strange to her employers, although she worries about the future. For now, though, she appears to be one of a certain type of girl—a girl who wants to be an actress, who's come in from the suburbs and never really worked before, a girl restaurants in the city employ a lot of. She always asks about flexibility in her interviews, citing auditions and rehearsals. Nadia is glad of the easy excuses, since she does actually need a flexible schedule.

The only problem with her lie is that the other girls ask her to go to auditions.

Sometimes Nadia goes, especially when she's lonely. Her boyfriend is busy learning about teeth and gets annoyed when she calls him. He has a lot of classes. The auditions are often dull, but she likes the part where all the girls stand in line and drink coffee while they wait. She likes the way their skin shimmers with nervous sweat and their eyes shine with the possibility of transformation. The right part will let them leave their dirty little lives behind and turn them into celebrities.

Nadia sits next to another waitress, Rhonda, as they wait to be called back for the second phase of the audition for a musical.

Rhonda is fingering a cigarette that she doesn't light—because smoking is not allowed in the building and also because she's trying to quit.

Grace, a willowy girl who can never remember anyone's order at work, has already been cut.

"I hate it when people stop doing things and then they don't want to be around other people doing them," Rhonda says, flipping the cigarette over and over in her fingers. "Like people who stop drinking and then can't hang out in bars. I mean, how can you really know you're over something if you can't deal with being tempted by it?"

Nadia nods automatically, since it makes her feel better to think that letting herself be tempted is a virtue. Sometimes she thinks of the way a ribcage cracks or the way fat and sinew and offal taste when they're gulped down together, hot and raw. It doesn't bother her that she has these thoughts, except when they come at inappropriate moments, like being alone with the driver in a taxi or helping a friend clean up after a party.

A large woman with many necklaces calls Rhonda's name and she goes out onto the stage. Nadia takes another sip of her coffee and looks over at the sea of other girls on the call-back list. The girls look back at her through narrowed eyes.

Rhonda comes back quickly. "You're next," she says to Nadia. "I saw the clipboard."

"How was it?"

Rhonda shakes her head and lights her cigarette. "Stupid. They wanted me to jump around. They didn't even care if I could sing."

"You can't smoke in here," one of the other girls says.

"Oh, shove it," says Rhonda.

When Nadia goes out onto the stage, she expects her audition to go fast. She reads monologues in a way that can only be called stilted. She's never had a voice coach. The only actual acting she ever does is when she pretends to be disappointed when the casting people don't want her. Usually she just holds the duffel bags of the other girls as they are winnowed down, cut by cut.

The stage is lit so that she can't see the three people sitting in the audience too well. It's one of those converted warehouse theaters where everyone sits at tables with tea lights and gets up a lot to go to the bar in the back. No tea lights are flickering now.

"We want to teach you a routine," one of them says. A man's voice, with an accent she can't place. "But first—a little about our musical. It's called the *Aarne-Thompson Classification Revue*. Have you heard of it?"

Nadia shakes her head. On the audition call, it was abbreviated ATCR. "Are you Mr. Aarne?"

He makes a small sound of disappointment. "We like to think of it as a kitchen sink of delights. Animal tales. Tales of magic. Jokes. Everything you could imagine. Perhaps the title is a bit dry, but our poster more than makes up for that. You ready to learn a dance?"

"Yes," says Nadia.

The woman with the necklaces comes out on the stage. She shows Nadia some simple steps and then points to crossed strips of black masking tape on the floor.

"You jump from here to here at the end," the woman says.

"Ready?" calls the man. One of the other people sitting with him says something under his breath.

Nadia nods, going over the steps in her head. When he gives her the signal, she twists and steps and leaps. She mostly remembers the moves. At the end, she leaps through the air for the final jump. Her muscles sing.

In that moment, she wishes she wasn't a fake. She wishes that she was a dancer. Or an actress. Or even a waitress. But she's a werewolf and that means she can't really be any of those other things.

"Thank you," another man says. He sounds a little odd, as though he's just woken up. Maybe they have to watch so many auditions that they take turns napping through them. "We'll let you know."

Nadia walks back to Rhonda, feeling flushed. "I didn't think this was a call for *dancers*."

Rhonda rolls her eyes. "It's for a musical. You have to dance in a musical."

"I know," says Nadia, because she does know. But there's supposed to be singing in musicals, too. She thought Rhonda would be annoyed at only being asked to dance; Rhonda usually likes to complain about auditions. Nadia looks down at her purple nail polish. It's starting to chip at the edges.

She puts the nail in her mouth and bites it until she bleeds.

Being a werewolf is like being Clark Kent, except that when you go into the phone booth, you can't control what comes out.

Being a werewolf is like being a detective who has to investigate his own crimes.

Being a werewolf means that when you take off your clothes, you're still not really naked. You have to take off your skin, too.

Once, when Nadia had a different name and lived in a small town outside of Toronto, she'd been a different girl. She took ballet and jazz dancing. She had a little brother who was always reading her diary. Then one day on her way home from school, a man asked her to help him find his dog. He had a leash and a van and everything.

He ate part of her leg and stomach before anyone found them.

When she woke up in the hospital, she remembered the way he'd caught her with his snout pinning her neck, the weight of his paws. She looked down at her unscarred skin and stretched her arms, ripping the IV needle out of her skin without meaning to.

She left home after she tried to turn her three best friends into werewolves, too. It didn't work. They screamed and bled. One of them died.

"Nadia," Rhonda is saying.

Nadia shakes off all her thoughts like a wet dog shaking itself dry.

The casting director is motioning to her. "We'd like to see you again," the woman with the necklaces says.

"Her?" Rhonda asks.

When Nadia goes back onstage, they tell her she has the part.

"Oh," says Nadia. She's too stunned to do more than take the packet of information on rehearsal times and tax forms. She forgets to ask them which part she got.

That night Rhonda and Grace insist on celebrating. They get a bottle of cheap champagne and drink it in the back of the restaurant with the cook and two of the dishwashers. Everyone congratulates Nadia, and Rhonda keeps telling stories about clueless things that Nadia did on other auditions and how it's a good thing that the casting people only wanted Nadia to dance because she can't act her way out of a paper bag.

Nadia says that no one can act their way out of a paper bag. You can only rip your way out of one. That makes everyone laugh and—Rhonda says—is a perfect example of how clueless Nadia can be.

"You must have done really well in that final jump," Rhonda says. "Were you a gymnast or something? How close did you get?"

"Close to what?" Nadia asks.

Rhonda laughs and takes another swig out of the champagne bottle. "Well, you couldn't have made it. No human being could jump that far without a pole vault."

Nadia's skin itches.

Later, her boyfriend comes over. She's still tipsy when she lets him in and they lie in bed together. For hours he tells her about teeth. Molars. Bicuspids. Dentures. Prosthodontics. She falls asleep to the sound of him grinding his jaw, like he's chewing through the night.

Rehearsals for the *Aarne-Thompson Classification Revue* happen every other afternoon. The director's name is Yves. He wears dapper suits in brown tweed and tells her, "You choose what you reveal of what you are when you're onstage."

Nadia doesn't know what that means. She does know that when she soars through the air, she wants to go higher and farther and faster. She wants her muscles to burn. She knows she could, for a moment, do something spectacular. Something that makes her shake with terror. She thinks of her boyfriend and Rhonda and the feel of the nitrous filling her with drowsy nothingness; she does the jump they tell her and no more than that.

The other actors aren't what she expects. There is a woman who plays a mermaid and whose voice is like spun gold. There is a horned boy who puts on long goat legs and prances around the stage, towering above them. And there is a magician who is supposed to keep them all as part of his menagerie in cages with glittering numbers.

"Where are you from?" the mermaid asks. "You look familiar."

"People say that a lot," Nadia says, although no one has ever said it to *her*. "I guess I have that kind of face."

The mermaid smiles and smoothes back gleaming black braids. "If you want, you can use my comb. It works on even the most matted fur—"

"Wow," says the goat boy, lurching past. "You must be special. She never lets anyone use her comb."

"Because you groom your ass with it," she calls after him.

The choreographer is named Marie. She is the woman with the necklaces from the first audition. When Nadia dances, and especially when she jumps, Marie watches her with eyes like chips of gravel. "*Good*," she says slowly, as though the word is a grave insult.

Nadia is supposed to play a princess who has been trapped in a forest of ice by four skillful brothers and a jaybird. The magician rescues her and brings her to his menagerie. And, because the princess is not onstage much during the first act, Nadia also plays a bear dancing on two legs. The magician falls in love with the bear, and the princess falls in love with the magician. Later in the play, the princess tricks the magician into killing the bear by making it look like the bear ate the jaybird. Then Nadia has to play the bear as she dies.

At first, all Nadia's mistakes are foolish. She lets her face go slack when she's not the one speaking or dancing, and the director has to remind her over and over that the audience can always see her when she's onstage. She misses cues. She sings too softly when she's singing about fish and streams and heavy fur. She sings louder when she's singing of kingdoms and crowns and dresses, but she can't seem to remember the words.

"I'm not really an actress," she tells him, after a particularly disastrous scene.

"I'm not really a director," Yves says with a shrug. "Who really *is* what they *seem*?"

"No," she says. "You don't understand. I just came to the audition because my friends were going. And they really aren't my friends. They're just people I work with. I don't know what I'm doing."

"Okay, if you're not an actress," he asks her, "then what are you?"

She doesn't answer. Yves signals for one of the golden glitter-covered cages to be moved slightly to the left.

"I probably won't even stay with the show," Nadia says. "I'll probably have to leave after opening night. I can't be trusted."

Yves throws up his hands. "Actors! Which of you can be trusted? But don't worry. We'll all be leaving. This show *tours*."

Nadia expects him to cut her from the cast after every rehearsal, but he never does. She nearly cries with relief.

The goat boy smiles down at her from atop his goat legs. "I
have a handkerchief. I'll throw it to you if you want."

"I'm fine," Nadia says, rubbing her wet eyes.

"Lots of people weep after rehearsals."

"Weird people," she says, trying to make it a joke.

"If you don't cry, how can you make anyone else cry? Theater
is the last place where fools and the mad do better than regular
folks . . . well, I guess music's a little like that, too." He shrugs.
"But still."

Posters go up all over town. They show the magician in front
of gleaming cages with bears and mermaids and foxes and a cat
in a dress.

Nadia's boyfriend doesn't like all the time she spends away
from home. Now, on Saturday nights, she doesn't wait by the
phone. She pushes her milk crate coffee table and salvaged sofa
against the wall and practices her steps over and over until her
downstairs neighbor bangs on his ceiling.

One night her boyfriend calls and she doesn't pick up. She just
lets it ring.

She has just realized that the date the musical premieres is the
next time she is going to change. All she can do is stare at the
little black book and her carefully noted temperatures. The ringing phone is like the ringing in her head.

I am so tired I want to die, Nadia thinks. Sometimes the
thought repeats over and over and she can't stop thinking it,
even though she knows she has no reason to be so tired. She gets
enough sleep. She gets more than enough sleep. Some days she
can barely drag herself from her bed.

Fighting the change only makes it more painful; she knows
from experience.

The change cannot be stopped or reasoned with. It's inevitable. Inexorable. It is coming for her. But it can be delayed. Once she held on two hours past dusk, her whole body knotted with cramps. Once she held out until the moon was high in the sky and her teeth were clenched so tight she thought they would shatter. She might be able to make it to the end of the show.

It shouldn't matter to her. Disappointing people is inevitable. She will eventually get tired and angry and hungry. Someone will get hurt. Her boyfriend will run the pad of his fingers over her canines and she will bite down. She will wake up covered in blood and mud by the side of some road and not be sure what she's done. Then she'll be on the run again.

Being a werewolf means devouring your past.

Being a werewolf means swallowing your future.

Methodically, Nadia tears her notebook to tiny pieces. She throws the pieces in the toilet and flushes, but the chunks of paper clog the pipes. Water spills over the side and floods her bathroom with the soggy reminder of inevitability.

On the opening night of the *Aarne-Thompson Classification Revue*, the cast huddles together and wish each other luck. They paint their faces. Nadia's hand shakes as she draws a new red mouth over her own. Her skin itches. She can feel the fur inside of her, can smell her sharp, feral musk.

"Are you okay?" the mermaid asks.

Nadia growls softly. She is holding on, but only barely.

Yves is yelling at everyone. The costumers are pinning and duct-taping dresses that have split. Strap tear. Beads bounce along the floor. One of the chorus is scolding a girl who plays a talking goat. A violinist is pleading with his instrument.

"Tonight you are not going to be *good*," Marie, the choreographer, says.

Nadia grinds her teeth together. "I'm not good."

"Good is forgettable." Marie spits. "Good is common. You are not good. You are not common. You will show everyone what you are made of."

Under her bear suit, Nadia can feel her arms beginning to ripple with the change. She swallows hard and concentrates on shrinking down into herself. She cannot explain to Marie that she's afraid of what's inside of her.

Finally, Nadia's cue comes and she dances out into a forest of wooden trees on dollies and lets the magician trap her in a gold-glitter-covered cage. Her bear costume hangs heavily on her, stinking of synthetic fur.

Performing is different with an audience. They gasp when there is a surprise. They laugh on cue. They watch her with gleaming, wet eyes. Waiting.

Her boyfriend is there, holding a bouquet of white roses. She's so surprised to see him that her hand lifts involuntarily—as though to wave. Her fingers look too long, her nails too dark, and she hides them behind her back.

Nadia dances like a bear, like a deceitful princess, and then like a bear again. This time, as the magician sings about how the jaybird will be revenged, Nadia really feels like he's talking to her. When he lifts his gleaming wand, she shrinks back with real fear.

She loves this. She doesn't want to give it up. She wants to travel with the show. She wants to stop going to bed early. She won't wait by the phone. She's not a fake.

When the jump comes, she leaps as high as she can. Higher than she has at any rehearsal. Higher than in her dreams. She jumps so high that she seems to hang in the air for a moment as her skin cracks and her jaw snaps into a snout.

It happens before she can stop it, and then she doesn't want it to stop. The change used to be the worst thing she could imagine. No more.

The bear costume sloughs off like her skin. Nadia falls into a crouch, four claws digging into the stage. She throws back her head and howls.

The goat boy nearly topples over. The magician drops his wand. On cue, the mermaid girl begins to sing. The musical goes on.

Roses slip from Nadia's dentist-boyfriend's fingers.

In the wings, she can see Marie clapping Yves on the back. Marie looks delighted.

There is a werewolf girl on the stage. It's Saturday night. The crowd is on their feet. Nadia braces herself for their applause.

Weredog of Bucharest

IAN WATSON

Shortly before driving into Bucharest proper, we stopped for a pee in some bushes. Twice en route we'd seen men vomiting into roadside shrubbery, probably on account of drinking bad tap water, so use of bushes seemed normal. A tall sign announced: *Parking, Kebab, Sexy Show, Motel, Telefon.* We only required the first of those, just for a few minutes. We'd been in Inspector Badelescu's black BMW (with 120,000 kilometres on the clock) for a little over an hour, but prior to leaving the island in the Danube, we'd had a few beers. Endless maize stretched around our roadside oasis, although a strong odour of pigs hung in the air, which must have been coming from the dilapidated barns nearby.

Slumped on their sides in the dust by the bushes, under some tree shade, were three tatty though sizeable mongrels, fawn-coloured with white patches. At our approach, two of the dogs raised their heads and regarded us with utter apathy in their lacklustre eyes. The third remained sprawled as though life was too exhausting, or the temperature too high, to bother moving. Oh, all of a sudden one pooch scrambled up and stood facing us, its ears half-cocked like bat wings, its tail half-lifted.

Badelescu stooped, scooped up a stone, and threw it, not for the mongrel to chase and fetch, but at the dog's flank. The animal yipped and scuttled away.

"Fucking things," he said to me amiably. "Don't worry about rabies, and I have my gun if they show their teeth. Most are too tired and weak with hunger. Welcome to Bucharest from its canine inhabitants."

"A million stray dogs in the city," Adriana, my impromptu translator, called after me—whether in warning or simply by way of explanation I couldn't be sure. Adriana was unconsciously beautiful in the way that so many young Romanian women were—graceful, long-legged, fine sensuous figure in tight jeans and blouse. On the whole, Romanian women didn't seem to realize they were gorgeous; because so many were, therefore this was normal. Adriana wore her dark silky hair in a very long ponytail, which I had held with great satisfaction in a tent on the island while with my other hand I gave her pleasure as her head tried to toss from side to side, but couldn't, while she groaned and cries jerked from her.

Adriana was staying to guard the car since she hadn't drunk so much, and it would have been more complicated for her to pee in bushes, the way we all had on the island.

So I sprayed the gritty soil, along with the Inspector, and Romulus—whose second name I couldn't remember—and Virgil Gramescu. At times Romanians could sound like the Lost Legion, which in a sense they were. Inspector Badelescu's first name was Ovid.

Quickly I returned to Adriana, who was smoking.

"Do you know, Paul," she said to me, "when the Mayor of Bucharest proposed exterminating all the strays, Brigitte Bardot flew here on a mercy mission to dissuade him? According to one version of the story, Brigitte donated a lot of money for a dogs' home. Consequently, two hundred strays live in luxury, then the extermination went ahead anyway. But it must have failed, or else the survivors bred very fast. The number of dogs on the streets is as high as ever."

"Are they dangerous?"

"Only in winter, if they form packs. Sometimes a baby or little child gets carried off."

Brushing back his oiled dark hair, Ovid Badelescu was about to say something when a jangle of bells sounded from within his shirt pocket, so he fished out his mobile.

And frowned, and queried, and queried again and again in Romanian.

He shut the phone and said, "Bad news. A young woman has been torn apart in an elevator in the centre of the city."

"Torn *apart*?" I exclaimed.

"Not literally limb from limb," he said. "I mean savaged to death, with terrible injuries. I must go there immediately. Do you want to see?" he asked me. "Or wait in the car, which might be tiresome in this heat? Virgil and Romulus can make their way home from there. Or you might prefer to have lunch with Adriana."

Have lunch, or visit an appalling murder scene? I was incredulous. "Do you mean see *the body*?"

The Inspector laughed. "No, an ambulance is taking it to the morgue. Although you can visit the morgue if you're really curious. I meant the scene of the crime. I've been called there because of a Jack the Raper murder I was involved with last year. Do I mean raper? No, ripper. Rapers don't often rip. They may strangle or stab, but not do complete ripping. Not usually."

"A *solved* murder?"

"The murderer might have been a Turk," he replied. "But he disappeared. Ankara couldn't trace him, nor Interpol in case he hid among the Turks in Germany."

I couldn't help wondering if he said Ankara and Interpol to enhance his importance. And I supposed I must attribute his comparative nonchalance, or what I took as nonchalance, first of all to the requirements of haste, and secondly to whatever other horrors he may have experienced in his job.

We'd been a mixed bunch on that cultural island in the Danube: lots of beautiful Romanian girls, and handsome youths, too, the annual event being sponsored by the Ministry for Youth Development. A Bulgarian kick-boxing champion who gave open-air classes, an astronomer who appealed to science-fiction fans, several musicians and poets, an American from an Institute for Human Development who believed that immortality is within our grasp, an angry German feminist. I could go on.

I would describe my own writings as psychological horror, or perhaps darkness, which illuminates the mundane world, paradoxically heightening our awareness, although I was published as Crime. Consequently, my "real world counterpart" was the Inspector, with his theories about order and disorder, darkness and light within society, and, of course, his wealth of practical experience, which he became intent on demonstrating to me, either for egotistical or for inspirational reasons, or maybe because he genuinely liked me. Hence his driving me back to Bucharest to show me things, which seductive Adriana was also intent on. In her case, maybe with a tentative motive of gaining an author from abroad as a husband, a foreign passport, a different life? Authors are esteemed unduly in some countries. Or maybe Adriana merely wanted some fun and to enjoy herself. When I explained that my surname, Osler, was originally a French name for someone who catches wild birds, Adriana had been highly amused.

I'd been persuaded to pay my own, fairly minimal, airfare from England by fellow crime author Max Rigby, who was moving slowly around Eastern Europe and who had already enjoyed the free hospitality of the island the year before. Currently, Max was

renting a flat in Bucharest, where I'd stay for a week. Other habi-
tués of the island were driving Max back to the city.

Max was seeking exotic foreign settings for future novels
because, frankly, in my opinion, his most recent book, set in
England, had seemed lacklustre and ho-hum. Competently
done, to be sure, but lacking the additional frisson of strange-
ness which distinguishes a competent book from something
exceptional. I'd said so myself in no uncertain terms in a review,
which I certainly *didn't* sign with my own name, concocting
instead an alias—Martin Fairfax (a reviewer should always seem
fair), which, ironically, as I realized later, was the name of a
minor character in one of my early books, long out of print.
Should I beware of impending Alzheimer's? Not so long as I
continued drinking red wine.

With so many Eastern European countries joining the EU,
and so many citizens of those countries settling in Britain for
jobs, not least about a million Poles, obviously one should expand one's repertoire, which was a reason why Max easily persuaded me to visit Romania.

Badelescu, though I suppose I should more familiarly call him
Ovid, placed a flasher on the roof of his BMW, and we sirened
our way past trolleybuses, trucks, a convoy of giant Turkish lor-
ries, decrepit Dacias, and flashier new cars, along tree-lined av-
enues, the trunks painted white.

I pointed, and asked Adriana, "Is that so you can see the trees
in the dark?"

"Do you know why we're giving a lift to Virgil?" she replied.
"He wouldn't get to the island otherwise. That's because his wife
crashed their car into the only other car on a huge empty boulevard." She zigzagged her hands as if steering two vehicles. "From
hundreds of metres apart they start trying to avoid each other.
Virgil's wife steers left, the other guy steers right. Then they

change their minds and directions a dozen times. Until *crash*. It was incredibly bad luck."

"And neither of them slowed down?"

"Why do that, on an empty boulevard?"

Presently, the dilapidated city mutated into a Futureville of huge honey-white buildings adorned with balconies. Part-way around a huge piazza, police vehicles clustered, on and off a broad pavement. Ovid kept his siren howling to herald his arrival until we had parked.

Bye-bye to Romulus and Virgil, who sauntered off with their rucksacks.

"Oh, look," said Adriana, pointing into the distance along a vast boulevard. "Ceauşescu's palace, there at the far end."

That was my first view of the dead dictator's megalomaniac structure, supposedly the second largest building in the world. Even dwarfed by distance it *loomed*. And the great bright apartment building where the murder had happened was in direct line of sight.

Ovid informed me, "This place was built for the Securitate, but it was only finished after the Revolution. Come on!"

The Securitate: Ceauşescu's secret police, whose surveillance of Romania's citizens was very exhaustive indeed, and whose network of informers, many of those against their will or wishes, may have comprised a significant percentage of the population.

"I don't want blood on my shoes," said Adriana.

If she went home, how was I going to find Max's flat? The Inspector might become too busy to drive me there, and I felt dubious about trusting myself to a taxi driver in an unknown city when I only knew a few phrases of Romanian that Adriana and others had taught me on the island. Ah, Max could come and fetch me, because my mobile now had a Romanian sim-card. However, Adriana spied a café. Yellow Bergenbier umbrellas-cum-sunshades outside sheltered tables and chairs. Half a dozen large mongrels lay nearby.

"I'll buy a magazine and wait for you in there, okay?"

Accordingly, in went Ovid and I to find the Boys in Blue busy on the ground floor examining an open lift, the floor and walls of which were very bloody. I'd been at two or three actual crime scenes before, yet here it was as if a madman had thrown crimson paint around. The smell, however, wasn't of paint but of a slaughterhouse. I presumed my presence was explained cursorily by Ovid, since various police nodded at me before, as I supposed, reporting circumstances to him in Romanian.

"So, Mr. Story Writer," Ovid said after peering assiduously, "what do you notice?"

"Less blood on the floor outside than I'd have expected," I suggested.

"And that was probably caused by us police and by the ambulance people. It seems there are some bloody tracks and drops on the sixth floor, but again not too much blood is in the corridor up there."

"So she was attacked inside the lift, with the doors shut."

"Precisely. And I think I know how."

Ovid stepped inside the lift fastidiously, crouched, and peered at the paneled rear wall, which was almost unstained. Then he inserted his little finger somewhere amongst the woodwork and pulled. The rear wall split in half, opening as two floor-to-ceiling doors. Behind was a space large enough for a couple of people to stand, or kneel, between the true rear wall and the false wall. And the true rear wall was bloody, as were the insides of the doors.

"Here," said Ovid, "is where the killer hid, to burst out suddenly between floors. I told you this building was made for the Securitate, but about six thousand special spies spied upon the secret police themselves by such bizarre methods as this. No doubt a microphone would have been hidden inside the elevator, but here's a back-up, just in case. A man sitting on a stool could look and listen through the tiny hole in the wall."

The sheer shock of being between floors in an otherwise empty lift when suddenly the wall opened and another person emerged! The victim might faint or even die at once of a heart attack.

Ovid explained in Romanian, and the lesser police looked at him in admiration.

Of course we climbed the white marble stairs to the sixth floor rather than using the lift.

It seemed to me that the tracks up there were rather narrow to be those of shoes or trainers. They became vague after not too many paces.

Adriana pointed through the café window at one of the tall white apartments around the piazza, blue sky showing through ornamental turrets along the edge of the rooftop.

"Sniper watchtowers," she said. "You could shoot down into any rebellious crowds."

We were inside for the air-conditioning. So were some bleached-blond youths wearing gold chains, sunglasses pushed up on top of their heads, sons of the new rich.

"You say the tracks of blood were narrow." She shuddered and crossed herself. "I think a werewolf killed that woman in the elevator. Probably the Inspector thinks so, too, but he wouldn't tell you that."

"Werewolves aren't real," I protested.

"In Romania they are. And weredogs, *priccoltish*. With a million dogs on the streets it can't be surprising if at least one is a weredog. It's the perfect place to hide. Unless," she added with what seemed at first a wonderful lack of logical connection, "Badelescu thinks a Turk did it. Maybe he hopes that's the answer."

"Why blame a Turk?"

"They ruled us for three hundred years; consequently, many Romanians don't like them much. Better a Turk than a werewolf. I'll see if there are any news reports yet."

Flipping open her phone, amazingly she googled.

"How can you do that?"

"You can do it anywhere in the city center."

I thought of old women draped in black guarding a single cow or a few geese by the roadside out in the country. Truly, the last shall be first technologically.

"No, nothing yet." Rather too soon for news.

"Will you take me to Max? And maybe I can see you tomorrow?" In fact, I felt a bit tired, but also I wanted to make notes about the murder scene.

"Tomorrow," she said. "I don't know. I'll phone. Yes, probably." She wasn't going to seem overeager, but she wanted me to feel eager.

Max's place proved not to be far, just beyond the boundary where Ceaușescu's architectural master plan had erased a vast area of the old city—houses, churches, whatever was in the way—to make space for ostentatious modernity.

The flat was on the top floor of a modest block. To the front, the outlook was upon a line of trees, then some open grass, then low houses with red roofs suddenly abutting a towering wall of vast white apartments. Directly below was a very modest old cottage to which were attached a clutter of small corrugated-roofed sheds, surrounded by rows of vegetables and bean poles—I even spotted some geese and hens—all within a green-painted picket fence.

Incongruously next to this relic of the past was a sizeable ultra-posh house in Art Deco style, gleamingly white.

"Probably an old lady died there and her heirs accepted an

offer they couldn't refuse," said Max. Max was short and burly and wore an assertively black moustache, although his hair had lightened and receded a long way. I didn't know if he dyed the moustache.

"So the old woman directly below hasn't died yet?"

"I've never seen her."

My room contained a double bed, a large wardrobe, and a bench press that seemed to have strayed from some gym. Frills were lacking, yet the furnishings sufficed for sport that I anticipated with Adriana. On the bed, I mean, not on the bench press.

"Chap called Silviu may be coming round to take us somewhere," Max told me. "Couple of days before I went to the island, Silviu told me the sad story of how his mother's son by a previous marriage had suddenly died from premature kidney failure. He begged me to lend him three hundred dollars for the funeral because his mother couldn't afford it. So I did. Very next day, I bump into Silviu and he proudly shows me this expensive new camera he just bought. You know, *innocently* shows me the camera because he's so excited and happy. I ought to have got mad at him. But it was my own fault. You don't lend money to people here unless you're willing to regard it as a gift. Some day they'll do something for you, perhaps. Well, Silviu phoned an hour ago and I said, 'Come and drive us somewhere tonight, right?'"

"Somewhere?"

"Educational. In your honour. Writers in the crime line need to research sleaze." So saying, Max cast himself upon a sofa and reached for an elegant, glossy English-language magazine, published for expats no doubt, its cover a stylish photo of giant terracotta garden urns. Thumbing to the back, he intoned: "Royal Orchid Male Sacred Spot Massage. A gentle digital technique for contacting these subtle places. In the internal way a lubricated finger will be inserted into the anus, and then it will gently massage around the chestnut-sized and -shaped prostate. This feels better when you are somewhat erect and excited and if it's done during the intimate massage (don't worry, the girls will take care of that). It will produce a very thrilling orgasm."

"You're making that up."

"I'm not. This is Bucharest. Take a look."

I looked, and it was true.

"I thought that mag was the local *Homes and Gardens*."

"And casinos and escorts."

"Um, I don't want a finger stuck up my bum, Max."

My writerly colleague grinned. "Do you have piles? Don't worry, we aren't doing any such thing. Tonight will only cost a few dollars for drinks. It's purely educational. Background research. Anyway, what kept you?"

"Ovid Badelescu got called to a murder site."

"Do tell!"

I proceeded to, but didn't inform Max about the concealed doors at the back of the lift—I might want to use that detail some day myself. I also excluded Adriana's notion that a werewolf was responsible. Or a weredog, hiding out among the multitude of anonymous mongrels.

Shortly before Silviu arrived, a long cry and a chorus of yapping from outside drew me to the window. The cry was like that of a muezzin calling worshippers to prayer. A middle-aged woman wearing a baggy multicoloured dress and headscarf was driving her horse and cart loaded with scrap metal and other rubbish that might be worth something. Her cry had excited the dogs. As I watched, she halted beside the humble cottage, dismounted, and rattled the picket gate with a stick. And waited.

Presently, a black-clad shape emerged from the cottage, cradling what I identified as a broken old clock of some bulk. With a surprisingly sprightly step, the old cottager bustled to her gate and handed over the relic, to receive in return, after humming and hawing, some scrap of paper, which might have been a banknote—if so, here in Romania it would have been thin plastic that looked like paper.

As the horse and cart and the scrap-woman's outcry proceeded onward, the strangest thing happened. Half a dozen strays sidled from different directions toward that garden gate. The black-garbed cottager glanced about, as though to ensure that no one was observing her—she wouldn't spot me at the window high up—then she offered her hand over the gate. Was she about to feed the strays with scraps? But she was holding nothing that I could see.

One by one those desolate dogs proceeded to lick, or slobber on, her palm—I was put in mind of nothing so much as movies of Italian gangsters kissing the hand of their Mafia godfather! This done, the cottager withdrew her hand, and then herself quickly back into her home.

Travelers in unfamiliar countries often misinterpret things and leap to the wrong conclusions, but I've always had a strong sense of intuition, a belief in quasi-magical linkages that others call coincidences. In my novels, such is the way that a dark crime is often solved. There's a logical sequence of circumstances, yet this is only revealed—illuminated, if you like—by illogical means, by an illogical route. That Ovid should have driven me directly to that blood-stained lift in the former Securitate building, then that I should come to Max's and overlook that cottage, cast adrift while time and town planning advanced, and that I should glimpse the owner, queen of canines, whom Max had never seen . . . this spoke to me inwardly, compellingly.

Silviu proved to be a tall, wispy person, wearing a somewhat soiled lightweight cream suit. His eyes seemed to me very blue, and his English was quite good. What an honour to be meeting a famous colleague of famous Max.

We descended to the street, to climb into an elderly white Dacia that had suffered bumps and scrapes through the years. Although it was early evening by now, the air was still sultry and cloying. I felt a strange mixture of reinvigoration due to my sighting of the crone of the cottage, and languor, as though I was surrendering to whatever the night might contain.

First, we went to an open-air restaurant to drink beer called Ursus and eat rolls of minced meat and salad, and spend, or rather, squander, some time. Time seemed to have a way of melting in this city. Apparently we were to meet a mad genius. But after an hour the man phoned, depressed—his father had a sudden brain tumour. Maybe an excuse, maybe true or half-true. And that was the last I heard of the genius. Silviu went off and brought back a newspaper, and the murder did feature. Silviu translated the story, but already I knew more than the reporter had discovered.

Then Ovid phoned my mobile.

"Paul, where are you?"

I consulted with Max, who took the phone and said, "We're at the meech"—I think—"place on," and he named a street. "But we're going to Herastrau afterwards."

They talked for a while, then Max ended the call and handed my phone back.

"He'll try and join us." Then, surveying our surroundings, he remarked that under Communism people went to restaurants for show, not for the food—to be seen in such a place, rich enough to buy a meal, of which they would then eat every morsel, instinctively, even if it burst them. Silviu listened politely and nodded. He had cleaned his plate, and I guessed that Max would be footing the bill, unless he and I shared it. I wondered if the crone of the cottage had ever been near a restaurant during her entire life. I thought of an appetite so voracious that a person would ravage a body bloody in a lift.

• • •

Herastrau proved to be a sizeable lake within a park. By now evening had arrived. We halted on a tree-lined roadway inside the park, behind a line of cars far more luxurious and up-to-date than Silviu's. Silviu seemed edgy. Dogs lay round in the gloom like mounds of earth. On a bench a shaven-headed man, dressed in a leather jacket, was lounging.

"It's all right, Silviu," said Max. "I'll give him a little money. Car insurance," he told me. "Even though Silviu's car is an old wreck, best to be on the safe side."

Evidently Max knew how much, or how little, to give. I felt a double sense of mild menace at Max's casual determination to show me how *au fait* he was with life here, and at the implications of my not knowing the ropes. My host, full of bonhomie, was also my rival. Which would explain, in retrospect, this particular outing tonight.

Scarcely had Max returned from paying Leather Jacket to keep an eye on the car than Ovid drew up behind us in his BMW. Getting out, Ovid waved casually at Leather Jacket, but Ovid certainly didn't bother to cross the road to say anything to the man. So probably Max had wasted his money, seeing that we were now associated with an Inspector of police. It struck me as only mildly sinister that Ovid should turn up immediately after us, almost as though we were back in Securitate times when everyone's exact whereabouts were monitored.

A short walk brought us to a big, though modestly lit, building on the shore of the lake. Two suited bouncers stood outside, smoking.

Inside, a few men sat at tables with beautiful girls, and a little crowd of likewise lovely tall girls were shuffling round in a slow dance to the background music. A trio of the Bleached Boys sporting gold looked like pimps in this setting.

"The girls aren't in their underwear here," Max pointed out.

"They can wear casual clothes, so there's no pole dancing, if you're disappointed. This is classy sleaze."

We sat and ordered beers, the cheapest option.

"Anything new about the lift murder?" I asked Ovid.

"Autopsy," he said. "Terrible claw-like injuries and animal-like bites. The Turk may have worn specially adapted gauntlets and not had his own teeth anymore but special false fanged ones. If he needs false teeth, maybe he's fifty or sixty years old, though very strong." After saying which, he winked at me. Was he teasing me? Or satirizing himself? And avoiding confiding whatever the police now knew?

When our beers arrived, girls came to sit with us. One plumped herself on my lap and wiggled about.

"You can talk free for ten minutes," whispered Max, "then she'll ask you to buy her a drink. That's only about ten dollars, so you decide."

"What's your name?" I asked my sexy burden, whose face was unusually broad, her eyes wide-spaced, though her figure was impeccable.

"Luciana. And what do they call you?"

Quite soon I said, "Where did you learn such good English?"

"In school, of course. I also speak German and Italian. A lot of Italians live in Romania, and Germans visit."

"So, Luciana, do you like working in this place?"

"It's better than my hometown. But I'd like a real job sometime."

"What do you mean by a real job?"

"Oh, a shop assistant, for instance."

"My God, speaking four languages you could at least be an interpreter or an air hostess."

Max whispered, "If you ask a schoolgirl in the countryside what she wants to be, she'll say a prostitute, so she can meet foreign men."

Ovid and Silviu were talking in Romanian all this time, ignoring the girls on either side of them, who reacted by chattering behind their backs, displaying nail varnish.

"Will you buy me a drink?" asked Luciana. "Or else I can't stay with you."

I decided to do so, as did Max for his own blonde companion.

"If you want to take yours to the flat," mentioned my host, "it's best you both arrange to meet outside, then the club doesn't get commission."

"Doesn't the club object?"

"No, it's understood. So long as you don't actually leave the premises along with her."

Prompted, Luciana squirmed and said, "I love sex. Will you take me home tonight for a hundred dollars?"

"Offer her two thousand lei."

"Oh no, that is much too little," protested Luciana. "Fifty dollars."

"But I already have Adriana," I told Max.

"Maybe you ought to have variety. In case you overvalue Adriana."

Evidently Max had my best interests at heart!

Just then Ovid's mobile jangled and his side of the conversation certainly intrigued Silviu and all of the girls.

Ovid looked across at me. "There's been another killing. Same MO. Modus operandi," he added. "I must go." He threw an arm around his neglected girl and hugged her. "Don't worry, the arm of the law will protect you." She giggled.

"May I come with you?" I asked.

"Yes. No. Yes. Why not? Taxi for you afterwards." He threw down some money.

"How much do I owe for the drinks?" I asked Max.

"We'll sort it out tomorrow. You'll need a key." He fished in his pocket. "Oh, do you mind if I take a girl home with me?"

"Of course not."

How could I possibly mind? Yet I did. Not for any moral reason, but because this seemed a bit, shall we say, oppressive, as regards myself rather than the girl. However, I was about to walk out on my host.

The crime scene, as I reckoned when a summoned taxi finally returned me, was only about three kilometres from Max's flat, in a big apartment block not completely fitted out inside, and consequently only semi-occupied. Not a lift, this time, but a coin-operated mini-laundry in the basement. The victim was another young woman. The discoverer was her boyfriend, when she failed to return to their flat; although he had been taken back upstairs for questioning, and the body was about to be zipped up by the time Ovid and I walked in. I glimpsed something from a butcher's shop, or abattoire, like paintings by Soutine of carcasses of beef. Flayed, was my impression. A torn, blood-soaked skirt and blouse, and other scattered garments, lay as if really needing the services of the half-full washing machine which yawned open.

I thought of Luciana and so many others like her, innocently vulnerable in the city, yet eager for money. In fact this murder had nothing to do with prostitutes, but my writerly brain was at work.

When I emerged from my bedroom relatively early, Max was through in the tiny kitchen drinking coffee boiled in a steel pot on a gas ring. His own bedroom door stood open. No evidence of any prostitute.

"Has she gone already?"

"I changed my mind. The girls ask less after midnight when they get worried they won't earn, but I couldn't be bothered to wait." *If that was true—if he hadn't just wanted to have an effect upon me.* "So what of the second atrocity?"

"Atrocities involve lots of people, not just one."

"Two now. Could be a cumulative atrocity? How many does it take? Actually, a single act of brutality qualifies as an atrocity."

I ignored this casuistry, even if he was right.

Dogs howled and yodeled, and a few moments later the building shuddered briefly.

"Minor earthquake, don't worry. There's glacial moraine under Bucharest. Some land moves horizontally, some vertically, some is mixed. That's why it's very expensive to build here . . . The *atrocity*," he pressed me.

So I described the brutal scene, though I did not mention my image of paintings by Soutine.

Max took me for a walk around his neighbourhood, which was distinctly run-down, although parts were being poshed up by new money, seemingly at random. In the middle of a potholed back street, asphalt burned and bubbled blackly.

Max laughed. "Some builder needs hot tar for a job, so he set fire to it. Obviously the middle of the street is safer than the sides." He laughed. "Romanians don't think of consequences. They'll run you over in the street because they don't think of prison as the result. I'm not kidding. They will not stop. Oops," and he caught my arm and dragged me well to one side because a battered pick-up truck was indeed heading our way, and to avoid the fire, the driver mounted the pavement. Max had hurt my arm with his grip, though for a perfectly good reason, so I tried not to show pain.

We must have seen a score of skinny, roaming dogs already, variously marked, although all of the same general build.

"Ha," said Max. "That crime scene reminds me of a joke. Which I've already *used*, by the way," he emphasized. "A forgetful man visits a shortsighted gypsy fortune-teller. She looks at his palm and exclaims, 'I see men with knives coming for you—and blood!' He starts sweating with fear. She examines his palm even more closely and finally says, 'You forgot to take off your pigskin glove.'"

"Ha-ha," I said. A perverse urge tempted me to add: "I'm glad you already used it."

"As for drivers and future consequences," he went on, as though I'd said nothing at all, "Romanian people choose to be suspended in eternity. It's still difficult for them to get over the dictatorship. Safer not to take responsibility."

"'Suspended in eternity' is quite a phrase. I suppose you'll be using that, too."

He nodded, appeased or otherwise I couldn't decide. Time was melting again, like the runny hot asphalt. Already it was afternoon. So Max led me circuitously to a café he favoured, for some beer.

Halfway through the second can of Ursus, Adriana phoned me.

"Are you free this afternoon?" I asked her. "What are we doing this afternoon?" I asked Max almost simultaneously.

"I need to buy a camera card," was Max's reply. "You can come or not."

I was, of course, eager for Adriana to visit me privately on my own, although not entirely for the obvious reason of possible sex. Max out of the way would suit me very well, doubly so.

Max had already buzzed off, and I didn't know when he'd be back. Given the vagaries of Bucharest, maybe hours as yet.

I kissed Adriana enthusiastically. "Lovely to see you! Look, do you think we could pop over the road for a few minutes? I'm very curious about the old woman in that cottage. If it's halfway possible, I'm dying to see inside and see her close to. Could we pretend that I want to buy some eggs?"

"I suppose so. She might sell some eggs."

"Oh, and don't tell Max, will you not?"

Adriana grinned. "How mysterious you crime writers are. Men of mystery are exciting."

The crone's door was intricately carved, and worn, as though it preceded the city or had been transported here from a farm in the country, perhaps one of the tens of thousands bulldozed under Ceauşescu for a dam or for socialist rationalisation.

The owner's face was rutted, like carved and varnished wood itself, though her brown eyes were alert. Blackness scarfed her and draped her. After Adriana explained in Romanian, the woman uttered a brief reply or a cackle.

"Tell her," I suggested, "that I'm a writer and, in addition to eggs, I'm very interested in her life here surrounded by modern city. I'll pay her for her time, twenty dollars, no make that thirty."

"Twenty," said Adriana, and complied.

Surprisingly, or unsurprisingly, the crone—Madame Florescu now, to be polite—admitted us into a gloomy room and stuck out a hand dark with dirt or the resin of age, into which I counted four five-dollar bills, which she sniffed before promptly disappearing them within her neckline as though she was some much younger entertainer who used her cleavage for tips.

I took in the items of rustic home-made furniture, the blackened pots and pans and jars of herbs and other stuff. Rather a lot of green candles stood around in old brass candlesticks, understandable if Madame Florescu had no mains power, as seemed likely. A faint sickly odour emanated from vases of marigolds and ox-eyed daisies which were red rather than white, and, strangely, from lilies-of-the-valley, which surely should be past their season, unless the Romanian variety was different or else the crone had patronised a florist's shop for blooms flown from far away.

Coincidentally, Adriana was translating, "A present from my

son," when she herself really noticed those flowers and gasped and crossed herself.

"My son visits me once a week of an evening after he finishes working hard, a good boy," Adriana continued dutifully interpreting despite whatever had shocked her.

"You would like him. He also can tell you remarkable things— in your own English. He's clever." And can do with some dollars himself, I thought. "You sleep only over the street. If you see a red Dacia outside here, probably on Thursday, come and knock. A red Dacia which says taxi, but my son is more than taxi-driver."

Thursday was the day after next. If only Max would leave me alone that evening.

Mrs. Florescu discoursed about geese and her water butt and her man who had been killed by the Securitate. Apparently her man was a black marketeer. After a reasonable time she dried up and looked expectant. My twenty dollars had run out as though all the while a taxi metre had been running in her head. I said that I'd love to hear more from herself and her son on Thursday. I was becoming hungry for Adriana before Max would return. Besides, rather than hearing more domestic details, I wanted to know what had visibly shocked Adriana.

I departed with three eggs clutched in my hand. Once we had recrossed the road, yet another dog wandered close. My body hiding what I was doing, in case Madame Florescu was looking out, I dropped the eggs to make raw omelette. The pooch sidled swiftly towards this in a flinching manner, sniffed, then lapped, crunchy eggshells included.

"Oh, Paul! Butterfingers. Isn't that what you say?"

Of course I didn't want Max to have a clue as to what I'd been up to, by leaving eggs in his fridge.

"The dog's need is greater than mine," I assured her. "To tell the truth, I don't like eggs much in any form."

• • •

"Yes, it was those flowers," Adriana confirmed once we were in the flat. "Those ones are used in the countryside to attract werewolves. Because of the smell."

"To *attract* werewolves?"

"Maybe to control, or to cause. My own mother warned me never to wear the, um, the little white bells."

I felt quite pleased with myself.

I felt even more pleased when Adriana amiably consented to test my double bed. The bench press was useful to dump our clothes on. Afterwards, she fell asleep, and looked very innocent, as though orgasm had drained away all cares.

The next day Max and I visited his Romanian publisher at home for lunch, by taxi. Only one of my books was published locally as yet—which was enough for me to be famous on the island—and I nursed hopes for more translations. Cezar, yet another displaced ancient Roman, was jolly and hospitable with beer, coffee, nuts, and nibbles. We sat, Romanian style, in a dingy courtyard, or patio-alley, running from front to back of his house. Inside, the house's bare floorboards were dirty and the place was full of tat, as I found when I visited the toilet.

A coil of incense set on bricks burned under the plastic patio table. Sometimes the air smelled of patchouli, sometimes of sewage. A guard dog was on a long chain secured to the inside of its kennel. A white cat with a fluffy tail ambled around. A sizeable though twisted tree arose through the concrete of the patio without any evidence of how rain could possibly reach its roots; maybe those had broken through to the sewer for sustenance.

Apparently the crime market was flooded; thus, a publisher had to be careful, but if I posted my best books to Cezar he would see. More time dissolved, until the ubiquitous Silviu turned up with his car. And the same camera as, presumably, I'd heard about from Max. Cezar duly admired the camera. Then Max handed Silviu a memory card in its little plastic box. Silviu proceeded to install the memory card and take photos of me and Max and Cezar. This made no sense to me at all. If Max resented lending, or rather, giving, the three hundred dollars to Silviu, why then present him with a memory card? Was that in exchange for today's use of petrol? As lanky Silviu focused, he looked like a tall, thin photographic tripod. Or bi-pod, I suppose.

Shortly after we left, to drive seemingly aimlessly around the city, rain began to fall heavily. Mighty fountains pluming skyward in vast piazzas fought back against the downpour. We stopped at a café, then when the storm stopped and the sky cleared towards the end of the afternoon, Max said, "Show you something." On foot we turned a few corners into a big boulevard, farther along which towered, as Max pointed out, the Intercontinental Hotel.

Spaced along the steaming pavement were prostitutes in mini-skirts, who proved assertive. One delicious girl, who looked no more than fifteen, already wore the scar of a Cesarean above her bared navel pierced with a gold ring. She smooched right up to me and placed her hand on my groin, brazenly massaging, and jerking her head towards a dark, deserted arcade. Max stood eyeing me, to see how I would extricate myself, which I did by backing away while wagging a reproving finger, even though I confess I'd become excited.

As we returned to the car, I said, "There's something *predatory* about them."

"Predatory, yes," agreed Max. "*Le mot juste.* They're Gypsies, hoping to prey on foreign businessmen from the Intercontinental. To the Gypsies we're just sheep to be fleeced. In fact, security on the hotel door could send out for better from his catalog."

Soaked dogs were lapping water.

• • •

The murders featured on TV by now, although the set in the flat was crap, even if we could have understood. Max brought out a litre bottle of sweet, strong, seductive, almondy Disaronno, and put on a CD of a Bulgarian pop starlet, then we proceeded to get quite drunk. I realized there was a need to match Max glass for glass. At the same time I didn't want a hangover, nor did I want to stay up half the night.

So when had Max been in Bulgaria? This led to anecdotes about bribing police and much else, a mixture of funny and disconcerting. Then we talked about personalities on the island, or rather Max did most of the talking since he'd previously known many of those present. Idly I wondered whether he had slept with Adriana the year before. Max's recounting became almost a non-stop monologue, which can be intimidating. He was talking at me, rather than with me. At some point sandwiches manifested themselves out of bread, ham, and mustard in the fridge. Finally I managed to finish the last of the bottle. Fingers and toes crossed for the following evening!

Fortunately, on Thursday Max didn't take me to experience more sleaze. Instead we went to tour Ceauşescu's palace, about which much could be said, but I shan't. Wonderfully, Max *would* be absent in the evening. Of course I could accompany him, but I pleaded a queasy stomach and headache. All that Disaronno.

At seven thirty I looked and saw a red Dacia parked outside the cottage. So I sallied forth.

Mihail Florescu, the dutiful son, looked to be in his late fifties, in cheap checked shirt and trousers, grey-haired and with a beer gut. Muscular, though. He welcomed me with delight, as did his mother, who bustled to provide some cubes of cheese and peanuts, while Mihail urged on me a big glass of orange juice. A plastic bucket chair for me. This time I'd brought a notebook. An oil lamp had been lighting the room, but now Mrs. Florescu proceeded to light the green candles as well, which produced blue flames.

"How can we help you to write?" asked Mihail, beaming. He meant "as a writer."

"Thank *you* for giving me your time," I replied. "Please accept a little compensation." Thirty dollars. I drank juice while he disappeared the money, then began, "I'm curious about those flowers, particularly the little white bells. I hear that in this country they are associated with werewolves."

Mihail looked blank, so I said, "Excuse me," then mimed a transformation, which must have been successful because he rattled away to his mother, and she to him.

"Yes," he said, "to keep away such things. My mother, all the dogs frighten her. Last winter, dog killed chicken."

My throat and tongue felt dry, so I emptied my glass, and realised that the orange juice must have been mixed with some strong spirit, maybe home-made, for all of a sudden I came over queer.

I must have passed out briefly, for mother and son were standing over me, regarding me attentively, and Mrs. Florescu was rubbing a smelly ointment onto my brow and cheeks. God, how parched I was. I croaked for a drink, although I was also feeling a mounting urge to pee. Probably Mrs. Florescu's toilet was a dark hole, and I could hardly excuse myself to use her garden, not with her vegetables there. I tried to clench myself tight, but my body felt incoherent. Suddenly I thought of the young Gypsy prostitute with such hunger for her flesh—oh, to be able to taste her, drink her juices. Which juices exactly? To my shame, spurts of pee began to pulse into my pants uncontrollably. A restless anxiety mounted. I was quivering—and then I found myself sliding out of the plastic seat, and glad to be nearer the floor on my hands and knees. Four limbs could support me better.

• • •

Dog rejoiced ragingly to be let out. Dog loped over empty wasteland. Moonlit. Twitching nose, taunted and teased. So thirsty. Dog-turds pungent. Potholed roadway. Lapped stale rain. Wrong liquid! *Howled*.

In every man: a dog. Turn man inside out, hairs bristle out all over. Dog fell over, scrambled up. Fellow dogs lay curled, muzzles resting on bums. Reek of bitch in heat far away?

The thirst! Not for dog blood. *Human!*

In moonlit street.

Big stick or long gun. Hairless head shone. Hairs crowded wide and black under nose, above mouth. Dried sweat, and cologne, and a fart.

Hunting for dog.

Dog hid amongst dogs. Other dogs shifted listlessly.

Dog cowered. Whimpers escaped. Dog buried muzzle in bum. Familiar fragrance of inside-oneself, comforting.

Human came.

Attack, rip with claws, grip throat with teeth so sharp! *No!* Dog feared bang-bang. Dog cringed among dogs. Lone eye watched.

Rattle of laughter.

Human noise: "*So how do you feel now, Mr. Martin Fairfax? How does it feel?*"

A camera flashed blindingly.

Head throbbing, I woke to daylight naked on that double bed beside the bench press. What a vile, terrible nightmare.

Then I saw my strewn soiled clothes, and discovered the state of my aching body.

I heard the crow of a cock. Was Max waiting patiently next door, drinking coffee?

At first I could hardly stand, weak as a decrepit old man.

Propelled by fear, I recovered some strength. Blessedly

186 | Ian Watson

Rigby—I couldn't bear to think of him any longer as Max—was absent.

I fled before even worse happened, wheeling my suitcase behind me to the nearest boulevard, flagging a taxi and saying, "Otopeni, *vǎ rog*," the name of Bucharest's airport, plus *please*. Of course the driver swindled me, though not grossly. And he *wasn't* Madame Florescu's son, even though paranoia whispered otherwise.

Rigby had set the trap cunningly.

Admittedly, his plan depended on such a crone as Madame Florescu living opposite his flat in such a home as she did. Although how exactly had Rigby located that particular flat? With Silviu's help, in line with what special requirements? Rigby's own research requirements, of which I knew nothing, yet which I'd let lure me like a bee to pollen!

Rigby must have paid the crone and her son quite a few more dollars than I did. And Silviu procured the hallucinogens, whatever those might have been? A cocktail of mandrake, henbane, LSD? Maybe some deadly nightshade and hemlock and mindaltering mushrooms thrown in?

No, how could Silviu, or Rigby, have known what to concoct? The crone must have known.

It couldn't be, could it, that I had truly been transformed? That the crone had thought I wanted to be transformed because of my miming? I'm quite light and short—even so, how heavy a weredog would I have become?

Fortuitous, indeed, that the bloody murders took place!

I would probably have been beguiled by the crone's cottage, even so.

What was Adriana's part in the conspiracy, gasping and crossing herself in timely fashion?

Bitch! I thought.

Bitch seemed entirely the wrong term of abuse. Or maybe entirely the right one.

So how do you feel now, Mr. Martin Fairfax? Such vindictiveness on account of a bad review. Rigby must have leaned on the editor of the mag, or maybe he'd read that early book of mine and the character's name stuck in his mind.

So I departed Romania with my tail, as it were, between my legs.

After I got back home and had recovered myself, I googled using automatic translation and discovered that a man had been arrested for the murders in Bucharest. The presumed perpetrator was a Turko-German drug smuggler, Günther Bey, sporting tattoos featuring samurai sword fights. Red dye used for sprays and pools of blood, I suppose.

It seemed to me that if the Turko-German's skin bore so much pictorial blood, it was unlikely that he felt a craving to replicate this upon the skins of unfortunate women. If he emulated Japanese gangsters, those people had a code of honour, only killing rivals and enemies within the fraternity.

Ovid had found half-a-Turk to fix up for the killings. It wouldn't do for a werewolf or weredog to be responsible. Romania was a modern country now, a member of the European Union.

So did those murders result from a crone applying a potion and a salve? Maybe her own good son, Mihail, was transformed? No, that was absurd.

Judging from the news, no more such murders happened. If I related my experiences as a short story, this should reflect badly on Rigby, though obviously I'd need to disguise his name.

I Was a Middle-Age Werewolf

RON GOULART

Sometimes bad luck just seems to gang up on you.

Take my situation on this past June 13. Things were lousy even before I turned into a shaggy grey wolf-man for the first time.

And I'm not even talking about the fact that I was two payments behind on the mortgage of my house here on the fringes of Beverly Hills. Back in the 1920s the silent-movie lover Orlando Busino lived in this sprawling Moorish-style mansion and romanced some of the loveliest actresses of the silver screen within these very walls. In the 1960s, the immensely, and briefly, popular rock group the Ivy League Jug Band staged excessive orgies here on a fairly regular basis. Obviously the roof didn't leak back then, nor did the pipes produce ominous keening noises in the midnight hours.

Also, I'm not alluding to my former wife, Mandy, whom you've no doubt heard of. She's a bestselling author of diet books under the name of Mandine Osterwald Higby. Such titles as *The Junk Food Diet* and *To Hell With Nutrition* have been on every bestseller list in the land for endless months. Rumors in the publishing trade were that Mandy was working on a memoir to be entitled *I Married an Asshole*. My attorney charged me $500 to tell me she had a perfect right to do that.

I am, by the way, Tim Higby. I'm forty-one, eleven pounds

overweight, and three inches too short. I make my living writing television comedies. I'm very fond of plaid shirts and was wearing one on that fateful night along with a venerable pair of khakis.

My most successful sitcom was *Uncle Fred Is a Pain in the Butt,* which ran from 2001 to 2003. Since then I haven't had another hit. Finally, four months ago, I was hired as a writer on *Nose Job*. That's the one about the wacky Hollywood plastic surgeon. It began plummeting in the ratings just after the first script I'd had a hand in aired. The show handler and the producers decided they need somebody younger to save *Nose Job* from extinction and, Lord knows, there are untold numbers of writers younger than I am in Greater Los Angeles.

So on the morning of June 13 I got an e-mail informing me I was no longer on the writing team. I'd been in the middle of writing a very funny script dealing with how this wacky Hollywood plastic surgeon misplaced the left ear of a patient.

As the day waned I was sitting in my living room, scene of many a seduction and many an orgy before my time of residence, and brooding over the fact that in addition to having to pay Mandy an enormous alimony each and every month, I was now going to be vilified in *I Married an Asshole*.

The cell phone, which I'd been able to keep up the payments on, played the opening notes of Thelonious Monk's "Crepuscule With Nellie."

I scratched at a sudden itch in my right palm, then picked it up. "Yeah?"

"Turn on the Gossip Channel."

"Why, Hersh?"

It was Bernie Hersh, one of my few close friends and, even at the advanced age of forty-seven, still a very successful television writer. "Just do, old buddy. On my way out." The call ended.

Putting down the phone, I scratched my hand yet again, and

then grabbed up the remote to bring the Gossip Channel into view. There on the screen was my daughter, whose agent had christened her Mutiny Skylark last year, and then sold her to the Will Destry Channel to star in *Posy Pickwick: Rock & Roll Detective.*

Beth, her real first name, was sitting on a purple sofa, hands folded in her lap and looking contrite. Well, as contrite as you can look while wearing a very low-cut yellow tank top and very minimal shorts. "It seems to me," she was saying to the stunning blonde interviewer, "that the executives at Destry, really wonderful people for the most part, Pam, have been excessive in this instance."

"They've just dumped you from *Posy Pickwick,* which, as of this week, is the top-rated YA show in the world."

"Except in Brazil," said my redheaded daughter, crossing her legs. "I do believe, in all modesty, Pam, and not to detract from the wonderful contribution of the entire *Posy* team and all the wonderful kids who act on my show with me, that this nearly universal international success is pretty much due to me."

"Sure thing, Mutiny. But the statement that Will Destry, Jr., released to the media just hours ago, states that you're being severed from the show for 'conduct unbecoming of a teenager and knocking over Charlie Chicken.'"

My daughter sighed. "I'd be a hypocrite if I didn't admit, you know, that I'm a little wild at times," she said, uncrossing and recrossing her legs. "I'm still not sure how I managed to drive my new SUV into that wonderful statue of Will Destry's most famous animated cartoon character. It makes me, you know, really sad, Pam."

My left side was commencing to itch. I scratched it.

"You also drove your Jaguar into the front window of the New Trocadero on the Strip last month, Mutiny," reminded Pam.

Beth held up her hand. "Let's get our facts straight, Pam," she said as she recrossed her legs. "I drove my *Mercedes* through the Troc window to avoid hitting a sweet little old lady tourist who'd fallen down in the crosswalk. My Jaguar I was using when I drove over Harlan Ellison's foot in the parking lot of Mexicali Rose's Hot Tamale Café, which was a very popular hangout for three weeks last March."

I realized I was still holding the remote. Setting it down on the coffee table, I scratched my right hand with my left and then my left with my right. "What have I got now? Some rare skin disease?"

"Excuse my being so personal," said Pam, leaning a bit forward. "But don't you feel it's time to stop your madcap ways, Mutiny?"

My enormously successful—until today—daughter began to sob quietly. Wiggling on the purple sofa, she tugged a petite pink hanky from a slit pocket of her crimson shorts. She dabbed at her eyes, sniffling. "As you and the majority of my wonderful fans around the world know, Pam, I'm the product of a broken home. I just know that if my parents got together again, it would work wonders for my overall deportment."

"Wonderful." I snatched up the remote to thumb the off button. Beth vanished.

The itch was spreading. I scratched at my right side, my left knee, my left buttock, and, as best I could, my upper back. "Jesus, maybe I've contracted some strange, highly dangerous Asian plague from eating Chinese imports."

When I stood up, I felt extremely woozy. When I sat down again my entire skeleton didn't feel right. I started to perspire, and as I wiped my itching palm across my forehead, I began to experience severe stomach cramps.

Apparently another symptom of this malady that was attacking me was drowsiness. I was getting very sleepy. As twilight began to close in outside, my eyelids fell shut. My attempt to open my eyes again failed, and in less than a minute, I fell deeply asleep.

Two things awakened me. One was the door chimes playing the first few bars of " 'Round Midnight" and the other was a loud animal howling.

"Nova Botsford," I recalled.

Nova is the Associate Producer of that very successful new sitcom, *Dump Truck.* That's the one about the wacky Hollywood garbage man. A handsome woman of forty-five or thereabouts, she's been described by those who've worked with her as impossible, tyrannical, sadistic, offensive, and meanminded. For some reason, though, Nova and I have always gotten along, and when she heard I'd been tossed off *Nose Job,* she phoned to tell me she was dropping by that night to talk to me. I figured maybe she could get me on the *Dump Truck* writing staff. I'd already made a few notes on some pretty funny garbage gags.

My legs were still a bit wobbly, but the itching had subsided. Maybe I'd suffered from a speeded-up version of some kind of one-day flu.

En route to the front door, I stopped at a wall mirror to check my appearance.

"Holy Christ," I observed, "haven't I undergone enough crap for one day?"

Apparently not. Looking back at me from the mirror was a furry-faced wolf-man. I knew it was me because of the plaid shirt.

"No wonder I was itchy." The fur had been starting to emerge just before I passed out.

Unbuttoning a couple of buttons of my shirt, I determined that my chest was covered with grey fur, too. So were my legs, I found after bending to pull up a trouser leg.

The door chimes sounded again, then Nova started knocking

forcibly on the oaken door. "Tim, yoo-hoo. Are you in there, darling? I haven't all the time in the world to commiserate with you."

"Damn, I've become a horror movie cliché and on top of that I'm contemplating seeking employment from a woman who likes to shout *yoo-hoo.*"

It then occurred to me that I was maybe only the victim of some sort of elaborate practical joke. I was drugged somehow and then worked on by a makeup man.

But, alas, several vigorous tugs at the newly-arrived fur on my chest convinced me that it was, unfortunately, real. Whatever I was the victim of, it wasn't practical jokers.

Nova whapped more profoundly on the door.

I started for the doorway, noticing that walking with hairy feet inside my loafers made me wobble some.

Putting my fur-rimmed eye to the spy hole, I gazed out into the night. The overhead light above my mosaic tile porch showed a very annoyed Nova Botsford standing out there. "Timmy?"

A cranky woman like her certainly would never hire a wolf-man to work on her show. I couldn't see her face-to-face, or anybody else for that matter, until I was over this. Whatever this was.

When I cleared my throat, it produced an unsettling snarling sound. "Nova," I called in a raspy, growly voice, "I've got bad news for you."

"We already talked about your getting the heave-ho from *Nose Job,* remember?"

"No, this is different bad news."

"You mean about your scrawny brat of a daughter being canned by Destry? I knew that two days ago, dear. Now, for Pete's sake, let me in."

"No, no, this is brand-new bad news," I explained. "I'm suffering from that new bug."

"Which bug?"

"The one that's going around. Just arrived from Asia Minor, I think. Extremely contagious, so you really can't come in."

"That's awful. You poor guy," she said. "But I can't afford to get the trots just now, otherwise I'd come right in to make you a cup of tea or something else to indicate I care."

"No, nope, don't think of it. *Dump Truck* can't function if you're under the weather, Nova."

"Exactly, I have to put *my* health first," she said through my door. "Oh, by the way, I thought I heard some kind of hound yowling in there. Did you get a dog?"

"That must've been me," I realized.

"What's that, Tim?"

"Neighbors have a pet wolf."

"A pet what?"

"Wolfhound. Russian wolfhound."

"Well, dear, you'd better get back to bed and take care of whatever the hell it is you've got," she said. "Good night, Timmy."

As her Porsche went roaring away into the night, I realized, "Damn, I was so preoccupied with being a wolf-man, I forgot to ask her about a job."

I walked lopsidedly back to the hall mirror for another look.

I was still covered with fur.

Returning to my living room, I figured I'd sit calmly down and try to decide what exactly to do about this latest catastrophe.

But then I suddenly realized that I wanted to go hunting.

Yanking off my shoes, I went loping into the kitchen. Howling once, I slipped out the back door, ran across the back lawn crouched low, and headed for the dark woodlands that stretched away behind the house.

Mostly I chased rabbits and, I'm pretty sure, the calico cat who belongs to the art director who lives two mansions down from me. I also went after some night birds, one of which might've been an owl.

Fortunately, I didn't catch anything and my interest in hunting waned after about half an hour. I was wheezing some as I headed for home. Probably from the exertion. "Jesus, I hope I'm not allergic to my own fur. Or maybe it's wolf dander that's causing the wheeze."

Back in my living room, I decided to call Bernie Hersh. I really needed somebody I trusted to take a look at me and confirm that I wasn't simply hallucinating. I only had to push one button on my phone with my clumsy fur-covered finger and say, "Hersh," to get the phone to dial his number.

"You've reached the residence of Bernard Hersh, one of America's most respected wordsmiths. Unfortunately, I'm home at the moment and have to answer the damn phone myself."

"It's Tim, Hersh. I have a serious—"

"I can e-mail you a list of rehab centers, therapists, priests, rabbis, and others who can deal with your nitwit daughter," he said. "I also know a guy who can put her in a sack and convey her to the jungles of Guatemala."

"This isn't about Beth, it's—"

"Whoever might she be? I'm alluding to your daughter, Mutiny Skylark, who was booted out by—"

"Listen," I cut in, "I've got a more pressing problem."

"Well, I might be able to help you find a new job, but—"

"You knew I was fired from *Nose Job?*"

"Everybody from Santa Rosa to Tijuana knows you were fired from the show. Let's have lunch tomorrow and—"

"Could you drop over here?"

"To pick you up tomorrow?"

"Tonight. Right now. Immediately."

"Are you ailing? Your voice does sound like you're in the throes of bronchitis or—"

"I need a reliable witness."

Hersh said, "Fifteen minutes," and ended the call.

"Did they move Halloween up a few months?" inquired Hersh as he crossed the threshold.

"I am a wolf-man, right? You can see that? I mean, I'm not simply suffering from hallucinations or delusions?"

"You look like a wolf, for sure, old buddy," he assured me as he shut my heavy front door. "Why have you made yourself up like that?"

"It's not makeup." I led him into the living room. "I just . . . suddenly changed." And, sitting uneasily down in a redwood and leather chair, I told him what had happened.

Hersh wandered over to a window to gaze up at the starry sky. "That's funny."

"What's funny, the fact that I've been transformed into a loathsome—"

"No, the fact that there's only a *half*-moon tonight."

"Hey, you're right." I tried to snap my fingers but discovered you can't do that with hairy fingers. "Traditionally werewolves only change during a full moon."

"Having scripted not only *The Werewolf Hunter* but *True Yarns from the Graveyard* and the unjustly short-lived soaper *Haunted Hospital,* I've become something of an expert on occult and supernatural stuff." He seated himself on the sofa. "In my opinion, this is unusual behavior for a werewolf."

"Maybe," I suggested, "this isn't anything supernatural at all. It could be a very nasty allergic reaction to something I ate."

Narrowing his left eye, my friend looked directly at me. "You really think so?"

My furry shoulders sank. "No," I admitted. "Now, wolf-men change back into human form comes the dawn, don't they?"

"*Traditional* wolf-men, yeah."

My nose started to itch, but when I tried to scratch it, it wasn't where it usually was. At the end of my furry snout it was and of a rubbery texture. "Let's get to *why* I'm in this current state."

"Have you been bitten by a werewolf of late?"

"C'mon, Hersh. Until I turned into one, I never actually believed that werewolves existed."

"Well, according to occult experts, there are only so many ways you can make a sudden transition like this," said Hersh. "If you haven't had any direct contact with a werewolf, then I'd guess that someone either put a spell on you or slipped you a potion."

"Would that work?"

"You are sitting there covered with fur from head to toe. Something did it."

"A magic potion, an evil spell. Who'd do anything like that to me?"

"Besides your erstwhile wife, you mean?"

Shaking my head, I raised my hairy hand to tick off my fingers. When I saw my wolf-man hand up close, I abandoned the notion. "Firstly, Mandy knows that most wolves don't earn enough money to pay much in the way of alimony," I explained. "Secondly, it's too late to change the title of *I Married an Asshole* to *I Married a Werewolf.*"

"Possibly," Hersh conceded.

"Third, and most important. She doesn't know diddly about black magic and sorcery."

"This is LA, Tim. There are more witches, warlocks, and sorcerers hereabouts than any other spot on Earth, except maybe San Francisco," he told me. "Take this guy Vincent X. Shandu, who's the hottest mystic going. Calls himself a necromancer and charges a thousand bucks an hour. Or Professor Estling, who—"

"Who the hell would pay a grand to turn me into a shaggy beast?"

"Some warlocks charge less. We'll have to find out who did the job."

"How?"

"When I was writing *Vampire Cops* for HBO, we had an occult detective as a consultant," Hersh said. "Name's Fletcher Boggs. I'll call the guy tomorrow and try to set up an appointment for you to—"

"What'll he charge?"

"A lot less than a thou."

"Okay," I said after about half a minute. "Talk to Boggs. Does he make house calls? I don't want to venture out in the world looking like this. Even with dark glasses and a hat—"

"Case like yours, he'll come here." He stood, moving toward the door. "I'll call you tomorrow, soon as I find out anything." He stopped just short of the doorway. "Or would you like to spend tonight at our place? Dottie is very understanding about—"

"Not that understanding," I said as I followed him to the door. "I'll be okay here by myself. And I really do appreciate your help."

Hersh took hold of the brass doorknob. "Do you mind if we don't shake hands?"

It had been, to put it mildly, a trying day. After attempting to pace back and forth across the living room, a process that usually helps me clarify my thinking, I decided to go up to bed. Pacing on furry feet, I found, didn't aid my thinking at all.

I usually sleep in a pajama top. That night, my first as a wolfman, the idea of taking off my clothes didn't appeal to me. Nor did the idea of brushing my teeth.

I'd sleep in my plaid shirt and khakis. Stretched out atop the bedspread, I propped up three fat pillows and picked up the book

I'd been reading from the bedside table. It was that bestselling self-help book, *Trample 'Em Underfoot: The Route to Success.*

Trouble was, it made me uneasy to look at my currently furry hands holding the damn book. Tossing it to the floor, I grabbed up the TV remote. After a couple of tries I was able to poke the *on* button with sufficient force to get the big set looming at the foot of the bed to come to life.

"Now some exclusive KMA-TV footage of the so-called Wolf-Man of Westwood," said the handsome, though aging, news co-anchor. "Pretty interesting stuff isn't it, Camilla?"

"Wolf-man?" I sat up.

The camera pulled back to include the stunning raven-haired Camilla Cardy. "It sure is, Will. And we want to thank viewer Wally Needham for donating this sensational footage that he was lucky enough to capture with his cell phone."

"As we reported an hour ago on KMA's *All Night All News,*" said Will Noonan in his deep, handsome voice, "the alleged wolf-man was first spotted earlier this evening prowling the side streets of Westwood Village. Thus far police have found no trace of him."

"Because of the proximity to the UCLA campus," added Camilla, "early reports suggested that this was nothing more than a college prank."

"Now that KMA has obtained exclusive pictures of this strange creature, however, we can confidently state that this is *not* a hoax or prank. Later in this hour we'll be talking to Professor Marshall Terping of the USC Zoology Department as to the true nature of this phenomenon."

Camilla said, "Let's take a look at this exclusive two-minute footage."

I leaned forward, eyes narrowing.

A very jiggly, long shot of the front of a Fanny's Undies

lingerie shop appeared. Coming out of the darkened store was a shaggy wolf-man. In his arms he clutched a tangled bundle of what looked to be lacy panties, half-slips, and frilly nightgowns. Clutched in his sharp teeth, dangling by one strap, was a white uplift bra.

The guy with the cell phone apparently got up the nerve to move closer at this point.

Dropping his collection of underwear, staring straight at the camera, and spitting out the bra, the wolf-man snarled at Wally Needham. Then he went loping away along the night street. In the distance a siren sounded, somewhere nearer a woman screamed. The film ceased.

The wolf-man had been wearing a plaid shirt.

Turning off the set, I dropped off the bed. "But that's not my plaid shirt," I told myself, starting to pace. "The shirt I'm wearing is the MacMurdie tartan. That wasn't."

Or was it?

I'd only seen his shirt up close for about half a minute and the color of the amateur footage was bad.

"No, that wasn't me. I know damn well I haven't been anywhere near Westwood," I told myself. After I'd morphed into a wolf-man, I'd chased rabbits. As far as I could remember. Besides, it would've taken quite a bit of time for me to get down there on foot. And I couldn't drive my six-year-old Volvo with furry feet.

But that meant there were two wolf-men, both fond of plaid shirts. A strange coincidence. But, no, that wasn't me.

"I don't have a lingerie fetish, either."

My pacing slowed. All at once I felt very drowsy again. Not bothering to climb back onto the bed, I curled up on the floor and drifted into sleep.

• • •

I was awakened by an immense thunking sound from outside, followed by a harsh metallic snapping and an assortment of birds cawing and cackling along with an anguished flapping of many wings.

"Someone's attacking the birdbath!" I exclaimed, popping up off the carpet.

As I started to run toward the bedroom door, I chanced to notice my feet. They were no longer furry. I stopped, held both hands up to my face. "Back to normal," I said, chuckling.

Ducking into the bathroom, hesitating a few seconds, I took a look in the mirror over the sink. I was no longer a wolf-man.

From out on my front lawn came more loud, angry bird sounds.

Barefooted, I hurried to the stairs. I was only halfway down when my oaken front door was unlocked and flung open.

"Popsy?" called my daughter.

"Beth, you can call yourself Mutiny Skylark, you can even call yourself Carmen Miranda," I said as I continued my descent, "but, damn it, don't call me Popsy."

"Sorry, Dad." Wearing cargo pants and a T-shirt that had END OF THE WORLD TOUR lettered across the front, my daughter entered the house.

I inquired, "What, pray tell, just occurred on the lawn?"

She shrugged one shoulder. "Nothing much."

"What's the condition of the birdbath?"

"Well, it sort of fell over."

"What caused that, Beth?"

"I accidentally drove into it with my Porsche."

"You seem to make a habit of driving into things."

She shut the door with a backward push of one foot. "I do, yeah. It's like you and your plaid shirts."

"Want a cup of herb tea?" I headed for the kitchen.

"Don't you have anything with caffeine in it?" she asked. "No, never mind. I know you don't." She followed me along the hall into the big white and yellow kitchen.

I took a half gallon of vanilla soy milk out of the yellow refrigerator, poured about a cup into my blender, peeled and cut up a banana, and tossed that in along with a spoonful of honey.

"Ugh," commented Beth as I pushed the *Blend* button.

After the machine had roared for about a minute, I turned it off and poured myself a glass and sat down at the raw-wood table. "You're really going to have to do something about your driving, kid."

She sat opposite me. "If you'd been around to teach me to drive, I'd—"

"What's going to happen with Destry?"

"I've got two of my agents, one of my attorneys, and a manager over talking to them."

"Maybe you ought to toss in a couple of personal trainers." I took a sip of my banana smoothie.

She rested an elbow on the table edge, studying me for a few silent seconds. "Can I ask you something, Dad?"

"Sure."

"How do you feel about Mom?"

"How did the residents of London feel about the Black Plague?"

"You aren't fond of her?"

"Not so you'd notice, no." I set down my glass. "What prompts this question?"

Beth leaned back in her chair. "You haven't felt differently lately?"

"As a matter of fact, I sure as hell have. But it has nothing to do with your mother," I told her. "Just last night I . . . never mind." I decided not to confide in Beth about my wolf interlude. She still lived with Mandy and I didn't want my former spouse to know what'd happened to me.

"You felt something last night?"

"Did you come here expecting to find me changed? You dropped in only two days ago, Beth, and your visits aren't usually that frequent."

"Well," she said, sighing in a disappointed way, "I was expecting you'd be more favorably inclined toward Mom."

"Why would I totally lose my powers of reason and assume an attitude like that? Why would I feel anything but fear and trembling about the woman who's going to immortalize me in a book entitled *I Married an Asshole*?"

My red-haired daughter took a deep breath, exhaled slowly. "Really effective sorcery and black magic is expensive," she began. "But, heck, I can afford it. Some friends of mine introduced me to a very effective sorcerer named Vincent X. Shandu and he—"

"I've heard of the guy. What the hell did you hire him to do?"

"Well, to bring you and Mom back together," she answered quietly. "So I'd have a *real* family again and wouldn't bang up so many cars and—"

"How was he going to do that?" I got up and stood looking down at my daughter, considerably pissed off.

"Well, with a magic potion. Guaranteed to be effective or your money back," she replied. "He took the recipe from a forbidden eighteenth-century magic book by an infamous black magician named Count Monstrodamus. He showed me his copy, the rare first edition. The one that's rumored to be bound in human skin and—"

"Have you already slipped me this damn potion?"

"Two days ago," she admitted. "I stirred it into your smoothie while you were pitting cherries to put on your bowl of granola."

I sat, slumped some. "Ask for your money back, hon," I advised. "I still can't abide your mother."

"It didn't work?"

"Oh, it was very effective but what it did was turn me into a werewolf."

She shot to her feet. "Shit, that jerk screwed up."

"That he did," I agreed. "Could you, do you think, contact this guy and have him whip up an antidote to whatever it was you actually slipped to me? Otherwise, come nightfall, the odds are I'm going to turn into a wolf-man yet again."

"Gee, I don't think I can do that right away, Dad," she answered apologetically. "See, I called him yesterday to ask why the potion was taking so long to affect you and all I got was his answering tape. Vincent is out of town."

"So where the hell did he go?"

"Into the desert to meditate."

"Which desert?"

She, sadly, shook her head. "He didn't say." Beth left her chair to come around and, tentatively, hug me. "I'm truly sorry you're a werewolf, Dad. That wasn't—trust me—my intention at all."

"Now we'll go get your car off the lawn and see if we can repair the birdbath." She stepped back and I stood.

"It's probably beyond repair."

"Well," I said, "let's hope I'm not."

The day was fading, slowly thus far, but fading nonetheless. I looked again at my watch. Almost 6:20 p.m. It was my impression that I was already commencing to itch a bit, which might be a prelude to another unwanted transformation. I unstrapped the watch and dropped it into my trouser pocket. Should I again turn into a wolf-man, I wouldn't be able to see the dial through all that grey fur.

Hersh had called at midday to tell me Fletcher Boggs, the occult investigator, had a sudden emergency case that had come up. Something involving poltergeists out in Malibu. Therefore, he wouldn't be able to consult with me until seven. And not at my place but at his home.

I was lifting my watch out of my pocket for another look when the door chimes played Monk. Sprinting down the hall, I yanked the door open. "Damn, Hersh, night is fast approaching and—"

"Relax, it's barely dusk." Turning, he started down my front steps. "Let's get going."

I was feeling increasingly itchy. As I slid into the passenger seat and buckled myself in, I asked, "Where exactly does Boggs live?"

My friend started his BMW. "Not far from here."

"And the town is?"

"Westwood."

I stiffened in my seat. "Westwood?"

"He has a cottage near UCLA."

"But Westwood Village is where that other wolf-man hangs out," I reminded him. "The police are trying to catch him. Christ, Hersh, if I turn into a werewolf before we reach Boggs, the cops may nab *me* as the Wolf-Man of Westwood."

"All you'll have to do is tell them you're really the Wolf-Man of Beverly Hills."

"I'm serious," I told him, my voice a bit froggy. "They'll start shooting at me with silver bullets; villagers will pursue me brandishing blazing torches."

"Don't fret. We'll reach the cottage long before nightfall."

"Night is already falling."

"Can you stop kvetching for a while?" He turned on the car radio. "I want to catch the news on KMA-FM. They're supposed to mention my new show on—"

". . . just in. The notorious Wolf-man of Westwood has surfaced again tonight. Just ten minutes ago he broke into a Venus' Boudoir lingerie shop and made off with an armload of frilly undies. Police expect to run him to ground soon. LAPD is sending over its special Occult SWAT team to—"

"Great," I observed as we entered Westwood Village. "Now a bunch of expert marksmen armed with high-powered rifles chock-full of silver bullets will be taking shots at me."

Hersh said, "You're not a wolf-man yet." He glanced over at me. "Oops."

I reached up a hand. It was furry. I touched my face with it. My face was furry. This time the transition from man to wolf had been swift. I hadn't even dozed off.

From about a few blocks away came the sound of sirens.

"Duck down," advised Hersh. "Keep out of sight."

I hunkered down on the floorboards with my knees near my chin and my furry arms circling my legs. The streetlights had just come on outside and every time we passed one the interior of the BMW was illuminated.

"Potential trouble up ahead. Stay down there; don't howl or make any noise."

"What sort of potential trouble?"

"People on the corner we're coming to, looking over the street and the sidewalks, about a dozen or more. Got digital cameras, cell phones. One guy's got a baseball bat," he explained quietly.

Just then Thelonious Monk began playing loudly in my pocket.

"Shut that damn phone off." Hersh halted at the corner stop sign.

More progressive piano came forth before I could tug out my cell phone and, very softly, answer it. "What?"

Hersh drove on, eyeing the world outside uneasily. "We'll be there in less than ten minutes. Keep a low profile, and a quiet one."

"I'm scrunched up as far as I can scrunch, Hersh."

"There's something I have to confess, Dad," came the voice of my daughter.

"Which of your damn cars did you smash into what?"

"No, no, this is about your current dilemma."

"We already talked about that, kid, and just at the moment I—"

"This is about why you turned into a werewolf, Dad. Did that happen again tonight, by the way?"

"It did. We can have a nice long chat about that at a later—"

"See, I did order that werewolf potion."

"Why in the hell did—"

The BMW suddenly went over something on the street we'd turned onto. Felt like part of a wooden box or something like that. The car bounced and I was thrown against the side of my improvised cubbyhole. I was suddenly visited by a very painful cramp.

"Hold on, Beth. I've got a cramp and I have to stretch my leg for a second."

I eased painfully up off the floorboards to try to straighten out my leg.

Simultaneously the car passed a light post and a bunch of college kids who were emerging from a Burger Oasis. They got a very brief glimpse of me before I hunkered back down.

"Oh, God," screamed a coed. "It's him!"

"It's the Wolf-Man!"

"Call the cops on your cell, Julie!"

Hersh gunned the motor and went bouncing along the night street. He skidded around a corner, drove down an alley to the next street over, slowed, and entered a darker, quieter, less frequented street. "I don't think they got my license number."

My leg still hurt, and my heart was beating at an unfamiliar rate. "Tell me about the potion, Beth," I said into the phone.

"Are you okay? What was all that noise?"

"Villagers spotted me, but we eluded them. None of them had flaming torches."

"Well, listen, Dad. I meant the werewolf gunk for Bryson Kranbuhl."

"Your mother's literary agent? The despicable oaf who suggested she write *I Married an Asshole?*"

"That Bryson Kranbuhl, yes. He's also been trying to sell the memoir as a TV serial. He's convinced that it can be the next *Survivor*," she continued. "I ordered the potion for him. I was hoping it would distract him and also inspire Mom to evict the guy. She, you know, isn't much of an animal lover. Bryson's been pretty much living with us since early this year."

"You're saying you got the two philters mixed up and gave me *his* potion?"

"No, Dad, I'm saying that imbecile Vincent X. Shandu screwed up and sold me two doses of werewolf potion and none of love potion," she explained. "I'm going to drive down to Palm Springs, since there's a lot of desert around there and maybe I can find him and—"

"No, nope. Don't *drive* anywhere," I cautioned her. "I think we have another way to work a cure. So you wait until—"

"We're there," announced Hersh, braking the car on what felt like a gravel driveway.

"Stay where you are until I contact you," I told my daughter. "Bye."

"Information from your nitwit offspring?" Hersh came around to my side of the BMW, opened the door, and helped me get myself off the floor.

"Yeah, now I know who the Wolf-Man of Westwood is," I replied as I emerged.

Fletcher Boggs was circling the straight-back chair I was sitting uncomfortably upon. He was a tall, broad-shouldered man of about sixty, tanned and with an impressive head of white hair. "Vincent X. Shandu is second-rate," he observed, halting in front of me and scrutinizing my face. "You're not much of a werewolf."

"Sufficient enough for me."

"You're not even an authentic wolf," the big occult investigator said, stepping back. "You aren't four-legged, you don't have a bushy tail; except for two canines, your teeth aren't even especially lupine."

Hersh had settled onto a low tan sofa across the cottage parlor. "Be that as it may, Fletcher, can you reverse the effect of the potion?"

Boggs frowned at him. "A defrocked veterinarian could do that." He returned his attention to me. "Tell me what your daughter told you about this stuff she fed you. By the way, is she going to get back on *Posy Pickwick*?"

"Negotiations are under way," I told him. "About the potion. Beth told me Shandu took it from a book of magic by a fellow named Count Monstrodamus, who flourished in the eighteenth century."

"Actually he flourished through several centuries," said the occult investigator. "The Count wasn't immortal, but he hung on for almost three hundred years. Sounds like Vince was borrowing from a copy of *The Vile and Unholy Spells, Potions and Incantations of the Infamous, Black-Souled Magus, the Notorious Count Monstrodamus, Late of Vienna*. Any idea which edition?"

"The first. The one that's supposed to be bound in human skin."

Boggs shook his head. "Bullshit. It's only goat skin," he said. "But the first edition version of the werewolf potion is slightly different from the one in later editions."

Hersh asked, "You have a copy?"

"Too expensive." He crossed to the PC that rested on a

tile-topped, iron-legged table against the wall. "I've modified my computer so it can access just about every forbidden sorcery book known to man."

"Who put that stuff on the Net?" I asked him.

"Various adepts." He seated himself at the computer. "I'll take a look at the Count's formula, then look up a surefire antidote. Did I mention my fee?"

"Not as yet."

"Since you're a buddy of Bernie's, I'll give you the discount. It'll run you, soon as you're satisfied with the cure, six hundred ninety-five bucks."

"I can afford that," I assured him.

I put on a fresh plaid shirt, buttoned several buttons and stepped into the john to observe my image.

I was my normal everyday self, as I had been since late last night when I'd swallowed the six ounces of Fletcher Boggs's antidote to the werewolf potion my madcap daughter had slipped into my morning smoothie. Considering what I was paying, I expected he'd serve me out of something more upscale than an old peanut butter jar.

The important thing, though, was that the stuff cured my lycanthropy in a matter of minutes. Outside of severe nausea, heart palpitations, double vision, and cramps for about a half hour, there were no side effects to speak of. Since last night I hadn't turned into a wolf-man again. And I noticed this morning that I didn't even need to shave. Hopefully I was cured.

I'd been in the kitchen less than a minute, when I heard a rattling crash out on the front half acre. That was followed by a large splash.

Setting the half gallon of vanilla soy milk that I'd just fetched out of the refrigerator down next to the blender, I ran outside.

Beth, wearing a bright yellow singlet, crimson cycling pants, and a silver cycling helmet, was stepping gingerly out of the fishpond. This was a few feet from where the birdbath once had stood.

A black ten-speed bike was partially submerged among the lily pads and agitated goldfish.

"Have you run out of cars, child?" I inquired, bending and hefting the bicycle out of the greenish water.

"I made a vow not to drive a car of any kind for six months."

"In church?"

"In the Will Destry offices," my daughter explained. "Part of the deal everybody worked up to put me back on *Posy Pickwick: Rock & Roll Detective.*"

"So you're gainfully employed again." I laid the dripping bike out on the lawn.

"I'm going to hire a chauffeur tomorrow, but today I used one of my bicycles to ride over to visit you."

"As I told you last night, I am no longer a werewolf. If all goes well, I never shall be again."

Beth said, "I've got some great news for you."

"Such as?"

"Mom has thrown Bryson out and fired him as her literary agent."

"Oh, so? What prompted that?"

My pretty red-haired daughter sat down on the stone bench beside the fishpond. "Well, I don't know if you've heard, but the police caught the Wolf-Man of Westwood last night."

"I thought that might happen."

"Bright and early this morning they looked into the cell they popped him in last night," she continued. "There was Bryson Kranbuhl. He told the cops who he was, but he didn't have any ID on him. They let him call Mom and she came down to Westwood to identify that jerk and bail him out."

"Sounds like an act of deep affection to me."

She shook her head. "Once she knew he was the Wolf-Man, she realized why Westwood was where he was always spotted," she said. "Mom had suspected that Bryson had a tootsie in Westwood and had been spending some afternoons and evenings with her. She also thought his impulse to swipe women's underwear was tacky. So he's out."

"What about *I Married an Asshole*?"

"She's shelved that for now while she rethinks the project," my daughter informed me. "So, Dad, this is a perfect time for you to get back together. Don't you think so?"

Crossing, I sat beside her and put a hand on her shoulder. "Probably not."

She looked sad. "Couldn't you at least drop by and have dinner with us some night?"

After a moment I answered, "That might be possible."

Beth smiled and clapped her hands together. "Neat. Then my efforts haven't been in vain."

"That's one way to look at it," I said.

Kvetchula's Daughter

DARRELL SCHWEITZER

The day my mother became a vampire, she ruined my life. *I* didn't know it at the time, and I'm sure *she* didn't have time to think about it—I have to admit that being dead and coming back to life more-or-less can be distracting—but that's God's honest truth and if I were of a slightly different persuasion I'd add "cross my heart and hope to die."

Give me a *break*!

It wasn't as if I were not *beside* myself with worry, what with Momma and Poppa off on their trip to Romania, *he* being, though he is my father and I love him, such a nebbish he never stood up to her about anything, so when he booked the two of them on that Dracula Fan Club tour or whatever it was with *non-refundable tickets,* you could have heard Momma's jaw drop in Brooklyn, as she observed at the time, and we don't live anywhere near Brooklyn.

My poppa, he was bats about bats, and about Dracula and Children of the Night and all that stuff. He had a vampire-movie collection like you wouldn't believe. I think it was the one thing Momma couldn't take away from him. After I went off to college and they were alone, he got even *battier,* and so they went on this tour that was supposed to last two weeks, and after they didn't come back and I didn't hear a thing from them for *six months,* you think I shouldn't worry?

It was one thing, that two weeks, during my spring break, me back in the old house, watching Poppa's movies when there was nothing else to do—he really does have a dubbed copy of *Mein Yiddishe Drakula*—and taking care of the cats. The cats, Elvira and Vlad. Poppa named them before Momma could. Just as well because *she* probably would have called them Pusscha and Poopsie.

Me, I am nothing like my mother, which is just as well, but I have to worry.

My *putzy*, sometime boyfriend Max, he says maybe they were carried off by the fairies, and I said no, in the Balkans you get carried off by the Gypsies. Ireland, fairies; Romania, Gypsies. Got it?

So Max, not worrying—I should have shot him—says, "Maybe Dracula turned her into a vampire . . ." and I have to laugh, despite my worries, because Momma is so *short*. What would she do, stand on a stepladder so she can reach people's necks to bite them?

Max has no idea what he is talking about.

Then the *packages* arrive, delivered by Gypsies. The truck says TRANSYLVANIAN PARCEL SERVICE, but I know these guys are Gypsies because what kind of delivery men wear scarves and earrings and make jokes about pulling one over on the *gajos* while hauling these *enormous* packages into the living room? I have to make sure the silverware doesn't disappear.

Max and I are left staring at these two boxes the size of phonebooths, which are marked DO NOT OPEN UNTIL SUNDOWN but today is Tuesday so the Shabbat rules do not apply, so what the hell does this mean? I want to know.

Nevertheless, it is getting late and starting to get dark, and God knows what's inside these packages, so we close the curtains. Then Max and I whack away at the first crate with hammers and big screwdrivers. Dirt pours out onto Momma's immaculate living-room rug, and the lid comes off, and inside is a *coffin* packed in more dirt. To get *that* open, we have to remove a whole bunch of *silver* nails, which are probably worth something, so I put them carefully aside.

The coffin lid *creaks* open just like in the movies. As soon as *Momma*, lying inside it, sees the hammer in my hand, and I see *her*, we *both* scream so loudly we could split the eardrums of everybody from Jersey City to Canton, China. She clutches her chest and says, "Go ahead, drive a stake through your poor mother's heart. You've already broken it!"

I let the hammer drop to the floor. It lands on my foot. While I'm hopping around in pain, I say, "I have?"

And Momma, she looks so *weird*, I should say *terrible*—her hair all frizzed up and tangled, her nails like *claws,* her *face* so pale and sunken like a balloon that's lost most of its air, and her *eyes* so dark and somehow *burning* that I can't look away from them. Momma, she turns to Max (who also drops his hammer but misses his foot) and says, "No mother, living or dead, wants to come home after so many trials and tribulations to find out her daughter's still messing with a *sheygets*."

"But, Mom—" I say.

"But *nothing*. When are you going to get a serious boyfriend, somebody with a future, somebody you can *marry, one of your own kind*?"

Max blurts out, "Who said anything about marriage?"

I stare at her, dumbfounded. Max is a bit of a doofus. He works in a flower shop and makes tie-dyed T-shirts on weekends and would have been a hippie if he'd been born a generation earlier. Maybe he's not such a good prospect, but this is a stupid time to bring this up.

Apropos of not knowing what else to say, I get defensive. "But, Momma, I *like* Max."

Max beams at me like a dope, "You *do*?"

I don't bother to explain that much of the time I'm not entirely sure of that because Max does have his shortcomings. But before I can utter another word Momma gets out of that coffin, opens her mouth to reveal *huge, dripping* fangs, and *slinks* over to Max in a way that no respectable short, *zaftig*, middle-aged woman should, and says, "Well, if you're going to marry him, he has to convert." She pronounces it *convoit*, her accent having somehow grown a lot thicker.

I stamp my foot (not the one the hammer landed on) and shake my finger at her. "Momma, we've been over this before! Get used to it! Max doesn't want to become a *Jew*!"

Momma's fangs somehow arc out of her mouth the way a rattlesnake's do and still (I have no idea how) she's able to say, "That's not what I have in mind."

Now there's a loud pounding from inside the other box. Momma pulls back, her fangs disappear back into her mouth, and she looks as close to normal as she is going to since stepping out of that coffin. She is Momma again and she's giving orders.

"Marsha, let your father out. We need to have a family discussion. Max, you help her."

So we let him out, carefully removing six more valuable-looking silver nails, which Momma cringes from and won't even look at. Soon the coffin lid creaks open and there's my father, dressed in black cape and black pants, white shirt, vest, medallion, and one of those bat-shaped ties I know Momma has always hated—it *doesn't* go with the outfit—and his eyes are red and gleaming and he makes a claw out of one hand as if he's trying to hypnotize me, and says in a thick, thick accent, *"I vant to drink your blllooodd!!"*

Then he trips over his cape and stumbles out onto the rug amid an *avalanche* of dirt that will be *impossible* to clean up. Somehow he twists around and lands on his butt, and there he is sitting in the dirt, staring up at me while his mechanical bat-tie flaps pathetically, only one of its wings working.

"Marsha?"

"Hello, Poppa."

I help him up, taking him by the hand.

"Brrr! Poppa, you're *cold*!"

"There's a lot to explain."

At our family conference, a *lot* that needs to be explained is explained. Max is there, holding on nervously to his hammer and screwdriver, as if that would do him any good. After all, he *might* become family, or at least Momma wants to allow for the possibility. Besides, he knows too much now.

"After all I've *given up* for you," she moans, meaning me, not Max. She doesn't care a rat's ass about Max.

And I break in, saying that I had to *give up* a whole semester at Bryn Mawr to be here minding the house *just in case* she and Poppa should somehow reappear out of nowhere, and I did take care of Elvira and Vlad just fine, and I can't help it if they hiss and run and hide when Momma comes near them. (They hide from Poppa, too; he's really unhappy about that.) And she has the nerve (I almost say *noive* but stop myself) to tell *me* to stop kvetching when she, my mother, is the world's greatest *kvetch,* a Niagara Falls of guilt poured out, a woman put on Earth by God to *complain* about how things aren't right and make people feel guilty about them. I think the only reason she doesn't want me *kvetching* is she's afraid I may have inherited some of her talent for it and she wants to make sure that if anybody in this house is going to *kvetch,* it's going to be *her*, no competition allowed.

And she says, "Besides, you're not going back to that snooty school, anyway."

And when I say, "What?" she *explains* that there have been some, uh, *changes,* like she and Poppa are technically dead now, but not in any sense that really matters; they'll just have to keep different hours. Then she tells the whole story about how Poppa *dragged* her on this Children of the Night Special tour of Transylvania, and after *days* of wandering into one crypt after another, something *happened* and now they're both vampires, which did not, I gather, change her disposition much, or stop her *kvetching*. Although she's vague on the details, I gather that after some months of bouncing around in crummy coffins listening to Gypsy jokes, and reaching people's necks, not with a stepladder, but by getting people to bend over to look at a map of Bucharest when she asked them for directions (even if she was in some other city), and realizing she was *still* being her old self, not *svelte* like the vampire women in movies, she *kvetched* all the way up the chain of command until Dracula himself couldn't stand her anymore and had her and Poppa nailed up in special coffins with silver nails so they couldn't get out. But *even then* she *kvetched* so much (he could still hear her; vampires have very good hearing), he finally gave up and shipped the two of them home.

She finishes deciding, "So the best thing for all of us, will be that I should bite you, and, *ugh*, your father can bite Max, and then we'll all be a vampire family together."

Max raises his hammer and his screwdriver and crosses them. When Momma glares at him, he drops them to the floor: *clunk, clunk.*

I put my hand to my throat. "Momma, gee, you'll never get any grandkids that way."

Then Poppa pipes up, which is amazing, since he never interrupts when Momma's Decided and Made Up Her Mind About What Is Best. Now he says, "Wait a minute, Honey Love"—a name he calls Momma when he's trying to wheedle something out of her—"sometimes it's useful for our kind to be cared for by mortals, like that nice Mr. Renfield we met—"

And Momma rears up, eyes blazing, fangs gleaming, and she says, *"No* daughter of mine is going to eat bugs!!"

"That may not be necessary, Honey Love—"

She nods to Max. "Now *he* can eat all the bugs he wants, but not Marsha Leibowitz."

So the family conference ends and I get to stay among the living, and so does Max, although Momma puts the whammy on him and before long he *does* eat bugs, insisting that they're organic and all-natural and taste like roasted peanuts, rather than simply disgusting. I can't imagine what I ever saw in him.

But he is really helpful around the house, once you get used to his gibbering, drooling, and constantly looking around for insectile snacks. The place seems to be overrun with bugs now and Momma will *not* allow me to call an exterminator. So, bugs and all, Max and I have to break up the basement floor with jackhammers—and I will *kill* anybody who asks if it ruined my nails—and dig a pit for the two coffins to rest side by side in their "native" New Jersey earth (with all the Transylvanian earth I could vacuum off the carpet thrown in for good measure), and, by day, that's where my parents sleep.

Yes, I know that vampires are *evil* and totally given over to Satan and a menace to be destroyed, yadda yadda yadda, but she's still my *mother,* and if you know *my* mother, you don't worry about such things as going to Hell. Hell on Earth is having to listen to her *kvetching,* which she can keep up until Hell freezes over unless she gets her own way.

Poppa has Max fix up a flat-screen TV on the inside of his coffin lid and hook up the VCR to it so he can watch tapes during the daytime.

I never return to Bryn Mawr, but after some whining I get to transfer to Columbia, which is in Manhattan, to which I commute as a day student. But I'm under strict instructions to get home every evening by dusk, so I can help her and Poppa out of their coffins and "see them off" for their "evening rounds," as Momma calls it. "Terrorizing the countryside" is what Poppa calls it, as he swirls out the door in that ridiculous outfit with the cape. If he doesn't turn into a bat and fly away, he'd like me and Max to think he does. I'm past caring.

Can you *imagine* what this does to my social life? Max has moved in. I can watch him eat bugs, or watch TV, or do my homework. I become very studious. I get straight A's. But believe me, romance is not on the roster.

The *scary* part of all this is that sometimes I am not sure I really *am* living with my parents anymore, or with two all-devouring *things*, who will gobble up even me at the end. When your parents are undead, you can never be certain they love you. It causes anxiety, believe me.

Then there is the one time I dare to bring over my best friend Sylvie for a night of shared homework and girl talk—and miraculously she is willing to put up with the bugs and the *stench* of the place. Did I tell you that vampire lairs *smell bad*? I could go on and on . . . I even convince her that Max is a retarded cousin the two of us should lock in the basement (we do, and he sits down there contentedly chomping on bugs). Things are going swimmingly, and I feel almost *normal* for once, when suddenly I'm not sure what is happening, and there is a *mist* sliding under the bedroom door, and that mist has red eyes in it and looks a bit like my mother. It might be a dream. I am not sure. I can't move. I want to call out, but I can't, and when I really do wake up, there is Sylvie on the bed next to me, pale as the other white meat with two holes in the side of her neck and her eyes crossed and rolled up.

Oy vey. So Max and I have to carry Sylvie out into a deserted lot and bury her in a cardboard box, which is very dangerous because the police might see us, but Momma likes her privacy and won't share the basement (which she now calls "the crypt") with just *anybody*. And most nights afterwards Sylvie comes floating to my second-floor bedroom window, tapping on the glass, asking to be let in, and before long she's as much a nuisance as Max.

But I feel sorry for her and maybe I am even afraid of her. It is not her fault, what happened. But she also has that hungry, hungry, *empty* look in her eyes, and sometimes I am not sure if it's even Sylvie, just those eyes and a mouth full of sharp teeth that talks like my best friend.

Everybody has their breaking point, and I have mine. I think I'm already past it. But what can I do? I am not made of glass, that I can literally *break*.

I get on the Internet. I go to lots of chat rooms. I become something of a celebrity, but everybody thinks I am making this up. People don't take me seriously. They tell me how much they like my stories. The editor of *Weird Tales* asks me to send him something. I also get people writing to know what flavor of bugs I like, and am I really a hunchback, because hunchbacks are supposed to be the servants of vampires—and I write back, *No, that's mad scientists, you dork!* because this is my *mother* you are talking about—and I get some *very* odd spam, a lot of it from a dead African oil minister turned zombie who wants to get together with me to share the $30 million he intends to smuggle out of his country in a coffin.

And then at last there is a message that merely says: *I think I can help you.—Heinrich.*

Heinrich?

Is your last name Van Helsing by any chance? I want to know.

No, it is Schroeder.

What do you want? I type.

I want to meet you, he types back.

Now this is *so* mysterious, and everything your mother ever warned you about when messing on the Internet, but when you have a mother like *mine,* maybe you take her warnings with a grain of . . . garlic? (And that's *another* thing—ever since the Big Change, there is *no* pizza allowed in our house, but I am babbling . . .)

I am thrilled. Also desperate. I am almost ready to fling myself into the arms of the zombie African oil minister, or certainly a mad scientist's hunchbacked assistant as long as his breath smells like garlic, and in such a deranged state of mind I tell my new friend Heinrich Schroeder that I would like to meet him.

So we make arrangements to get together.

At night.

Alone.

In a lonely graveyard near Hoboken.

This breaks *so* many rules that it just adds to the thrill. So I stay late after school. I eat a light supper at a Pizza Hut, and then wait some more, until it is dark. Yes, I know Momma will be mad, but I don't *care;* I'm that desperate. In any case, I know she can take care of herself, and that idiot-retard Max will be able stop eating bugs long enough to cope with any vampire-hunters who might want to sprinkle holy water into the basement or whatever else they might do.

It'll be *okay.* I tell myself that over and over as I get off the PATH train in Hoboken and walk down a dark street between dingy buildings, until I come to another street, which is even darker and dingier, and my footsteps are going faster, faster, tap-tap, tap-tap, like in the movies when the girl is about to get jumped, only I don't get jumped, and eventually I climb through a broken fence and into an old, deserted graveyard. There *are* such places in the New York area. Not everything is modern and built-up. Probably nobody has been buried here for a hundred years, and if anyone or anything climbs up out of a grave to get me, I'll just tell him or it who my parents are.

Not that such a thing happens. Heinrich is waiting for me on a bench, in the one spot where a little light from a streetlamp shines through the gnarly trees.

When he stands up to greet me, like a perfect gentleman, I see that he is *big*. My head doesn't even come to his shoulders. He is broad-shouldered, like two or three linebackers crammed into one body, and I can see that he's one of these guys whose face is always hairy no matter how many times he shaves, but maybe my senses are getting sharper from hanging around vampires so much, because I can *smell* him in a *good* way, not BO but an *alive* odor that excites me more than I can understand, and when he takes my hand in his and his grip is firm and so hard it almost breaks my hand, but *warm*, I'm instantly *in love!* Before we even say a word, we fall into each other's arms, on the ground, rolling in the leaves, heaving with such passion that a decent girl like me (ahem!) will have to leave out some of the details.

Later we talk quite a lot, and I pour my heart out to him, the whole story, and he is *so* understanding. He has seen and experienced strange things, too, he says. He believes me. He *knows* I am telling the truth.

I look into his eyes. I may never look anywhere else again.

"You have to get away," he says.

"But I don't want to hurt Momma's feelings."

"She's a minion of evil, a blood-drinking demon of darkness."

"I know, but she's my mom. Besides, one tries not to be judgmental about alternate lifestyles."

"That's the college girl talking, not the real you," he says, and takes me in his arms again and once more we are rolling on the ground, making hay in the dead leaves, if you will pardon the expression, and *oh!* I have never felt anything like this and *oh!* goes on and on, and *oh!* I don't care what Mom and Dad think, I just want to be with Heinrich.

"I might have a few deep, dark secrets of my own," he says afterwards. "I am glad you are not judgmental."

Then I suggest that maybe we should take the silver nails and nail my parents back into their coffins. It won't be such an inconvenience for them because they're immortal, so we could live out our lives and maybe let them loose again when we're eighty or so—but at the first mention of *silver,* Heinrich hisses and recoils as if I'd handed him a live snake.

Which is very odd. But do you expect me to have a *normal* boyfriend?

Then Heinrich has to leave. He leaves, quickly.

"I love you!" I shout after him, but he's vanished into the darkness.

There is indeed hell to pay when I get home, close to dawn, about the same time Momma and Poppa do, and even Poppa is beside himself with rage, his eyes burning red, his fangs dripping. He's gotten his bat-tie repaired. Both wings are flapping furiously.

"*You* are one *disobedient* minion!" Momma screams as she *oozes* toward me in that odd, rolly-polly *slink* that is so hard to describe. Her eyes are all fire, too, and her fangs are out.

"Damn it, Mother! I'm not a minion! I'm your daughter!"

Just then Max shambles into the room, a gigantic, live cockroach wriggling between his teeth. His back has been broken in several places, almost tied into a pretzel, though he doesn't seem to feel any pain. Vampires really do have powers science can't understand. Max is now a genuine hunchback of the finest quality, two-humped like a dromedary.

"Now *that's* a minion!" I shout.

Momma shouts, too, orders to Max, who is surprisingly agile despite his condition, and surprisingly strong, not to mention *horrible* smelling, as he grabs me and drags me up the front stairs like a sack of laundry, while both of my parents are hovering over me, their faces hideous masks with red eyes and gleaming fangs, like something seen in a dream, and the cockroach in Max's teeth seems to be saying, "You're a naughty, naughty girl and you're *grounded for life!*"

Maybe they've put the whammy on me, because there is a gap in my memory, and when I wake up I am on my bed in my bedroom. The first thing I do is put my hand to my throat to see if I feel warm, and I do. That calms me a little, but I get up woozily and only gradually discover, to my increasing rage, that the door to my room has been nailed shut, and there are boards nailed over all the windows.

My little prison consists of the bedroom and the adjoining bathroom. Someone or something (probably Max, who seems to have razor-sharp teeth these days) has *gnawed* a bit of the bottom of the door away, enough to make a slot where food can be slid in to the prisoner.

There's a bowl of soggy Cheerios on a plate, but there's a bug swimming in it and I push it back out.

So that's how it is.

Yes, it is. I can't go to college anymore. I can't go anywhere. I am held prisoner, starving, occasionally able to nibble on the less disgusting things Max provides. (The lunch meat isn't too bad. I can even manage the stale doughnuts.)

Every evening I hear my parents rise from their coffins. I hear everything. I think my senses *are* heightened beyond what is normal. The lids creak, I think, because they like it that way. They *could* oil the hinges, but it would be against proper vampire style. They go out. They come in a little before dawn, exchanging a few pleasantries. "Did you have a good time, Morris?" "Yes,

Honey Love." Sometimes I overhear a few words about "What are we going to do with our daughter? What *can* we do?" followed by assurances (from Poppa) that all parents go through this with teenaged daughters and things will work out.

Yes, they will. Thank God for the Internet. Max is too addled and I don't think my parents ever quite understood what computers are for, particularly a wireless connection through a laptop. (They've ripped out my phone.) If I am typing away, they think I am doing my homework.

("*Could* we let her go back to school?" Poppa asks. "She's still working so hard." Momma just hisses like a snake and that settles that.)

I type away, day and night. By day, idiot Max the hunchback is there to make sure I don't escape. At night, my old friend Sylvie still hovers outside the window like a Halloween version of Tinkerbell in a trailing shroud, tapping her skeletal fingers on the windows, asking me to let her in. I don't, but she's still out there, certain to make sure I can't go *out*.

Where *did* she get the shroud, anyway? She was wearing jeans and a top when we buried her. But I can't bring myself to care anymore.

I type and type. I find Heinrich again, and we exchange e-mails fast and furious.

I too am a creature of darkness, he types. *You might not be happy with me. I have a terrible secret.*

Yeah, yeah. I DON'T CARE!

You sure?

YES I AM SURE. COME AND GET ME!

I shall rescue you, then, as a knight would rescue a maiden imprisoned in a tower. It's very romantic, really.

Yes, it is, and I spend my days and nights dreaming of him, imagining that I am with him, that he is in my bed, doing things a nice girl like me doesn't talk about. I spend hours before my mirror trying to make myself presentable for him. We talk over the Internet every day, sometimes all day, but the one thing I can't understand is why I have to *wait*. Why can't he come and get me *right now?*

These things have to be done right, for the sake of romance, he types.

I don't care!

But you should, my sweet. There is, too, the matter that my power will not be at its greatest until the end of the month.

I have experienced enough of his power to last me a lifetime and I want more, but I do, ultimately, have to wait. The routine goes on. I listen to what Mom and Dad say to each other every morning after they come back from terrorizing the countryside. I can even hear the soundtrack of the movies Poppa plays inside his coffin.

I cross the days off the calendar.

28th, 29th, 30th.

And then, just after sundown, the front door *explodes* like it's been dynamited, and I hear Max yelping and then such *screams* and snarls as you've never heard before, like there's a rabies outbreak at the zoo, and furniture is crashing.

Then Max is whimpering outside my door.

"It might hurt the Master and Mistress! It might hurt them!"

Crash! Smash! *Howl.*

It?

I pound on the door.

"Max, can you hear me?"

He whimpers and whines and slobbers. I hope I have his attention.

"Max! *Let me out!*"

"Can't!"

The chaos downstairs continues. It doesn't sound as if Mom and Dad are getting the best of it. The whole house begins to shake and sway. If this goes on much longer, the place may be ripped off its foundations.

"Max! *I can help them!*"

Max stops whimpering, and, in a voice that sounds almost like his old self, asks a surprisingly intelligent question. "But why should you help them after what they've done to you?"

"Max! They're my *parents*! Can't you understand that?"

Then he's tearing away the boards nailed to the door, and in a moment, I'm walking downstairs into what used to be the living room, with Max shambling somewhere behind me.

There isn't much of the downstairs left. The walls are out. The TV is smashed to bits and smoldering. Most of the furniture is in splinters. Wading through what used to be the dining room, a huge, hairy Thing faces off against my parents, circling as they do. Momma's dress is in tatters. Poppa's cape is gone, and his vest and starched shirt are shredded, and *everybody's* claws are covered with I-don't-want-to-know-what. Everybody's eyes are blazing like furnaces. They lunge at one another, jump out of the way, parry, and thrust with their whole bodies like fencers.

"Stop it! All of you!" I scream at the top of my lungs, and somehow, like my hearing and my sense of smell, my voice has become something it didn't used to be, and the whole house shakes with the sound of it, and they all stop and turn toward me, their eyes still blazing, fangs gleaming.

Quickly I reach into one of the few surviving pieces of furniture, a little sideboard cabinet, and take out two of the long silver nails I had carefully placed there when we opened my parents' coffins for the first time.

It's trite, I know, and not what you'd expect from someone of my background, but I actually hold up the two long nails like a *cross* as I say, "Now everybody back off."

They do, equally recoiling from the silver nails.

"Mom, Dad . . . is that you, Heinrich?" The Big Hairy

Thing nods, breathing heavily. "Mom, Dad, you have to learn to let go. I'm grown-up now. You have your life—or unlife or whatever it is—and I have mine. I'm not a *minion*. I'm your *daughter*. I ask you to respect that. Do you think you actually can? Do you?"

The fire fades from their eyes, and their fangs retract. Heinrich, a.k.a. the Hairy Thing, just stands there, panting.

Before anyone can say anything, I continue.

"Mom, Dad, I've got an announcement to make. I'm not the same as I once was. I've been . . . *bitten.*"

For an instant I can see Momma's eyes beam with pride, in the sense of *our little girl has grown up,* but then she seems just confused, because she knows it isn't what she thought.

I turn to show her the bruise on my neck, which I've had for a month now. "That ain't a hickey, Momma."

She just looks stupefied.

"Momma, I want you to meet Heinrich. I love him."

The Hairy Thing leans over, as if to lick my face the way a dog would, but then whines and draws away from the silver.

That is when I realize my hands are smoking and the silver nails are burning *me*. I let them drop to the floor, and before anyone can react, I rush over to the window, tear aside the drapes, and let the light of the *full moon* flood what is left of the dining room.

I begin to change then. Fur grows on my arms and legs. I feel my whole body melting, falling down, hardening into something else. My senses are much sharper than they've ever been before. It's as if I can hear a cloud passing across the face of the moon, like silk wiped across glass, and I can hear every sound of the night. I can see in ways that I've never seen before, *through* things, sensing heat and *life*. Were I so inclined I could tell Max where every bug in the whole damn house is hiding.

But I am not so inclined. Heinrich nuzzles me behind the ear.

We play. I try to say something more to my parents, and I think I actually do manage to say, "His middle name is Wolfgang."

And my mother sputters, "But he's *not Jewish*!" and she is sobbing in Poppa's arms. "We've lost our daughter!"

"No," Poppa says, "It'll be all right, Honey Love, as long as the . . . er . . . cubs are brought up Jewish."

Howling, Heinrich Wolfgang Schroeder and I leap through the window, out into the night.

What beautiful music we make.

And Bob's Your Uncle

CHELSEA QUINN YARBRO

Sometimes when it was night and Uncle Bob and Mom were fighting, Jake would go to the park and sit on the swings, listening to the rush of traffic on Franklin Boulevard and enjoying the dark. Everyone said the park was dangerous at night, but Jake had never had any trouble there, in spite of all the rumors of bad things happening. Jake thought it was far more dangerous to remain at home when the adults were fighting: Uncle Bob was using his fists and Mom was throwing things. Just last week she'd smashed his PlayStation by accident; Uncle Bob thought it was funny.

Uncle Bob wasn't Jake's real uncle, or so his mother had explained a year or so ago. "But, Jake, he's like family. He takes care of us, not like the rest of our relatives; you know what they're like . . ." She stopped and went on in a more subdued but injured tone, "Since your father died . . ."

Jake couldn't remember his father, not really: the man had vanished when he was four, and that was more than half his lifetime ago. He relied on his mother to keep his father's memory alive, but the things Mom said about his father changed over time; Jake could still remember when Mom had said it was a good thing he wasn't alive anymore—that was shortly before she met Bob. "I get it that you want to have a guy around." He shifted awkwardly in his slightly-too-large running shoes. Jake was small for his age and was often mistaken for being younger than nine, and it didn't help that, being undersized, his clothes made him look like a kid since he wore younger children's apparel because it fit, a constant reminder about how dissimilar he was to his classmates; he hated the teasing he endured. Along with that, he also hated it when his mom got down on one knee to look him in the eye, and he knew from Mom's voice what was coming next. "But does it have to be him? Uncle Bob?"

She dropped down on one knee, so that she had to look up into his face. "Listen, Jake, you're almost ten, and you can understand things very well. You're really mature for your age, and you've always been a bastion for me. I couldn't have made it this far without you." She often called him a bastion when she was about to ask him to do something unpleasant. "If you can just try to get along with him. Just a little."

"I do try. He's the one who picks the fights." He rarely let himself be dragged into Uncle Bob's ranting, but for the last six months, the verbal barrage had increased and had been punctuated with vigorous slaps which Uncle Bob justified by blaming Jake for making him angry. Jake's mom always tried to make Jake understand that Uncle Bob didn't mean it—it was just that work was so hard and he thought it was unfair to be denied another promotion, or that he had had a bad week at poker, or that he was really tired and didn't want anything noisy around him.

"Well, Jake, I need you to try harder. If you aren't willing to help improve the family, then I think you may need an extra two hours in your room." It was her usual threat, one she never actually followed through on: Jake would have loved more time in his room, even if it wasn't very big and at the opposite end of the L-shaped house from the bathroom. At least his room was quiet, and it had two windows, either of which he could leave through if he wanted to.

"That would be okay with me," said Jake, disheartened to have his mother take Uncle Bob's side again. "I can do homework, and read."

Esther Sparges frowned. "Don't you have anyone you'd like to study with? You have friends at school—everyone does. Wouldn't one of your friends like to have you over to play games or work on projects together?" She had that wheedling note in her voice, as if she were offering him a treat rather than trying to get rid of him.

"Not really," he said, not wanting to admit that he had no friends at school, just a couple of geeks he hung around with occasionally, who had the same taste as he did for spooky video games; he was especially fond of *Shape Shifter*.

Shaking her head, Esther got to her feet and began to pace. "I wish I knew what to do with you, Jacob Edwin Sparges, I really do. You're a good kid, but you get up Bob's nose every time you open your mouth. I hate being put in the middle of you two." She clutched her elbows, her hands working. "It's never easy when you have to blend a family. I wish you could make just a little more effort."

Only we aren't a family, thought Jake, and we aren't blending. "Yeah."

"If I could work something out with your Aunt Judy, but she believes everything Denny and Jennine tell her. They're all against him, my whole family, and won't give him a break," Esther said aloud to herself. "Judy's very closed-minded; she just doesn't listen to reason about Bob."

Jake went very still. "What do you mean?" He tried not to hope.

"Well, if you could stay with her for a while, until Bob and I work a few things out, it would be a lot easier on all of us, and that means for you as well as Bob and me. You've been one of her favorites, and it isn't as if she has kids of her own." She flung her arms wide in exasperation, then grabbed her elbows again. "You'd like to spend time with her, wouldn't you?"

"Prob'ly," Jake said, not wanting to sound too willing.

"But she says she won't help me until I get rid of Bob. She says Bob's bad for me—as if she knows." She touched the livid smudge on her jaw and scowled. "It's not as if men grow on trees."

"Sure, Mom," said Jake, wishing he had some excuse to get out of the dining room and have some time for himself, so that he could think.

There was a sound of the front door opening. Esther said, "Run along and do your homework. I'll call you when dinner's ready."

Glad for this opportunity, Jake bolted from the dining room and headed to his own place where he could read in peace.

Later that night, when Mom and Uncle Bob were starting to shout again, Jake slipped out the window and hurried off to the park. It was chilly so he had put on his anorak and pulled up the hood, but he wasn't really warm as he sat on the swing, not moving, and stared out into the darkness beyond the lights on the four tall poles around the playground, casting more glare than illumination. He figured he would remain for another hour and then head home; the yelling should have stopped, and the two of them would be in their bedroom, making up for all the bad things they'd said. At least his homework was done and he would probably be able to get some sleep before he had to be up again. It felt better here alone than it felt in his bedroom right now. He had been scratching in the sand with a long, thin branch, making patterns at his feet when he noticed shining eyes at the edge of the light.

"Who's there?" he called out. His question was met with

silence. Jake felt a moment of fear, but then he realized it wasn't a person looking at him; it was a big, black dog, with a long muzzle and a thick coat. As Jake stared at the creature, it gave a tentative wave of its tail. Jake got off the swing and started toward it, going slowly so as not to frighten the animal.

The black dog sat down and waited for the boy.

"Hey, fella," said Jake, coming up to the side of the dog and holding out his hand to be sniffed, all the while being careful not to do anything sudden or to look the dog directly in the eyes. "You're a big guy, aren't you?" He noticed the dog was well-groomed, but lacked a collar and instead had a peculiar kind of cloth with strange marks on it knotted around his neck, which seemed unusual. There was no license, no tags, nothing on the cloth. "You have a chip, boy? So they can find you if you get lost?"

The long head nudged Jake's hand, its black nose deep in Jake's palm.

Jake closed his eyes and swallowed hard. This little gesture of friendship nearly overwhelmed him and he felt his throat tighten. Most of the time he didn't think about being lonely, but now it was all he could do to keep from crying. He bent his head to the dog's ruff and felt the soft fur touch his face, and waited until he could speak without sounding like a little kid. "I wish I could take you home with me, fella, but I can't. Mom would have a fit, and Uncle Bob would probably go through the roof." He couldn't stand the thought of this splendid dog getting hurt, especially if Uncle Bob did the hurting. "I'm sorry. I'd like to take you home, I really would." It would be great to have someone at home who was on his side, even if it were only a dog.

The dog nuzzled Jake's face, then gave him a swipe with his long, red tongue.

Jake laughed to keep from sobbing. "It isn't fair, fella," he stated. "If you want to come with me, and I want you to come with me, there shouldn't be any problem about it. But there is."

As he rested his jaw on Jake's shoulder, the dog made a musical kind of whine.

"I know, fella, I know," said Jake, ruffling the fur behind his ears. "You got to belong to someone, anyway, I guess, so you have an owner. You're too neat and well-fed to be a stray."

The dog made a groaning sound and flattened his ears in pleasure as Jake continued to scratch around the base of his ears; he took another swipe at Jake with his tongue.

"I like you, too, fella," Jake said, and thought as he stroked the dense, soft fur, *But sometimes things don't work out the way we'd like.* He was quoting Mom now, and he sighed. "Looks like we both have people at home. That's a good thing, isn't it?" He thought of the many warnings Mom had given him about strange animals and the many dangers they represented. He decided she was wrong about this dog, cloth collar or not.

The dog gave a soft yip followed by an energetic yawn.

"I sure hope you're all grown-up, fella, because you got really big feet. If you get much larger, you'll need a barn for a doghouse." He examined the large paw, and was rewarded as the dog lifted his foot into his hand. "Really big paw, fella." He sat down next to the dog, trying not to think about all the things his mom would be upset about if she could see him now. "You gotta have a name of some kind. Fella sounds really dumb. Maybe I can't keep you, but I can call you something better than fella." He leaned against the dog's shoulder and thought. "Why not Ben?" he said after a long pause. "Like for Franklin Boulevard. Sure beats calling you Diogenes I. Vlamos for the park. Ben's better."

The dog lay down, head raised, paws stretched out in front of him, alert and content at once.

Jake draped his arm over the dog and pretended, just for a little while, that Ben was his dog and that they were out for Ben's night-time walk and just taking a break from their rambles. After about ten minutes, the dog noticed something approaching, and a low, rumbling growl grew in his chest. "What is it?" Jake asked, trying to figure out what Ben had smelled, because it had to be an odor, since Jake couldn't discern any reason for this change.

A guy in a county park ranger's uniform came into the playground light, a flashlight in his hand. As the light flickered over the big black dog and the youngster beside him, the ranger said something under his breath. Aware that Jake and the dog were watching him, the ranger's attempt to smile failed utterly because his face was lit from beneath by the flashlight, making him appear sinister. "Kind of late for you to be out, isn't it, son?" He had a nice voice—deep but not booming; it kind of made up for the weird light on his face.

"Ben's gotta be walked," said Jake, scrambling to his feet. Next to him Ben stood up.

"Yes, he does, but it's a little late for walking a dog." He saw the set look in Jake's face and tried to soften his remarks. "He's a real handsome dog—that ruff makes him look wolfish."

"I think so, too," said Jake, realizing it was true.

"Still, it's after ten. There's a ten o'clock curfew for youngsters like you."

"My mom had to work late, and somebody's gotta walk Ben," said Jake, making a big show of shrugging.

"Without a leash?" the ranger inquired.

"He's easier to handle if I just hold his collar. That's why it's cloth," Jake improvised. "When I'm taller, I'll get to use a leash."

"How old are you, son?" The ranger had taken a notebook out of his pocket.

"Nine. I'll be ten in two months."

"What grade are you in?"

The black dog whined a little and looked as if he wanted to move on.

"Fourth, at Burbank," Jake said. "Look, I gotta get going. Ben's hungry."

"Next time don't wait so long to take him out. This isn't a safe place for a kid after dark, and the curfew is real, you know." The ranger bent down to make sure Jake could see his concern; Jake longed to hit him. "You should be home in bed."

"I'll keep that in mind," said Jake in the same tone he used with Mom when she lectured him about Uncle Bob's problems.

"Are you sure you can get home okay?" the ranger asked as Jake and Ben went to the paved walkway leading out of the park.

"Yeah. We know the way, don't we, Ben?"

The big dog gave a merry little croon.

The ranger looked displeased but he said nothing more; he scribbled something in his notebook and waved to Jake before continuing on his rounds.

Jake and Ben walked together for about half a mile, as far as West Sycamore; Jake had spent most of the time trying to figure out how he could keep Ben without Mom or Uncle Bob finding out about him. At the intersection, Jake turned right and headed for the last quarter mile between him and home, but Ben halted, refusing to go farther. Jake pulled on the cloth around Ben's neck, but to no avail. He let go of the collar and pointed down West Sycamore.

"It's not a long way, Ben. Three blocks down and turn into Barrington Court. It's the rear unit of number twenty-two," said Jake, trying not to plead. "Come on. It's not hard to find."

Ben moved away from the boy; he was now out of reach and putting more distance between them by moving sideways. As Jake came toward him, he threw back his head and howled, a sound so eerie and forlorn that Jake stopped still. Ben wagged his tail, turned, and hastened off into the night, Jake trying to follow him.

Two blocks later, Jake gave up and turned around, his head down and a feeling of tremendous loss weighing heavily upon him.

The middle-aged woman in the boxy tweed suit at the door had to call out twice to be heard over the vacuum cleaner; when Esther turned the machine off, she gave Jake's mother a tentative smile through the worn screen. "Missus Sparges?" she repeated. "Missus Esther Sparges?"

Esther made a grimace that was supposed to be a friendly expression. "Yes?" She stayed away from the door.

"I'm Isobel Matthews—from Luther Burbank Elementary—Jake's school? We sent you a letter a month ago about your boy, but we haven't heard anything from you, and we really do need to talk." She pressed her lips together, then explained. "I'm a psychologist for the district, and Ms. Davidson—your son's teacher?—has expressed some concerns about him."

"My boy's fine," said Esther, bristling. "If she says otherwise, she's wrong."

"I don't mean that he's disruptive, or that his grades are falling. Nothing like that," said Isobel hastily. "Quite the opposite; Jake is very quiet and self-contained. He has artistic talents. He's good at science. He's an excellent student."

"Then why are you here?" Esther demanded, setting her vacuum cleaner aside and coming up to the screen.

"Because he's showing signs of serious depression: that can be dangerous in children Jake's age. There's reason to be worried. He's withdrawn, he keeps to himself, he spends his lunchtime alone, he writes stories about a hero with a secret identity, he wants nothing to do with school activities beyond his classroom work, he is—"

"Oh, God, you psychologists have to find something wrong with everyone, don't you?" Esther glowered at Isobel. "Look, you've got Jake all wrong. He's kind of shy, and he's real sensitive about being small. He's had a rough time of it. Why can't you leave the poor kid alone?"

"Because he's at risk, Missus Sparges." She paused. "May I come in? This isn't the sort of discussion one should have on the porch."

Esther hesitated. "I think our conversation is over," she said, trying to be authoritative and ending up sounding petulant.

"Oh, I hope not, Missus Sparges, for your son's sake," said Isobel. "I hope you'll give me a chance to explain so he won't end up in serious trouble."

"That won't happen; not to Jake."

"It very well may, if we can't find out what's bothering him and try to do something about it." Isobel wanted to encourage Esther, so she added, "You don't want to see him hurt by this, do you?"

"Look, lady, I think Jake still hasn't got over his father's death, and that makes him quiet and . . . thoughtful."

"When did his father die?"

"Five years and seven months ago," said Esther a bit wistfully, an emotion that faded and was replaced by truculence. "He was okay, and then he was real sick, and then he was dead. At thirty-one, he got sick and died. And I was left with bills that ate up all the insurance money and a four-year-old to raise." She was afraid that sounded bad, so she added, "It hasn't been easy for either of us."

Isobel had seen information about this in Jake's file, but didn't mention it to Esther. "Would you like me to refer you to a counselor, or to one of the community support groups? You might be eligible for food stamps and money to help cover the costs of raising a child. I'd be glad to help you through the process, if you like. It might make it easier for both of you, and that would take some of the stress off you and Jake." She tried to be reassuring but could tell by Esther's frown that she wasn't succeeding.

"No, I wouldn't." She knew she had been too blunt, so she added, "Thanks. We've managed this far, we'll get along the rest of the way."

"I hope you're right, Missus Sparges," said Isobel, doing her best to engage Esther's attention in a more positive way. "But for the sake of your boy, I hope you'll consider having him evaluated for depression. It won't cost you anything. The district has to pay for it."

"You mean you'll pay to find out we have to buy him drugs and things, and you aren't going to buy those for him, are you?" There was a touch of panic in her eyes now, and she took hold of her elbows. "If you want to hook a kid on legal drugs, you go right ahead and do it, so long as it isn't my boy."

"But Missus Sparges, I hope that he won't need anything more than counseling, or perhaps some kind of therapy. We won't know that until he's been interviewed by the district psychiatrist. I need to have your permission to set up the appointment."

"Well, you don't have it," said Esther.

"But it could be very important," Isobel persisted. "This could head off trouble down the line. The teen-age years are very vulnerable ones, especially for a boy like Jake. Depressed children can act out in very damaging ways. Think about those terrible school shootings—"

"Oh, God, not the Columbine thing again. Jake's nothing like those two lunatics, nothing at all like them."

"I agree," said Isobel promptly. "But if he goes untreated, he could end up in that kind of hidden anger that took hold of those boys. He might not go on a rampage, but he could do something desperate." She pressed on the screen. "Let me explain it to you, so you can make up your mind what you want to do."

"I've already made up my mind what I want to do. It's you who's having trouble getting the message." She really wanted a cigarette right now, and more than that she wanted this Isobel Matthews to go away. Then she had a sudden inspiration. "Besides, Jake will be spending six months back east with my sister Judith, and that would fu—screw up any therapy, wouldn't it? Maybe, if he's still having trouble when he gets back, we can talk about it again." She reached for the front door, prepared to close it on Isobel.

"Here," said Isobel, holding out her card. "If you change your mind, call me. I want to help you, Missus Sparges, and your son."

"If you want to help, go away," said Esther, ignoring the card and shutting the door with what she intended to be finality.

"Esther, honey, that kid of yours is bad news—what have I been telling you all along?" Uncle Bob was stretched out on the sofa, a six-ounce glass of tequila in one hand and an open Negra Modelo on the coffee table beside him.

"They're just picking on him because he's not like the other kids in his class," said Esther, with a conciliatory smile. "You know what teachers are like these days: anyone a little bit different they want on Ritalin or some kind of drug. They all seem to want cookie-cutter kids in class."

"They're right in Jake's case; he needs something," said Bob with an angry chuckle. "Think about it. The kid's always skulking around. And the games he plays!"

Esther knew better than to defend her boy too vigorously, so she looked down at her shoes. "I'm going to call Judith again; see if I can talk some sense into her, you know?"

"Judith!" he scoffed. "She's not gonna do you any favors,

honey. You know how she is. She's jealous that you got a man and she doesn't."

"I gotta try, for Jake's sake."

Bob grew sulky. "Well, if you're gonna be stubborn about it—I just wanted to spare you some disappointment when your sister says no again." He propped himself on his elbow and drank a mouthful of tequila and chased it with a generous swig of Negra Modelo. "When's dinner?"

"Half an hour. It's in the Crock-Pot. Can't you smell it?"

"Hard to tell. They're redecorating the fourth floor and all I can smell is paint." He finished off his tequila and frowned at Esther. "So, are you going to get your begging out of the way?"

"After dinner," said Esther. "And keep your voice down. Jake's in his room. I don't want him to overhear us."

"Fat chance. That kid is lost in a book or playing his video games." He gave her an accusatory stare. "You bought him that PlayStation gizmo. You know we can't afford it."

"I paid for it out of my tip money," she said sullenly.

"Oh, crap!" He sat up, his face darkening. He stabbed an accusatory finger in her direction. "You think you're doing him a favor? That he's grateful to you for it? He should have had to work to earn the money himself."

"Bob, he's nine." Esther could hear herself whine and felt ashamed.

"Nine, nineteen, no difference. He can run errands, cut lawns, do odd chores, all kinds of things. That way he'll know the value of his things." He sneered at her. "You make nine sound like he's just learning to talk. Keep coddling him like this and you'll turn him into a faggot. Wouldn't Judith like that?"

"He's a *kid*, Bob. He needs to spend his time studying and learning. Jake's bright and very imaginative, and he likes trying things out. That's what kids do. That's their job." Esther reached to take away Bob's beer, but she was a fraction of a second too late, for Bob anticipated her move and threw the beer at her, cursing her as he did. The bottle struck her shoulder; Esther screamed and shouted obscenities. She rushed toward the kitchen door and slammed it closed as Bob struggled up from the sofa, calling down maledictions on her and her boy as he hurried toward the closed door.

"You *bitch*!" Bob roared.

Esther shrieked as Bob kicked at the kitchen door. "Don't you wreck my house, Bob!"

"You gotta learn sense, woman! That kid is weird!" Bob bellowed, kicking harder and yelling when he hurt his ankle. "You gotta draw a line with him! He's gotta know what's real and what isn't."

Down the hall Jake was listening and becoming more disheartened by the second. He guessed dinner would be late, if at all, and he was hungry, but not hungry enough to take on Mom and Uncle Bob when they got like this. He pulled a Kit Kat bar out of his school satchel and unwrapped it, biting into it slowly to get the most out of it. What he really wanted was some of the pot roast he could smell all the way from the kitchen, but that was out of the question. He glanced at the clock: 6:48. Mom and Uncle Bob would be at it for another hour or so—it was their usual pattern—and then another hour of resentful silence, and then, for some reason that made no sense to Jake, they would end up making energetic love. "Well," he said quietly, "the pot roast probably won't be ruined. The Crock-Pot cooks real slow, Mom says."

"Esther, you gotta listen to reason!" Uncle Bob shouted.

"Leave me alone!" was her answer.

Slowly Jake finished the Kit Kat bar and opened one of his windows. Then he picked up his school satchel and climbed out onto the lid of the garbage can, jumped down, and started walking in the direction of Diogenes I. Vlamos Park. It was almost sunset and he could find a place in the bushes where he wouldn't be noticed. He reckoned that three hours should be about right.

When it got dark Jake left the thicket of bamboo where he had been hiding, and he made his way over near the playground. Little as he wanted to admit it, he was hoping he might find Ben wandering about in the park; he wanted so much to see the big dog again and to make the most of the companionship the animal provided. He kept away from the well-lit swings and instead went over to the jungle gym, where there were more shadows and he would not be as readily seen. He climbed up into the bars and sat watching the traffic through the trees, trying to keep from feeling sorry for himself; he wished he'd brought his PlayStation and a couple of games. He knew it was useless for his mom to call Aunt Judith. She wouldn't want to take him. No one wanted to take him. Desolate and alone, he did his best not to think at all. After a while, he began to doze, and as he dozed, he thought he saw Ben coming, and he smiled. Only it wasn't really Ben, it was a tall, angular man with a long head wearing a kind of parka with a fur collar. He held the cloth with the strange writing on it in one hand; he offered it to Jake.

"Wouldn't you like to be one of the pack, Jake? Have a place where you'd always be wanted?" the man-dog asked. "Have somewhere you'd always belong? Wouldn't it be good to have friends and comrades?"

Muzzily Jake answered, "Not . . . gonna happen."

"It will if you'll let it," said man-dog Ben. "Put on the . . . collar; tie it loosely around your neck and wait a little while."

"Why?" Jake asked, feeling a bit more awake, but certain he was still dreaming.

Ben didn't answer his question, but asked one of his own. "How much do you know about wolves, Jake? Not Hollywood wolves, the real animals?"

"I seen some things on Discovery. I know they eat mice, mostly, and stay with the same mate." In the way of dreams he felt he could hear himself speak.

"You're a good boy, Jake, a clever one. You know how to keep secrets and you could go far." Ben came and leaned against the jungle gym. "It's not a bad life with the pack. We could use a youngster like you."

"To be a wolf?" Jake almost giggled. This was better than any video game.

"Well, yes, whenever you put on the collar." He held it up again. "We don't hunt very often—in the city, we don't have to. But every now and then, we will settle on . . . You know how there are some wolves who give all wolves a bad name? We look for humans who are like that: they give humans a bad name. We don't need to wait for a full moon, or to be cursed, or any of that nonsense. We keep our activities under control, at least we do after our first kill, which is kind of an initiation, to see if the life will suit you. After that first kill, we don't do anything . . . impulsive. The pack agrees on the prey, and then we put on our collars, seek out the offender . . ." He stopped as if trying to find a way to explain.

"Then what?" Jake demanded, excited by what he heard even though it was only a dream.

Ben frowned with concentration. "When we have him cornered, we go in as a pack, and . . . and . . ." Suddenly he smiled. "And Bob's your uncle!"

Certain now that this had to be a dream, but fully alert, Jake sat up so quickly that he banged his forehead on one of the jungle gym's bars. "And Bob's your uncle?" he repeated.

"And everything works out," said Ben. "We're safe; we leave no incriminating evidence behind us, and we go back to our jobs and families except on those nights when our pack meets." He put his large, thick hand on Jake's shoulder. "Think about it, okay? We'd be glad to have you."

Jake's thoughts were suddenly racing, and possibilities flared in his mind. This was so much cooler than *Shape Shifter*! Dream or no dream, he was suddenly all for trying this promise of a secret identity life, just to see what it was like; he took the collar and held it up, squinting at the arcane writing on it. "What does it say?"

"It tells your body how to change," said Ben as if it were the most ordinary thing in the world.

"This dream gets better and better," Jake exclaimed as he tied the collar around his neck, expecting nothing much to happen. Almost at once he felt a straining of his arms and a lengthening of his feet, his heels rising and making a sharp bend in his legs. His neck and shoulders changed, and his ears did something creepy on his head. His nose thrust out of his face and his teeth rearranged themselves in his suddenly much longer mouth. Looking down he saw his hands condense into paws with long, hard nails, and he felt the base of his spine tingle as his tail appeared. For a minute or so he itched fiercely as the fur sprouted, and then he could see more clearly in the night and was overwhelmed by the rich sea of odors everywhere.

Ben patted his head. "Good boy, Jake. Give it a try. See how it feels. Make the most of your first kill."

Jake tried to say all right, or even cool, but his mouth could no longer accommodate the shape of the words, so he yipped, then started off, clumsily at first, but gaining balance and confidence as he hurried toward 22 Barrington Court to find out what Uncle Bob and Mom would think of him now.

The Bank Job

GREGORY FROST

Iancu Svekis sat in the chair beside the bank manager's desk. He sat still, his outward calm belying the turmoil of impatience within. He awaited word that the transfer of funds from Romania had gone through as it should have done by now; he awaited also the return of his passport. While Pascu had confirmed in a phone call that he would have as much money as he needed to continue his quest here, the bank manager—Erica Langdon was the name on her cubicle plaque—had explained that with all the antiterrorist checks and verifications nowadays, things like this took much longer than in the past. He ought to have been gone by now, and with a full wallet. Instead, tired and unshaven and hardly presentable so far as he was concerned, he was sitting unattended when the robbers showed up.

There were three of them, and one—a blonde woman—must have been in the bank awhile, in plain sight. He had no doubt looked right at her earlier. Now she wore a Wonder Woman mask and pressed a gun to the neck of the guard while her crew strode in carrying two canvas satchels and waving their weapons as if no one would notice them otherwise. One had an autoloader, a carbine with a profile that reminded Svekis of a shark. "Hands up! Everybody move!" shouted the taller robber. He sported a George Bush mask.

The guard went to his knees compliantly, but one of the tellers reacted by hitting an alarm button in her cage, and George Bush shot her. The low Plexiglas barrier on the front of her counter splintered and she fell.

People screamed then. Seventeen customers and three tellers hit the floor. Erica Langdon ran to the fallen teller, and the killer might have shot her if Wonder Woman hadn't spun him around and punched him in the chest. "What in *hell* are you doing?" she yelled.

"She hit the button!"

"Yeah, and?"

When he didn't respond, she shoved him backwards. "I wanted her to do that, you stupid shit. I *told* you someone would."

She swung about and faced the robber with the carbine. He had on an imitation hockey goalie's mask. "You and your fucking brother!" She thrust a finger at the guard. "Let's try not to shoot the damn cop at least, okay? Just stand over him!" He nodded and took his place. "Jesus," she snarled. She shoved a satchel into the hands of George Bush. "Go collect their cells from them." She walked into the midst of the crouching customers. "All right, who's the manager? Who's in charge here?"

In the distance sirens sounded.

Svekis continued to sit, to observe, as motionless as the furniture, amazed at how quickly a plan could unravel. The thought made him wince. His wife was dead because of an unpredictable unraveling. Nothing he could have done about that, but he was here for this one.

Erica arose from behind the teller's cage. "I'm the manager," she answered the robber. Her terror and anger had her trembling.

"Great. Buzz me into the back now. How's your girl?"

"Unconscious, but—but not dead. The barrier . . ."

"That's good. No one else needs to get hurt here, okay? But you get it that we mean business, right?"

Erica nodded.

"Buzz me in and get the rest of your people out of there. I want 'em on the floor out here like everybody else." She took one empty satchel the others had brought. Erica released the electronic lock, and Wonder Woman went through the doorway. The vault stood wide open, and the robber led Erica inside. Svekis studied the other two.

Beside the kneeling guard, Hockey Mask shifted back and forth on his feet, anxious. Bush the Idiot strode up and down through the trembling crowd of hostages, collecting cell phones in his bag like an oversized trick-or-treater. It wasn't until he was walking back toward his brother that he looked at Svekis.

"Hey! Hey, you. What the hell are you doing?"

Svekis looked around himself. "Nothing," he replied.

"Yeah? Well, you better do your nothin' over here on the floor." When Svekis didn't move, he pointed his gun. "Now!"

Wonder Woman had come out of the vault. "What's the problem, dickhead?"

Bush pointed at Svekis. "Him."

She set the satchel on the counter. "Here, get the drawer money."

She unlocked the door and came out from the back, but left the door ajar. Behind her, Erica stood in the vault doorway. She stared at him fearfully. He smiled to her.

"We got cops!" shouted Hockey Mask. Flashing, colored lights striped the side of him.

"Good, that's what I want. You stand right there and let them see you, the guard, and that gun, so they don't think they can rush in here," she answered. She walked over to Svekis. "You got some nerves, Pops."

He lowered his head. "Not really. I am too tired to react to anything today."

"Bad week, was it?"

He thought of the *strigoi* he'd battled, the child and mother who would go on living because of him, the horror of that unbridled hunger he'd slain. "You would not believe."

"Yeah, I'm sure. You want to sit here, that's okay with me, but you don't try to call anybody, okay?"

"Yes."

"What's your name, in case I have to yell at you all by yourself over here."

"Iancu." When she continued to stare, unmoving, he added, "In your language, it's John."

"John." She repeated it as if doubting it. "You give him your phone, John?"

He dug into the pocket of his raincoat and handed her his phone. "He did not ask me for it," he said.

"Thank you." She turned and carried his phone away, but hadn't gone ten steps when the desk phone beside Svekis rang. She turned back to answer it. He pretended not to notice her, but he had already satisfied himself that her clothing was bulky and ill-fitting as if she was wearing extra layers against the cold. Except, it wasn't all that cold outside.

"That's right," she said into the phone and gestured at Bush Mask. He went through the open security door and then walked down the line, pulling cash out of the teller drawers. "We got twenty people in here, and we want twenty people to go home tonight, right? One of them's hurt already so we're going to send her out. Play nice and she'll be the only one. No. I'll tell you what. You get us a touring bus. You know, something a rock band would like. You get the bus and you bring it up outside. Then you call us back. Bye."

She nodded to herself, and headed back across the lobby. In the middle she stopped and asked, "What's that smell?" She looked over the customers huddled below. "Somebody here shit himself?"

Finally, and with great hesitation, one man raised his hand. He kept his head bowed.

"Great. Well, we're gonna be here awhile, folks, so maybe you need to go take care of your mess. And the rest of you, too. You need to pee, don't leave it till you're pissin' on the floor." She snatched the satchel from Bush. "Go out there and lead them to the bathroom," she told him. "One at a time, got that? And don't shoot anybody else, for Christ's sake."

The embarrassed man got up and walked uncomfortably across the lobby to a set of restrooms. They were locked but Erica was already holding out the keys. "They're for employees," she explained.

Bush Mask and the man went into the nearer bathroom. Wonder Woman went back into the vault.

When the bathroom door opened again, the man emerged first. He was wiping his sleeve across his face. It was clear that he'd broken down. He quickly sat and grabbed his knees as if he could hide from everybody. A few others raised their hands to be allowed into the bathroom. Bush Mask surveyed them all. Svekis raised his hand, too. The mask twitched, and Svekis heard him snort, no doubt amused that the old man he'd intimidated had finally broken. Thus it was that he let one woman into the ladies room and came back for Svekis while Wonder Woman returned to the vault and Hockey Mask watched the cops outside. "Come on, geezer," he said, and all but prodded Svekis with the nose of the automatic.

Svekis got up heavily. He drew a deep breath, but kept his shoulders hunched, his head down. His rumpled London Fog disguised the solidity of him. He walked ahead of his captor, waited while the door was unlocked, then let himself be shoved inside. "Try not to mess the place any worse, huh?" Bush Mask said.

Inside were two urinals and a single stall. Polished chocolate brown tiles covered the walls and floor. The room reeked, the smell coming from the trash bin. No doubt the frightened customer had thrown out his soiled underwear. The window of frosted glass was wired inside and out. There was a vent in the wall past the sinks, perhaps the size of a notebook, and a narrow closet door behind which would be shelves of toilet paper, cleaners, and mops.

Svekis went to the stall and closed the door. He took off his coat and hung it on the door hook, then followed with his shirt and trousers. Even as he stripped down, the roar of transformation filled his ears and a redness rose behind his eyes, blood becoming like acid in his veins. His body creaked like a tree about to snap in a high wind, but distantly. He was falling away from it, into pure white pain. Ribs flexed and curved in, his muscles following, reshaping. It took every last shred of conscious control not to cry out. He doubled over in the narrow space, pawing at the metal wall. His senses plunged into shadow. In shadow he was reborn.

The tall old man hadn't come out after ten minutes. Bush Mask figured he'd had a stroke or something, and stuck his head into the restroom. "Hey, let's go!" he shouted.

When nobody answered, he went in. He had the good sense to keep his gun leveled at the stall. Nobody stood in front of the urinal or at the sink. Except for the broom closet, there was nowhere else. He walked to the closet and checked the handle. It was locked. He turned and saw that the slats had been removed from the air vent high up in the wall, but the hole was so small that nothing bigger than somebody's head could have fit through it.

Under the door of the nearer stall, he could see the tips of the old guy's shoes on the floor. "Goddamit! Whadja do, have a coronary on me? She's gonna blame me for it, you bastard." He

254 | GREGORY FROST

kicked at the stall door. It wasn't latched, and banged wide open, revealing an undershirt, boxer shorts, and socks beside the shoes on the floor.

For a brief instant he imagined that the old man had somehow flushed himself down the toilet. Instinctively he looked behind the door and found that the rest of the old man's clothes were hung on the hook there. "What the hell?" he said. Where could the guy have gone, naked?

The wall switch by the door clicked. The lights went out. Fear drove him then. He backed out of the stall and up against the sink. Wan light came in through the frosted glass of the window, showing the darker wire within like strands of spider webbing. He held his gun ready. He sensed movement, started to turn, and came up against orange eyes glowing in the dark, and a solid form surrounding them that was furred blue-gray in the light from the window, a snout against his cheek, the smell of its furious breath like a color. Bright red.

He opened his mouth to scream, but a sharp crack resounded off the tiles and amid searing pain he felt himself flying through the air.

One of the women finally went to Wonder Woman and said, "Please, I've *got* to use the bathroom!"

"Well, then—" She turned about, realized that Andy's idiot brother was nowhere in sight. "Great," she said. She went over to Andy in his hockey mask, setting the second satchel—the one full of cash—down beside the guard. "Your brother's screwing up again. *Deal* with him. Now."

Shaking his head, Andy crossed the lobby in strides of anger. She was half-hoping he'd just shoot the idiot.

He skidded at the men's room door, slipped, and fell onto one elbow. Scrambling up, gun in hand, he shouted, "Jesus!"

Gun at the ready, he shouldered open the door to the

bathroom. She could see how dark it was, but instead of going in, he backed away, all the way to the wall. The hostages were all staring. She could not let this happen.

She hauled the guard to his feet, pushed her pistol to his cheek, then walked him to the restroom.

One side of Andy's clothes was smeared in blood. On the floor lay a puddle of it that had leaked from under the door. She cautiously nudged the door open again. Lobby light slashed across the dark room, across the simian halloween mask of George Bush.

"God *damn* it," she said. She let go of the guard and reached cautiously around the wall until her fingers found the light switch. She held her gun ready to shoot. "I told him not to . . ." The overhead light fluttered on. A headless torso lay in the middle of the room. There was blood in sprays across the stall, all the way to the ceiling. The mask, she saw now, was still attached to the head. The gun lay in the middle of the floor.

Andy started to babble. "That's Markie, that's—he's dead, oh, Christ, what the hell, what the hell—"

She backed out into him, then grabbed onto him as much to hold herself up as to shut him up. "I don't know what the hell. Who'd he take in here, who was the last to use the bathroom?"

They turned and looked at the crowd that was looking back at them. The horrified guard gaped, too. She turned and faced the manager's cubicle.

The old gent, John, sat exactly as before. If anything he looked more rumpled, pale, and exhausted than half an hour ago. His head hung low, but he seemed to be watching from beneath his brows, as if too tired to face things head-on.

The phone beside him began to ring then, and she made herself walk calmly over to the cubicle to answer it. She stared down at him while she talked, until he finally glanced up. He wasn't as old as all that, she decided, just thin and weather-beaten, like a cowboy, someone who lived hard. It was the white hair that made him seem older.

"Glad to hear it," she told the cop on the phone. "Outside in ten minutes. We bring out the hostages with us, so no Annie Oakley shit. I'll tell your driver where we're going. You don't need to know, and you don't follow. Anybody follows and nobody gets off the bus, understand?" Oh, he understood, all right. She hung up.

Andy came over. She told him, "The bus is ready. Pick out your group and let's get the hell out of here. Whatever happened in there, I don't know, okay? I'm sorry. Your brother was a dickhead but whatever's in there is staying the hell in there. We're not going to go in after it. Nobody else gets to go to the bathroom, period." Andy moved off shakily.

"What happened to your friend?" John asked her. He had an accent she couldn't place.

She faced him, stared into nearly golden irises. Something in his gaze closed around her like a steel trap, pinning her. The moment passed, and she threw off a shiver, blinked, and took a step back. Instead of answering, she found herself telling him, "You'll be joining us on the bus."

"Yes," he answered, "of course."

The transfer of hostages went smoothly. Svekis could appreciate that they'd given this a lot of thought.

The robbers split the hostages into two groups. The only one left behind was the guard, trussed up in the vault. Everybody got a Halloween mask, and each group was bound by a clothesline rope looped around their wrists and held by the robber in the middle of the group. The groups shuffled out to the bus like two bent, ungainly centipedes. They clambered up the steps and past the driver—no doubt a cop—and through a privacy curtain into the back. Wonder Woman told the driver to turn off the interior lights. Then she assigned everybody their seats. She put Svekis at the back.

Hockey Mask, meanwhile, had pulled out a knife and was cutting the rope between the rows and using each length to tie the duos together. He pushed their masks up, too, to make it harder for them to see, but Svekis couldn't tell if that actually had a purpose or if he just enjoyed it.

The woman returned to the front and sat down behind the driver and quietly gave him orders.

The bus lurched into gear.

She got up and walked up the aisle again. A speaker crackled to life. The woman counted off the rows as she passed them, touching the people in the aisle seats as she said their number. She came to Svekis as she said, "Eleven." Then she passed him and said, "Twelve." Turning back, she headed toward the front again, passing her partner as he finished tying up their hands. Her voice blared like that of a tour guide. "You all sit in your seats, and when you're told to get off—when I call your number—you get up and get out. The bus will slow down enough for you to jump, but we're not stopping. So try not to break something. What you do after you get out, I don't care, but if you want to live, you'll follow my orders. I told you your numbers. You don't get up unless you're called."

The bus rolled along through the city. After ten minutes the speaker crackled again and she called out, "Three!" Two people scrambled up and ran clumsily, strung together, to the front of the bus. He heard her say to the driver, "Just slow enough that they can jump." Svekis looked out the window. The area was deserted, full of warehouses. It would be a while before they found anyone to help them. Alternatively, they might be mugged. He sat back and waited his turn.

The bus rolled along out of the city proper and toward the western suburbs. They entered an area of tenement rowhouses, and two more were let go.

Hockey Mask had passed by him after tying his hands, and now Wonder Woman followed into the very back of the bus. He listened to the rustle of her clothes, to the sound of a zipper, to other noises. He had a good idea what they were up to.

The speaker crackled again, and the woman called out, "Twelve. Get up, get out. Now."

Svekis watched a fashionable pair of slacks, a turquoise blouse, and dark hair pass him. The mask was different, too. She carried a small, full backpack over one shoulder. No doubt it was loaded with the contents of one satchel. She held her hands out in front of her, rope looped around her wrists and connected to the man behind her in the jeans, windbreaker, and another backpack. They walked down the aisle and through the curtain. The door hissed open and the bus slowed for a moment.

Then, over the speakers, she said, "Go on," as if she were still inside the bus. Svekis smiled. It was a clever trick.

The bus picked up speed. He tore off his mask. He'd already made one hand transform so that he could slip it out of the ropes. Standing, he glanced to the rear where her and her partner's clothes lay in heaps beside both discarded satchels. He knelt and rifled through both bags. He found his cell phone, but that was all.

He rose and walked down the aisle. Passengers lifted their heads at his passing, instinctively fearful. Most of them had left their masks askew. They kept their tied hands in their laps, too.

Even as he reached the curtain the woman's voice blared over the intercom: "Take your next right and drive for two miles until you go under the interstate."

Svekis stepped up beside the driver. "How is the door opened?" he asked. The driver glanced up in astonishment.

"But she said—"

"I must insist." He placed his hand on the driver's shoulder, and the driver pointed to the handle that operated the door. "Thank you. Now, please, don't slow down any further. Do exactly as you were instructed." The door opened with a hiss, and Svekis sprang into the night like a man jumping off a cliff.

They'd parked the Toyota on a tree-lined street a block from the nearest regional train stop. The plan had been for her and Andy to take the car and for Markie to jump on the next train back into the city. Nobody would expect that. She changed the plan now. She would take the train and he could drive off alone. That way they wouldn't match anything anyone was looking for; but with Markie dead, they needed to get out of town soon.

They stood on the sidewalk beside the car. A man was walking his dog, a white terrier, in their direction. She stepped up to Andy and said loudly, "I'll see you when you get back, sweetheart," then gave him a big kiss. "Drive safely. Don't speed."

The dog-walker looked away, a shy smile on his face. Just what she'd hoped. They stood together, waiting while he rounded the corner and went on up the street. She pulled away. "I mean it about the speed," she said.

"Yeah, I got it in one."

Around the corner, the terrier started barking. She took that as her cue and started up the street. She heard the car door open. She was thinking about how they'd actually pulled it off—her plan so carefully worked out. By now the bus had reached the interstate and was waiting for her to tell them to let the next passengers go. She switched on the walkie-talkie and said, "Okay, six, get up and get out." The thing was supposed to have a ten-mile range. If it did, they'd go a while longer, and she would broadcast one more set of orders, send the bus out into the 'burbs for another half hour. If not, they'd shortly be looking for a man and woman in masks. She was halfway up the street before she realized that the car door had never closed.

She turned around, walking backwards. The Toyota sat there against the curb. The driver's door hung open wide. She couldn't see if Andy was in the car or not. What the hell could he be doing, putting his bag of loot in the trunk? Idiot. For a second she considered going back, and she slowed her pace. Something was wrong back there. Instinct compelled her to move, to get off the street. She turned and picked up speed.

The thing came out of the darkness beside her, a moon-colored blur moving in swift smears across the night, across a lawn from shadow to shadow, and then suddenly right before her. Golden feral eyes met hers. She ought to have been terrified but it was as if she'd expected this, as if someone had told her it was coming. The rich, dark voice—real or imagined—said, "You've borrowed something of mine, I'm afraid, that you should not have."

She thought of words to say but couldn't find them before the eyes swelled like twin suns and drank her down.

"It was terrible," said the branch manager. Iancu Svekis nodded.

"A tragedy, I'm sure," he said.

"They *could* have killed them. You know, that's what everybody's scared will happen in a robbery. That one girl—the one they shot—she's going to be okay."

"That's good to hear."

"But you were there, right? I had to call Erica, because she'd put through your wire transfer and she knew what was going on with it—"

"Yes," he said heavily, "I was there."

"That thing in the bathroom—she said even the cops can't figure it out. They think maybe it was a gang thing, but nobody saw any gang, did they?" Svekis said nothing, but she went right on. "Of course, finding the bodies in that car trunk along with the money—that's got everyone thinking it's a gang thing, too. It's so *weird*." When he only sighed, she seemed to understand that he didn't want to talk about this any further.

"Anyway," she said, and handed him back his passport, "everything's fine, your money was transferred from overseas into your new account. Here's the documentation and the number. You can draw on that at any of our branches anywhere from here to Boston. There's a list of addresses in here, too. But you should get your ATM card in about ten days."

"Thank you." He took the envelope she held out and started to get up.

"I was wondering," she said. "Can I ask you one more thing?"

"Yes?"

"Um, Erica wanted to know how you got your passport back. She said she was sure they scooped it up when they were cleaning out the tellers."

He looked at her with some concern. "Oh, no," he assured her. "They left it on her desk and I took it back when they weren't watching."

"Wow. That was pretty brave."

"I did not, you know, think of it that way. Perhaps brave, perhaps foolish. But then, stealing is foolish." He tucked the envelope into his jacket and reached out. "Thank you," he repeated, and she shook his hand. No one was watching, and he only needed to hold on to her for a few moments.

He left her sitting, staring off into space. Someone would notice eventually and shake her back into the here and now, but she would remain vaguely confused as to what had occurred and to whom she'd been speaking just before she dozed off.

Svekis pushed open the door and walked out into the light.

La Lune T'Attend

PETER S. BEAGLE

Even once a month, Arceneaux hated driving his daughter Noelle's car. There was no way to be comfortable: he was a big old man, and the stick-shift hatchback cramped his legs and elbows, playing Baptist hell with the bad knee. Garrigue was dozing peacefully beside him in the passenger seat, as he had done for the whole journey; but then, Garrigue always adapted more easily than he to changes in his circumstances. *All these years up north in the city, Damballa, and I still don't fit nowhere, never did.*

Paved road giving way to gravel, pinging off the car's undercarriage . . . then to a dirt track and the shaky wooden bridge across the stream; then to little more than untamed underbrush, springing back as he plowed through to the log cabin. *Got to check them shutters—meant to do it last time. Damn raccoons been back. I can smell it.*

Garrigue didn't wake, even with all the jouncing and rattling, until Arceneaux cut the engine. Then his eyes came open immediately, and he turned his head and smiled like a sleepy baby. He was a few months the elder, but he had always looked distinctly younger, in spite of being white, which more often shows the wear. He said, "I was dreaming, me."

Arceneaux grunted. "Same damn dream, I ain't want to hear about it."

"No, wasn't that one. Was you and me really gone fishing, just like folks. You and me in the shade, couple of trotlines out, couple of Dixie beers, nice dream. A *real* dream."

Arceneaux got out of the car and stood stretching himself, trying to forestall a back spasm. Garrigue joined him, still describing his dream in detail. Arceneaux had been taciturn almost from birth, while Garrigue, it was said in Joyelle Parish, bounced out of his mother chattering like a squirrel. Regarding the friendship—unusual, in those days, between a black Creole and a *blanc*—Arceneaux's father had growled to Garrigue's, "Mine cain't talk, *l't'en* cain't shut up. Might do."

And the closeness had lasted for very nearly seventy years (they quarreled mildly at times over the exact number), through schooling, work, marriages, family struggles, and even their final, grudging relocation. They had briefly considered sharing a place after Garrigue moved up north, but then agreed that each was too old and cranky, too stubbornly set in his ways, to risk the relationship over the window being open or shut at night. They met once a week, sometimes at Arceneaux's apartment, but more usually at the home of Garrigue's son Claude, where Garrigue lived; and they both fell asleep, each on his own side of the great park that divided the city, listening to the music of Clifton Chenier, Dennis McGee and Amédé Ardoin.

Garrigue glanced up at the darkening overcast sky. "Cut it close again, moon coming on so fast these nights. I keep telling you, Jean-Marc—"

Arceneaux was already limping away from the rear of the car, having opened the trunk and taken out most of the grocery bags. Still scolding him, Garrigue took the rest and followed, leaving one hand free to open the cabin door for Arceneaux and then switch on the single bare light in the room. It was right above the entrance, and the shadows, as though startled themselves to be suddenly awakened, danced briefly over the room when

Garrigue stepped inside, swung the door to, and double-locked it behind them.

Arceneaux tipped the bags he carried, and let a dozen bloody steaks and roasts fall to the floor.

The single room was small but tidy, even homely, with two Indian-patterned rag rugs, two cane-bottomed rockers, and a card table with two folding chairs drawn up around it. There was a fireplace, and a refrigerator in one corner, but no beds or cots. The two windows were double-barred on the inside, and the shutters closing them were not wooden, but steel.

Another grocery bag held a bottle of Calvados, which Arceneaux set on the table, next to the two glasses, deck of cards, and cribbage board waiting there. In a curiously military fashion, they padlocked and dropbolted the door, carefully checked the security of the windows, and even blocked the fireplace with a heavy steel screen. Then, finally, they sat down at the table, and Arceneaux opened the Calvados and said, "Cut."

Garrigue cut. Arceneaux dealt. Garrigue said, "My littlest grandbaby, Manette, she going to First Communion a week Saturday. You be there?" Arceneaux nodded wordlessly, jabbing pegs into the cribbage board. Garrigue started to say "She so excited, she been asking me, did I ever do First Communion, what did it feel like and all . . ." but then his words dissolved into a hoarse growl as he slipped from the chair. Garrigue was almost always the first; neither understood why.

Werewolves—*loups-garoux* in Louisiana—are notably bigger than ordinary wolves, running to larger skulls with bolder, more marked bones, deeper-set eyes, broader chests, and paws, front and rear, whose dew claw serves very nearly as an opposable thumb. Even so, for a small, chattery white man, Garrigue stood up as a huge wolf, black from nose to tail-tip, with eyes unchanged from his normal snow-gray, shocking in their humanity. He was at the food before Arceneaux's front feet hit the floor, and there was the customary snarling between them as they snapped up the meat within minutes. The table went over, cards and brandy and all, and both of them hurled themselves at walls and barred windows until the entire cabin shook with their frenzied fury. The wolf that was Arceneaux stood on its hind legs and tried to reach the window latches with uncannily dextrous paws, while the wolf that was Garrigue broke a front claw tearing at the door. They never howled.

First madness spent, they circled the room restlessly, their eyes glowing as dogs' and wolves' eyes do not glow. In time they settled into a light, reluctant sleep—Garrigue under a chair, Arceneaux in the ruins of the rug he had torn to pieces. Even in sleep they whined softly and eagerly, lips constantly twitching back from the fangs they never quite covered.

Towards dawn, with the moon gray and small, looking almost triangular because of the moisture in the air, something brought Arceneaux to the barred window nearest the door, rearing once again with his paws on the sill. There was nothing to see through the closed metal shutters, but the deep, nearly-inaudible sound that constantly pulsed through his body in this form grew louder as he stared, threatening to break its banks and swell into a full-throated howl. Once again he clawed at the bars, but Garrigue had screwed down the bolts holding them in place too tightly even for a *loup-garou*'s deftness, and Arceneaux's snarl bared his fangs to the black gums. Garrigue joined him, puzzled but curious, and the two of them stood side by side, panting rapidly, ears flattened against their skulls. And still there was no hint of movement anywhere outside.

Then the howl came, surging up from somewhere very near, soaring over the trees like some skeletal ancient bird, almost visible in its dreadful ardency. The werewolves went mad, howling their own possessed challenges, even snapping furiously at each other. Arceneaux sprang at the barred windows until they shivered. He was crouching to leap again when he heard the familiar whimper behind him, and simultaneously felt the brief but overwhelming pain, unlike any other, of distorted molecules regaining their natural shape. Coming back always took longer, and hurt worse.

As always afterward, he collapsed to the floor and lay there, quickly human enough to curse the weakness that always overtook a returning *loup-garou*, old or young. He heard Garrigue gasping, *"Duplessis . . . Duplessis . . ."* but could not yet respond. A face began to form in his mind: dark, clever, handsome in a way that meant no good to anyone who responded to it . . . Still unable to speak, Arceneaux shook his head against the worn, stained floorboards. He had better reason than most to know why that sound, that cold wail of triumph, could not have been uttered by Alexandre Duplessis of Pointe Coupee Parish.

They climbed slowly to their feet, two stiff-jointed old men, looking around them at the usual wreckage of the cabin. Over the years that they had been renting it together, Garrigue and Arceneaux had made it proof, as best they could, against the rage of what would be trapped there every month. Even so, the rugs were in shreds, the refrigerator was on its side, there were deep claw-marks on the log walls to match the ones already there, and they would definitely need a new card table. Arceneaux pointed at the overturned Calvados bottle and said, "Shame, that. Wish I'd got the cap back on."

"Yeah, yeah." Garrigue shivered violently—common for most after the return. He said, "Jean-Marc, it was Duplessis, you know and I know. Duplessis *back*."

"Not in this world." Arceneaux's voice was bleak and slow. "Maybe in some other world he back, but ain't in this one." He turned from the window to face Garrigue. "I killed Duplessis, man. Ain't none of us come back from what I done, Duplessis or nobody. You was there, Rene Garrigue! You saw how I done!"

Garrigue was hugging himself to stop the shivering, closing his eyes against the seeing. Abruptly he said in a strangely quiet tone, "He outside right now. He *there*, Jean-Marc."

"Naw, man," Arceneaux said. "Naw, Rene. He gone, Rene, my word. You got my word on it." But Garrigue was lunging past him to fumble with the locks and throw the door wide. The freezing dawn air rushed in over the body spilled across the path, so near the door that Garrigue almost tripped over it. It was a woman—a vagrant, clearly, wearing what looked like five or six coats, sweaters, and undergarments. Her throat had been ripped out, and what remained of her intestines were draped neatly over a tree branch. Even in the cold, there were already flies.

Arceneaux breathed the name of his god, his *loa*, Damballa Wedo, the serpent. Garrigue whispered, "Women. Always the women, always the belly. Duplessis."

"He carry her here." Arceneaux was calming himself, as well as Garrigue. "Killed her somewhere back there, maybe in the city, carry her here, leave her like a business card. You right, Rene. Can't *be*, but you right."

"Business card." Garrigue's voice was still tranquil, almost dreamy. "He know this place, Jean-Marc. If he know this place, he know everything. *Everything.*"

"Hush you, man, hush now, mind me." Arceneaux might have been talking to a child wakened out of a nightmare. "Shovel out back, under the crabapple, saw it last time. We got to take her off and bury her, first thing. You go get me that shovel, Rene."

Garrigue stared at him. Arceneaux said it again, more gently. "Go on, Rene. Find me that shovel, *compe'*."

Alone, he felt every hair on his own body standing up; his big dark hands were trembling so that he could not even cover the woman's face or close her eyes. *Alexandre Duplessis, c'est vraiment li, vraiment, vraiment*; but the knowledge frightened the old man far less than the terrible lure of the crumpled thing at his feet, torn open and emptied out, gutted and drained and abandoned, the reek of her terror dominating the hot, musky scent of the beast that had hunted her down in the hours before dawn. *The fear, Damballa, the fear—you once get that smell in you head, you throat, you gut, you never get it out. Better than the meat, the blood even, you smell the fear.* He was shaking badly now, and he knew that he needed to get out of there with Garrigue before he hurled himself upon the pitiful remains, to roll and wallow in them like the beast he was. *Hold me, Damballa. Hide me, hold me.*

Garrigue returned with the rusty shovel and together they carried the dead woman deeper into the woods. Then he stood by, rubbing his mouth compulsively as he watched Arceneaux hack at the hard earth. In the same small voice as before, he said, "I scare, me, Ti-Jean," calling Arceneaux by his childhood nickname. "What we do to him."

"What he did to us." Arceneaux's own voice was cold and steady. "What he did to *ma Sophie*."

As he had known it would, the mention of Arceneaux's sister immediately brought Garrigue back from wherever terror and guilt together had taken him. "I ain't forgot Sophie." His gray eyes had closed down like the steel shutters whose color they matched. "I ain't forget nothing."

"I know, man," Arceneaux said gently. He finished his work, patted the new grave as flat as he could make it—*one good rain, two, grass cover it all*—and said, "We come back before next moon, clean up a little. Right now, we going home." Garrigue nodded eagerly.

In the car, approaching the freeway, Garrigue could not keep from talking about Sophie Arceneaux as he had not done in a very long while. "So pretty, that girl, that sister of yours. So pretty, so kind, who wouldn't want to marry such a fine woman like her?" Then he hurriedly added, "Of course, my Elizabeth,

Elizabeth was a fine woman too, I don't say a word against Elizabeth. But Sophie . . . *la Sophie* . . ." He fell silent for a time, and then said in a different voice, "I ain't blame Duplessis for wanting her. Can't do that, Jean-Marc."

"She didn't want him," Arceneaux said. There was no expression at all in his voice now. "Didn't want nothing to do with him, no mind what he gave her, where he took her, never mind what he promised. So he killed her." After a pause, he went on, "You know how he killed her."

Garrigue folded his hands in his lap and looked at them.

So low he could barely be heard, he answered, "In the wolf . . . in the wolf shape. Hadn't seen it, I wouldn't have believed."

"Ripped her throat out," Arceneaux said. "*Ma colombe, ma pauv' p'ti,* she never had no chance—no more than him with her." He looked off down the freeway, seeing, not a thousand cars nor a distant city skyline, but his entire Louisiana family, wolves all, demanding that as oldest male he take immediate vengeance on Duplessis. For once—and it was a rare enough occurrence—he found himself in complete agreement with his blood kin and their ancient notions of honor and retribution. In company with Garrigue, one of Sophie's more tongue-tied admirers, he had set off on the track of his sister's murderer.

"Duplessis kill *ma Sophie,* she never done nothing but good for anyone. Well, I done what I done, and I ain't sorry for it." His voice rose as he grew angry all over again, more than he usually allowed himself these days. He said, "Ain't a bit sorry."

Garrigue shivered, remembering the hunt. Even with an entire werewolf clan sworn to avenge Sophie Arceneaux, Duplessis had made no attempt to hide himself, or to flee the region, so great was his city man's contempt for thick-witted backwoods bumpkins. Arceneaux had run him to earth in a single day, and it had been almost too easy for Garrigue to lure him into a moonshiner's riverside shebeen: empty for the occasion and abandoned forever after, haunted by the stories of what was done there to Alexandre Duplessis.

It had taken them all night, and Garrigue was a different man in the morning.

After the first scream, Garrigue had never heard the others; he could not have done otherwise and held on to his sanity. Sometimes it seemed to him that he had indeed gone mad that night, and that all the rest of his life—the flight north, the jobs, the marriage, the beloved children and grandchildren, the home—had never been anything but a lunatic's hopeless dream of forgetfulness. More than forty years later he still shuddered and moaned in his sleep, and at times still whimpered himself awake. *All the blood, all the* shit . . . *the* . . . *the* . . . sound *when Ti-Jean took that old cleaver thing . . . and that man wouldn't die, wouldn't die . . . wasn't nothing* left *of him but open mouth, awful open mouth, and he wouldn't* die . . .

"Don't make *no* sense," Arceneaux said beside him. "Days burying . . . four, five county lines—"

"Five," Garrigue whispered. "Evangeline. Joyelle. St. Landry. Acadia. Rapides. Too close together, I *told* you . . ."

Arceneaux shook his head. "Conjure. Conjure in it somewhere, got to be. Guillory, maybe, he evil enough . . . old Fontenot, over in St. Landry. Got to be conjure."

They drove the rest of the way in near-silence, Arceneaux biting down hard on his own lower lip, Garrigue taking refuge in memories of his wife Elizabeth, and of Arceneaux's long-gone Pauline. Both women, non-Creoles, raised and encountered in the city, believed neither in werewolves nor in conjure men; neither one had ever known the truth about their husbands. *Loups-garoux* run in families: Arceneaux and Garrigue, marrying out of their clans, out of their deep back-country world, had both produced children who would go through their lives completely unaware of that part of their ancestry. The choice had been a deliberate one, and Garrigue, for his part, had never regretted it. He doubted very much that Arceneaux had either, but it was always hard to tell with Arceneaux.

Pulling to the curb in front of the frame house where Garrigue lived with Claude and his family, Arceneaux cut the engine, and they sat looking at each other. Garrigue said finally, "Forgot to fish. Grandbabies always wanting to know did we catch anything."

"Tell them fish wasn't biting today. We done that before."

Garrigue smiled for the first time. "Claude, he think we don't do no fishing, we goes up there to drink, get away from family, get a little wild. Say he might just come with us one time." Arceneaux grunted without replying. Garrigue said, "I keeps ducking and dodging, you know? Ducking and dodging." His voice was growing shaky again, but he never took his eyes from Arceneaux's eyes. He said, "What we going to do, Ti-Jean?"

"Get you some sleep," Arceneaux said. "Get you a good breakfast, tell Claude you likely be late. We go find Duplessis tomorrow, you and me."

Garrigue looked, for a moment, more puzzled than frightened. "Why we bothering that? He know right where we live, where the chirrens lives—"

Arceneaux cut him off harshly. "We find him fast, maybe we throw him just that little bit off-balance, could help sometime." He patted Garrigue's shoulder lightly. "We use what we got, Rene, and all we got is us. You go on now—my knee biting on me a little bit."

In fact—as Garrigue understood from the fact that Arceneaux mentioned it at all—the bad knee was hurting him a good deal; he could only pray that it wouldn't have locked up on him by morning. He brought the car back to Noelle, who took one look at his gait and insisted on driving him home, lecturing him all the way about his need for immediate surgery. She was his old-est child, his companion from her birth, and the only one who would ever have challenged him, as she did now.

"Dadda, whatever you and *Compe'* Rene are up to, I *will* find it out—you know I always do. Simpler tell me now, *oui*?"

"Ain't up to one thing," Arceneaux grumbled. "Ain't up to nothing, you turning such a suspicious woman. You *mamere*, she just exactly the same way."

"Because you're such a bad liar," his daughter replied tenderly. She caressed the back of his neck with a warm, work-hardened hand. "*Ma'dear* and me, we used to laugh so, nights you'd be slipping out to drink, play cards with *Compe'* Rene and your old zydeco friends. Make some crazy little-boy story—*whoo,* out the door, gone till morning, come home looking like someone dragged you through a keyhole backwards. Lord, didn't we *laugh*!"

There had been a few moments through the years when pure loneliness had made him seriously consider turning around on her and telling her to sit herself down and listen to a story. This moment was one of them; but he only muttered something he forgot as soon as he'd said it, and nothing more until she dropped him off at his apartment building. Then she kissed his cheek and told him, "Come by for dinner tomorrow. Antoine will be home early, for a change, and Patrice just *got* to show his *gam'pair* something he drew in school."

"Day after," Arceneaux said. "Busy tomorrow." He could feel her eyes following him as he limped through the lobby doors.

The knee was still painful the next morning, but it remained functionally flexible. He could manage. He caught the crosstown bus to meet Garrigue in front of Claude's house, and they set forth together to search for a single man in a large city. Their only advantage lay in possessing, even in human form, a wolf's sense of smell; that, and a bleak awareness that their quarry shared the very same gift, and undoubtedly already knew where they lived, and—far more frightening—whom they loved. *We ain't suppose to care, Damballa.* Bon Dieu *made the* loup-garou, *he ain't mean us to care about nothing. The kill only. The blood only . . . the fear only. Maybe* Bon Dieu *mad at us, me and Rene, disobeying him like we done. Too late now.*

Garrigue had always been the better tracker, since their childhood, so Arceneaux simply stayed just behind his left shoulder and went where he led. Picking up the werewolf scent at the start was a grimly easy matter: knowing Duplessis as they did, neither was surprised to cross his trail not far from the house where Garrigue's younger son Fernand lived with his own wife and children. Garrigue caught his breath audibly then, but said no word. He plunged along, drawn by the strange, unmistakable aroma as it circled, doubled back on itself, veered off in this direction or that, then inevitably returned to patrolling the streets most dear to two weary old men. Frightened and enraged, stubborn and haunted and lame, they followed. Arceneaux never took his eyes from Garrigue, which was good, because Garrigue was not using his eyes at all, and would have walked into traffic a dozen times over if not for Arceneaux. People yelled at him.

They found Duplessis in the park, the great park that essentially divided the two worlds of the city. He wore a long red-leather coat over a gray suit of the Edwardian cut he always favored—*just like the one we tear off him that night, Damballa, just like that suit*—and he was standing under a young willow tree, leaning on a dainty, foppish walking stick, smiling slightly as he watched children playing in a sandbox. When Arceneaux and Garrigue came up with him, one on each side, he did not speak to them immediately, but stood looking calmly from one face to the other, as his smile broadened. He was as handsome as ever, velvet-dark and whip-lean, unscarred in any way that they could see; and he appeared no older than he had on the night they had spent whittling him down to screaming blood, screaming shit, *Damballa* . . .

Duplessis said softly, "My friends."

Arceneaux did not answer him. Garrigue said inanely, "You looking well, *Compe'* Alexandre."

"Ah, I have my friends to thank for that." Duplessis spoke, not in Creole, but in the Parisian French he had always affected. "There's this to say for hell and death—they do keep a person in trim." He patted Garrigue's arm, an old remembered habit of his. "Yes, I am quite well, *Compe'* Rene. There were some bad times, as you know, but these days I feel as young and vigorous as . . . oh, say, as any of your grandchildren." And he named them then, clearly tasting them, as though to eat the name was to have eaten the child. "Sandrine . . . Honore . . . your adorable little Manette . . ." He named them all, grinning at Garrigue around the names.

Arceneaux said, "Sophie."

Duplessis did not turn his head, but stopped speaking.

Arceneaux said it again. "Sophie, you son of a bitch—*pere de personne, fils de cent mille*. Sophie.*"

When Duplessis did turn, he was not smiling, nor was there any bombast or mockery in his voice. He said, "I think you will agree with me, Jean-Marc, that being slashed slowly to pieces alive pays for all. Like it or not, I own your poor dear Sophie just as much as you do now. I'd call that fair and square, wouldn't you?"

Arceneaux hit him then. He hadn't been expecting the blow, and he went over on his back, shattering the fragile walking stick beneath him. The children in the sandbox looked up with some interest, but the passersby only walked faster.

Duplessis got up slowly, running his tongue-tip over a bloody upper lip. He said, "Well, I guess I don't learn much, do I? That's exactly how one of you—or was it both?—knocked me

unconscious in that filthy little place by the river. And when I
came to . . ." He shrugged lightly, and actually winked at Arceneaux. He said softly, "But you haven't got any rope with you
this time, have you Jean-Marc? And none of your little—ah—
sculptor's tools?" He tasted his bloody mouth again. "A grandfather should be more careful, I'd think."

The contemptuous lilt in the last words momentarily cost
Garrigue his sanity. Only Arceneaux's swift reaction and strong
clutch kept him from knocking Duplessis down a second time.
His voice half-muffled against Arceneaux's chest, Garrigue heard
himself raging, "You touch my chirren, you—you touch the
doorknob on my grandbabies' house—I cut you up all over again,
cut you like Friday morning's bacon, you hear me?" And he
heard Duplessis laughing.

Then the laughter stopped, almost with a machine's mechanical *click*, and Duplessis said, "No. You hear *me* now." Garrigue
shook himself free of Arceneaux's preventive embrace, nodded
a silent promise, and turned to see Duplessis facing them both,
his mouth still bleeding, and his eyes as freezingly distant as his
voice. He said, "I am Alexandre Duplessis. You sent me to hell,
you tortured me as no devils could have done—no devils would
have conceived of what you did. But in so doing, you have set
me free, you have lost all power over me. I will do what I choose
to you and yours, and there will be nothing you can do about it,
nothing you can threaten me with. Would you like to hear what
I choose to do?"

He told them.

He went into detail.

"It will take me some little while, obviously. That suits
me—I want it to take a while. I want to watch you go mad as I
strip away everything you love and cannot protect, just as you
stripped away my fingers, my face, my organs, piece by piece by
piece." The voice never grew any louder, but remained slow and

thoughtful, even genial. The soulful eyes—still a curious reddish-brown—seemed to have withdrawn deep under the telltale single brow and contracted to the size of cranberries. Arceneaux could feel their heat on his skin.

"This is where I live at present," Duplessis said, and told them his address. He said, "I would be delighted if you should follow me there, and anywhere else—it would make things much more amusing. I would even invite you to hunt with me, but you were always too cowardly for that, and by the looks of you, I can see you've not changed. Wolves—God's own *wolves*—caging themselves come the moon, not even surviving on dogs and cats, mice and squirrels and rabbits, as you did in Joyelle Parish. *Lamisere a deux . . . Misere et Compagnie*—no wonder you have both grown so old, it's almost pitiful. Now *I*"—a light inward flick of his two hands invited the comparison—"I dine only on the diet that *le Bon Dieu* meant for me, and it will keep me hunting when you two are long-buried with the humans you love so much." He clucked his tongue, mimicking a distressed old woman, and repeated, "Pitiful. Truly pitiful. *A tres—tres—tot* . . . my friends."

He bowed gracefully to them then, and turned to stroll away through the trees. Arceneaux said, "Conjure." Duplessis turned slowly again at the word, waiting. Arceneaux said, "You ain't come back all by yourself, we took care. You got brought back—take a conjure man to do that. Which one—Guillory? I got to figure Guillory."

Duplessis smiled, a little smugly, and shook his head. "I'd never trust Guillory out of my sight—let alone after my death. No, Fontenot was the only sensible choice. Entirely mad, but that's always a plus in a conjure man, isn't it? And he hated you with all his wicked old heart, Jean-Marc, as I'm sure you know. What on earth did you *do* to that man—rape his black pig? Only thing in the world he loved, that pig."

"Stopped him feeding a lil boy to it," Arceneaux grunted.

"What he do for you, and what it cost you? Fontenot, he come high."

"They all come high. But you can bargain with Fontenot. Remember, Jean-Marc?" Duplessis held out his hands, palms down. The two little fingers were missing, and Arceneaux shivered with sudden memory of that moment when he'd wondered who had already taken them, and why, even as he had prepared to cut into the bound man's flesh . . .

Duplessis laughed harshly, repeating, "My insurance policy, you could say. Really, you should have thought a bit about those, old friend. There's mighty conjuring to be done with the fingers of a *loup-garou*. It was definitely worth Fontenot's while to witch me home, time-consuming as it turned out to be. I'm sure he never regretted our covenant for a moment."

Something in his use of the past tense raised Arceneaux's own single brow, his daughters' onetime plaything. Duplessis caught the look and grinned with the flash of genuine mischief that had charmed even Arceneaux long ago, *though not* ma *Sophie, never— she knew.* "Well, let's be honest, you couldn't have a man with that kind of power and knowledge running around loose—not a bad, bad man like Hipolyte Fontenot. I was merely doing my duty as a citizen. *Au 'voir* again, *mon ami. Mon assassin.*"

Watching him walk away, Arceneaux was praying so hard for counsel and comfort to Damballa Wedo, and to Damballa's gentle wife, the rainbow Ayida, that he started when Garrigue said beside him, "Let's go, come *on*. We don't let that man out of our sight, here on in."

Arceneaux did not look at him. "No point in it. He *want* us to follow him—he want us going crazy, no sleep, no time to think straight, just wondering *when* . . . I ain't go play it his way, me, unh-uh."

"You know another way? You got a better idea?" Garrigue was very nearly crying with impatience and anxiety, all but dancing on his toes, straining to follow Alexandre Duplessis. Arceneaux put his hands on the white man's arms, trying to take the trembling into himself.

"I don't know it's a better idea. I just know he still think we nothing but a couple back-country fools, like he always did, and we got to keep him thinking that thing—*got* to. Because we gone kill him, Rene, you hearing me? We done it before—this time we gone kill him *right*, so he stay dead. Yeah, there's only two of us, but there's only one of him, and he ain't God, man, he just one damn old *loup-garou* in a fancy suit, talking fancy French. You hear what I'm saying to you?"

Garrigue did not answer. Arceneaux shook him slightly. "Right now, we going on home, both of us. He ain't go do nothing tonight, he want us to spend it thinking on all that shit he just laid on us. Home, Rene."

Still no response. Arceneaux looked into Garrigue's eyes, and could not find Garrigue there, but only frozen, helpless terror. "Listen, Rene, I tell you something my daddy use to say. Daddy, he say to me always, *di moin qui vous lamein, ma di cous qui vous ye.* You tell me who you love, I tell you who you are." Garrigue began returning slowly to his own eyes, looking back at him: expressionless, but present. Arceneaux said, "You think just maybe we know who we are, *Compe'* Rene?"

Garrigue smiled a little, shakily. "Duplessis . . . Duplessis, he don't love nobody. Never did."

"So Duplessis ain't nobody. Duplessis don't exist. You gone be scared of somebody don't exist?" Arceneaux slapped his old friend's shoulder, hard. "Home now. Ti-Jean say." They did go to their homes then, and they slept well, or at least they told each other so in the morning. Arceneaux judged that Garrigue might actually have slept through the night; for himself, he came and went, turning over a new half-dream of putting an end to Alexandre Duplessis each time he turned in his bed. Much of the waking time he spent simply calling into darkness inside himself, calling on his *loa*, as he had been taught to do when young, crying out, *Damballa Wedo, great serpent, you got to help us, this on you . . . Bon Dieu can't be no use here, ain't his country, he don't speak the patois . . . got to be you, Damballa . . .* When he did sleep, he dreamed of his dead wife, Pauline, and asked her for help too, as he had always done.

A revitalized Garrigue was most concerned the next morning with the problem of destroying a werewolf who had already survived being sliced into pieces, themselves buried in five different counties. "We never going to get another chance like that, not in this city. City, you got to *explain* why you do somebody in—and you definitely better not say it's cause he turn into a wolf some nights. Be way simpler if we could just shoot him next full moon, tell them we hunters. Bring him home strap right across the hood, hey Ti-Jean?" He chuckled, thinking about it.

"Except we be changing too," Arceneaux pointed out. "We all prisoners of the moon, one way another."

Garrigue nodded. "Yeah, you'd think that'd make us—I don't know—hold together some way, look out for each other. But it don't happen, do it? I mean, here I am, and I'm thinking, I ever do get the chance, I'd kill him wolf to wolf, just like he done Sophie. I would, I just don't give a damn no more."

"Come to that, it come to that. Last night I been trying to work out how we could pour some cement, make him part of a bridge, an underpass—you know, way the Mafia do. Couldn't figure it."

Garrigue said, "You right about one thing, anyway. We can't be waiting on the moon, cause he sure as hell won't be. Next full moon gone be short one *loup-garou* for certain."

"Maybe two," Arceneaux said quietly. "Maybe three, even. Man ain't going quietly no second time."

"Be worth it." Garrigue put out his hand and Arceneaux took

it, roughness meeting familiar lifelong roughness. Garrigue said, "Just so it ain't the little ones. Just so he don't ever get past us to the little ones." Arceneaux nodded, but did not answer him.

For the next few days they pointedly paid no attention to Duplessis's presence in the city—though they caught his scent in both neighborhoods, as he plainly made himself familiar with family routines—but spent the time with their children and grandchildren, delighting the latter and relieving the men of babysitting duties. Garrigue, having only sons, got away without suspicions; but neither Noelle nor Arceneaux's daughter-in-law Athalie were entirely deceived. As Athalie put it, "Women, we are so used to men's stupid lies, we're out of practice for a good one, Papajean," which was her one-word nickname for him. "I *know* you're lying, some way, but this one's really good."

On Saturday Arceneaux, along with most of his own family, accompanied Garrigue's family to the Church of Saints Philip and James for Manette Garrigue's First Communion. The day was unseasonably warm, the group returning for the party large, and at first no one but Arceneaux and Garrigue took any notice of the handsome, well-dressed man walking inconspicuously between them. Alexandre Duplessis said thoughtfully, "What a charming little girl. You must be very proud, Rene."

Garrigue had been coached half the night, or he would have gone for Duplessis's throat on the instant. Instead he answered, mildly enough, "I'm real proud of her, you got that right. You lay a hand on her, all Fontenot's *gris-gris* be for nothing next time."

Duplessis seemed not to have heard him. "Should she be the first—not Jean-Marc's Patrice or Zelime? It's so hard to decide—"

The strong old arms that blocked Garrigue away also neatly framed Duplessis's throat. Arceneaux said quietly, "You never going to make it to next moon, *Compe'* Alexandre. You know that, don't you?"

Duplessis looked calmly back at him, the red-brown eyes implacable far beyond human understanding. He said, "*Compe'* Jean-Marc, I died at your hands forty and more years ago, and by the time you got through with me I was very, very old. You cannot kill such a man twice, not so it matters." He smiled at Arceneaux. "Besides, the moon is perhaps not everything, even for a *loup-garou*. I'd give that a little thought, if I were you." His canine teeth glittered wetly in the late-autumn sunlight as he turned and walked away.

After a while Noelle dropped back to take her father's arm. She rubbed her cheek lightly against Arceneaux's shoulder and said, "Your knee all right? You're looking tired."

"Been a long morning." Arceneaux hugged her arm under his own. "Don't you worry about the old man."

"I do, though. Gotten so I worry about you a whole lot. Antoine does, too." She looked up at him, and he thought, *Her mama's eyes, her mama's mouth, but my complexion—thank God that's all she got from me* . . . She said, "How about you spend the night, hey? I make gumbo, you play with the grandbabies, talk sports with Antoine. Sound fair?"

It sounded more than fair; it sounded such a respite from the futile plans and dreaded memories with which he and Garrigue had been living that he could have wept. "I'm gone need take care some business first. Nothing big, just a few bits of business. Then I come back, stay the night." She prompted him with a silent, quizzical tilt of her head, and he added, "Promise." It was an old ritual between them, dating from her childhood: he rarely used the word at all, but once he did he could be absolutely relied on to keep it. His grandchildren had all caught on to this somewhat earlier than she had.

He slipped away from the party group without even signaling to Garrigue: a deliberately suspicious maneuver that had the waiting Duplessis behind him before he had gone more than a block from the house. It was difficult to pretend not to notice that he was being followed—this being one of the wolf senses that finds an echo in the human body—but Arceneaux was good at it and took a certain pleasure in leading Duplessis all over the area, as the latter had done to him and Garrigue. But the motive was not primarily spite. He was actually bound for a certain neighborhood *botanica* run by an old Cuban couple who had befriended him years before, when he first came to the city. They were kind and brown, and spoke almost no English, and he had always suspected that they knew exactly what he was, had known others like him in Cuba, and simply didn't care.

He spent some forty-five minutes in the crowded little shop, and left with his arms full of brightly-colored packages. Most amounted to herbal and homeopathic remedies of one sort and another; a very few were gifts for Damballa Wedo, whose needs are very simple; and one—the only one with an aroma that would have alerted any *loup-garou* in the world—was a largish packet of wolfbane.

Still sensing Duplessis on his track, he walked back to Noelle's house, asked to borrow her car briefly, claiming to have heard an ominous sound from the transmission, and took off northeast, in the direction of the old cabin where he and Garrigue imprisoned themselves one night in every month. The car was as cramped as ever, and the drive as tedious, but he managed it as efficiently as he could. Arriving alone, for the first time ever, he spent some while tidying the cabin, and the yet-raw grave in the woods as well; then carefully measured out all the wolfbane in a circle around the little building, and headed straight back to the city. He bent all his senses, wolf and human alike, to discovering whether or not Duplessis had trailed him the entire way, but the results were inconclusive.

"Way I been figuring it over," he said to Garrigue the next day, drinking bitter chicory coffee at the only Creole restaurant whose cook understood the importance of a proper *roux*, "we lured him into that blind pig back on the river, all them years ago, and he just know he way too smart for us to get him like that no second time. So we gone do just exactly what we done before, cause we ain't but pure-D country, and that the onliest trick we know." His sigh turned to a weary grunt as he shook his head. "Which ain't no lie, far as I'm concerned. But we go on paying him no mind, we keep sneaking up there, no moon, no need . . . he smell the wolfbane, he keep on following us, we got to be planning *something* . . . All I'm hoping, *Compe'* Rene, I'm counting on a fool staying a fool. The smart ones, they do sometimes."

Garrigue rubbed the back of his neck and folded his arms. "So what you saying, same thing, except with the cabin? Man, *I* wouldn't fall for that, and you *know* I'm a fool."

"Yeah, but see, see, we know we fools—we used to it, we live with it like everybody, do the best we can. But Duplessis . . ." He smiled, although it felt as though he were lifting a great cold weight with his mouth. "Duplessis *scary*. Duplessis got knowledge you and me couldn't even spell, never mind understand. He just as smart as he think he is, and we just about what we were back when we never seen a city man before, we so proud to be running with a city man." He rubbed the bad knee, remembering Sophie's warnings, not at all comforted by the thought that no one else in the clan had seen through the laughter, the effortless charm, the *newness* of the young *loup-garou* who came so persistently courting her. He said, "There's things Duplessis never going to understand."

He missed Garrigue's question, because it was mumbled in so low a tone. He said, "Say what?"

Garrigue asked, "It going to be like that time?" Arceneaux did not answer. Garrigue said, "Cause I don't think I can do that again, Ti-Jean. I don't think I can watch, even." His face and voice were embarrassed, but there was no mistaking the set of his eyes, not after seventy years.

"I don't know, me." Arceneaux himself had never once been pursued by dreams of what they had done to Alexandre Duplessis in Sophie's name; but in forty years he had gently shaken Garrigue out of them more than once, and held him afterward. "We get him there—just you, me, and him, like before—I know then. All I can tell you now, Rene."

Garrigue made no reply, and they separated shortly afterward. Arceneaux went home, iced his knee, turned on his radio (he had a television set, but rarely watched it), and learned of the discovery of a second homeless woman, eviscerated and partly devoured, her head almost severed from her body by the violence of the attack. The corpse had been found under the Viaduct, barely two blocks from Arceneaux's apartment, and the police announced that they were taking seriously the disappearance of the woman Arceneaux had buried. Arceneaux sat staring at the radio long after it had switched to broadcasting a college football game.

He called Garrigue, got a busy signal, and waited until his friend called him back a moment later. When he picked up the phone, he said simply, "I know."

Garrigue was fighting hysteria; Arceneaux could feel it before he spoke the first word. "Can't be, Ti-Jean. Not full moon. Can't *be*."

"Well," Arceneaux said. "Gone have to ask old Duplessis what else he sold that Fontenot." He had not expected Garrigue to laugh, and was not surprised. He said, "Don't be panicking, you hear me, Rene? Not now. Ain't the time."

"Don't know what else to do." But Garrigue's voice was slightly steadier. "If he really be changing any damn time he like—"

"Got to be rules. *Le Bon Dieu,* he wouldn't let there not be rules—"

"Then we got to tell them, you hear *me?* They got to know what out there, what we dealing with—what coming *after* them—"

"And what we are? What they come from, what they part of? You think your little Manette, my Patrice, you think they ready for that?"

"Not the grandbabies, when I ever said the grandbabies? I'm talking the chirren—yours, mine, they husbands, wives, all them. They old enough, they got a right to know." There was a pause on the other end, and then Garrigue said flatly, "You don't tell them, I will. I swear."

It was Arceneaux's turn to be silent, listening to Garrigue's anxious breathing on the phone. He said finally, "Noelle. Noelle got a head on her. We tell her, no one else."

"She got a husband, too. What about him?"

"Noelle," Arceneaux said firmly. "Antoine ain't got no were-wolf for a daddy."

"Okay." Garrigue drew the two syllables out with obvious dubiousness. "Noelle." The voice quavered again, sounding old for the first time in Arceneaux's memory. "Ti-Jean, he could be anywhere right now, we wouldn't know. Could be *at* them, be tearing them apart, like that woman—"

Arceneaux stopped him like a traffic cop, literally—and absurdly—with a hand held up. "No, he couldn't. Think about it, Rene. Back in Louzianne—back *then*—what we do after that big a kill? What *anybody* do?"

"Go off . . . go off somewhere, go to sleep." Garrigue said it grudgingly, but he said it.

"How long for? How long you ever sleep, you and that full belly?"

"A day, anyway. Slept out two whole days, one time. And old Albert Vaugine . . ." Garrigue was chuckling a bit, in spite of himself. He said, "Okay, so we maybe got a couple of days—*maybe*. What then?"

"Then we get ourselves on up to the cabin. You and me and him." Arceneaux hung up.

It had long been the centerpiece of Arceneaux's private understanding of the world that nothing was ever as good as you expected it to be, or as bad. His confession of her ancestry to Noelle fell into the latter category. He had expected her reaction to be one of horrified revulsion, followed by absolute denial and tearful outrage. Instead, after withdrawing into silent thought for a time, and then saying slow, mysterious things like, "So *that's* why I can never do anything with my hair," she told him, "You do know there's no way in the world you're going without me?"

His response never got much beyond, "The hell you preach, girl!" Noelle set her right forefinger somewhere between his Adam's apple and his collarbones, and said, "Dadda, this is my fight, too. As long as that man's running around loose"—the irony of her using the words that Alexandre Duplessis had used to justify his murder of the conjure man Fontenot was not lost on Arceneaux—"my children aren't safe. You know the way I get about the children."

"This won't be no PTA meeting. You don't know."

"I know you and Uncle Rene, you may both be werewolves, but you're *old* werewolves, and you're not exactly in the best shape. Oh, you're going to need me, cause right now the both of you couldn't tackle Patrice, never mind Zelime." He was in no state to tackle her, either; he made do with a mental reservation: *Look away for even five minutes and we're out of here, me and Rene. You got to know how to handle daughters, that's all. Specially the pushy ones.*

But on the second day, it didn't matter, because it was Noelle who was gone. And Patrice with her. And her car.

After Antoine had called the police, and the house had begun to fill with terrified family, but before the reporters had arrived, and before Zelime had stopped crying for her mother and little brother, Arceneaux borrowed his son Celestin's car. It was quite a bit like renting it, not because Celestin charged him anything, but because answering all his questions about why the loan was necessary almost amounted to filling out a form. Arceneaux finally roared at him, in a voice Celestin had not heard since his childhood, "Cause I'm your father, me, and I just about to snatch you balder than you already are, you don't hand me them keys." He was on the road five minutes later.

He did not stop to pick up Garrigue. His explanation to himself was that there wasn't time, that every minute was too precious to be taken up with a detour; but even as he made it, he knew better. The truth lay in his pity for Garrigue's endless nightmares, for his lonesome question, "It gone be like that time?" and for his own sense that this was finally between him and the man whom he had carved to obscene fragments alive. *I let him do it all back to me, he lets them two go. Please, Damballa, you hear? Please.*

But he was never certain—and less now than ever before—whether Damballa heard prayers addressed to him in English. So for the entire length of the drive, which seemed to take the rest of his life, he chanted, over and over, a prayer-song that little Ti-Jean Arceneaux, who spoke another language, had learned young, never forgotten, and, until this moment, never needed.

"*Baba yehge, amiwa saba yehge,*

"*De Damballa e a miwa,*

"*Danou sewa yehge o, djevo de.*

"*De Damballa Wedo, Bade miwa . . .*"

Rather than bursting into the cabin like the avenging angel

288 | PETER S. BEAGLE

he had planned to be, he hardly had the strength or the energy to open the car door, once he arrived. The afternoon was cold, and he could smell snow an hour or two away; he noticed a few flakes on the roof of Noelle's car. There was flickering light in the cabin, and smoke curling from the chimney, which he and Garrigue mistrusted enough that they almost never lighted a fire. He moved closer, noticing two sets of footprints leading to the door. *Yeah, she'd have been carrying Patrice, boy'd have been too scared to walk.* The vision of his terrified four-year-old grandson made him grind his teeth, and Duplessis promptly called from within, "No need to bite the door down, Jean-Marc. Half a minute, I'll be right there."

Waiting, Arceneaux moved to the side of the house and ripped down the single power line. The electric light went out inside, and he heard Duplessis laugh. Standing on the doorstep as Arceneaux walked back, he said, "I thought you might do that, so I built a handsome fire for us all—even lit a few candles. But if you imagine that's going to preclude the use of power tools, I feel I should remind you that they all run on batteries these days. Nice *big* batteries. Come in, Jean-Marc, I bid you welcome."

It was not the shock of seeing Noelle tied in a chair that almost caused Arceneaux to lose what control he had and charge the smiling man standing beside her. It was the sight of Patrice, unbound on her lap, lighting up at the sight of him to call *"Gam'pair!"* He had been crying, but his face made it clear that everything would be all right now. Duplessis said pleasantly, "I wouldn't give it a second thought, old friend. I'm sure you know why."

"Fontenot," Arceneaux said. "Never knowed the old man had *that* much power."

"Oh, it cost me an arm and a leg . . . so to speak." Duplessis laughed softly. "Another reason he had to go. I mean, suppose everyone could change whenever he chose, things might become a bit . . . chaotic, don't you agree? But it certainly does come in handy, those nights when you're suddenly peckish, just like that, and everything's closed."

Noelle's eyes were terrified, but her voice was surprisingly steady. She said, "He broke in in the night, I don't know how. I couldn't fight him, because he had Patrice, and he said if I screamed . . ."

"Yeah, honey," Arceneaux said. "Yeah, baby."

"He made me drive him up here. Poor Patrice was so frightened."

Patrice nodded proudly. "I was *scared, Gam'pair.*"

"He tried to rape me," Noelle said evenly. "He couldn't."

Duplessis looked only mildly abashed. "Everything costs. And it did seem appropriate—you and little Rene working so hard to entice me up here. I thought I'd just take you up on it a bit early."

Arceneaux took a step, then another; not toward Duplessis, but toward Noelle in the chair. Duplessis said, "I really wouldn't, Jean-Marc."

Noelle said, "Dadda, get *out* of here! It's you he wants!"

Arceneaux said, "He got me. He ain't getting you."

Duplessis nodded. "I'll let them go, you have my word. But they have to watch first. That's fair. Her and the little one, watching and remembering . . . you know, that might even make up for what you did to me." His smile brightened even more. "Then we'll be quits at last, just think, after all the years. I might even leave some of the others alive—lagniappe, don't you know, our greatest Louzianne tradition. As your folks say down in the swamp, lagniappe *c'est bitin qui bon*—lagniappe is lawful treasure."

Arceneaux ignored him. To Patrice he said, "Boy, you get off your mama's lap now, I got to get those ropes off her. Then we all go get some ice cream, you like that?"

Patrice scrambled down eagerly. Noelle said, "Dadda, *no*. Take Patrice and get *out*—" just as Duplessis's voice sharpened and tightened, good cheer gone. "Jean-Marc, I'm warning you—"

The ropes were tight for stiff old fingers, and Noelle's struggling against them didn't help. Behind him, Arceneaux heard Patrice scream in terror. A moment later, looking past him, Noelle went absolutely rigid, her mouth open but no sound emerging. He turned himself then, knowing better than they what he would see.

Petrifying as the sight of a werewolf obviously is, it is the transformation itself that is the smothering fabric of nightmare. On the average, it lasts no more than ten or fifteen seconds; but to the observing eyes and mind the process is endless, going on and on and on in everlasting slow-motion, as the grinning mouth twists and lengthens into a fanged snarl, while the body convulses, falls forward, catches itself on long gray legs that were arms a lifetime ago, and the eyes lengthen, literally reseat themselves in the head at a new angle, and take on the beautiful insane glow that particularly distinguishes the *loup-garou*. Alexandre Duplessis—cotton-white, except for the dark-shaded neck-ruff and the jagged black slash across the chest—uttered a shattering half-human roar and sprang straight at Arceneaux.

Whether it was caused by the adrenaline of terror or of rage he couldn't guess, but suddenly the ropes fell loose from the chair and his fingers, and Noelle, in one motion, swept up the wailing Patrice and was through the door before the wolf that had been Duplessis even reached her father. The bad knee predictably locked up, and Arceneaux went down, with the wolf Duplessis on him, worrying at his throat. He warded off the wide-stretched jaws with his forearm, bringing the good knee up into the *loup-garou*'s belly, the huge white-and-black body that had become all his sky and all his night. Duplessis threw back his head and bayed in triumph.

Arceneaux made a last desperate attempt to heave Duplessis away and get to his feet. But he was near to suffocation from the weight on his chest—*Baba yehge, amiwa saba yehge, de Damballa e a miwa*—and then the werewolf's jaws were past his guard, the great fangs sank into his shoulder, and he heard himself scream in pain—*Danou sewa yehge o, djevo de, Damballa come to us, they are hurting us, Damballa come quickly . . .*

. . . and heard the scream become a howl of fury in the same moment, as he lunged upward, his changing jaws closing on Duplessis's head, taking out an eye with the first snap. Wolf to wolf—the greatest sin of all—they rose on their hind legs, locked together, fangs clashing, each streaked and blotched with the other's blood. Arceneaux had lost not only who he was, but *what*—he had no grandchildren now, no children either, no life-long downhome friend, no memories of affection . . . there had never been anything else but this murderous twin, and no joy but in hurting it, killing it, tearing it back once again to shreds, where it belonged. He had never been so happy in his life.

In the wolf form, *loups-garoux* do not mate; lovemaking is a gift for ordinary animals, ordinary humans. Yet this terrible, transcendent *meshing* was like nothing Arceneaux had ever known, even as he was aware that his left front leg was broken and one side of his throat laid open. Duplessis was down now . . . or was that some other wolf bleeding and panting under him, breath ragged, weakened claws finding no purchase in his fur? It made no difference. There was nothing but battle now, nothing but hunger for someone's blood.

Most of the lighted candles had been knocked over—some by Noelle's flight to the door, some during the battle. The rag rugs that he and Garrigue had devastated and not yet replaced were catching fire, and spreading the flames to dry furniture and loose paper and kindling. Arceneaux watched the fire with a curious detachment, as intense, in its way, as the ecstasy with which he had closed his wolf jaws on Duplessis's wolf flesh. He was aware, with the same disinterest, that he was bleeding badly from a dozen wounds; still, he was on his feet, and Duplessis was sprawled before him, alive but barely breathing, lacking the strength and will to regain the human shape. Arceneaux was in the same condition, which was a pity, for he would have liked to give his thanks to Damballa in words. He considered the helpless Duplessis for a moment longer, as the fire began to find its own tongue, and then he pushed the door open with his head and limped outside.

Noelle cried out at first as he stumbled toward her; but then she knew him, as she would always have known him, and knelt down before him, hugging his torn neck—Duplessis had come very near the throat—and getting blood all over the pajamas in which she had been kidnapped. She had no words either, except for *Dadda,* but she got plenty of mileage out of that one, even so.

The cabin was just reaching full blaze, and Patrice had worked up the courage to let the strange big dog lick his face, when the police car came barreling up the overgrown little path, very nearly losing an axle to the pothole Garrigue had been warning them about for the last couple of miles. Antoine was with them, too, and Garrigue's son Claude, and a police paramedic as well. There was a good deal of embracing among one group, and an equal amount of head scratching, chin rubbing, and cell-phone calling by the other.

And Jean-Marc Arceneaux—"Ti-Jean" to a very few old friends—nuzzled his grandson one last time, and then turned and walked back into the blazing cabin and threw himself over the body of the wolf Alexandre Duplessis. Noelle's cry of grief was still echoing when the roof came down.

When Garrigue could talk—when anyone could talk, after the fire engine came—he told Noelle, "The ashes. He done it because of the ashes."

Noelle shook her head weakly. "I don't understand."

Garrigue said, "Duplessis come back once, maybe do it again, even from ashes. But not all mixed up together with old Ti-Jean, no, not with their jaws locked on each other in the other world and the *loa* watching. Not even a really good conjure man out of Sabine, Vernon Parish, pull off that trick. You follow me?"

"No," she said. "No, Rene. I don't, I'm trying."

Garrigue was admirably patient, exhausted as he was. "He just making sure you, the grandbabies, the rest of us, we never going to be bothered by *Compe'* Alexandre no more." His gray eyes were shining with prideful tears. "He thought on things like that, Ti-Jean did. Knew him all my life, that man. All my life."

Patrice slept between her and Antoine that night: the police psychologist who had examined him said that just because he was showing no sign of trauma didn't mean that he might not be affected in some fashion that wouldn't manifest itself for years. For his part, Patrice had talked about the incident in the surprisingly matter-of-fact way of a four-year-old for the rest of the day; but after dinner he spent the evening playing one of Zelime's mysterious games that seemed, as far as adults could tell, to have no rules whatsoever. It was only when he scrambled into bed beside his mother that he asked seriously, "That man? Not coming back?"

Noelle hugged him. "No, sweetheart. Not coming back. Not ever. You scared him away."

"*Gam'pair* come back." It was not a question.

You're not supposed to lie to children about anything. Bad, bad, bad. Noelle said, "He had to go away, Patrice. He had to make sure that man wouldn't come here again."

Patrice nodded solemnly. He wrapped his arms around himself and said, "I hold *Gam'pair* right here. *Gam'pair* not going anywhere," and went to sleep.

ABOUT THE AUTHORS

PETER S. BEAGLE was born in New York City in 1939 and raised in the borough of that city known as the Bronx. He originally proclaimed he would be a writer when he was ten years old; subsequent events have proven him either prescient or even more stubborn than hitherto suspected. Today, thanks to classic works such as *A Fine and Private Place*, *The Last Unicorn*, *Tamsin*, and *The Inkeeper's Song*, he is acknowledged as America's greatest living fantasy author; and his dazzling abilities with language, characters, and magical storytelling have earned him many millions of fans around the world. In addition to stories and novels, Peter has written numerous teleplays and screenplays, including the animated versions of *The Lord of the Rings* and *The Last Unicorn*, plus the fan-favorite "Sarek" episode of *Star Trek: The Next Generation*. His nonfiction book *I See by My Outfit*, which recounts a 1963 journey across America on motor scooter, is considered a classic of American travel writing. He is also a gifted poet, lyricist, and singer/songwriter. For more information on Peter and his works, see www.peterbeagle.com or www.conlanpress.com.

HOLLY BLACK writes contemporary fantasy for teens and younger readers, including the Modern Faerie Tale series, *The Spiderwick Chronicles*, and her graphic novel series, *The Good Neighbors*. She lives in Amherst, Massachusetts, with her husband, Theo.

The winner of both a Bram Stoker and World Fantasy Award, P. D. CACEK has written more than two hundred short stories, appearing in such anthologies as *999*, *Joe R. Lansdale's Lords of the Razor, Night Visions 12, Inferno,* and the inaugural YA anthology of horror fiction from Scholastic, *666: the Number of the Beast.* Although Cacek will probably always consider herself a short story writer, she has written four novels to date and is currently finishing up a fifth, *Visitation Rites,* a good old-fashioned ghost story. A native Westerner, Cacek now lives in Fort Washington, Pennsylvania . . . in a haunted house across from a haunted mill. When not writing, she can often be found either with a group of costumed storytellers called the Patient Creatures (www.creatureseast.com) or haunting local cemeteries looking for inspiration. You can visit her website at www.pdcacek.com

Esther M. Friesner is a Nebula Award winner and the author of thirty-four novels and more than one hundred fifty short stories, in addition to being the editor of seven popular anthologies. Her works have been published in the United States, the United Kingdom, Japan, Germany, Russia, France, Poland, and Italy. She is also a published poet and a produced playwright. Her articles on fiction writing have appeared in *Writer's Market* and *Writer's Digest Books.* Her latest publications include *Nobody's Princess* and *Nobody's Prize,* from Random House; and *Temping Fate,* from Dutton/Penguin. She is currently working on *Sphinx's Princess* and *Sphinx's Queen*—two books about young Nefertiti, for Random House—and *Burning Roses,* for Penguin. Educated at Vassar College, receiving a BA degree in both Spanish and Drama, she went on to receive her MA and PhD in Spanish from Yale University, where she taught for a number of years. She is married, the mother of two, and lives in Connecticut.

Gregory Frost is a writer of fantasy, horror, and science fiction who has been publishing steadily for more than two decades. His latest work is the fantasy duology *Shadowbridge* and *Lord*

Tophet, published by Del Rey Books. His other works include *Fitcher's Brides*, *Tain* and *Remscela* (another duology comprising a retelling of the Irish epic *Tain Bo Cuailnge*), the fantasy novel *Lyrec*, and a Nebula-nominated science fiction work *The Pure Cold Light*. Much of his best short fiction is collected in *Attack of the Jazz Giants and Other Stories*. This collection includes his acclaimed novelette, "Madonna of the Maquiladora," a finalist for the James Tiptree, Jr., Award, Nebula Award, Theodore Sturgeon Memorial Award, and Hugo Award.

Frost's short work has appeared in *The Magazine of Fantasy & Science Fiction*, *Asimov's Science Fiction*, *Weird Tales*, *Realms of Fantasy*, and numerous anthologies. For two years he served as principal researcher for Grinning Dog Pictures, a Philadelphia film and television production company, on two productions for the Discovery Global Network series *Science Frontiers*, one of which, "Wolf Man: The Myth and the Science," examined the folklore of werewolves, the psychological illness known as lycanthropy, and the history of Inquisitional trials of accused werewolves, establishing that most were afflicted with ergot poisoning. It was the highest-rated show of the year on Discovery Europe Network. Frost has also acted in two very, very, very "B" horror films, including S. P. Somtow's *The Laughing Dead*. His website is www.gregoryfrost.com. Blog: "Frostbites," is at http://frostokovich.livejournal.com.

RON GOULART, in addition to being a mystery writer (twice nominated for an MWA Edgar) and a science fiction writer (once nominated for an SFWA Nebula), is also the author of more than a dozen nonfiction books in the popular fiction field. These include *Comic Book Culture* (2000, trade paper 2007), which was nominated for an Eisner Award, *The Comic Book Encyclopedia* (2004), and *Good Girl Art* (2008), an illustrated history of women characters in comic books from the 1930s to the present.

His next book will be *Good Girl Art Around the World* (2009). He's sold more than six hundred stories and articles in his long and colorful career. He and his wife, also a writer, live in ramshackle splendor in a rustic patch of Connecticut.

TANITH LEE was born in 1947. She became a full-time professional writer in 1974 and made a tremendous splash with her first fantasy novel for adults, *The Birthgrave*, in 1975. She has so far written nearly 100 books and more than 265 short stories, plus radio plays and TV scripts. She lives on the Sussex weald with her husband and coconspirator artist/writer, John Kaiine, and two tuxedo cats. She reports that she has numerous short stories and novellas out or due in anthologies from Ellen Datlow, Marvin Kaye, Gardner Dozois, and Leah Wilson. Others are forthcoming in *Weird Tales*, *Realms of Fantasy*, and the UK's *Nature*. Her most recently published adult fantasies were the *Lion Wolf* trilogy: *Cast a Bright Shadow*, *Here in Cold Hell*, and *No Flame but Mine* (Tor MacMillan). Three *Piratica* novels for young adults have appeared from Hodder Headline. Norilana Books (USA) will be reissuing all the existing *Flat Earth* novels, plus two new *Flat Earth* books through 2009 and 2010. She has won numerous awards, including the World Fantasy Award and the British Fantasy Award.

HOLLY PHILLIPS is the author of the award-winning collection *In the Palace of Repose* as well as innumerable short stories published in markets as diverse as *The New Quarterly* and *Asimov's Science Fiction*. She lives on a big island off Canada's western coast and is currently engaged in a heroic struggle to keep her website (www .hollyphillips.com) up to date even as she works on her newest novel. Holly's newest dark fantasy *The Engine's Child* was published by Del Rey in November 2008. Keep your eyes peeled for the gorgeous cover art by David Ho!

MIKE RESNICK is, according to *Locus*, the most awarded short fiction writer, living or dead, in science fiction history. He is the author of fifty-five novels, more than two hundred short stories, and two screenplays, and is the editor of fifty anthologies. He is currently the executive editor of *Jim Baen's Universe*. His work has been translated into twenty-two languages.

LISA TUTTLE is a native Texan (born and raised in Houston) who has been an honorary Brit for more than twenty-five years. She presently lives in a remote, rural region of Scotland, so urban settings provide her an enjoyable escape into fantasy. Over the course of her career she's sold around one hundred short stories and seven novels, most recently the contemporary fantasies *The Mysteries* and *The Silver Bough*. Some of her short stories may be found in *A Nest of Nightmares*, *A Spaceship Built of Stone and Other Stories*, *Memories of the Body: Tales of Desire and Transformation*, and *Ghosts and Other Lovers*. She has edited *Skin of the Soul: New Horror Stories by Women* and has also written several children's books.

CARRIE VAUGHN survived her air force brat childhood and managed to put down roots in Colorado. She lives in Boulder with her dog, Lily, and too many hobbies. A graduate of the Odyssey Writing Workshop, she's had short stories published in such magazines as *Realms of Fantasy* and *Weird Tales*. Most of her work over the last couple of years has gone into her series of novels about a werewolf named Kitty who hosts a talk radio show for the supernaturally disadvantaged. These include *Kitty and the Midnight Hour*, *Kitty and the Silver Bullet*, *Kitty Goes to Washington*, and *Kitty Takes a Holiday*.

IAN WATSON taught literature in Tanzania and Japan, then futurology at an art school in Birmingham, UK, before becoming a full-time writer thirty-three years ago, after his first novel, *The Embedding,* won a couple of prizes. Thus he was encouraged onto the slippery slope resulting so far in about thirty novels and almost a dozen story collections, variously SF, fantasy, and horror. A year's work with Stanley Kubrick produced the screen story for *A.I. Artificial Intelligence,* directed by Steven Spielberg. *Space Marine,* one of four ground-breaking future-Gothic novels that Ian wrote for the Warhammer forty thousand milieu, changes hands on eBay for such large sums that it's banned by its own publisher from ever being reprinted. Recently, Ian completed a book of wild and witty stories in collaboration with the Italian surrealist Robert Quaglia, with whom he stayed in Romania to experience "Weredog of Bucharest." Ian's website is at www.ianwatson.info, though he and his Spanish translator, Luisa, and his Hungarian publisher, Peter, also maintain a website of startling interest (www.ajeno.wired.hu) to honor the as yet almost unknown Colombian poet of erotic anguish Miguel Ajeno.

Upon his return from Korea, GENE WOLFE earned a BS in mechanical engineering from the University of Houston. He was a working engineer for seventeen years and an editor at an engineering magazine for eleven more. Many of his early stories appeared in Damon Knight's original anthology series *Orbit.* Wolfe has been writing full-time since 1984. His titles include *The Fifth Head of Cerberus, Peace, The Shadow of the Torturer, Soldier of the Mist, Nightside, The Long Sun, The Knight, The Wizard, Pirate Freedom,* and *An Evil Guest.* He and Rosemary have been married for more than fifty years; they have four children and three grandchildren.

CHELSEA QUINN YARBRO has been a professional writer for forty years and has sold eighty-five books and more than ninety works of short fiction, essays, and reviews. She also composes serious music. She lives in her hometown—Berkeley, California—with three autocratic cats. In 2003, the World Horror Society presented her with a Grand Master Award; the International Horror Guild honored her with a Living Legend Award in 2006. She is probably best known for her series of novels about the vampire the Comte de Saint-Germain.

ABOUT THE EDITORS

DARRELL SCHWEITZER co-edited *Weird Tales* magazine for nineteen years and co-edited (with Martin H. Greenberg) the successful 2007 anthology *The Secret History of Vampires*. He was also editor of *Discovering H. P. Lovecraft, The Thomas Ligotti Reader, The Neil Gaiman Reader,* and *Weird Trails: the Magazine of Supernatural Cowboy Stories*. As author he has published three novels, *The White Isle, The Shattered Goddess,* and *The Mask of the Sorcerer*. His nearly three hundred published stories have appeared in *Postscripts, Cemetery Dance, Interzone, Twilight Zone Magazine, Amazing Stories, Alfred Hitchcock's Mystery Magazine,* among others. His story collections include *Refugees from an Imaginary Country, Nightscapes* (which contains another Kvetchula story), and *Necromancies and Netherworlds* (with Jason Van Hollander). He has also published essays and interviews and is an award-winning poet. His most recent book is a collection of verse, *Ghosts of Past and Future*. He has been nominated for the World Fantasy Award four times and won it once. Despite all this, he could not be restrained from sneaking a ghastly lycanthropic limerick into this book, but we have decided to hide it here in the bio-notes where it will do the least harm:

> *A werewolf, who howled at the Moon,*
> *remarked, "I will be changed soon,*
> *from man into beast*
> *to enjoy a red feast,*
> *without use of knife, fork, or spoon."*

MARTIN H. GREENBERG is the CEP of Tekno Books and its predecessor companies, now the largest book developer of commercial fiction and nonfiction in the world, with more than two thousand published books that have been translated into thirty-three languages. He is the recipient of an unprecedented three Lifetime Achievement Awards in the Science Fiction, Supernatural Horror, and Mystery genres—the Milford Award in Science Fiction, the Bram Stoker Award in Horror, and the Ellery Queen Award, respectively—and is the only person in publishing history to have received all three awards.